# Shenandoah Dreams

**A Vineyard Romance**
Romance, history, adventure.
Get swept into the exciting Winds of Change series.

# Winds of Change

### * * *

## Shenandoah Nights
BOOK ONE

## Shenandoah Crossings
BOOK TWO

## Shenandoah Dreams
BOOK THREE

WINDS OF CHANGE

3

# SHENANDOAH DREAMS

LISA BELCASTRO

*Blessings,*
*Lisa Belcastro*

OAKTARA
www.oaktara.com

*Shenandoah Dreams*

Published in the U.S. by:
**OakTara Publishers**
www.oaktara.com

Cover design by Yvonne Parks at www.pearcreative.ca
Cover image © Alison Shaw at www.alisonshaw.com
Author photo © 2013 by Heidi Wild Photography

Copyright © 2014 by Lisa Belcastro. All rights reserved.

Cover and interior design © 2014, OakTara Publishers. All rights reserved. No part of this publication may be reproduced, stored in a retrieval system, or transmitted in any form or by any means without the prior written permission of the publisher. The only exception is brief quotations in professional reviews. The perspective, opinions, and worldview represented by this book are those of the author's and are not intended to be a reflection or endorsement of the publisher's views.

Scripture quotations are taken from the King James Version of the Bible.

ISBN-13: 978-1-60290-380-7 • ISBN-10: 1-60290-380-8
eISBN-13: 978-1-60290-478-1 • eISBN-10: 1-60290-478-2

*Shenandoah Dreams* is a work of fiction. References to real people, events, establishments, organizations, or locales are intended only to provide a sense of authenticity and are used fictitiously. All other characters, incidents, and dialogue are drawn from the author's imagination.

Printed in the U.S.A.

\* \* \*

## To Kayla

You are God's precious gift to me. From the moment the nurse put you in my arms, I loved you with an emotion more powerful than any I'd ever known. I have watched you grow, learn, explore, and mature into an amazing and beautiful young woman. I can't believe you're sixteen! Remember, when you were four years old, you signed that little pink slip of paper saying that Mommy could go to college with you! Just reminding you.

I love you, my Little Pumpkin!

# 1

THE AROMA OF POPCORN FILLED THE AIR as Melissa Smith strolled through the entry gates of the Martha's Vineyard Agricultural Fair. She'd made a habit of stopping in on opening day alone to see how her fair entries had done and to relish the moment. But, first thing first.

Melissa followed her nose to the vendor selling her favorite snack, gladly avoiding the longer lines at the ice cream sundae and cotton candy booths. As she munched on the buttery goodness, she chuckled at the irony of kids filling up on sweets and goodies and then running to the carnival rides that were sure to mix and tumble the snacks in their unsuspecting bellies. Shaking her head, she slid her camera bag around to her left side and started back toward the Ag Hall.

"Miss Smith. Miss Smith." Enthusiastic young voices shouted from the Ferris wheel. "Come ride with us!"

Melissa turned to her right and waved as the silver gondola carrying two of her English students ascended into the bright noonday sky. "Maybe next time," she called.

Melissa watched the girls make one round, waved at them again, and then made her way across the grassy field to the large, weathered building that housed all the non-breathing, non-shedding fair entries. She had entered six photos in the adult amateur divisions, all of them taken last summer while she chaperoned the Holmes Hole student cruise aboard the schooner *Shenandoah*.

The *Shenandoah* had captured Melissa's artistic eye. Once aboard, she'd rarely been without her camera in hand or within arm's reach. Photographing the students, the crew, the sails, the rigging, the sea and shores in the changing light throughout the day had added to her ultimate pleasures during last year's weeklong voyage. And she was eager to see if any of her images had won a prize.

Inside the hundred-year-old reconstructed barn, Melissa paused and took in the beauty of the post-and-beam building. Just as she was with the *Shenandoah*, Melissa was impressed with the care taken to maintain the old barn. In 1995, a team of fifty or so Vineyarders had gone to New Hampshire to disassemble the century-old structure, pack it carefully onto numerous trucks, transport it back to the Island, and then reassemble it.

Captain John Roberts had done something similar when he purchased the original *Shenandoah* from a shipyard in southern Maine. The centuries-old ship was not seaworthy, but many of the original beams and planks were salvageable. Every board in good condition was reused, fastened, and hammered to create an impressive replica of the eighteenth-century *Shenandoah*. And Melissa would be on her soon.

Smiling, Melissa moseyed past the cakes, cookies, and brownies, past the arts and crafts, and around the corner to the photography walls. She wadded up her empty popcorn container, then nervously tossed the glassine bag from one hand to the other while she searched the panels for her pictures. Her portrait of Captain Roberts, his gaze focused on the horizon and a long stretch of sea visible behind him as he sailed *Shenandoah* across the Vineyard Sound, had won an honorable mention.

Her favorite image, a tight shot of the sails aglow in the morning light, had taken second place. A great sense of accomplishment filled her. She'd been toying with the idea of shooting specific angles and images and then creating a line of stationery to sell at some of the Island gift shops. Between these awards and the new wide-angle lens she'd ordered in July, she felt a surge of confidence to set and achieve her new goal.

"Congratulations, Melissa. I love that shot of the sails."

Melissa turned to see her neighbor Alexandra Simmons and realized the striking blonde had been glancing over her shoulder. "Thanks, Alex. It's easy to take a good picture on the *Shenandoah*. Everywhere you look there is beauty and magic."

"Would appear so from your viewpoint."

Melissa smiled, but not being one to focus too much on herself, she brought up the next big event most Islanders and tourists attended on the third Friday of August. "Are you going to the fireworks in Oaks Bluffs tomorrow? I'm hoping to capture the flavor of the event. I'd love to shoot your famous blanket buffet, the essence of an Islander's love of the event."

"Wouldn't miss them or the chance to cook for the masses." Alex was known for laying out a veritable feast, turning her picnic blanket into a five-star dining event. "I'm trying a new lemon-blueberry tart recipe with candied lemon peel. Might be a magazine cover in the making. See you by the gazebo?"

"I'll be there—with my appetite and the camera." Melissa tapped her wadded-up popcorn bag on her camera case.

"See you then. Time to find my boys so I can get home and start cooking." Alex bent to pick up a grooming box filled with brushes, ointments, and baby oil. "One day Brendon or Kevin will remember their supplies," she said with slight exasperation and marched toward the animal barns housing the Holsteins her sons would show on Saturday.

Melissa stifled a giggle. If parents only knew how many excuses and creative stories a teacher heard throughout the year when homework wasn't done, a book wasn't read, or a test wasn't passed. That Alex lugged their brushes instead of insisting one of her sons run back to the truck and gather his own tools was one of the reasons the boys expected to get away with late homework or missing books. But Melissa didn't want to think about the complexities of how the home environment affected the classroom. Not today, not with the fair in full swing, not with her photos of the *Shenandoah* garnering a few prizes.

Shifting her focus back to her pictures, Melissa realized she was counting the days until she was back on the *Shenandoah*. Stepping onboard was like stepping back in time. The ship sailed by wind power…only wind power. No electricity, no hot water, no showers, no twenty-first-century conveniences. Leaving behind her computer, answering machine, television, and all electronics was a break Melissa delighted in. A couple of kids would complain for a day or two about their lack of cell phones, games, and gadgets, but they all came around by week's end.

*A week isn't long enough.* She ran her hand over the mat of the sail picture. *Shenandoah* was beautiful, serene, and calling her name. Melissa walked over to the nearest trashcan about five feet away and discarded her empty popcorn bag. Time for an ice-cold drink before a visit to the animals.

"Leaving so soon? Gloating over those ribbons, I bet."

A frosty pall covered Melissa. She knew that voice. Gayle Burroughs. Her ex-husband's third wife. The woman who blamed her for Bryce's death.

"Don't be feeling too high and mighty. We both know you should be in jail for murder."

Melissa sucked in her breath. Fear chilled her body, freezing time and her ability to move. Gayle's words wrested the warmth of the summer air and stole the oxygen out of the barn. Melissa struggled to draw a shallow, ragged breath before turning around to face Gayle.

"You should be behind bars, not winning blue ribbons!"

The accusations weren't new, but Melissa dropped her gaze to the floor. There was no truth to Gayle's bitter allegations, but Melissa's fear of what her ex-husband's widow might do was real. Almost three years had passed since Bryce's car crash and death two weeks later, and Gayle appeared more intent on blaming Melissa every time their paths crossed.

The woman stood clutching an old purse under her left arm, her right arm pressed against her chest as her fingers clung to the shoulder strap. Her eyes darted left and right in a frenzied, nonstop movement. *Menacing* was the first word that came to Melissa's mind when she came face to face with Gayle.

Melissa couldn't help but wonder if there was a gun in the grungy yellow bag. She wasn't going to stick around and find out. Faking a calm she didn't feel, Melissa took a step away from Gayle.

"Not so fast, goody two shoes."

A surprisingly strong hand clamped onto Melissa's left forearm. She stopped and looked back to find Gayle glowering at her.

"I know you were jealous when he left you." Gayle's voice rose another octave. "I know you wanted him back. I know you probably lured him away that night. I'll prove it, too—just you wait."

The last sentence came out in a shriek. Melissa wanted to jerk her arm free but saw the vehemence in Gayle's murky brown eyes. Without glancing around the photo area, Melissa was certain fair-goers were now witnessing and hearing Gayle's crazy claims.

"Gayle! Melissa! What's going on?"

The knot in Melissa's stomach unwound a bit when she spotted her friend hurrying toward her. Kendra Natale stepped between them, forcing Gayle to release her grip on Melissa's arm. Kendra placed one hand on each woman's back and gently guided them closer to the wall of pictures.

"Oh, Miss, you won. Well done. No wonder I heard you two shouting," Kendra said with a smoothness Melissa wished she possessed. Kendra could negotiate her way out of a mousetrap and leave with the cheese.

Gayle's eyes narrowed and zeroed in on Melissa. "We'll finish this another day." She patted her purse with her right hand. "Kendra," she said with a curt bob of her head and then strode off.

Melissa reached out to steady herself on Kendra's shoulder. The five-foot, seven-inch tower of strength wrapped her arms around Melissa and rubbed her back.

"Shake it off, hon. She's a whacko, a certified loon. I feel sorry for her. What's it been—three years? And she's still looking for someone to blame," Kendra murmured.

Stepping back, Melissa sighed. "I know, Ken, but why me? I don't doubt for a second Bryce was out cheating on her, but why does she suspect me?"

"Who knows? Probably her own guilt. She cheated with him when he was married to you, so it makes a weird kind of sense that she'd fear he would go back to you."

"I wouldn't have done so much as shake his hand. Forgiveness is one thing. Letting him back into my life wasn't ever going to happen."

"Ha! You got that right. You were the lucky one. You kicked his butt to the curb. Poor Gayle bore the shame of pitying glances and awkward condolences."

A shard of painful memories pierced Melissa's heart. "Bryce was a train wreck."

Kendra frowned. "A train wreck? Bryce was multiple train wrecks. You know it, and I know it. And you are sworn to secrecy."

Protectiveness squashed her own upsetting recollections. Melissa gently squeezed Kendra's right hand. "My lips are sealed. Forever."

"I know they are. Now let's get out of here and get on with enjoying this beautiful day."

The two friends walked through the Ag Hall and back to the entrance by the carnival rides, where sunlight welcomed them. Kendra paused just outside the large barn doors. "You got time for lunch before you sail off into the sunset?"

"Other than packing and some errands, next week is wide open."

Kendra smiled. "Monday, then? Twelve-thirty at Owen Park?"

"Perfect. You in a rush, or can you hang out for a bit?"

"Let me go tell Jamie that I'm going to have lunch with you, and I'll meet you back here in five minutes."

"Great." Melissa hadn't gone but ten steps when her two Ferris-wheel-riding students called her name once again, ponytails flopping as they ran.

Melissa grinned when the two girls raced to a halt in front of her. At age eleven and just entering the sixth grade, Mya, pronounced "me-yuh," and Lizzie were still excited about school and their teachers.

"Hi!" they said simultaneously with great enthusiasm.

"Hello, girls. Looks like you're enjoying the fair." Melissa smiled as she listened to their bubbly banter.

"It's awesome!" declared Mya Wright, her large brown eyes alive with excitement. "We've ridden the tilt-a-whirl five times, the scrambler three, and now we're gonna try the rockets. Well, maybe the rockets. Lizzie's afraid she's gonna be sick when we go upside down."

"You could come with us—or go with Mya if you want." Lizzie's unspoken plea for help was quite clear.

Melissa scrunched up her face. "No, thanks, Lizzie. I'd be sick in two seconds if I rode that machine."

Lizzie Rubello nodded, her grimace a dead giveaway to her fear and

5

dread. "I love rides, Miss Smith, but even some high school kids have puked their guts out on that thing."

The poor girl. Melissa pointed left to the stretch of arcade games on the back part of the field. "Maybe you girls should save your tickets and play a few games instead. The fair is here for another three days. There's plenty of time to try a new ride."

Kendra walked over and joined them. "How's it going, girls?"

Lizzie grimaced.

"Did you ride that horrible thing?" Kendra pointed to the rockets.

"We were just discussing their other options," Melissa said.

"Such as avoiding anything that goes upside down for the next three days?" Kendra joked and pretended to gag. "Every August Islanders and visitors flock to the Fairgrounds from the time the gates open until late-night closings, and even though we're small compared to many fairs, they always manage to bring in two or three terrifying rides that I wouldn't be caught dead on. Why can't we all enjoy the food and animals and games and forget the stomach-tossing disasters?"

Everyone laughed. Melissa thought Kendra made a fine point. She loved the hometown feel of their fair and how Islanders entered everything from vegetables to artwork to baked goods for judging. Crowds cheered for their favorite pot-belly in the pig races, clapped during the dog show, gasped as the draft horses pulled unbelievable weights, and then hooted and hollered as women competed with fervor in the skillet toss.

"I'm with you, Kendra. I don't need to go on another ride for the rest of my life," Melissa said.

While she loved the tamer aspects of the fair, most kids of all ages loved the rides. Many of the younger ones could be found at the steamship dock, watching the big flatbed trucks roll off the ferry with the carnival rides secured on the back. "Ooohhs" and "Aaaaahs" were common exclamations, as were bets on who would ride which ride first.

"What do you say, Lizzie? Should we hijack the ferry next year and take the Rebel Rockets over to Hyannis?" Melissa jested.

"Yes!" Lizzie agreed with a shout.

Mya winked at Lizzie and gave her an affectionate bump. "Come on, I'm hot. Let's split a sundae and go see the pigs. We can pick our favorites for the races."

Lizzie beamed at her friend. "Yeah, ice cream would be soooooo much better."

Mya glanced into the Ag Hall. "Did you enter a pie or cake, Miss Smith?"

Melissa shook her head. "No. I submitted a few photos from last year's *Shenandoah* trip."

"How'd you do?" Lizzie asked.

"She won a couple of ribbons," Kendra bragged.

"That's cool. Maybe you'll take one of me next week," Mya said with a grin. "I'm gonna own the *Shenandoah* diving contest. I've been practicing off the bridge every time we go to State Beach."

"I'll have my camera ready." Melissa patted her camera bag.

Lizzie walked over, leaned toward Melissa, and whispered, "Thanks."

"You're welcome," Melissa whispered back. "I wouldn't go on that ride if you paid me."

Lizzie stepped back. "I can't wait for our school trip. It's going to be the best week of school."

Though school was not officially in session until the Wednesday after the incoming sixth graders returned from their class trip, Melissa knew that Holmes Hole students considered their *Shenandoah* trip to be the start of the school year. Each of the five Island elementary schools sent their graduating fifth graders on a summer sail. Holmes Hole was the final school to go during the last week of summer break.

Melissa had signed up as the woman teacher chaperone the summer after her divorce was final. She'd needed to get away and couldn't afford a weeklong vacation. Working as a chaperone, she'd been paid to sail aboard the two-hundred-year-old schooner. Not a bad way to make money. This would mark her fifth year.

She smiled at Lizzie. "My favorite week, too. Best week of the year. You girls are going to have a fantastic time. "

"Can't wait! See you next Sunday. Bye, Mrs. Natale," Lizzie said, then skipped off with Mya.

Melissa and Kendra meandered through the rides, waving to a few students and friends before they got in line for frozen lemonade and gyro sandwiches. A couple of Melissa's sixth-grade students from last year were working the garbage detail, earning free entry into the fair every day they volunteered.

She sipped the cool beverage, allowing the chilly sweet and sour flavors to melt in her mouth. No frozen lemonade on the *Shenandoah*. No frozen yogurt, ice cream, or ice cubes two hundred years ago, at least not at a store or fair booth.

Melissa could live without a few luxuries for the daily peace she felt while sailing with students for that one week. After the encounter with Gayle,

7

she was doubly ready to go. If that week could become two, or four, or even fifty-two, Melissa wouldn't complain.

She was looking forward to the cruise more this year than ever before. Captain Roberts had called two days earlier to let her know they'd changed locations of the boys' and girls' cabins because they had far more boys than girls going on the Holmes Hole trip. The new sleeping arrangements gave Melissa an additional reason to anticipate the journey. She'd have her own cabin—a first. Even better, Cabin 8 was the only cabin onboard that was completely intact with its original boards from over two hundred years ago. The boys and men who'd bunk there before probably never appreciated how close they were to history. Melissa thought she would.

During the past sails, she'd gotten a taste of what life might have been like two hundred years ago, and she liked it. This year she'd be one step closer to that romantic notion being a reality.

Kendra grinned. "Those two are really looking forward to their *Shenandoah* trip."

"Me, too. It's going to be my best school trip yet."

# 2

THE DOG DAYS OF AUGUST WERE COMING TO AN END. For an entire week, unusual humidity had saturated everything and everyone, but now it had finally broken. Yesterday was nice. Today promised to be blissful. Melissa thoroughly enjoyed the cool morning air, the warm days, and the breezy nights typical of Martha's Vineyard in late summer. If the current weather held, Holmes Hole was going to have another fabulous sailing week aboard the *Shenandoah*.

Melissa glanced at the front door, where large, reusable grocery bags sat filled and waiting to be loaded into the car. Her packing was nearly done. Just a few more items to pick up in town and one last drive over to Edgartown for some hard-laid cotton cord, molding clay, fabric swatches, colored twine, yarn, and bottles of glue. If only she hadn't spent so much time getting caught up in editing her recent photographs and left her last-minute errands until Saturday morning.

Thinking of the numerous hours she'd spent at the computer over the last five days, Melissa realized she needed another 32-gigabyte memory card for her camera. She'd uploaded her pictures of the Ag Fair, the Oak Bluffs Fireworks, and Illumination Night onto her computer. She had some great shots—additional images to use for her note cards. The business concept was becoming more of a reality as each day, each photo, each idea came into clear view. She'd taken over three hundred pictures of last year's class trip, and she'd shoot twice as many this year.

She wrote *memory card* on her list of tasks for the day and walked over to the sink to refill her glass. The sun was shining outside the small rectangular window that looked over her deck and backyard. She'd watered the potted flowers and herbs the night before and knew her best friend, Cindy, would be by a couple of times during the week to check on the plants and lawn. She drank the last of her water, rinsed out the glass, and turned it over to dry on the wooden rack to her left.

Spike rubbed up against her leg and meowed. Melissa reached down briefly and scratched the top of his head. He threaded his way in and out of her legs in a figure-eight until she bent over and picked him up—all twenty-two pounds of him. Spike was, above anything else, affectionate. He loved people and loved attention. He'd been that way since he'd clawed at Melissa's door six winters ago on a chilly January day. As a scrawny, dehydrated kitten, he'd moved in that night and made himself right at home. Though she hadn't wanted a pet, Melissa's heart warmed up to the snowball with a large gray tabby saddle on his back.

"Are you excited for your vacation, handsome? You seem kind of restless this morning. Relax, bud. Your food, toys, and blanket are in the car. I know it's only nine o'clock, but Cindy has already texted twice and asked when his royal highness would be arriving. I think she loves you more than you love her." Melissa cradled Spike to her chest, his white belly exposed and in want of rubbing. "I love you more, though. Try not to forget me when you're being fed fresh steak, chicken, and seafood."

After five minutes of snuggle time, about four minutes longer than he normally liked to be on his back, Melissa hefted Spike onto her shoulder and walked across the wood floors in her great room. "I guess we'd better get moving if I'm going to drop you off and get my errands done before the tourists are out in full force."

Spike walked willingly into his cat carrier, an act Melissa knew was against the norm for felines and for which she was exceedingly grateful. She placed her shopping list into her purse, slung the paisley bag over her left shoulder, and lifted Spike off the floor. His green eyes stared up at her as they moved toward the car. She'd told him he would be at Cindy's for eight days, and she'd swear he understood every word of her explanation. Something in his gaze, though, the intensity of his focus, gave Melissa a moment of unease.

"What is it, Bud? You're staring at me like I'm leaving you forever. You love it at Cindy's. You know she'll feed you salmon off her plate. If she spoils you like she did over Memorial Day weekend, I won't be able to lift you when I return. "

As Melissa set the carrier on the passenger seat, still Spike had his eyes trained directly on her. She left the car door open and ran back to the house to load her craft bags. After stowing everything in the back seat, she turned Spike's crate to face the driver's side and closed the passenger-side door. When she sat behind the wheel, Spike meowed and stared at her through the front grate.

"You thinking of pouncing on me when I open that door? I'm not a mouse, you know." She chuckled, but the uneasy feeling began to move across her shoulders and down her spine. "Okay, Spikester, I've got to drive. Can you please focus on something else? Look out the window and stalk a bird. You're giving me the willies."

The scenery on the six-mile drive to Cindy's house in West Tisbury did not capture Spike's attention. Melissa loved going to Cindy's. Her home, an old Island farm, had been in Cindy's family for over a century. Though she lived inland, surrounded by fields and gardens, her family had a fascinating sailing history. Cindy's great-great grandfather was Captain Benjamin Clough, a whaling captain. In the 1840s, on the whaling ship *Sharon*, he quelled a mutiny, and the owners rewarded him with a new ship.

Born in Maine, Captain Clough met and married Charlotte Downs of Tisbury. Cindy could always be counted on to tell the romantic tales of the Cloughs raising their family on Island and their daughter Annourilla marrying Henry Richmond Flanders, whose father was Captain Stephen Flanders. Her Island roots were centuries old, which was the reason she'd kept her maiden name years ago when she married Rick Kensington. The home they lived in had been passed down to her and would be passed down to Cindy and Rick's children.

As Melissa thought about Cindy's history with whaling and the Vineyard, Spike continued to stare at his human mother. By the time she'd put her old Volvo station wagon in park, Melissa's neck hairs were standing on end. The stunning dahlias, roses, and hydrangeas that welcomed visitors to the Flanders's farmhouse did nothing to subdue Melissa's uneasiness.

"Spike!" she snapped a little too loudly. He flinched but did not look away. "What's up with you today? I've gone on this trip four times already. Each time you've had a blast at Cindy's. This time will be no different. Now quit!"

"Ahoy, mateys," Cindy called as she pushed open her screen door. "Is the number-one cat ready to be pampered and spoiled?"

Melissa shrugged before giving Cindy a hug. "I don't know. Something's wrong with him. Look at him. He hasn't taken those green eyes off me. From the second I walked him out of my living room, he's had this intense, penetrating glare."

Cindy raised her perfectly polished right hand and waved off Melissa's concerns. "He knows you're leaving, and he's going to miss you. That's all. Don't read anything into it. Besides, you can't take him along."

While Melissa unloaded Spike's food, bowls, toys, and blanket from the backseat, Cindy walked around to the passenger side and grasped the handle on the cat carrier. Spike let out a long, low meow. The hairs on the back of Melissa's neck rose once again.

"What was that?" Cindy raised the crate higher to peer in at Spike.

"See? That's what I'm talking about. His highness is not himself."

Lowering the crate, Cindy nodded at Melissa. "Let's get him inside and let him out. Maybe he needs to go to the bathroom."

Hoping her friend was right, but knowing that Spike had been outside roaming in the yard for over an hour that morning, Melissa didn't believe his odd behavior had anything to do with his bladder control. Once inside Cindy's 3,000-square-foot farmhouse, they opened the carrier and waited for Spike to exit and make a run for the kitty door. Instead, he stepped out and began a new figure-eight path around and between Melissa's legs.

"Okay, how much catnip did the Spike-man have this morning?" Cindy asked, only half joking.

"None. Maybe he's sick." Melissa's stomach flip-flopped at the thought. "Maybe I should run him down to the vet's and have him checked today."

In his typical feline fashion, totally in tune with her words and thoughts, Spike batted Melissa's leg and hissed.

Cindy squatted and ran her hand along Spike's back as he continued rubbing against Melissa's legs. "I don't think he's sick, Miss. I think he's worried, stressing that you're leaving. Just like a little kid. Remember when Patrick was four and he'd cling to me all morning before I dropped him at daycare in the afternoons? That went on for weeks. Spike is acting the same way. Maybe you should head out, and we'll have tea when you get back."

With a troubled heart, Melissa stared down at her feline friend. Patrick, now twenty-four and working in Maine, had been a bit of a momma's boy. Spike, however, had never shown any signs of worry or stress before. Not that Melissa traveled often, but Spike had spent a few nights or weekends at Cindy's over the years, and he'd never been out of sorts. She couldn't shake the feeling that something was wrong, yet it felt ridiculous to cancel her plans because her cat didn't want her to leave.

She scooped him up off the floor and hugged him tightly. "Eight days, Bud, eight days," she whispered into his ear. "Be a good boy. I love you to the moon and back."

When Spike nuzzled into her neck, tears welled in Melissa's eyes. She couldn't explain the sudden sadness at leaving Spike. It was irrational to cry over leaving her cat for a few days. Fortunately, she and Cindy had shared many tear-filled moments during long talks, nights out at the movies, or simply camped in front of the television during a sappy commercial. At the moment, Melissa felt like a snapshot of a Hallmark ad for pet cards.

Spike lifted his head and looked into her eyes. Neither moved for a good sixty seconds; then Spike blinked and jumped down.

"That—" Cindy pointed to the cat with his back to them—"was weird."

Melissa wiped the tears from her eyes. "I know. Can't explain it."

Cindy wrapped her arms around Melissa and squeezed. "Miss, go have a great time. He'll be fine. I promise. You know I won't let anything happen to him."

"I know. Until this morning, I was looking forward to the sail. He's just not himself." The hairs on her neck had relaxed, and Spike was no longer staring at her, but Melissa still felt uneasy. She wasn't given to superstition, didn't read horoscopes or get her palm read. But today her cat had unnerved her.

Cindy stepped back. "Go run those errands, have some chocolate, and forget about Spike's abnormal behavior. Turn on your cell phone at night, and I'll be sure to send you a daily Spike update to let you know he's fine and living the good life."

"Thanks, Cin." Melissa smiled. "Love you."

"Love you too, Miss. Now go before the traffic to Edgartown is backed up for miles."

With one last hug, Melissa was out the door and driving up State Road. She made the left onto the West Tisbury-Edgartown Road and drove in a haze past the airport, past Morning Glory farm, past her turn, and all the way to the stop sign near the Edgartown School.

When Melissa realized where she was, she smacked her right hand to her head, hoping she'd knock some sense into herself. She switched on her left turn signal, drove by Cannonball Park, and back toward Post Office Square and the craft supply store. When she'd found a parking spot, she grabbed her purse and headed into Yarn, Lore, and More.

Within minutes, her arms were laden with school trip essentials. Melissa carried the glue, twine, cord, and yarn to the register. Totally distracted, she placed her stuff on the counter and waited for the cashier to ring her up.

"Hellooooo, Melissa."

She turned at the teasing male voice to find Brant Gates, his daughter, Starr, and her friend Kayla standing in line along with a few other people. Behind her. Where they'd probably been waiting until she stepped in front of them.

"Hi, Brant. Sorry. Did I cut in front of you three?"

"No worries. We've got time." He stepped up to the second register and paid for his purchases. Melissa walked out of the store with Brant, Starr, and Kayla. "You heading out with the school again tomorrow afternoon?" Brant asked as they paused on the sidewalk.

"I am."

Starr edged around her dad. "Who's going to take care of Spike, Miss Smith? Can he come stay with us?" Though she had grown about an inch in the last year, Starr was still small for her six years. And a huge cat fan.

Kayla, a good four inches taller than her best friend, smiled. "Oooh, I could sleep over and we could babysit him together."

Melissa shook her head. "Sorry, girls. Spike is staying with Mrs. Flanders for the week. At least, I hope he is."

The girls gave each other knowing looks and nodded.

"Dad, Dad, let him stay with us. Pleeeeaassseee," Starr begged.

Brant rolled his eyes and laughed. "Melissa, if you're unsure whether Cindy can cat-sit, I have two munchkins here who are eager for the job. I'm sure he'd be no trouble."

Rubbing her right hand up and down her left arm, Melissa shook her head once again. "No, he's already at Cindy's. Just ignore me. Spike has my brain on another planet. Today he was acting like I was never coming back. He's never behaved like that before. Guess I'm more upset than I thought."

"I bet he's just going to miss you," Starr offered, reaching for her father's hand. "I would miss Daddy if he went away for a week."

Kayla made an exaggerated happy face. "Lily says she's going on the *Shenandoah* in a couple of years, but I don't think I'm going to miss her. She's bossy and never lets me into her room. If she's gone for a week, I'm going to use her computer."

Starr giggled. Melissa forced a short laugh and glanced down at the girls. "One day you'll both go sailing on *Shenandoah*, and you'll have the time of your lives. I promise. I love it. And I shouldn't let that silly cat upset me. He'll be fine with Mrs. Flanders, and I'm going to have a great trip. I'll be back next Saturday to bring Spike home, and then he'll be jumping all over my desk, complaining that I'm working too long on the computer."

Melissa affectionately tapped Starr's brown head and Kayla's blond one. "And then I'll stare at Spike all night and see how he likes it."

The girls laughed. Brant dropped one hand onto a shoulder of each child and looked at Melissa. "They say cats have a sixth sense. Maybe Spike knows something about your trip that you don't. Maybe this year will offer new excitement and adventure."

Though a hint of trepidation crawled across her skin, Melissa forced a smile. "You could be right. I'll be staying in a different cabin this year—the only one that's exactly the same as it was over two hundred years ago." Melissa glanced at Starr and Kayla. She hoped they could sense her excitement. "Who knows? Maybe I'll discover secrets or unravel a mystery."

# 3

MELISSA DROVE CAREFULLY THROUGH THE LATE-AFTERNOON TRAFFIC. A distracted father in a bright yellow T-shirt, pushing a stroller with one hand and holding an exuberant toddler with the other, stepped off the curb and onto the crosswalk—without checking for oncoming vehicles.

"Sheeesh," Melissa exclaimed, then braked and waited for the family to make it safely across the road. She'd left her house with ten minutes to spare, knowing full well that August Sundays could be a nightmare in downtown Tisbury. The Summer Sails Tall Ship office was located about a hundred yards beyond Five Corners, the worst intersection on the Island, possibly on the entire Eastern seaboard.

Five streets, five sidewalks, and the steamship ferry all converged at this one small dot on the Island map. If the Steamship auto ferry didn't load and unload from and onto one of the five intersecting streets, the situation might not be as hairy as it was. But cars did roll on and off the ferry there, and harried drivers honked and yelled as they ended or began their vacations.

Knowing the 3:45 ferry docked at Tisbury's Vineyard Haven port at 4:30, Melissa had left her house at four to avoid the worst of the madness. With great care, she had planned to spend a quiet day before assuming responsibility for twenty-eight students for six nights and seven days.

She was thankful she'd gotten her errands done the day before. She'd slept in an extra hour, then had gone to church. Not the most exciting service with the visiting pastor, and the music she and the other choir members had sung consisted of older, slower hymns that made her want to crawl back into bed. Cindy had poked her twice when her eyelids drooped. Melissa grinned, thinking about her friend's immense pleasure at her sleepiness. *Ah, well, you can't stay awake through every service.*

Steering around a neon orange Jeep, Melissa mastered Five Corners and pulled onto the sand lot next to the Tall Ships office. She slipped off her sandals, breathed in the heady scent of salty sea air, and barefooted over the narrow stretch of beach toward the water.

"Good afternoon, Andy," Melissa called out as she neared the wooden dock that extended a hundred feet out into the harbor. At six o'clock, the students and their parents would congregate by the ice house about twenty-five feet in. She watched Andrew Roberts tie off a skiff to the launch platform at water level. In his mid-twenties, Andy was the youngest of Captain Roberts' three sons. He had served as first mate on two of Melissa's previous class trips, though he dropped his family childhood nickname and went by Drew on the ship. "Are you sailing with us again this year?" she asked.

Andy looped the last line around a pylon and climbed up the ladder to the main dock. "Not this year. But I see you're back and ready for another week on the Sound." He extended his right hand and shook Melissa's. "I think you're the only teacher who returns year after year. How many trips is this?"

Melissa almost blushed. She knew most school chaperones did one or two years and then bowed out. The kids could be draining. Two years ago, her group had been more challenging and less enjoyable than her worst teacher nightmare. Fortunately, last summer had been a dream and had reignited her desire to sail another summer.

"This is my fifth year. Hard to believe. But I do love being on the water. Best week of school, hands down."

Andy laughed. "You can't fool me, Melissa. I was on that cruise two years ago. I would have thrown a couple of those brats into the sea myself if jail had not loomed on the horizon."

"I had similar thoughts myself. Thank God last year's class was easy and enthusiastic. I think we'll have a good group this year. Most of the students were talking it up in June before the end of school."

"That's a relief." Andy pointed toward the parking area. "Need some help unloading?"

"That would be great. I've got about six large bags and one box, plus my duffel."

With Andy's help and only one trip back to her car, Melissa had all her items secured in the small motorboat. After her bags were neatly lined up, he unclipped the walkie-talkie from his belt and paged the boat office. "Drew to base. Who's reported in?"

A moment of silence followed, then a crackle of static before the office manager replied. "Andy, this is Vera. Pete, Avery, and Nathan are hanging out drinking coffee. I believe Justin and Caleb are saying good-bye to their girlfriends around the back. I do hope the children don't arrive before their farewells are complete."

Melissa stifled a chuckle. Vera McCormick was sixty-eight years old and knew everybody on the Island. She also knew their life stories. One wouldn't call her a gossip…rather a well-connected, well-informed woman of the community.

Andy pressed the talk button again. "Can you send the guys down to the dock, Vera? Ask Nathan to grab the keys for the second shuttle boat."

"Be glad to. Those boys have had enough affection to last them a week." Vera harrumphed and signed off.

Picturing Vera stomping around the corner of the building and ordering the crew to report for duty, Melissa covered her mouth with her hand to stem the giggle building within. Andy rolled his eyes and smiled.

A few minutes later, five crewmembers sauntered onto the dock. Melissa recognized Pete Nichols, an Islander and last year's galley boy, and Justin Vaughn, a stocky young man who'd been with them last summer as well.

"Hey, guys," Andy greeted them, shaking hands as they reported for another week of duty. "Let's get Melissa's gear out to the ship and help her settle in before the families arrive. Nathan, please motor everyone out in the dory. Wait for Melissa to unpack, then bring her back to organize the kids."

"Will do, Drew." Nathan turned and extended his right hand. "Nathan Brown. Bosun and all-round great guy."

Melissa chuckled and shook his hand. "Nice to meet you, Nathan. As this is the end of the season and you're in good humor, I'll trust that you are a great guy. I'm sure the students are going to have fun with you."

At well over six feet and probably in his early twenties, Nathan looked like an overgrown boy. His brown hair was almost shoulder-length, though not long enough for a ponytail. He wore a lopsided grin that seemed to match his wide brown eyes and scruffy stubble. What truly gave away his sense of humor—and his inner child—was his Snoopy T-shirt. He was either into retro clothing or a kid at heart. Melissa opted to believe in the kid.

"Oh, we'll have fun. I've been known to cannonball from the rigging. The kids go crazy."

"Now that I want to see." Melissa picked up her duffle while the crew loaded boxes of dry goods and two large plastic containers of homemade cookies into the motorboat. Once seated and ready to depart, Melissa called up to Andy, "See you Saturday. I hope I don't miss your strict enforcement of curfew."

"You won't. Zane Warren has filled my shoes better than we hoped. He'll keep your students in line and be sure you have plenty of quiet time in your cabin at night."

Melissa smiled and waved good-bye. The dory rose and fell across the *Governor's* wake as the steamship ferry carried tourists and Islanders to the mainland seven miles away. Melissa released a long, slow sigh as they moved closer to *Shenandoah*.

She simply loved the ship. Captain Roberts had reconstructed and remodeled the original 1770 schooner back in the early sixties. Melissa wasn't yet born when he'd purchased the ancient vessel in 1958, but she became an admirer during her many trips from Vineyard Haven to Woods Hole as the ferries passed the *Shenandoah* on her mooring ball in the harbor. A sleek, tall ship with her black hull and long masts. Melissa had longed to sail on her years before the opportunity presented itself.

She sighed again, contentment and quiet anticipation filling her mind and soul.

"Lots of chaperones sigh as they leave the dock. Are you happy or wishing we would turn around so you could go home?" Nathan asked.

"Thrilled, if truth be told."

"Miss Smith's a return customer," Pete Nichols offered.

Nathan nodded. "Oh, yeah? Got the sailing bug, do you?"

"I love *Shenandoah*. She's magnificent. I don't know that I'd want to be on a powered sailboat, but there is something wholly romantic about cruising on a true wind-powered tall ship, and a historic one to boot."

They drew alongside the *Shenandoah*, and someone lowered the rope ladder over the side. Once onboard, Melissa headed below to her cabin, eager to check out the ancient bunk. Goosebumps rose on her arm as she entered—the same uneasy feeling that had troubled her yesterday when she dropped off Spike at Cindy's. She couldn't explain it.

Shaking out her arms, she inhaled a long, slow breath. As she pictured the *Shenandoah* gliding across the water under full sail, she exhaled, imagining the rise and fall of the bow. She could almost feel the wind in her hair. The goose bumps receded.

Melissa walked slowly around the cabin, trying to figure out what characteristics defined her new sleeping quarters as eighteenth century. The room was smaller, and there were only two sleeping bunks, as opposed to the three or four she'd had in the past. Other than the obvious, she couldn't pinpoint any significant differences from her previous cabins.

She didn't know what she had expected, but she was slightly disappointed. Her initial goose bumps and all of Spike's fussing for a smaller cabin made no sense.

Pete knocked on the door and placed her bags along the empty wall to the right of the entrance. "Best bunk on the boat," he said, motioning his right hand in an arc.

"You think so? I guess I was expecting some eighteenth-century markings or secret messages. Are you a history buff, then?"

Pete laughed. "History? I guess. But I'm talking about space, not old news. This bunk is the only quarters other than the captain's where you're not sharing a room with ten other guys or a bunch of kids."

"Don't forget the doghouses." Melissa noted the two tiny cabins on deck that did bear a slight resemblance to oversized doghouses. Each unit held a cot and a small side table with just enough floor space to stand. The doghouses were given to the first mate and cook, an honor on the ship, but not spacious.

"Ha. I'd rather be in the crew's quarters than a doghouse. I need room to move, if you know what I mean." Pete smiled and left Melissa to organize her belongings. She stowed her clothes in the locker, hung her towels on the wall hooks, and laid out the twenty-eight student activity packets on her bunk.

She ascended the companionway ladder and surveyed the deck. Melissa had hoped Zane would be near or in his doghouse so she could introduce herself. She turned around and noticed Justin and Caleb standing by the starboard icebox and receiving instructions from a man in khaki pants and a navy blue polo shirt. He had to be the first mate.

From the back, Melissa couldn't tell how old he was, but his attire set him apart from the rest of the crew in their traditional shorts and tees. His black hair was close-cropped, neater than any other member of the crew Melissa had seen in years past.

When he swiveled in her direction to point out something to Justin, Melissa was surprised. Zane had to be thirty if he was a day. Definitely not what she was expecting. She walked midship and waited for him to finish his instructions.

"You must be Melissa. Zane Warren. Pleasure to have you aboard." His words were formal, but his engaging smile and friendly tone immediately made Melissa feel at home.

"Nice to meet you, Zane. I wanted to check in, see what needed to be done, and find out if there were any changes from the previous pre-board routine."

A gull swooped down and landed on the rail near the galley. Perhaps it smelled the boxes of fresh-baked cookies sitting on the counter.

Zane ignored the bird and lifted the clipboard he held in his right hand. "I've inspected all the cabins, so you don't need to worry about that. If you have any items to distribute before the students arrive, you can do so now. Otherwise, we're good to go, and I can have Nathan escort you back to the dock when he's done inventorying the bosun box."

"I'll sit here and relax until he's ready. I always arrive a bit early so I can enjoy the ship while she's still somewhat serene. Thanks for giving me even more time to dream." Melissa was impressed. First time anyone had done cabin inspection for her. She was accustomed to counting the towels, washcloths, basins, and metal cups left on every child's bunk. The job was simple and normally completed in under an hour. But it was nice to have it done and have extra free time. If Zane continued to make her job easier, he would soon be her favorite first mate.

She walked toward the bow and leaned against the windlass. The anchor was lowered, the ship secure. No one would be going anywhere tonight. Tomorrow, Captain Roberts would arrive and, winds being agreeable, they would set sail. She wondered where they would anchor Monday night, where the winds would take them. She closed her eyes, tilted her face toward the lowering sun, and imagined the week ahead. Time slipped away.

"All hands on deck."

"All hands on deck."

The words, being repeated on and below deck, brought Melissa back to the moment at hand.

Zane had paged the crew. It was time to pick up the students.

Her fifth cruise was about to begin.

# 4

"Victoria, walk. Don't run," Melissa called through the open door to the lanky brunette hustling down the passageway, probably to comfort Amber.

"Okay," Victoria yelled back, though Melissa couldn't tell from her seated position on her bunk if the young lady had altered her pace. Victoria—not Vickie—had probably slowed to a walk. Melissa had once made the mistake of calling her "Vickie" in front of the girl's grandmother. The older woman had politely yet firmly informed Melissa that her granddaughter's name was Victoria Katherine Lally, "which may be shortened to Victoria." Whenever Melissa sent papers home to parents, she made a conscious effort to address a special envelope to: *The Parents of Victoria Katherine Lally.*

There had been a great deal of paperwork for the *Shenandoah* trip, some of which should have prevented anyone getting caught with banned items. Though every child was personally handed a list of what they should bring and what they could not bring aboard, and each parent was emailed the packing list as well, inevitably one or two students tried to sneak an electronic device into their backpack or suitcase.

Amber, a feisty strawberry-blonde with more personality than an eleven-year-old girl needed, had managed to stash her phone somewhere clever in her duffle to get past the first inspection on the dock. Unfortunately for her, Amber was unaware Melissa had every child's cell number. Once everyone was aboard, lined up with their luggage, and waiting for cabin assignments, Melissa began dialing.

"What time is it? Summertime, it's our vacation…" The lyrics from the latest *High School Musical* movie blasted from Amber's hunter-green duffel bag. "I'll shut it off. I promise," Amber had pleaded as she rummaged frantically through her bag. Flinging a pair of cargo shorts onto the deck, she shoved her right hand into a side pocket as she tried in vain to silence Troy, Gabriella, Sharpay, and Ryan. "Don't take it. Please."

Melissa had marched across the fifteen feet between them and held out her hand. "Sorry, Amber, but you know the rules. No phones. Please pass me your cell."

Her pale, freckled cheeks had tinged instantly with hints of red, but Melissa couldn't ascertain whether from embarrassment or anger. Nearly an hour later, Amber had yet to come out of her quarters. Melissa had surrendered the phone to Zane for lockup in the captain's safe and couldn't give it back to Amber if she wanted to, which she didn't. She just hoped the young lady would adjust her mood before Zane's introductory meeting.

Melissa checked her watch: *7:55*. Pretty soon the ship's bell would ring eight times, signaling 2,000 hours or 8:00 p.m. When the bells had rung earlier, Caleb and another crew member had walked the passageways informing the boys and girls that they had thirty minutes left to stow their gear and make their bunks before Zane expected them all in the saloon.

In years past, the Sunday night gathering had been no ordinary meeting. The first mate, after giving instructions and warnings, had always excused himself and then returned bearing trays of homemade cookies. The cook and crew would pour ample glasses of milk and water, and the incoming sixth-graders would revert to six- and seven-year-olds, dunking and munching until they were too full to eat another bite. After the lecture, of course.

Melissa picked up her camera. She walked into the corridor and reached behind to pull her cabin door shut. The door stuck a bit, probably swollen from the extreme heat and humidity they'd had this summer. She tugged gently until the latch clicked into place. She'd have to mention it to Nathan. If he wasn't in charge of repairs, he would know who was. Not now, though. She needed to get to the saloon before the stampede for sweets began.

No sooner had she entered the room when shouts arose at each end of the ship, and crew members led eager youngsters to the long, rectangular tables situated on either side of the saloon. Amber was smiling, a positive sign that day one would end well for all.

"Sit down and listen up!" Galley boy Pete Nichols raised his voice over the din.

Mya Wright and Lizzie Rubello were the first to claim their seats on the wall benches on the port side. Melissa placed her camera on the table and sat beside Lizzie. She waved to fellow teacher and chaperone John Masters as he came in behind Israel Mendez, a rugged young man who played soccer on the youth summer travel league and was sure to be a great addition to the middle-school team.

"Are you excited, Miss Smith? Are you going to take pictures of the cookies? I've heard there's hundreds of them!" Lizzie's excitement could not be contained.

Melissa smiled. "Not hundreds, but certainly a few dozen. Enough for you all to get a sugar buzz."

Lizzie rubbed her hands together and flashed a toothy smile. "Yum!"

Zane, dressed in khakis and a clean white button-down shirt, entered the saloon, and the room went quiet. Every child onboard had heard tales about the Sunday night trays of goodies. They might not know the treats were stashed in the galley, but Melissa would bet every child had heard the warning that desserts would come out only if the class gave the first mate their full attention. Hence their still bodies and focused eyes, diligently watching Zane.

"Welcome, Holmes Hole!" Zane waited for a second, then cupped his hands around his mouth and shouted, "Welcome, Holmes Hole!"

The students cheered, clapped, and stomped. Melissa grinned. Zane may look stuffier than your average first mate, but a rowdy side definitely lurked beneath his tailored appearance.

When the room had quieted to a dull rumble, Zane glanced around and winked at a few of the kids. "Who knows where we are on the ship?"

Max raised his hand. "The dining room."

A crewmember behind Melissa sounded a gong.

"No cookies for Max," Zane joked. "Anyone else want to guess?"

Nicole raised her hand. "The galley."

The gong sounded again. Nicole shrugged.

Zane chuckled. "Let me ask you, Holmes Hole, do your parents know you're out tonight in a saloon?"

A few of the boys elbowed each other. The girls snickered and giggled. Melissa soaked in the festive energy.

"That's right—a saloon. For many of you," Zane stepped left, giving underage Travis Briscoe a man-to-man fist bump, "this is your first time in a saloon. Let's be clear, though, it's a dining room, not a bar. Milk, water, and juice, ladies and gentlemen. You'll have to go elsewhere for your beer and wine."

While most of the kids were laughing, a loud voice started chanting, "Cook-ies, cook-ies, cook-ies, cook-ies." Within seconds, all twenty-eight students were clapping and chanting, "Cook-ies, cook-ies."

Zane raised his hands and waited for a hush to fall over the room. "Cookies are coming. First, let's review basic shipboard etiquette." In less than ten minutes, the children knew how to go up and down the companionway ladder safely, whom to ask for help with what, what time meals would be served, when they could be on deck, and where the heads—or toilets as they are called on land—were and how to work them.

"Now, there are three rules you must never, ever break." Zane turned around slowly, making eye contact with everyone in the saloon. Melissa's appreciation of the new first mate grew as he connected with the boys and girls in his care. Who knew why someone his age was working a summer job, but whatever his reasons, he clearly enjoyed kids.

When he had come full circle, Zane stopped. "Remember what I'm about to say, and we'll all have a great cruise."

"Number one: Do not mention feeling seasick. You will only feel worse if you complain to your friends. This is a large ship. Most of you won't notice when she's moving. For those of you who do notice, get up on deck and look out at the horizon. The feeling will pass and will not return.

"Number two: Do not talk about missing your parents, your dog, your cat, or your siblings. Homesickness can be contagious. It's worse than the flu. Not only will you feel miserable, but you'll make others miserable. The best remedy is to stay active and have a good time. We'll be sure you work and play hard. In a day or two, you'll be asking to stay aboard and join the crew."

Some of the girls shook their heads, while a few boys nodded enthusiastically.

"Now, number three. You'll ask a lot of questions on the ship. We'll ask you some, too. Ninety-nine point nine percent of the questions you ask are awesome and reflect great intelligence on your part." Zane winked at Amber.

Melissa noticed a sparkle in the girl's blue eyes and wondered if she'd approached Zane and asked for her cell phone back.

Erasing his smile, Zane narrowed his eyes. Melissa knew what was coming, but some of the kids leaned forward, eager to find out what the forbidden fruit was.

Zane spoke very slowly. "Do. Not. Evv-ver. Ask. Captain Roberts. When. We. Will. Sail. Is that clear? Never!"

Nearly every head in the room nodded in unison. Melissa caught a few telling glances between three of her more rambunctious male students. Sooner or later, one of them, if not all three, would stir up trouble. Greg, Anthony, and Trace were good kids but relished pushing the proverbial envelope.

The crewmembers who had lined up on the far wall now stepped forward. Zane motioned for Melissa and the other chaperones to stand. "I know you're all eagerly awaiting Chef Nick's famous snack, so let me quickly introduce to you the men and woman who will supervise your cruise."

Zane raised his left hand and gave Nathan a thumbs-up. "Some of you have already met our ship boatswain, or bosun, Nathan Brown. Nathan will supervise your shipboard duties. You might want to share your cookies with him."

After introducing six of the nine crewmembers, Zane stepped toward Melissa. "I'm guessing you all know your teachers from Holmes Hole, Miss

Smith and Mr. Masters." The first mate paused for the clapping to die down. "Miss Smith will oversee the ten girls and Mr. Masters the boys. Helping them are Mr. Saunders and Mr. DeMello."

For a moment, Melissa wished she'd opted to include a female parent chaperone. Every other year, there had been more girls than boys cruising, so they'd asked one mom and one dad to accompany their children. With eighteen boys, Melissa had originally been pleased to have the extra guy help. Now, analyzing the numbers—thirty-five males to eleven females—she wished one of the females was her age. *Ah, well, at least I have a cabin to myself.*

After the chaperones sat down again, Zane and Chef Nick walked toward the galley. Pete strode to the center of the saloon and put his index finger over his lips. The students lowered their voices but cracked huge, expectant smiles.

Within minutes, Zane and Nick, each holding two platters piled with goodies, marched back into the room and made a grand show of pacing off their strides to the tables, Zane starboard and Nick port. Before the trays had settled onto the tables, arms were reaching and cookies were grabbed.

Melissa angled her camera, capturing crumbs on lips, chocolate-stained fingers, sugary smiles, spilled milk, and empty platters. When their bellies were full, the students headed back to their cabins to grab toiletries and then went up on deck to wash off, brush their teeth, and prepare for lights out.

By ten, doors were closed, flashlights were turned off, and Melissa was nestled in her bunk with the sheet tucked under her chin. She could hear the boys across the hall joking with one another, and a few higher-pitched giggles reached her room as well. She smiled, knowing full well Monday night would be much quieter after a day of chores, and Tuesday would be nearly silent.

Melissa turned on her cell and read Cindy's text: *Spike is great. He had a little steak with his dinner—lol. Did you win a new iTouch or cell phone?*

Shaking her head, Melissa grinned and replied: *One cell phone turned over to the first mate. We won't make a fortune on eBay—ha! Give Spike a hug and tell him I miss him. Love you.*

She reached over the bed rail and placed her phone on top of *Tristan's Gap.* She thought about switching on her flashlight and reading for a bit but decided a good night's sleep would be a better choice. She had about fifty pages left in Nancy Rue's gut-wrenching novel. If Melissa opened the book now, she wouldn't put it down until after eleven. Sleep was necessary for the week ahead.

She listened to the sounds in the harbor: a motor boat trolling by, a rowdy group toasting and partying on a nearby ship, and the peaceful lap of the waves against the black hull of *Shenandoah.* The last thing she remembered hearing was the late ferry coming into port just before ten thirty.

*

"Ye must be relieved the Townshend Act has been repealed."

"Aye, Adam, we must all be grateful, though the cost was dear. Five men, five families. I fear the violence has only yet begun."

In her sleep, Melissa tossed and turned. The bed had become increasingly uncomfortable throughout the night, and her dream was too vivid, the men too loud, and the tension too real. She refused to open her eyes. She would will herself back to sleep, think of something positive, and focus until her mind settled. She'd somehow gotten her back up against the wall, and the hard wood was not helping her relax.

Without peeking, she fanned the fingers of her left hand against the wall to help her slide to the middle. The wood was rough. She gave a gentle shove to shift her weight to the center of the bunk. As she slid her hand along the board, a splinter pierced her skin. She let out a short, high-pitched "eek." She snatched her hand away from the wall and shifted her weight, tucking her injured hand under her head.

*Now I discover the eighteenth-century connection! I'll never get back to sleep.*

"Did ye hear that? Something within moved about the cabin."

Melissa froze. The voice sounded as though it was in her cabin. She waited, eyes squeezed shut. If one of the students was playing a prank, she would not give in so easily.

"There had best not be rats aboard."

*Rats?* That did it. She opened her eyes, blinked a few times to adjust to the dim pre-dawn light, and found herself staring at a wall of wood. She glanced over her shoulder. More wood.

*What is going on?*

The door latch clicked and the hinge squeaked as someone entered her cabin. "I shall see to it, Captain."

Her sense of fun and games was over. This was not a good way to begin Monday. Whoever the two boys were, they were about to get into trouble. Big trouble.

Melissa pushed hard on the board in front of her, and the wall gave way. Before she could stand or scream, she fell into a black hole.

# 5

MELISSA WOKE WITH A START, her heart pounding and her hands aching. It took her a second to realize she had balled the sheets and clenched them in her fists. Slowly, she opened her fingers, wiggling each one to initiate productive blood flow. "God in heaven, what was that?" she whispered with a shaky voice.

She laid her right hand on her chest and felt the rapid, hard beat beneath her palm. She'd been falling—through blackness. Her impression wasn't of a thrill ride, but that she'd tumbled backward into nothingness.

It had to have been a dream. It simply had to, but the sensation had been vividly real. As her heart raced under her cotton Garfield nightshirt, Melissa turned her head to the side and looked around the cabin for assurance of her whereabouts. The orderly lineup of craft supply bags against the opposite wall imbued her with much-needed comfort.

She brought both hands up to her face and gently massaged her temples.

How many times had she heard or read about people having dreams of falling? Dozens. But she wasn't one of those people. Her dreams were nice, calm, sometimes boring, sometimes fantasy, with the occasional bad one when she was overtired or overstressed. Falling through black holes had not been something she'd encountered before.

Yet the dream was intense. The falling sensation, careening backwards through a dark tunnel, unable to see or hear anything, had not felt like a dream. And now she was slightly seasick, though she knew the *Shenandoah* was anchored to a mooring ball and resting quietly in the calm harbor.

Melissa sat up and looked at her watch. Five forty-four. Early. She had more than an hour before the students would be summoned for morning duties at seven. Swabbing the deck was a daily chore on *Shenandoah.* The students learned quickly that what was portrayed as fiction in pirate movies on the big screen was a fact of life for sailors on the high seas in the eighteenth century.

In a short while, the girls and boys of Holmes Hole Elementary would be dashing for mops and sponges, grabbing quickly so as not to get stuck with the scrub brushes. Whoever ended up with a brush would be on their hands and knees, scouring the deck. Melissa smiled, remembering the years past and the shocked expressions of some of the students when they discovered they were required to do chores.

As the corners of her mouth turned up, her lips cracked. She swallowed to dampen her tongue and found her throat also exceedingly dry. She ran her index finger over her lips. They were definitely chapped. Ignoring the lightness in her head and the queasiness of her stomach, Melissa stood and walked three steps across the room to her cosmetic bag. She pulled out her tube of lip balm and applied the ointment to her lips. *I didn't think I was outside that long yesterday.*

She put the tube back in her case and snatched her bottle of water off the floor, chugging a good ten ounces before taking a breath. Feeling slightly more normal, Melissa dabbed at her mouth with the hand towel hanging on the wall hook and then lowered the bottle to the floor. The water was refreshing, but she needed coffee. At least two cups.

Since the coffee was in the galley and not her own kitchen, Melissa changed out of her nightshirt into jean shorts and a school T-shirt, wrapping a gray sweatshirt around her waist before tackling her hair. As she finished knotting the sleeves together, her left ring finger throbbed.

A tiny splinter was causing her finger to turn reddish. She pinched the surrounding area and pulled the annoying speck out between two fingernails. The day was definitely off to a rough start. And her bed-head undoubtedly required some attention before she saw another human being.

When she was a child with long, thin hair down to her waist, Melissa's mom had taught her to begin at the ends, so she did. Melissa gathered her shoulder-length, sandy-blonde mess into her left hand and began brushing out the snarls. Listening to the tangles break and release, Melissa searched her memory to recall any details she could about her dream, before she fell.

*Okay, so where did I fall from?*

A good question. She had no recollection of flying or floating, no happy thoughts of traveling to Greece or jet-setting to Paris or Rome, no alarming visions of crashes or jumping. She released her hair and brought the brush to her scalp and started combing down each side of her center part. "Egad." She stopped midstroke. "Rats. I remember something about rats."

The brush rested halfway down the right side of her head, the bristles filled with hair. Melissa finished the stroke and tapped the back of the brush against her left palm. "Rats? Really? Why rats?"

She continued tapping the brush as she mused. Nothing came to mind. Spike was a mouser, but he'd never brought home a rat. She couldn't recall the last time she'd seen one anywhere.

"Let it go." She dropped the brush back into her cosmetic bag and slipped her feet into her red flip-flops. She needed a strong cup of coffee and a view of the harbor.

First, though, she had to tidy her bunk. Last night Zane had emphasized his expectation that every bunk would be made before breakfast. Or else. He hadn't specified what the "or else" was, but Melissa did not want to draw double duty on kitchen detail. Washing dozens of plates was not in her plans.

Five minutes of straightening and Cabin 8 was ready for inspection. Melissa craved coffee, but her lightheadedness and queasiness were gone. She walked to her door, lifted the handle, and gently pulled. The door didn't budge. Melissa checked to make sure the screw eye hook wasn't fastened. It wasn't. She pulled a little harder, and the door squeaked open.

*Coffee now. Get the door fixed later.*

Standing in the passageway, Melissa could hear the students stirring. If she didn't hurry, they'd be up before she had enough caffeine to function. She hustled through the saloon to the galley, following the mouthwatering aroma of fresh-brewed nectar of the gods.

"Knock, knock," Melissa said, hoping she didn't startle Nick, who was adding salt and diced potatoes to a large pot of water. Monday's breakfast of scrambled eggs, bacon, toast, and home fries was in full prep.

"Come on in. Coffee's on the stove. Just brewed the second pot." Nick reached overhead and placed the box of salt on the lower shelf. Two thin slats of wood held all the spices and baking needs securely in place should the ship ever hit nasty weather.

At the moment, Melissa cared only about a mug to hold her coffee and a spoon to stir in the cream. After filling a white ceramic mug nearly to the rim, she added a drop of cream, swirled in the milky substance, and took that first sip. "Ahhhhh, the day can commence."

Nick laughed. "Don't know how people function without it."

"Me either. I don't care about the pros and cons of caffeine. I need it. Some days more than others. I'll have two cups this morning."

"Didn't sleep well?" Nick's gaze never shifted from the knife he held in his hand and the green pepper he was slicing.

Melissa swallowed a mouthful of coffee. "Weird dreams. You don't have rats on board, do you?"

The stocky young man stopped slicing and looked over at Melissa. "Never seen one. You, ah, didn't see one, right?"

"No," Melissa said, shaking her head. "Someone was talking about rats in my dream. Then, next thing I knew, I was falling through a black tunnel."

"Were there rats in the tunnel?"

For a second, Melissa was going to answer him. Then she saw a corner of his mouth turn up, followed by a grin. His full beard framed his sense of humor perfectly. She couldn't help but chuckle along with him. "I know. Ridiculous. Two guys talking about rats."

The chef picked up a red pepper and placed it on the cutting board. "I've heard stranger, which we won't go into."

Melissa took another sip of coffee. Nick's rhythmic carving of the peppers into thin strips lulled her into a relaxed stance. Leaning against the doorframe, she savored her morning coffee.

Working as masterfully as a five-star chef, Nick had the peppers ready in less than five minutes. "Are you interested in a second cup? Might want to act fast before I start dicing up these onions."

Melissa slammed her mug onto the counter. "Act! Oh, my gosh! That's it."

The young chef with the white apron tied around his waist nearly dropped the onion he was holding. "What did I do?" He caught the onion in midair and placed it back on the cutting board.

"Sorry. But you said 'act,' and I remembered the men in my dream were discussing the Townshend Act." With what she hoped was an explanation for her dream, Melissa peered out into the passageway and beyond down to the saloon. Cabin 8 wasn't far from the saloon. Surely some of the guys had been up early talking and she'd overhead them. "I must have caught the tail end of someone's conversation on the Townshend Act."

Nick cocked one eyebrow. "The what?"

Melissa rolled her eyes. "Exactly. Something to do with something in history, but for the life of me I haven't a clue."

"Well, you're in luck. There's a history professor onboard. I bet Zane will know what your Town Act is."

"No kidding? Zane's a history professor? " Melissa wanted to jump for joy. "See, there you go. Zane was probably talking shop last night, and the conversation carried down to my bunk. Is he on deck?"

"Yup."

"Thanks." Melissa cut through the galley and reached the bottom of the tiny three-rung ladder.

"How about that second cup of coffee?"

Melissa shook her head. "Don't need it. I'm awake now."

# 6

MELISSA CLIMBED OUT OF THE GALLEY HATCH and scanned the deck for Zane. He stood at the helm, papers in hand, reading as Pete Nichols stood to his left. With new knowledge about his more formal occupation, Melissa grinned as she took in his khaki shorts and navy blue polo shirt, both of which appeared to be starched. *Yes, he does dress more as a history teacher than a first mate.*

With eager anticipation, Melissa strode quickly toward Zane.

He greeted her with a warm smile. "Good morning, Miss Smith. How was your first night onboard?"

Melissa grimaced. "Not as restful as I'd hoped. Normally I sleep like a baby, but I had the strangest dream last night. I'm hoping you can help me out. I've heard you're a history buff."

Zane folded the papers in his right hand and passed them to Pete. "Not sure how much help I'll be in the dream-interpretation department, but I'll give it a shot. What happened?"

Taking a step toward Zane and Pete, Melissa surged ahead with her question, despite a moment of self-doubt at sounding a tad foolish. "Were you in the saloon last night, talking about the Townshend Act, by any chance?"

"The Townshend Act?" Zane asked with a touch of amusement. "Can't say I was discussing anything about the Revolutionary War last night. Don't recall being in the saloon either. Why do you ask?"

His response eliminated her easy, hoped-for answer in one simple sentence. Melissa did her best to contain her disappointment and explained, "In my dream last night, I heard two men discussing the Townshend Act. I was hoping, after Nick mentioned you were a history teacher, that you were talking shop in the saloon and I'd merely overheard your conversation in my sleep. Guess not."

"Sorry. Can't help you there. But out of curiosity, what were you doing in the dream?"

Melissa shook her head, more confused than she could express. "Nothing. Listening. I think I was hiding, or maybe trapped. I was boxed in, until I was falling."

Pete stared up at the ropes and beams overhead. *Shenandoah's* masts skyrocketed over eighty feet in the air off the deck. Falling from that height was often fatal, as crewmembers on eighteenth-century schooners witnessed many times during rough seas or high winds.

Pete leaned closer to Melissa and pointed aloft while feigning a shiver. "Falling? I've had a few of those dreams. Usually I'm falling from the rigging. Hate it."

"No one will be climbing to the top of the rigging or falling from the yardarms under my watch," Zane said, waving off Pete's comment. The first mate focused on Melissa. "Who did you hear talking in the dream?"

"I don't know who the men were. At first, I assumed they were two male students, but maybe not. I was in my bunk, or at least I thought I was in my bunk. Whoever was talking mentioned five men being dead and repealing the Townshend Act, and then someone said something about rats." She shivered. "The next thing I knew, I was falling backward into a black hole. I couldn't see anything. I think I was screaming before I woke up."

Her face grew warm as she realized how strange her unusual dream sounded. Avoiding Zane's eyes and trying to make light of the scenario, she glanced up at the tall masts and grinned as if the dream didn't matter to her. "At least I wasn't falling from there or into the water."

The sky was ablaze with bright gold light as the sun rose, and the ship's dark brown beams glistened and warmed under the radiant colors. She should be aiming her camera and taking pictures instead of thinking about black holes and ancient history. Lowering her gaze, she smiled at Zane and Pete. "I don't know why this dream has affected me so much. Sounds rather silly now."

Pete chuckled. "Well, you were saying yesterday how much you wanted the cabin to be as it was years ago. Guess you got your wish."

His words brightened Melissa's mood. Pete was right. She had hyped up the old cabin in her thoughts and in conversations with friends. Maybe the entire dream was just her mind creating the scenario she romanticized about. "You know, Pete, maybe my brain conjured up the whole thing. Wouldn't be the first time my fantasy life was more active than my real life."

"I'm sure that's all it was," Pete said, then checked his watch.

"Almost 0700," Zane told Pete. "You need to report to Nathan and prepare for the new crew."

Pete saluted Zane and Melissa and marched toward the bow where Nathan and six other guys gathered. The "new crew" would be the Holmes Hole students, and they were about to start their first day on the job.

Melissa turned toward Zane. "Out of curiosity, what is the Townshend Act, and why did five people die for it?"

Zane gained an inch in height as he assumed a teacher's stance and gathered his thoughts on a subject obviously close to his heart. "I thought you'd never ask."

Melissa stepped back and sat on top of the roof of the captain's quarters. Zane rested his forearms on the wheel and contemplated his lone student. Melissa gave him her undivided attention, and he began.

"The Townshend Act, though not widely recognized, served a pivotal role in America's history. In 1767, Charles Townshend, Britain's Chancellor of the Exchequer, introduced new taxes on glass, lead, paint, paper, and tea. The Stamp Act had been repealed and the British government hoped to offset some of the imperial expenses in the colonies. In December of said year—"

"Can you simplify the history to the basics?" Melissa asked. "I do want to understand, but I'm hoping not to revisit that dream tonight."

"Of course, sorry. Got carried away." Zane gave her a lopsided grin.

"Oh, I know how that goes. Don't get me started on my favorite list of young adult novels or why some of the so-called classics should be relegated to the dungeons of the school storage facility."

The two shared a knowing chuckle. Melissa sensed they would become friends, and in due time she would ask why he was on a ship instead of in the classroom. Until then, she needed a brief, as-short-as-possible history lesson.

Rubbing her hands together, she encouraged Zane to continue, hoping his memory would jiggle something in hers. "Okay, hit me with a tad more info on the Townshend Act."

Just as Zane was about to expound on his favorite topic, Pete rang the ship's bell and a herd of children ascended the companionway ladders midship and near the stern. Melissa stood, rotating to her left to observe the hustle and bustle. While Zane had been educating her, Pete had laid out the cleaning tools. Twice Melissa refrained from advising a child where to find a cleaning implement or which one not to pick up. When every student was equipped with a broom, mop, brush, or sponge, Nathan demonstrated the proper way to wash down the deck.

When he finished explaining the procedures, Nathan gave the recoil rope a powerful tug and started the ship's generator. The engine, used once a day in the mornings to pump fresh water onto the deck for the daily cleaning, amplified the noise level. Bear, the second mate who looked nothing like his namesake, passed Nathan the water hose, and the chores on *Shenandoah* commenced.

"Ah, the joys of slave labor," Zane joked. "We've got a few minutes until they reach the stern. Where were we?"

"Simplifying history," Melissa quipped.

"Right." Zane bobbed his head once in agreement. "The British needed money to offset their expenses in America. Taxes were the quickest way to score unearned income. But they should have known better. The Stamp Act had been met with hostility, followed by organized resistance until the tax was lifted. The Townshend Act fared no better. Sam Adams, while famous today for Boston Lager, was one of the most outspoken opponents of the Stamp Act and the Townshend Act."

The noisy student crew, some standing, some on hands and knees, mopped and scoured their way closer to the helm. Zane raised his voice. "Already high tensions rose again. Colonists rebelled, taunting British soldiers, shunning their rules, and boycotting British goods. The situation reached its pinnacle on March 5, 1770. The Twenty-ninth Regiment, led by Captain Thomas Preston, arrived at the Customs House to relieve the previous shift, already being mocked by locals, and were met by a large, angry crowd."

Zane paused as water trickled toward their feet. Twenty-eight fully engaged students were ten to fifteen feet away, all busy talking, laughing, scrubbing, or trying to appear as though they were working hard. Zane winked at Amber, who was pushing her broom over the pine boards with tenacity. Amber responded with a thumbs-down, though she wore a smile. Once Amber spotted Melissa observing their exchange, she lowered her gaze to the deck and pushed harder on the broom.

"Seems you've made a friend," Melissa said to Zane.

"We made peace is more like it."

"Ah, did she come looking for her phone last night?"

The first mate clucked his tongue. "One could say that. I believe she would have used her toothbrush as a sword if she could have."

Melissa boxed her thumbs and index fingers into a frame and dramatically scanned Zane's body from head to toe. "You appear to be without injury."

Zane laughed. "She's a firecracker, that one. Gave me what-for until I informed her yelling at the first mate was the quickest way to earn galley duty three times a day, every day. When her mouth and hands stopped moving, I made her a deal. She accepted." He pointed to the bow. "Shall we head for dry land?"

"Not so fast. What was the deal?" Melissa asked, water swirling around her red flip-flops.

When he shifted his focus to the horizon, Melissa knew Zane had a heart of gold. "I suggested that by the end of the week she wouldn't miss her phone.

She said, 'As if,' and I made a small wager." Now he grinned at her.

Opening her mouth wide and drawing her right hand up, Melissa feigned shock and outrage. "You bet one of my students?"

A chortle escaped Zane's lips. "Bet. Wager. Perhaps those aren't the best words to use. Let's say I promised her a T-shirt if she didn't have a good time."

"I love it!" Melissa clapped her hands together. Cool water washed over her feet. Zane's toes were also being showered by the hose and eager students.

"Time for our retreat," he said.

Melissa followed Zane up the port side to the open area mid-ship, by the iceboxes. She had one more question for him. "Though I can't for the life of me figure out how my brain conjured up anything to do with the Revolution, why did the men in my dream mention five people dying?"

Zane leaned against the cap rail and grabbed the nearest section of rigging with his right hand. He looked solemn, as though he had witnessed the deaths. "Paul Revere's famous engraving depicts the Boston Massacre as a one-sided British attack. Hardly true, but great propaganda for the Patriots and excellent merchandising on his part. The facts appeared irrelevant to Revere."

"How so?" Melissa asked.

"When the Twenty-ninth Regiment arrived at the Customs House, the Colonialists were belligerent, shouting, throwing snow and ice and who knows what else at the British soldiers. Church bells had been rung. Many people came out in the cold night because they thought a building was on fire. Within minutes, hundreds of men formed an angry mob raging at the small British contingent. Samuel Adams had instigated a minor revolt. Revere portrayed the British as standing in a line and opening fire on helpless victims. Inaccurate representation, but Revere garnered great support for the Patriots when the print came out. Sam Adams must have been thrilled."

Melissa sat on the portside icebox. "I have a vague recollection of the Boston Massacre. I guess I always thought the British did attack the Colonists."

"Many people believe that. Just the name makes it sound like the British slaughtered random civilians. Calling it the Boston Massacre was another stroke of genius credited to Sam Adams, though he didn't coin that phrase until three years later as he rallied the crowds for the Boston Tea Party.

"The truth is, there was no massacre. Captain Preston swore under oath that he ordered his men not to fire. Speculation had it that his soldiers couldn't hear him with all the shouting and they did open fire, but only after physical assaults and verbal taunts from the angry mob."

"I had no idea," Melissa mused. "And I still haven't the faintest clue why I was dreaming about this when I know nothing about it. Please go on."

Zane lowered his hand from the rigging and rested his palms on his khakis. "Five men died, three on the spot, and two a few days later. Crispus Attackus, an escaped slave, was the first to die. He has since been regaled as the most famous African-American to fight and surrender his life in the Revolutionary War. A month later, while Preston and his men were incarcerated and the atmosphere in Boston was layered with intense hatred, the British repealed the Townshend Act."

Though the morning air was warm and the sun was shining, Melissa shuddered. "What happened to the British soldiers?"

"Captain Preston was tried in October, defended by none other than Sam Adams' second cousin and our future president, John Adams. Preston was acquitted. A month later, the eight soldiers charged with murder were also represented by Adams and a couple of his contemporaries. Only two of the soldiers were found guilty of manslaughter."

"Wow. Guess I zoned out on that bit of history when I was in school." Melissa couldn't fathom how she'd dreamed about this.

"Many believe the Boston Massacre was the first armed confrontation in our fight for freedom. The Tea Party wouldn't occur for another three years, when Samuel Adams would once again incite the masses. Your dream carried you back to the year *Shenandoah* first sailed and the start of the American Revolution." Zane rose and walked toward the ice chest. Though he stood in front of her, his gaze was far away, centuries away.

She studied him. "You're passionate about this."

"Greatest war this country fought. Best time in history, when politicians were honorable and men believed in a cause enough to die for it. My ancestors were there. I was born too late." Without making eye contact, Zane said, "In an ideal world, I would teach American history during the school year and sail during the summer. "

"Sounds perfect to me. How's that working out?"

"Not ideal yet." Zane shuffled to the bulwark, head down, then placed his hands on the rail. He drew in a deep breath before pivoting to face her. "Enough about me, enough about death, and enough about long-ago events. I was reading the weather report when you first came up. We're in for a great day of sailing. As long as there's no mutiny onboard, I suspect, with the winds as they are now, we'll anchor off Cow Bay tonight. First things first, though. Let's have some breakfast."

Melissa's stomach growled in agreement.

Zane waved at Pete to ring the breakfast bell.

# 7

"Miss Smith, can I come in?" Victoria stood outside Melissa's open door, knocking softly.

"Of course, Victoria. What's up?"

The tall, willowy brunette scraped the big toe of her right foot back and forth on the floorboard where she stood. "I was wondering..." The words hung in the air as she inched her toe forward as far as it could reach and then dragged it back as slowly as possible. "Well, can I call home? It's my sister's birthday, and I wanted to talk to her."

Melissa crossed the tiny cabin in two steps and wrapped her arm around Victoria's shoulder. "Are you missing your family?"

Water pooled in the girl's big brown eyes. "Kinda. But it really is Tanya's birthday. Honest."

"I'm sure it is. Did your family have a party this weekend?" Melissa gave Victoria's shoulder a squeeze before letting go.

"Nope. We're going out to dinner on Saturday night after I get home. Tanya will probably choose The Black Dog because she loves their clam chowder."

"That sounds fun. Will you have cake, too?" Melissa hoped her questions and comments would give Victoria something positive to think about.

A hint of a smile appeared on Victoria's face. "My mom is baking Tanya's favorite white chocolate-raspberry cheesecake."

"Yum. I love cheesecake. Lucky you!" Melissa said with an extra dash of oomph.

Though she didn't verbally agree, Victoria wiggled her head with an affirmative response. Melissa pulled a tissue out of one of her supply bags. She passed it to Victoria and waited while the girl dried her eyes.

"How about we see how the day goes? In a few minutes we'll be back up on deck, the food is going to arrive, and you'll be busy packing and storing. Before you know it, we'll be sailing and swimming. I bet you'll feel better once you're busy. And I promise to check on you before lights out. Okay?"

Melissa waited while Victoria sorted through her emotions. The girl was always polite and often more introspective than vocal. "Okay," was all Victoria said. She trudged, head hung low, out of Melissa's cabin and walked into Pete.

"Hey, there." He placed one hand on either side of her shoulders to steady her. "Chin up, eyes up. Got to see where you're going on a ship. Wouldn't want you tumbling overboard." His joke was lost on the sad young lady.

"Sorry," Victoria mumbled, shuffling down the passageway to her cabin.

"Homesick or in trouble?" Pete asked Melissa.

"Homesick."

"It's the first day. She'll be okay." The galley boy tapped his watch. "Came to tell you that the meat and produce have left the dock. Ten minutes or so 'til our cargo arrives. Then we'll get her refocused right quick."

Melissa nodded. "I told her as much. Any word on when Captain Roberts will board?"

"As fate would have it, he's coming out with the food and ice. He wants to catch the morning breeze while it's blowing strong. The winds are perfect, southwest, and *Shenny* will sail right off her mooring ball. Won't need the yawl to push her out into open waters."

"Wonderful. There'll be a ship full of smiling faces."

Pete headed up the ladder. Melissa loaded her camera bag with sunscreen, lip balm, hair ties, mints, and a small bag of ginger chews in case any of the students became queasy once the ship was in motion.

Her cabin had passed first inspection without a tick in the negative column. Five years of shipboard experience had paid off. Melissa knew that ship-shape meant her towels and loose clothing were hung neatly on pegs, her gear was stowed in the built-in chest under her bunk, her teacher supply bags were lined up against the wall, and her sheet and blanket were pulled taut over the bunk without a wrinkle to be seen. She had even fluffed her pillow and leaned it against the wall at the head of her mattress. Zane had been impressed and given her a perfect score.

Draping the camera bag over her right arm, she smoothed out the small wrinkle her camera had left on the navy wool blanket. Melissa picked up her nearly empty water bottle and pulled her cabin door shut. It stuck once again. She left it slightly ajar and headed above to find Nathan.

The nine crewmembers were all milling about. Melissa could see the yawl boat and a larger motorboat approaching the *Shenandoah*. She hustled over to speak with Nathan before the second round of work orders was given.

The bosun had traded his Snoopy T-shirt of last night for Scooby Doo. Melissa chuckled. "I'm not going to ask if you want a Scooby snack."

Justin laughed and clapped Nathan on the back. "He ate enough at breakfast to tide over both Scooby *and* Shaggy until lunch."

"You're one to talk." Nathan shrugged off Justin's comment and faced Melissa. "How's it going, Miss Smith?"

"Great. Except my door is sticking. Could you take a look at it?"

"Sure thing. I'll see to it this afternoon when the kids are swimming."

"Thanks." Melissa left the crew to their prep work and made her way to the bowsprit. Though she would not climb all the way out on the twenty-foot beam as many in the crew and quite a few students did, she loved watching the action of the ship while standing at the base and gaining a higher angle. John and the two male chaperones were talking by the galley hatch, and Pete rang the ship's bell, calling for all hands on deck.

Melissa took her camera out of the bag and attached a filter onto the lens. The morning light made for some wonderful pictures, but as the sun rose, the brightness also bleached out the images during the middle hours of the day.

Snapping as she moved, Melissa captured the excited faces, high-fives, fist-bumps, and numerous gestures and faces her students made as they migrated into their five work groups.

"Hey, Miss Smith, how about a shot of us?" Mya made a goofy face and gave Lizzie rabbit ears.

Melissa took their picture, laughing at their silliness. "Now I think you'd best get to your teams before you end up with extra galley duty."

The previous night Zane had read through their group assignments. As the kids moaned and groaned that they weren't working with their friends, Zane had refrained from telling them that Melissa and John had created the groupings. Years ago, Captain Roberts had stipulated that no two children from one cabin should serve on the same work team. He hoped the students would learn to support and function with others they might be less comfortable with. With groceries several feet away, they were about to begin their first task as teams.

"Attention," Zane called, "let's sound off. Is everyone with their group? Get there quickly if you're not."

A couple of girls separated and ran to their groups. Melissa watched as Amber, Lea, and Maddie moved boldly to stand beside the crewmember in each of their groups. Those girls were natural-born leaders. When Maddie winked over at Lea, Melissa hit the shutter button. She hoped like crazy that she'd captured the moment. She'd check her pictures later when she was out of the sun and the morning chores were done.

Caleb saluted Zane. Amber copied him and grinned directly at Melissa's camera. She was definitely enjoying herself, the confiscated cell phone already a distant memory.

"Group One: Amber, Haley, Israel, Greg, Max, and Mr. DeMello, reporting for duty," Caleb said.

As each group checked in, Zane weaved his way through the students and high-fived each and every kid. If he was looking to build camaraderie, the first mate was gaining ground by the minute. The children were juiced and ready to haul, sort, and pack.

"Listen up," Zane shouted above the excited voices.

The deck became quiet. Melissa zoomed in on eager faces, her own enthusiasm bubbling over into her pastime. For a moment, she wished she'd brought her computer so she could upload her pictures each day and give a slide presentation during the captain's talent show on Friday night. She lowered her camera when Zane addressed the teams.

"The captain and his Corgis are about to board. Let's have everyone single file in two rows, one on starboard, the other on the port side. When his feet hit the deck, let's give Captain Roberts a loud Holmes Hole welcome."

Zane walked to the boarding ladder and then glanced over his shoulder. The students, adults, and crew were standing at attention as commanded.

Melissa felt the sizzle of the children's excitement in the air. When a large, rugged hand grabbed the top of the ladder, she heard Haley whisper to Greg, "Look, there he is."

Stifling a chuckle, Melissa knew Haley was correct. A second later, a Tall Ships ball cap appeared, followed by a head of gray hair atop a smiling, sun-weathered face. Captain Roberts, well into his sixties, boarded the ship with as much enthusiasm as the students awaiting his arrival.

"Good morning, everyone," he said, waving to all the work teams.

Zane, whose arms had been resting by his side, raised his hands palms up and signaled the students.

The children roared, "Good morning, Captain Roberts."

"Are you ready to meet Noah and Cassie?" Captain Roberts asked.

The children clapped and cheered.

Out of sight, over the side of the ship and from down in the yawl boat at water level, a cacophony of barking rose into the crisp morning air. Anyone within earshot was alerted as to who was next to arrive. Captain Roberts turned to face the gangway. As the barking grew louder, the students broke rank and clustered *en masse* behind the captain.

Suddenly, a red and white Corgi head bounced over the cap rail. The girls squealed. Amber, Lizzie, Shelby, and Ashleen made a beeline for the fur ball, who acted as though their adoration was completely expected. Within seconds, a second set of ears crested the bulwark. The smaller dog yipped and wriggled in Drew's arm, then trotted slowly to join her littermate amid the circle of children.

Noah was a tank of a dog, and quite striking with his wide-set ears, white stripe down the center of his face, and deep red coat. Though only about a foot tall, he was solid muscle and master of his domain, which was the *Shenandoah.* He had half a dozen girls kneeling on the deck, telling him how handsome he was.

Melissa raised the viewfinder to her eye and zoomed in on Noah licking Shelby's face. Shelby's giggles spurred the pup on, and he soon had the petite brunette on her back, fending off the wet, black nose and long, pink tongue.

Cassie, short for Cassiopeia, sat daintily at the feet of the students. Last year she had jumped and played along with Noah. Though they were both around ten years old, Cassie had aged much quicker than her brother. Travis bent over and scooped up the little lady. The black-headed tri lathered him with kisses, and then rested her head against his chest. Melissa zoomed in on the tender moment. She knew Travis's mom, Rachel, would love the picture. The image evoked the compelling bond between man and dog. If she'd shot the picture she hoped, Melissa would ask Rachel's permission to use the photo in her new line of cards.

After five minutes of doggie playtime, Captain Roberts called Noah and Cassie to his side. Zane stood beside the captain, his arms crossed over his chest exactly like Captain Roberts. Melissa thought the image was priceless.

She wanted the shot but didn't want to appear obvious. Melissa looped the camera strap over her head and adjusted it around her neck. She lifted the camera to about chest high, then glanced over at her subjects. Zane was moving, motioning for Bear to join him.

Melissa lowered the camera and waited for the coming announcement.

"We've got a breezy southwest wind calling our name. Let's make light work of sorting through the fruits, vegetables, dairy, and meats so we can get *Shenny* under sail," Zane said.

The children clapped and hooted. When they'd calmed down, Zane issued the work orders. "Groups one and two, you've got the fruits and vegetables. Take the starboard icebox. And let's pay attention. Watermelons go on the bottom, apples in the middle, grapes go on the top. Got it?"

Roscoe, group two's crew leader, was as compact and solid as Noah and equally good-looking. He nudged Travis and David. "Ah, yeah, we've got it."

"Good. I don't want any bruised apples. Now, groups three, four, and five, you'll be storing the diary and meats. One word, lads and lasses—ice. And plenty of it!"

The crews lined up mid-ship. Nick, Bear, and Pete climbed down the ladder into the two motorboats along with Drew. The guys formed a conveyor line, passing food up to and over the cap rail. The crew leaders passed off the goods to their teams, and the job was done in less than half an hour.

"Where are the bananas?" Lea asked. "I eat one every afternoon as a snack."

"Bananas are bad luck. No bananas on the boat." Pete picked up a green grape, tossed it high, and caught it with his open mouth. "Grapes are good." He tossed another even higher than the first and caught it between his teeth.

"Can I try?" Lea asked.

"Me, too," Israel shouted.

"Me, too," Amber added.

Justin grabbed a bag of grapes and passed it around. Pete held one between his thumb and forefinger and circled it outstretched for all to see. "One rule, troops. You toss it, you eat it, whether you catch it or drop it."

The concept of eating grapes off of the deck must have appealed to the boys and girls. They tossed and dropped and retrieved and chewed. Melissa shot a couple dozen pictures, then sat on the bosun box and basked in the sunshine.

Drew had departed in the larger motorboat. Four members of the crew hauled the yawl boat up to the stern rail and tethered off her lines. Zane and Captain Roberts were at the helm, probably charting their course.

The sky was a gorgeous Dodger blue. Melissa loved using that phrase. She had discovered the color while painting the interior of her house. Brant had given her a large palette of blue paints. She'd Googled the Dodger color, wondering if the name had anything to do with the baseball team. Sure enough, there were two Dodger blue colors. One darker and grayer, the shade of their uniforms. And the other, the sky blue painted around the ballpark. Gazing at the sky, it was definitely in the Dodger Blue shade.

Melissa rested her head against the pin rail behind her, feeling peaceful. Life on the *Shenandoah* was the best. Maybe she was born too soon. And female. No woman she'd heard about or read about had owned and captained her own schooner in the eighteenth century. But if she'd lived as a man in those days, she could have worked on a schooner, or perhaps owned one. "Maybe *Shenandoah*," she said aloud, giggling at her fanciful thoughts.

"Dare I ask what's so funny?" John Masters asked.

Melissa shaded her eyes and peeked at John. "I was sitting here imagining myself the proud owner of the *Shenandoah*...in the eighteenth century, no less. Oh, and I was male."

John chuckled. "Doesn't hurt to dream."

Shaking her head, Melissa stood. "All my recent dreams seem to be a couple hundred years too late. I think I'd best focus on today and the future."

"You picked a good day to focus on. The weather and winds are perfect. Any second now, they'll raise the sails and we'll be at sea." John's voice held the exact mixture of peace and awe she was feeling about the ship.

Not quite six feet tall, with salt-and-pepper hair and closer to fifty than forty, John was one of the few single male teachers at Holmes Hole. He was handsome. She wouldn't describe him as Paul Newman or George Clooney attractive, but he definitely had appeal. Just not to her. Friends had hinted and suggested over the last couple of years, but neither she nor John had ever made so much as a flirtation with one another. Which had been fine.

Standing on the *Shenandoah* with the warm summer air caressing her skin and the sunlight bouncing like diamonds on the water, Melissa still felt nothing but friendship for John. She smiled at her fellow teacher-chaperone. "You're in for a treat. Few experiences in life equal a week on *Shenny*. Let's get down by the mainsail. I want to take some pictures. You'll probably want to be on the lines hoisting away."

John rolled his eyes. "I have no choice. Greg, Trace, and Anthony challenged the male chaperones. Larry accepted on behalf of the three of us. Frankie was watching, and there was no way Larry was going to decline in front of his son."

Her fellow teacher walked to the chain box and lightheartedly lifted a length of chain, pretending to do bicep curls with an unbelievably heavy weight. He feigned a hearty grunt as he curled the chain, then dropped the iron back into the box. "I'm ready," he boasted, brushing his hands together loudly.

Melissa enjoyed a good chuckle. The man was kind of funny. She'd never noticed that aspect of his personality in school. Then again, their classrooms were at opposite ends of the building. Biology was nowhere near language arts.

"How exactly is this competition going to work?" she asked.

"They'll be on one sail; we'll be on the other. They have a stopwatch. You can see where this is going. Their testosterone has kicked in. The boys' and Larry's."

"I hope you all realize that everyone helps to hoist the sail. Your victory could be won or lost depending on who else is working the lines with you."

John nodded slowly, that patient, nearly resigned nod when a negative outcome is inevitable. "Yeah, I'm aware of that. And I've noticed that those little skunks are whispering to all the boys in their class. I'm fairly certain who will be on our team, so to speak."

Melissa spotted the three boys in question and chuckled. They were flexing their muscles and ribbing one another. She liked them all, though she knew they would most likely be a handful in the classroom this year. Not today, though.

She gave John the thumbs-up sign. "They're all yours."

"The battle is on. I've got to find Chip and Larry. I hope they ate their Wheaties this morning." He turned with a shake of his head and walked toward the main hatch. About ten steps from Melissa, John stopped and glanced over his shoulder at her. "Do me a favor. If we lose, spare us any photographs memorializing our defeat."

"No worries. What happens on the *Shenandoah* stays on the *Shenandoah*." She winked. She wasn't flirting, not at all, she told herself. She was being friendly. And funny.

John pressed his hands together and gave a short but exaggerated bow. "Thank you, O kind one."

When he swung around and continued on his way, Melissa wondered if he had been flirting. She mulled it over for a minute, applied a healthy dose of logic to the situation, and determined that they had never been together outside of work. Their actions and comments were normal for friends on vacation. And they were friends, on vacation. Not together as friends, though. Just two people on a boat who knew each other. And they were friendly toward each other.

Her throat was dry. All of a sudden she needed to find her reusable water bottle and take a long, refreshing drink. Scanning the ship to remember where she'd left it, Melissa spied John chumming it up with Larry and Chip. He wasn't looking at her…didn't so much as peer over at her.

If he was interested, she figured he'd be stealing casual glances in her direction. He wasn't. Thank goodness. Satisfied there was no attraction to deal with, she reversed direction and walked back to the bowsprit. She found her water bottle on the deck beside the starboard chain box and guzzled. Tap water had never tasted so good. She consumed about a third of the pink bottle.

"Weigh anchor," Zane called. He strode in her direction, bringing students with him. Melissa surveyed the throng moving toward the bow and, seeing that Captain Roberts was alone at the helm, made an instantaneous decision to join him.

The students rushed past her. Half the boys, eager to show off their strength, begged to help Bear and Tucker retrieve the anchor. Bear, clearly enjoying his role of command, launched his personal selection process. Four students would work the windlass with Tucker and Bear. The task required muscle. The windlass resembled an iron seesaw, only one with a huge length of chain and a heavy anchor attached to it. The two side arms, which operated the winch that reeled in the chain and raised the anchor, required sheer strength to push them up and down.

When Melissa had first witnessed the mechanisms of the windlass five summers ago, the up-and-down motions of the push-and-pull device had brought to mind movie scenes of two men on an old-fashioned hand car, riding down an early railroad track while grunting and sweating. She'd never thought they were having fun. The students, however, rather enjoyed the shipboard activity.

Having participated in the moment numerous times, Melissa kept walking and settled herself comfortably on the roof deck of the captain's quarters. Captain Roberts was folding the wheel cover. The only true indication that he was ready to set sail came when he removed the white sailcloth cover. But she had a couple minutes to ask him some questions while Bear razzed the boys a bit and then raised the anchor.

"Morning, Captain."

"Good morning, Melissa. Ready for another week on the water?"

"I'm ready for a year on the water," she blurted out.

Captain Roberts chuckled. "Spoken like a true seafarer."

A strong breeze blew Melissa's hair into her eyes. She twisted into the wind, brushed the hair off her face, and dug in the outside pocket of her camera bag for an elastic hair tie. Once her hair was gathered into a ponytail, Melissa smiled at Captain Roberts. "I'm probably doomed to live on land because I need these modern devices." She held up an olive green, fabric-covered elastic hairband. "These, as well as others."

Captain Roberts waved off her answer. "You can purchase those in any port. Worst-case scenario, you use a bit of twine or a bandana. I see it in you. You love the thrill of being at sea."

"I'm a convert, that's for sure. Though I'd like to bring along my cat, my microwave, and my computer for starters. I was daydreaming this morning about owning my own schooner and sailing in the eighteenth century."

"Ah, so you would have been a man," he said with more authority than jest.

The captain lived by the more old-fashioned rules of sea life. He had three sons who had started serving as deckhands when they were ten. Each one worked hard and earned any position he acquired on their ships. But he would not employ his only daughter, who adored sailing more than all three of his sons put together. Once she had turned twelve and developed breasts and an attraction to boys, Tess was prohibited from staying overnight with the all-male crew, and that ruled out any job on the *Shenandoah*.

Melissa shrugged. "I know. I said as much to John, the other teacher-chaperone, a few minutes ago. Do you know of any women who owned and captained their own schooners in the eighteenth century?"

He leaned toward her and whispered, "If you promise not to tell my daughter, I'll let you in on some little-known facts."

Melissa brought her index finger to her mouth. "My lips are sealed. Tess won't hear a peep from me."

"That girl is going to be the death of me. She is determined to sail on my boat, and there is no way I can grant her wish." Captain Roberts rubbed his forehead with his three middle fingers. "I know of no schooner or honest sailing vessel owned and captained by a woman during the eighteenth century.

"However, and this is never to be an option for Tess, though I fear she might fancy giving it a shot, history has recorded two, possibly three, women pirates in that era. Maria Lindsey, who some say sailed in Canadian waters and others say was a fictionalized character, is speculated to have been sailing at the early part of that century. Maria Cobham is questionable. Many believe she and Maria Lindsey are one and the same.

"Of no doubt is the notorious Shipping Queen, as Ingela Gathenhielm was called. She originally began privateering in the Baltic Sea with her husband, Lars, aboard his ships. When he died in 1718, Ingela took over his pirate empire."

Melissa stood and crossed the six feet between herself and Captain Roberts. She wrapped her fingers around the spokes on the wheel and pretended to steer. "I have no desire to be a pirate. In the movies, life normally ends badly for them. I think I'm stuck on land in the twenty-first century."

The captain covered one of her hands with his. "All this talk about times gone past. If you're serious about wanting to spend more time on a ship, do it. Bring your cat, too. Sailors consider them good luck. And they do build ships with electricity. You could have a computer and a microwave." He spoke the last words teasingly.

A shout from the bow ended their conversation.

"Anchor retrieved," was echoed from windlass to helm.

"Hoist the mains'l," Captain Roberts called back.

John, Larry and Chip lined up with a mostly girl contingent. As they hauled on the line, five deckhands grabbed on, and the sail rose rapidly. The boys' team booed and hissed. When it was their turn to man the line of the foresail, Chip timed them. Melissa left her camera bag beside the captain and relocated atop the paint box for a better angle.

The second Chip's watch surpassed the chaperones' time and he yelled out their win, cheers arose. Melissa couldn't shoot the pictures fast enough. She jumped down from the paint box and scooted closer to the action. John spotted her and raised his fist high in the air. She grinned behind the camera. He waved back at her, obviously having seen her grin. Melissa felt awkward, uncertain of their exchanges throughout the morning. She lifted her hand for a brief wave, then hurried back to the stern.

"Off the hook at 1100 hours with a few hours of fair tide to go. A great start to the day," Captain Roberts said as she approached, though he didn't look directly at her. He didn't seem to expect a response. His gaze stayed on the waters ahead as *Shenny* sailed out of the harbor and around East Chop. Melissa eased away, leaving the captain in his glory and making an escape to her cabin. *To get a hat,* she told herself on the way down.

By noon they'd spotted Edgartown Light. The gorgeous summer afternoon passed in the blink of an eye. Melissa finished her book in the shade of the boom and started a second one. Around three, they dropped anchor in Cow Bay. Every child onboard had swum in the waters before, most having been driven by their parents from either Oak Bluffs or Edgartown and then having parked somewhere along the four-mile stretch of State Beach.

The view and the swimming from the boat were much sweeter. Especially during the first three weeks in August, when the beaches were packed full of Islanders and tourists and parking was at a premium. After a solid hour of jumping, diving, and goofing off in the ocean, Zane hollered for the students to board.

Melissa tapped John on the shoulder. "Mind if I head below and flip through my pictures?"

"Go ahead. We got this. Let me know if you captured a good one of me winning." He grinned.

"Sure thing." As she climbed down the ladder, she found herself wondering yet again if he was flirting with her. She had no interest, absolutely none, in dating John…or anyone. One bad marriage was enough for her.

# 8

THE SATISFIED MUMBLES OF BOYS AND GIRLS, who had gobbled down heaps of vegetable lasagna and now were gabbing amongst themselves with mouths full of Nick's double-chocolate brownies, filled the saloon. Melissa sat at the starboard table with Captain Roberts. She enjoyed his nightly talks after dessert. Over the years, she'd learned different sailing topics, been enthralled by folklore stories, grinned at the many superstitions, and tried to sort facts from exaggeration in his stories.

The light faded quickly outside, and darkness crept through the skylights. Tucker turned the wick up higher in the oil lamps, suffusing the room with a warm glow. In a different situation, say, with one man and no children, it might have been romantic.

Melissa reined in her sentimental notions. Too many times in one day she'd thought about dating. Something strange was definitely happening during this cruise. She had no interest in dating and no interest in the Townshend Act either.

Hoping to clear her vision, or at least the ideas running through her mind, Melissa rubbed her eyes. When she opened them, she saw Amber returning from the head. The little minx convinced one of the boys to slide down on the bench, and she managed to claim the seat to Zane's right. The first mate had definitely made a new friend.

Several arms reached across the table, trying to score what was left of the brownies. More than two-thirds of the sweets were consumed. Captain Roberts had about half an hour of their attention span before the sugar high wore off and the students began yawning and nodding off. Melissa couldn't wait to hear what his topic would be. She needed something else to concentrate on, and his forty-plus years on the water gave him more than enough material. None of which had ever included dating or marriage.

The captain pushed his plate toward the center of the cherry table, leaned back slightly, and tapped his right index finger sharply five times, gaining everyone's attention. "Who inquired if we had any bananas this morning?"

A dozen or so heads turned toward Lea. Ever the extrovert, Lea shot her left hand into the air. "I love bananas, especially with peanut butter. But I guess I can survive on grapes for a week."

Melissa smiled at the girl's confidence, as did Captain Roberts. "I'm pleased to know you'll survive," Captain Roberts joked. He allowed the chuckles to die down before elaborating.

"Bananas have been around for centuries and are one of the most popular fruits in the world. However, sailors consider bananas bad luck. As early as the 1700s, men going out to sea have believed that having bananas on board, even one banana, was an omen of disaster."

"No way," was shouted by several disbelieving children.

"Yes, way," the captain replied. "In the early 1700s, when Spain ruled the South Atlantic and Caribbean trade routes, sailors and landlubbers observed that nearly every ship that disappeared at sea or met with a tragic end was carrying bananas in their cargo hold." He looked at Lea. "I speak the truth. Your bananas quickly acquired a bad reputation."

"How was that the banana's fault?" Lea asked, frowning at the captain as if he'd started the superstition.

Wiping his mouth with a napkin, Captain Roberts took a moment to respond. "It's not a matter of blame, but rather of circumstance. Sailors are one of the most superstitious lots around. After numerous reports of banana ships disappearing, no captain in his right mind wanted to sail with them aboard."

Anthony raised his hand. "So if all the captains wimped out, how did bananas get shipped around the world before trains and planes?"

"Good question, young man," Captain Roberts said. "Some ships continued to transport bananas. Fast ships, because the fruit ripens quicker than most. But they had problems, too. Large poisonous spiders with a lethal bite chose to hide in banana bunches. When unsuspecting deckhands thrust their hands into the hold to grab some fruit, they would find themselves the victims of spider bites. Their deaths did nothing to eliminate mariners' superstition about bananas."

Melissa had heard this superstition before. She wasn't one to crave bananas, so she'd never missed them while onboard. But she loved watching the children's faces as they processed the information. Many were awed or impressed. And most bobbed their heads in agreement.

"Now," Captain Roberts added, and Melissa wondered where he was going next. She hoped no ghost stories. "Who knows the significance of Friday the thirteenth?" he asked.

"Bad luck," Jake answered.

Amber stood with her arms on her hips. "My mom says if you walk under a ladder and see a black cat on Friday the thirteenth, you are doomed for life."

"Scary movies," Lea said.

"Something with hotels, too," Ashleen chimed in. "When we went to Boston over spring break, the hotel didn't have a thirteenth floor. The elevator went from twelve to fourteen. Which is really stupid, if you ask me, because we all knew that the fourteenth floor was really the thirteenth."

Melissa laughed along with the students and crew. Ashleen was a hoot. A bit sassy, but funny and bright.

Captain Roberts grinned as well. He wagged his finger at Ashleen. "You're observant. And correct. We don't have fourteen floors on the ship, nor do we currently have a cabin thirteen. Years ago, when I took out adult cruises, we had fifteen cabins, including a number thirteen. Never had any problems with it."

"What I won't do, though, is depart for a voyage on a Friday. Been told it was bad luck since I first rowed a boat. For centuries, ships have remained in port on a fine Friday and started their journey on another day. I don't tempt fate. No sense taking chances now."

A yawn escaped Melissa's lips. She quickly covered her mouth with her hand. Many of the students were yawning as well. The sugar rush had plunged, and the kids were crashing.

Captain Roberts must have noticed the drooping eyelids. "That's all for tonight, gang. Time for shut-eye. Work begins at 0700."

Some mutterings and gripes were spoken under their breath as the kids rose from the table.

Captain Roberts stood and placed his large hand on Jake's shoulder. "One last bit of advice—a minor superstition. Don't sleep with your head toward the bow." Captain Roberts winked.

As the students filed past, Melissa overheard someone ask where the bow was. Then a female voice wondered if he was joking or if she should sleep in a different direction.

John Masters cupped his hands around his mouth and called out, "Ten minutes, boys and girls. In ten minutes we want to see everyone above and washing up for bed."

After scrubbing her face and brushing her teeth, Melissa stood by the main hatch, supervising the girls as they got ready for bed. They were rather sweet, sharing their toothpaste as only a couple of them had carried some up, passing around their tubes of face wash, and divvying up corners of towels from the three who remembered to cart one topside.

Victoria was smiling and laughing with the rest of them. She hadn't mentioned her sister or a desire to call home at any other point during the day. Melissa dreaded having to bring it up now before bed.

Amber was the first to climb down the companionway ladder. Shelby and Haley were hot on her heels, everyone else forming a line and chatting nonstop.

"Good night, girls," Melissa said.

"Good night, Miss Smith," they replied in unison.

"Keep it to a dull roar. I'll check on you shortly."

Victoria was the second to the last to go below. "Enjoy your day?" Melissa asked.

Victoria turned to face the wall so she could descend the ladder properly. Without glancing at Melissa, she muttered an "Uh-huh" and slipped off to her cabin. The answer suited Melissa.

With all her charges below, Melissa decided to stargaze a little before she walked the passageway and turned out her own light. She'd never taken an interest in what constellation was what, but she loved the beauty of the night sky. And on the Island, especially out at sea, few lights dimmed the natural glow. All the stars seemed to radiate a white-gold radiance against the near-black sky.

"Magnificent, isn't it?" Pete Nichols had come up beside Melissa while she'd let her mind wander.

"To say the least." Melissa stretched. "Perfect end to a great day."

"My shift is over. I'm ringing the bell and heading below. Have a good night. Hope you dream of starry skies and sailing."

"My thoughts exactly. See you in the morning."

Pete rang the ship's bell four times. Ten o'clock. Melissa heard the melodic echo across the *Shenandoah* as she headed to her cabin. She switched on the flashlight she left hanging on the wall and then drew the door shut behind her. Once again it dragged and stopped about half an inch from the frame. Nathan must have forgotten to fix it. She tugged hard until the latch clicked into place.

Shining the flashlight about the cabin, she crossed to her bunk and switched on the battery-powered light Captain Roberts had installed over the bunk beds in all the cabins. Oil lamps were a fire hazard with the students. A shame, but safety for the students overrode historical accuracy. A fire onboard would be disastrous.

Melissa dug her cell phone out of her purse to check her messages. Cindy had texted twice. She and her husband, Rick, had spent the day Up Island at Squibnocket Beach with her cousins, who owned a house in Chilmark. *Don't worry,* she texted. *Spike is content, purring in my lap as I type, and stuffed to the gills (pun intended). He does love his salmon.*

Melissa sent a quick reply: *Sounds heavenly—the beach, not an obese Spike. Great day here. Just love* Shenny. *Dropped anchor at Cow Bay. Give Spike a pat from me. Hugs and love to all.*

Spike was happy, which was a relief after his strange behavior before she left. She guessed Cindy had been right. He was probably just upset that his human mommy was leaving. *Ah well, he's being spoiled now.*

She changed into her nightshirt and crawled into bed. The white sheets were cool and crisp, as was the air drifting in through the skylight vent. She reached up and turned the hatch lever to the right, leaving the window open just a crack.

"Oh, wait!" She bolted upright. "Which direction is the bow?"

Melissa drew a mental map of the ship. The girls' quarters were on the bow end of the *Shenandoah*. So that meant…her head was toward the bow.

"Yikes!" Melissa threw back the covers, stood, and remade her bed, this time with her head toward the stern. She wasn't superstitious, not really, but she wasn't taking any chances. She was going to get a good night's sleep, without any Colonial sailors or talk of war, politics, or rats.

Satisfied her new arrangements would ensure a restful sleep, Melissa snuggled into the blankets, opened her book, and lost herself in Tristan's story. She heard the five bells at ten-thirty and kept reading, hoping to finish the twenty-three pages remaining. At eleven, with six pages to go, Melissa couldn't keep her eyes open. She'd reread the last page twice already. Closing the book, she turned out the light and fell blissfully to sleep.

*

"She sails well."

"My nephew is most enamored with her."

The men chuckled. Melissa rolled over. They were too noisy.

"That he is. The lad was born to sail."

"He is a lad no longer. Twenty and five, with no wife and no declared intentions to settle. Elizabeth frets he will join with Samuel and the Sons of Liberty."

"I perceive no occasion upon whence Benjamin would inflict violence upon another without just cause. Samuel and his mob have displayed a grave lack of character. A fault I cannot conceive within Benjamin."

"Eli has said as much to Elizabeth. The recent events have placed men and women on edge. Though it galls Elizabeth to agree with me, life at sea appears a much safer choice. Not a musket fired from Maine to Milton."

A finger of fear slid across Melissa's shoulders. She shivered in her sleep and reached for the blanket.

"Ye must be relieved the Townshend Act has been repealed."

"Aye, Adam, we must all be grateful. Though the cost was dear. Five men, five families. I fear the violence has only yet begun."

Melissa moved her hand across and over her body. She patted around the bed, certain she'd kicked off the sheet and blanket.

"Did ye hear that? Something within moved about the cabin."

"There had best not be rats aboard."

*Rats? Gross!* Melissa kicked her right foot in a knee-jerk reaction. Her toes smacked into the wooden rail. She opened her eyes. No bedrail. Just wood. Where was the bedrail? Where was she?

Images, recent memories, scrolled rapidly through her mind. It took about five seconds for Melissa to realize she was having the same dream as the night before. Only now she was awake...or at least she felt as though she was awake. Her toes were throbbing, she was lying on the cabin floor with a board blocking her view, and she'd clearly heard a man mention rats. Again!

The latch on her door clicked, and a dim shaft of light shone over the sheet of wood in front of her.

"I shall see to it, Captain."

*Not before I see who you are.* She quietly eased herself onto her knees and then shoved as hard as she could against the wood. In an instant she pitched backwards, careening once again into the black hole.

# 9

"No!" SHE SCREAMED. She could hear her own voice from the dream world but also ringing in her ears. Then she realized she wasn't dreaming.

Melissa opened her eyes. She was sitting up in her bunk. Her nightshirt was drenched in sweat. Someone was knocking on her door.

"Miss Smith? Miss Smith, are you okay?"

"Yes," she tried, but only hoarseness scratched through her vocal cords.

The knocking continued. "Miss Smith?"

She couldn't speak. Her throat was parched and sore. Melissa stood, intending to open the door, but a wave of dizziness threw her backward onto the bunk. She landed with a loud thud.

"Miss Smith!" The door flew open. Tucker darted across the room. "Miss Smith, are you okay?"

She wanted to laugh. It was obvious she wasn't okay, and the young man, probably only eighteen or nineteen, looked as though he'd seen a ghost. He lowered himself to a squatting position and reached for her wrist. He then pressed two fingers on her pulse.

Her heart was racing. She didn't need him to tell her that. Her pulse rate wasn't her biggest concern, though. Her head was pounding, and the entire room appeared to be spinning. When she'd stood, she'd felt as though the floor was dropping out from under her. *Dizzy* was an understatement.

Tucker lowered her arm. "Do you take any medications? For blood pressure or heart disease or…well…anything else?"

She heard the concern in his voice, as well as the maturity. Knowing she needed to say something, she tried to swallow but found herself unable. She looked up at Tucker and then pointed to her water bottle.

He passed it to her. "Sip it. Don't drink too much, too quickly."

The water felt divine. A cough drop or throat lozenge would be even better. She'd ask Nick in a little bit. She'd seen a medical kit and a chest of herbs on one of the shelves yesterday when she popped in to ask for a teabag. She'd go down there soon…when she could stand without spinning.

"You were moaning. Loudly."

"Sorry. Nightmare, I think."

"I was in the…ah…head. I closed the door as quietly as I could. Didn't want to wake the three boys next to you. At first I thought the noise of the hand crank had startled you; then I realized you were in trouble."

Melissa met his gaze. "I'm okay."

"You don't look okay," he countered and then reached for her wrist and took her pulse again. "Better," he said after a minute.

He was young enough to be her son, though she had no children. She'd married late and married the wrong man. Tucker would have been a wonderful son. She imagined his mother loved him very much.

"Thank you, Tucker. I'm feeling much better. Don't look so worried. I'm sure you've seen a few shaky people in your life. Say, your friends after a party?" Melissa was trying to be funny, to lighten the mood. Tucker's expression didn't change, though. She placed her hand in his and squeezed. "Honest, I'm starting to feel better."

He looked at her, through her, searching her face. "I don't want to be rude, but…" Sadness flashed in his eyes. "Are you sick? With cancer?"

"No. Oh, gosh, no. I promise, Tucker." Melissa patted the blanket beside her. Tucker shifted and sat on the bunk next to her. His care and concern instantly made sense. "Does someone you know have cancer?"

She watched him ball his fists and then slide his hands over his army green cargo shorts. He dropped his chin to his chest. "My mom," he murmured, the grief in his voice louder than the words he spoke. "She died last summer."

"Oh, Tucker, I'm so sorry." Melissa moved her hand in a circular motion on his back. "Was she here on the Island? Did you take care of her?"

"We lived on the Cape. During my senior year, we spent a lot of time at hospitals and going to Boston. Nothing helped. I tried, but…" He choked up.

"I imagine you were wonderful with her," she said gently. "You have been extremely caring with me. You'd make a good doctor."

Tucker brought his head up and turned slightly to face her. "I hope so. I took a year off after high school to be with my mom. I got into BU. Start next week. This is my last cruise. Needed to work every day I could."

"Wow, Tucker! Boston University is a great school. I bet your mom is looking down and feeling rather proud of you."

"When I first came in the room, and you were sweating and wobbling back and forth on the bed, you reminded me of my mother toward the end. She had trouble standing. Any movement could make her sick."

Melissa took another sip of water and placed the bottle on the floor beside her right foot. "I'm sorry. And I promise you, I don't have cancer. I had a nightmare. Guess it spooked me more than I realized."

Tucker smiled for the first time in fifteen minutes. "Must have been some dream!"

"I think it was. Though it's all a bit fuzzy now. I hope I didn't wake any of the students."

They both glanced at the open door. Tucker shook his head. "I don't think so. They're all so tired after yesterday, they were probably groaning in their sleep and didn't notice anyone else making noise. If I hadn't been consciously aware of attempting to be quiet, I might not have heard you either." Tucker grinned, and Melissa was relieved to see most of the worry gone from his eyes.

"Would you mind asking Mr. Masters to meet me on deck by the galley in half an hour?"

"Um, are you sure you're gonna be able to climb up there? I could ask him to come here." Tucker observed her like a doctor examining a patient.

Melissa smiled. "I feel much better, Doc. Honest. I just need to get into some clean clothes and beg Nick for a cup of tea. I think the sea air might do me some good."

"Go slow." Tucker's eyes radiated warmth and concern. He'd be a great doctor.

Tucker exited her cabin, leaving her door ajar. Melissa took a moment to collect her thoughts. She bowed her head and prayed, "Dear Lord, please bless Tucker. He has been through so much. Help him to prepare for college, and be with him as he pursues a career to help others. Thank you for sending him to help me this morning. I'm not sure what's wrong, and I ask for your healing. Please also watch over the children and crew on the ship. Amen."

Melissa took Tucker's advice and moved unhurriedly about the cabin. She pushed the cabin door shut, at least as far as it would go without a struggle. She didn't have the stability to shove on it, at least not without the fear of falling over. She hung her damp nightshirt on a peg. She'd wash it later and hang it in the sun to dry.

Fortunately, her clothes were stored in the built-in footlocker under her bunk. Melissa sat on the mattress as she slipped on a pair of jean shorts. She bent over and retrieved a light cotton T-shirt out of the middle locker. After pulling it on over her head, she gently brushed her hair. She couldn't think why she'd asked Tucker to go find John. She really needed to talk with Zane. John was a biology teacher, not a history buff.

She put the brush on the bed and massaged her temples. Maybe she was coming down with something. She definitely didn't feel normal. She rose slowly, feeling dizzy as the blood rushed to her feet. Melissa waited for the room to stop whirling before inching toward the door. She'd make her bed and tidy her cabin later.

Walking into the passageway, Melissa felt nauseated again. The distance between her cabin and the galley couldn't be more than forty feet. Fifty, tops. She wasn't sure she was going to make it, but she plodded along anyway. When she reached the black potbelly stove, only about fifteen feet from where she began, she rested both hands on the cast iron antique. Fortunately, it was still early, and the kids hadn't stirred yet. She didn't want any of them seeing her hunched over and looking as if she would toss her cookies.

"Breathe, just breathe," Melissa whispered, encouraging her body to find its equilibrium again. After about thirty seconds, she stood and judged what appeared to be, in her woozy condition, a vast space between the stove and galley. Though only about twenty-five feet, she moved cautiously through the saloon until she reached the steps on the stern side. She paused, resting her palm against the wall to recharge for the climb up the three short steps.

Melissa wiped her brow with the back of her right hand. She was sweating again. Maybe she really was coming down with something. She'd never before had dreams that made her feel sick. Nothing made sense. She needed a cup of tea, more water, and fresh air.

Bracing her left hand on the wall, Melissa placed her right foot on the first step and then brought up her left. She took a breath and prepared for the next step. Seconds felt like minutes, but she conquered the middle step. And then the third. She was inches from the galley, and she was going to faint.

She lunged forward, grabbed the doorframe for support, and whimpered, "Nick..."

"Good morning Melis—" Nick put down the spoon in his hand as soon as he saw her and rushed to Melissa's side. He wrapped one arm around her waist and placed his other hand on her upper arm. "Nice and easy, let's get you over to the ladder so you can sit yourself down."

Outweighing her by close to a hundred pounds, Nick all but carried Melissa across the tiny galley. He maneuvered her around and gently eased her back so she could rest against the third rung.

In a matter-of-fact, unfazed manner, Nick asked, "What can I get you?"

"Do you have any herbal tea?" Melissa asked weakly. "And a glass of water, too, please."

"Of course." He poured her a glass of water and then stepped to the rack containing tin canisters. He brought down a can and gave her the options. "Lemon zinger, ginger-peach, or mango tango delight?"

"Ginger-peach sounds perfect. The ginger will be good for my stomach."

He crossed to the stove, where he already had a pot of water on the back burner. Nick began feeding Bessie, as the oven was affectionately called, around five in the morning. She ate a large amount of coal and gave off a good deal of heat. The pot of water Nick had boiled an hour ago would retain much of its higher temperature.

Nick dipped the tip of his right index finger into the liquid. "The water's warm, but not boiling. Want me to heat it up, or is sort of hot good enough?"

Melissa felt her face. A damp sheen covered her skin. "Lukewarm is probably good. I'm still a little flushed."

"Honey?" Nick asked.

"Please."

Nick hummed a soothing melody while he poured the water over her tea bag and stirred in a dollop of honey. He brought the mug to Melissa.

"You don't by any chance have throat lozenges in that medical kit up there, do you?"

"Maybe. I had a boy a few weeks ago who had a nasty cough. I don't know how you teachers deal with all those sick kids bringing their germs to school every day." He opened the box and rummaged around. "Sorry, nothing doing. Must have given the pack to the whooping cough victim."

"No problem." Melissa chuckled. "The tea is helping."

He stepped closer. "Now that I've escorted you across my galley, made you tea, and breathed the same air as you, please tell me you don't have the flu," he said, sort of jokingly.

Melissa shook her head slowly. "I don't think so. I had another falling dream. I woke up screaming and sweating. When I tried to stand, I nearly passed out. The floor was spinning, and I was nauseated. Tucker came to my rescue."

Nick stroked his beard with one hand. "Falling? Two nights in a row, huh? Dizzy and sick to your stomach in the mornings. I have a younger brother. I seem to recall my mother complaining of similar symptoms when she was—"

"Don't even go there." Melissa cut him off, chuckling. "Of all the ideas. I never heard of pregnant women having falling dreams, but I can guarantee you I am not pregnant."

Nick grinned. "I didn't think you were. But you perked up pretty quick."

"Hellooooo down in the hole," John called, peering his head over the open galley hatch.

Melissa leaned to the right and cocked her head, glancing up. "Morning, John."

"Heard you weren't feeling well. Everything okay?"

She placed her tea mug on the counter, grasped a ladder rung, and stood. "Life is looking up. I think I'm going to live."

"Well, that's a relief. No burials at sea my first time out," John deadpanned.

Nick chortled. "Not in the next hour at least. We'll see how the kids behave."

"Hey, don't be messing with my students," Melissa teased, then stared up at John. "I'm coming up. Would you please reach down and take my mug?"

Melissa made it up the ladder and took one stride to the rail, grasping a section of rigging for support. She gazed out over the water. State Beach was empty. She could see runners and bikers moving along the pathways on the pond side of the road. Though she couldn't see them, people were probably shellfishing across the sand bar in Sengekontacket Pond. Behind her, the sun rose off the port side. She was enjoying a quintessential Vineyard morning. Absorbing the beauty of her surroundings soothed her with a calming peace she hadn't felt below deck. She sighed in appreciation.

John came up beside her. "Nice, huh?"

"Gorgeous. We really do live in paradise." Melissa rested both arms on the cap rail, settling her chin in her hands, and relaxed for the first time that morning.

"Ten months out of the year, at least," John joked.

Many Islanders shared his viewpoint. July and August could be crazy, with 100,000 people congregating and sharing one small Island, everyone wanting their section of beach, prime parking spaces, and a front-of-the line pass. Tempers were often high in the summer. Residents breathed an audible sigh of relief the Tuesday after Labor Day. One could almost feel the Island rise a foot or so from freedom of the weight of the summer people.

"You look good," John said. There was no hint of a suggestive tone.

"I feel better. Good to be awake, good not to be experiencing a nightmare, and good to be standing here." Melissa lifted her face and let the late summer breeze dry her skin.

"Want to talk about the dream?" John asked.

She didn't respond. Instead, she kept her eyes closed and absorbed the rays of sunshine streaking across the early sky.

# 10

DID SHE WANT TO TALK ABOUT HER DREAM? The question hung in the air between John and Melissa. Neither had moved. John now lived up to his school reputation as a patient man, leaning peacefully against the cap rail, granting Melissa the space and time she needed to collect her thoughts.

After a minute or two had passed, Melissa turned to sit at John's right between two lines of rigging. The sun was well above the horizon, painting the sky with gorgeous brushstrokes of orange. Maybe tomorrow she'd come up early and photograph God's artistry. Maybe tomorrow she'd wake up from a restful night's sleep. Maybe tomorrow she wouldn't be standing here attempting to dissect the two most out-of-this-world dreams she ever had.

"I don't know where to begin," she offered, her heart and mind still uncertain how her story should unfold.

She reflected on her waking moments. She had been scared, having fallen through total blackness. Tucker was banging on her door, the sound almost pulling her away from the blackness. When she'd tried to stand, though, the room had spun. Really spun.

She couldn't tell John that, no matter how many times she blinked, the revolving room never stopped moving. And the floor—God help her. When she'd glanced down, the floor resembled a kaleidoscope of rearranging forms. The combination of the whirling room and disappearing floor had made her physically sick. How could she explain those aspects without sounding certifiably crazy?

The historical components were easy to explain. She turned slightly to face John. "I think I'm having fantasies about Colonial Boston. The dream, though it was closer to a nightmare, was pretty much the same as yesterday. Strange guys talking about events from the Revolutionary War."

"Melissa," Zane called from the main hatch. He strode across the deck, stopping a couple feet in front of her. "Tucker just told me you're sick. How are you feeling? What can I do for you?"

Such a guy, stating the problem and immediately planning to fix it. She wanted to tease and ask if he could resolve her nightmare, but she'd also heard his concern. "I'm fine." Melissa waved a hand. "I was dizzy, and a little queasy, but a cup of tea and all this fresh air have cured me."

John draped an arm around her shoulder. "She was just starting to tell me about her dream."

Zane's brow puckered. "Another war dream?"

"Who had a war dream?" Pete asked as he climbed up from the galley.

"Melissa," John replied.

"So much for stars and sailing." Pete referenced his parting comment the night before. "Any black holes this time?"

"She fell again," Nick hollered up.

Melissa wanted to go below. To the solitude of her cabin. She was feeling more and more foolish as the men analyzed and remarked on her nighttime activities. What she wouldn't give to be able to talk with Cindy or Kendra. Girlfriends would be sympathetic. The men around her were analytical. Though, in fairness, all four had expressed concern. She just felt a little ridiculous talking about her bad dreams to a bunch of guys who were definitely in the manly man category.

Then there was John's presence to deal with. He suddenly felt more male than the others combined.

He still had his arm around her…awkwardly, as a line of rigging and the metal pulley attached to the cap rail separated their bodies. She knew he probably thought he was being protective, but she couldn't figure out what she had said or done that gave him any indication she wanted his protection. His arm didn't feel bad. Nor did it feel good. She felt uncomfortable, though. Too aware of him, less able to focus on herself. Was he thinking they were more than teacher friends? He'd never touched her at school. Why now?

Too much to think about.

Pete turned and walked away without another comment.

Zane was staring down at her. "Melissa?"

"Hmmm? What? Sorry, I was thinking." She didn't mention she was pondering the significance of John's arm around her. She shifted her weight, reaching up with her right hand to grab the line beside her. As she shifted and leaned right, John extracted his arm.

Zane lowered himself down to the top of the galley roof. "I'm curious, so humor me, okay? And we've got twenty minutes until the indentured servants scrub the deck for their breakfast." Zane's green-gray eyes were warm and glinted with humor. She sensed he was drawing her out without grilling her. "What was the history lesson in last night's dream?"

"You know, it's funny, but it was almost like I was reliving Sunday night's dream, only I'd arrived a few minutes earlier."

"What do you mean, 'earlier'?" Pete asked, having returned with a white five-gallon bucket. He turned the bucket over, placed it on the deck, and sat between Melissa and Zane.

"I'm fairly certain the two guys talking were the same ones from the night before. I still couldn't see anybody, but they sounded the same and, the more I think about it, the more the conversations seem identical."

"Did you try to see them?" Pete asked.

"Identical how? Same bit of history?" Zane inquired before Pete finished his question.

Melissa looked down at Pete and across to Zane. "I did try, Pete. At least I remember thinking in my dream that I should see who was coming into my cabin. That's the last thing I remember—trying to see around the board in front of me—before the falling started again. But I did hear them. The part about the Townshend Act was the same. But that came after. At first they were talking about a ship—"

"What ship?" Zane interrupted.

"I don't know." Melissa closed her eyes and massaged her forehead with both hands. She searched her memory. The characters in her dream hadn't mentioned what boat they were on, yet she'd felt as if she was still on *Shenandoah*. "I think I was here, on *Shenny*, but probably because it was my dream and I couldn't imagine myself on another ship. But it's highly unlikely anyone from the war was on this ship. I don't think Sam Adams ever stepped foot on *Shenandoah*."

Pete drummed on the bucket. "I wish. Free beer for life."

"Last time I saw your résumé, you weren't twenty-one." Zane's tone had gone from friendly to authoritative.

"A man can dream." Pete gave the bucket a loud one-two bang. "We could have a beer named after us, maybe even be on the can."

"I can see it now." John extended his arms overhead and slid his hands apart in a long arc to create a banner. "Sam Adams Shenandoah Lager."

"Never happen," Zane said. "Captain doesn't allow liquor on the ship."

John shook his head. "I don't think the Boston brew house would be asking Captain Roberts' permission. The almighty dollar would prevail."

Everyone laughed, heads nodding in agreement.

Zane slapped his thigh. "Melissa, you have brought alcohol onboard a dry schooner. This act is punishable by either walking the plank or being tarred and feathered. The choice is yours." The green in Zane's eyes was bright and as inviting as a lush spring lawn.

Melissa leaned back and brought the edge of her right hand to her forehead with great flourish. "Oh, no, I couldn't stand to be tarred and feathered. Such cruel punishment for a lady. I fear I shall be faced with walking the plank."

"Good thing you like to swim," John joked.

*Ba-dum-tsh.* Pete played out a rim shot on the bucket.

"I do," Melissa agreed. "But I'd rather swim at night when the water is warmer than the cool evening air. Maybe walking the plank tonight would clear my head before I closed my eyes. Then I could leave Sam Adams and Ben in the past."

"Ben?" Zane asked.

"Benjamin Franklin, I think," Melissa replied.

Zane stood. "So you've added another statesman to your dream, huh?"

"Guess so. I've got Ben Franklin, Sam Adams, Adam somebody. And some guy whose name I don't know, but he's probably George Washington." Melissa buried her face in her hands. "Do I sound as crazy as I feel?"

Someone patted her shoulder. She lowered her hands and peered up.

Zane was smiling, not mocking her in any way. "I think we spend too much time trying to interpret or figure out our dreams instead of simply enjoying the ride. Don't worry about it." He looked at his watch. "Pete, we've got five minutes. Time to rally the troops."

With a quick *rat-a-tat-tat* on the bucket, Pete stood.

Nick called up from the galley. "Pete, if you're done being Matt Flynn, and Maroon 5 can wait to release their next hit single, you could report for duty."

The chef's assistant shrugged and stepped toward the galley hatch with the drum bucket under his arm. John and Melissa stood.

Zane headed toward the bow, then paused and glanced back. "Melissa, if you discover who fired the shot heard 'round the world, be sure to come to me first. I could write a dissertation that would have me teaching at Harvard."

"Ha, ha." She shooed him away. "I'm hoping I've had the last of my historical dreams."

A clamor arose at the base of the main companionway. "Dream time is definitely over," John said.

A second later, the bell rang and students raced up the ladder. "Ready or not, here we go." John grinned at her.

Students scurried toward the brooms and mops. The sun was out, the air was warm, and twenty-eight children were laughing and talking, with two arguing over the last push broom. Normality had finally returned to her life. She nodded and went below to grab her camera.

# 11

Melissa was relieved to be back up on deck. Nick's delicious breakfast of pancakes, fresh fruit, and sausage had been wasted on her. She'd picked at one flapjack, barely eating half of it. She did manage to consume a bowl of fruit, disappointed to miss the blueberry pancakes and real maple syrup.

Worse still was her abominable grade on the morning's cabin inspection. She'd received a seven out of ten, which any teacher knew was a C-minus. To make matters worse, she knew Zane had been kind with the seven. If she'd had to grade herself, she would have written down a five.

When Melissa had returned to her cabin after breakfast, she'd discovered that her nightshirt wasn't the only item in need of washing and drying. The sheets on her bunk were damp and also needed changing, a clear reminder that the nightmare had been very real.

Every sailor learned one of the golden rules of life on the water quickly: damp or wet clothes on a ship do not dry efficiently below deck, below the waterline. Appalled at the thought of sleeping on soggy sheets, Melissa had stripped them off, leaving the blue wool blanket and the pillow on the floor, along with the nightshirt she needed to drown in some of Nick's dish soap, her camera bag, and the two craft bags she'd also planned to carry topside.

Unfortunately, Zane had appeared while she was at the linen locker. When she'd walked into her cabin and found him standing there with his checklist, she'd felt like the cartoon of the young child writing a letter to Santa in the much-forwarded email: *"Dear Santa, I can explain."*

Which is nearly what she'd said to Zane.

"I know it looks bad, but I have a good reason." She lifted the sheets in her hands and extended them in his direction.

"You probably do have the most unusual excuse I've heard all summer," Zane had offered with a smile. Then he'd looked at his watch and tapped the pen to his clipboard. "But you know better than anyone that I can't let you off the hook and then insist the students are ready for 9 a.m. inspection. Someone might suggest I was playing favorites."

She'd heard the kidding in his voice and clutched the fresh linens to her chest in pseudo defeat. "Guess it wouldn't do for the teacher to be the first mate's pet."

"That would be a resounding no." Zane lowered the clipboard and pointed to her bags in the center of the floor. "Are those two going above? I could have Caleb or Justin haul them up for you."

"Thanks for the offer, but I've got to sort through the craft bags and make sure I have all the fabric paint for their T-shirts. I found some neon tubes at a store in Vineyard Haven, and I'm not sure which bag I put them in," Melissa explained.

Four other reusable cloth bags, overflowing with supplies, were neatly lined up against the portside wall.

"I'll leave you to prepare for the day," Zane said. "Glad you're feeling better."

The slight warmth of embarrassment crept up her neck. The guys had been very kind and sympathetic earlier, but she didn't want to think too long or too much about her strange dreams and weird physical reactions. "Thanks, me too," she'd murmured, wishing the morning hadn't happened.

After Zane moved on to inspect the girls' cabins, Melissa had straightened up her bunk and sorted through her supplies. Though the walls were no longer spinning and all signs of queasiness and dizziness were gone, the cabin had felt claustrophobic. The longer she was in there by herself, the more uneasy she'd felt. The walls and floor boards seemed to taunt her, though she knew that was ridiculous. With a shudder, she'd left everything in the center of the floor and headed down to see how the girls were doing.

Half an hour later, buoyed by their energy and giggles, Melissa had told the girls she would meet them on deck and had swung into her cabin to pick up the supplies and her camera.

Now the fresh air and flurry of activity on deck reminded Melissa why she loved sailing on *Shenny*. The air radiated positive energy. Captain Roberts was standing by the helm, though the canvas cover had yet to be removed from the wheel. Crewmembers were preparing the lines for the moment their captain called for the anchor to be raised. All the students had gathered midship, eagerly awaiting the call to haul on a halyard and hoist the sails.

"You'll be walking the plank this morning, Mr. Masters," Greg sneered in his best pirate voice. Already five-foot-six with a husky build and black hair, Greg personified a young pirate.

His two cohorts, Trace and Anthony, were painting beards onto their prepubescent chins using shoe polish, presumably that Nathan loaned them from the bosun box. Melissa couldn't help but grin that they were wearing the eye patches they received in their goodie bags on Sunday night. She dug out her camera and shot some pictures.

Anthony, black beard fully applied, extended his right arm and pretended it was a sword. "We're going to cut off your legs after we beat you raising the sail today."

John rolled his eyes and laughed. Greg, Trace, and Anthony had organized at least a half dozen of their classmates to form the Holmes Hole Pirate Gang. "All pirates will be tarred, feathered, and then keelhauled for good measure."

"Keelhauled? That sounds like some sissy girl thing, like when they knead bread in home economics," Trace challenged.

With great amusement in his voice, John offered, "When your legs and hands are tied together and you're dragged under the boat, scraping against the barnacles until every inch of your skin is torn to shreds, you let me know how 'sissy' keelhauling is."

"Ha," Anthony proclaimed, both hands on his hips. "You can't do that to us. You'd be fired."

John pretended to tie an imaginary rope. "Might be fun to try, though. Who wants to go first?"

They all laughed. Melissa captured the glint in John's eyes. He looked happier than the students.

The smiles, the bustle of activity, and the spirited conversations were pieces of the many aspects Melissa loved about the school cruise. No classroom assignment had ever inspired the animated expressions on the face of every student aboard. If Melissa could bottle this experience and sell it to other teachers for use throughout the year, she'd be a billionaire. Wealthy enough to own a wooden sailboat and hire a captain to transport her around the world.

"Miss Smith, you look happier than my sister did when she got a cell phone for her birthday," Lizzie said.

Melissa chuckled. "You students just gave me a great idea that would make lots and lots of money."

"What's that?" Lizzie tugged on Mya's arm and stepped closer to their teacher. "Do you mean really rich like the summer people with the big houses on West Chop?"

Ah, she should have seen that one coming. Many people viewed Martha's Vineyard as a playground for presidents, celebrities, business executives, and other well-to-do summer visitors. Tourists and tabloid readers had no idea about the poverty level on the Island. Numerous families struggled to get by. Few year-rounders had the funds to own a small home, never mind waterfront property. Most worked long hours, often at more than one job.

Melissa had six students in her class last year who were on the free lunch program and another four who received reduced-price lunches. That made nearly half her class. And she knew those parents were working their butts off to provide as best they could for their children. But jobs were scarce in the off-season, and prices were high year round. Holmes Hole Elementary had filed for additional government funding so the school would be able to provide breakfast to those in need. For some children, the food they received at school was their biggest, or only, meal of the day.

Those sobering thoughts brought Melissa back to Lizzie's innocent question. She affectionately draped an arm around the girl's shoulder. "If it were possible to bottle all your energy and enthusiasm on this class trip and then sell it to other teachers, I bet I would be able to buy a big house on West Chop. But I don't think a house is where I'd spend my fortune. Spike and I are pretty happy in our little cottage. I could do a lot of good things, though. Say, more books for my classroom and yummy snacks every morning?"

"My mom could bake the snacks," Mya chimed in. Her mother managed Naturally Good, a wholesome deli/bakeshop on State Road in Vineyard Haven that sold a wide selection of organic foods, gluten-free choices, and edibles made with Island-grown ingredients.

"Oh, I love that idea, Mya. I crave her soups when the cold weather hits, especially the butternut squash and apple. We could have those sunrise granola bars and yogurt parfaits and jumbo muffins. Yum. Lots of great choices. I'm getting hungry just thinking about all the options." Melissa rubbed her stomach. She really was hungry. An apple would help placate her appetite until lunchtime. She'd snatch one out of the fruit box after they were underway.

"All hands line up," Bear hollered.

Lizzie reached for Melissa's hand. "Come with us, Miss Smith. Be on our team this time."

"I'd love to." Melissa allowed Lizzie and Mya to lead her to the end of the group on the starboard side.

"I need six volunteers to weigh anchor," Bear said, grinning mischievously and moving toward Melissa's row of students. He pointed at Mya, Israel, and Ashleen. "I choose you, you, and you as willing volunteers." He strode across the deck and aimed his index finger at Amber, Chris and Travis. "And one, two, and three more willing volunteers."

Chris rolled his eyes, but Amber clapped her hands together and took off in a dash toward the bow. Bear laughed. "Now that's what I'm talking about. Volunteerism at its finest."

While the students mingled around the windlass and cheered their friends on, John came up beside Melissa. "How are you feeling?"

She cringed. She didn't want any of the students to hear about her nightmares and their ill effects on her disposition, nor did she want to rehash her physical condition. "I'm better. Ready to enjoy this gorgeous day."

John patted her back. "That's a relief. I mentioned your seasickness to Captain Roberts, and he—"

Melissa spun to her left to face John. "Oh, no, please tell me you didn't fill him in on this morning's episode?"

John's smile vanished, replaced by an apologetic shaking of his head. "Sorry, Melissa. I saw you talking with him yesterday and thought you had told him about your falling nightmare."

Melissa reined in her irritation. It would do no good to snap at John, though she was fairly ticked at him. She glanced beyond him to the ocean and breathed in the beauty of the day. Careful to watch her tone, Melissa corrected John. "I did talk with the captain yesterday, but I managed to ask questions without telling him about my dream. It's slightly humiliating. I'm too old for crazy dreams and nightmares. Heck, I had only a handful of them as a child."

John put his index finger on his lips, his smile returning. "Shhh, you're not old. I bet you're not even forty yet. And if you're old, what does that make me?" He gave her a gentle nudge, then put both hands into the pockets of his Bermuda bathing suit shorts.

Melissa smirked and pointed to the ship's brass bell, which she knew was at least a hundred years old. "An antique?"

John clasped his hands over his heart. "Ah, you wound me."

A cacophony of cheers erupted before Melissa could respond to his silly gesture. The anchor was up and it was time to sail. Melissa pretended to ring the bell and then turned around to join in the clapping. Trace stood on the cap rail and leaped off into the middle of his pack of friends.

"Quit your skylarking, all you sailor wannabes. Let's move. There'll be no slacking off on my ship," Bear hollered at the overzealous students. Ten seconds later, he grabbed Trace in a headlock and maneuvered him toward the bulwark.

Some of the kids started yelling, "Toss him overboard!" And, "Throw him into the water!"

Pretending to give Trace a noogie, Bear ruffled his hair and released him. Trace stood from his bent-over position and brought both arms to 90 degrees, flexing his muscles for all to see. "I win," he shouted.

Everyone knew it had all been fun and games, but his friends went along with Trace's claim of victory, giving him high-fives and slaps on the back. Bear eyed Trace's cohorts and slowly counted off the five boys silently, lifting one finger at a time while pointing to each boy. "You five win, all right. Galley duty! Five new slaves to scrub pots."

"No way!" they protested.

Most of the girls were giggling and quite thrilled with Bear's punishment. Bear laughed. "Just kidding."

"Well, I'm not kidding," Zane snapped. "Get yourselves into two teams, one on each line of the sails. Now, or they'll be the devil to pay."

Melissa wondered what was wrong with him; then he winked at her. The man had the imposing teacher act down pat. Probably not a good match for the elementary grades, but the high school could use his skills.

She chuckled and jumped into the melee of children rushing down the starboard side toward any open spot they could find on the line stretched out on the deck. As she fell in behind Mya and Ashleen, she remembered John's last comment. Glancing over her shoulder, she spied him hustling across the deck. She couldn't resist a parting comment, or didn't want to, so she yelled, "Ancient One, you'll live."

She waited a second for his response, but none came. He didn't so much as turn in her direction. Probably for the better. He might have thought she was flirting with him, and she most definitely did not want him to think that. Her dating days were over, and she wouldn't want to do anything to encourage anyone that she might feel differently. She was just being nice.

Much nicer than the rope felt in her hands. As they hauled right over left, pulling on the line to raise the sail, the rope felt abrasive against Melissa's palms. She'd forgotten the gloves she normally wore. She didn't bother with professional manicures as Cindy did, but she was an avid user of hand cream. Her bathroom cabinet held at least four different lotions to keep her hands soft. Pulling back on the line, feeling the rope's burn across her smooth palm, Melissa prayed she had remembered to pack the thick healing ointment.

When Zane called for the crew to drop the line, Melissa was relieved. She rubbed her palms together, decided to skip raising the foresail, and went in search of her camera bag. No one would question her lack of participation if she was taking pictures. Locating her bag atop the fruit box, Melissa removed her camera and focused on the students and the sails.

She listened as the wind slapped against the canvas, a sound she'd come to love. *Shenandoah* had caught wind and was cutting through the blue-black waters. Low curling whitecaps energized the water around them. The air was warm and invigorating.

"Take a picture of me, Miss Smith," Lea asked, her face beaming as she worked the line.

"How could I not?" Melissa snapped five or six shots of Lea in action.

"Hey, I want a picture too," Nicole fussed.

"Me, too," came another.

"I'm going to take everyone's picture. Now focus on the job at hand and pay attention to Zane and Bear." Melissa spoke her instructions kindly and with a smile. She would do nothing to dampen their enthusiasm. She was still trying to figure out how to bottle it.

Melissa walked toward the bow, to the front of the long row of students all seemingly attached by their hands to the rough, brown rigging.

Bear called out instructions, keeping them in sync. "Heave."

"Rest."

"Right over left."

"Left over right."

"Always keep one hand on the line!"

His directions were simple, yet critical to the safety and success of the crew's efforts.

The expressions on her students' faces varied from focused concentration to overexertion to pure delight to I'd-rather-be-at-the-head-of-the-line-with-the-real-crew. Melissa photographed from every angle, zooming in on fingers gripped around rope, feet braced on the deck, eyes and mouths saying more than words, and the sail as it inched up the foresail mast.

"Pull," Zane commanded. The kids grunted and tugged until Zane called for them to hold the line. The crew tied up and the students waited for Zane or Bear to give the final command.

"Up behind," Zane shouted, and the kids released the line so it hit the deck in one loud crack. Success.

With the two large sails raised and *Shenandoah* gliding gracefully toward East Chop, Captain Roberts called for the outer and inner jib to be unfurled. Several of the boys asked if they could help Roscoe, Nathan, Avery, and Caleb man the lines.

While the students were immersed in the fact that they were sailing toward East Chop Lighthouse, and a couple were taking bets on whether or not they would run into a steamship ferry carrying more tourists off Island than on, Melissa figured the time had come for a talk with Captain Roberts about her dreams. Since John had opened that can of worms, she needed to close it.

She walked down the port side, weaving between John and seven of the male students who were discussing theories on where and how the *Shenandoah* could ram into one of the ferries. When she heard Anthony suggest, "If the bowsprit sliced into the side of the ferry and we impaled ourselves…," Melissa shook her head and picked up the pace. *Boys will be boys.*

She rounded the roof deck and approached the helm. "Good morning, Captain Roberts. Fantastic day, isn't it?"

"Good morning, Melissa. How are you feeling?"

She did her best not to cringe. There was something discomforting about having every adult male on the ship asking how she was feeling and what her nightmares were about. Melissa was convinced that the entire crew knew, and someone, probably John or Pete, had surely told Larry and Chip, too. Thank God no one had mentioned anything around the students.

Melissa drew her five-foot, seven-inch frame to its full height and looked Captain Roberts directly in the eye. "I feel great. I can't explain the last two mornings. I don't normally have nightmares, and I've never been seasick before."

"I know you haven't." Captain Roberts extended his hand, motioning for her to sit on top of the roof deck. Melissa sat and waited. Over the years, she'd come to appreciate what she'd heard about the captain: "He's a man of few words, but pay attention when he speaks."

"You didn't mention anything yesterday when we spoke," he said. His voice contained no accusation.

"I didn't think much about it yesterday. Seemed like a weird dream. I would have felt even more ridiculous coming to you with a childish falling dream."

"And this morning? You alarmed the men. Perhaps not so childish." Once again, his words were direct, yet gentle.

"What did John tell you?"

"He was more concerned about your physical condition than your dreams."

That made sense. And easier to deal with. Better to have people thinking she woke up with a touch of seasickness than that she was crazy.

"Today was different. Though the dream was nearly identical, the nausea and dizziness almost caused me to pass out. Tucker was heroic, by the way. What a nice young man."

"Yes, I'm proud to have him onboard. He helped you this morning?"

The captain's question surprised Melissa. She'd assumed Tucker or Zane would have reported the morning events to the captain. She reined in the hint of anger that once more formed against John.

Glancing to her right, she saw the white conical lighthouse on Telegraph Hill or East Chop, as it was formally known. Gazing at the historic beauty, Melissa focused on gratitude for where she was and what she had in her life. *I shouldn't be angry at John anymore. I should have let it go earlier.* Withholding forgiveness was a sin. She knew that.

God had blessed her in so many ways. She was on *Shenandoah* viewing East Chop from the water on a centuries-old schooner. Not many people could say that. *Why can't I be a beacon like the lighthouse? John was concerned; he wasn't gossiping. God, please take my anger and teach me gratitude.*

Melissa released her hold on the annoyance and envisioned it as a balloon rising the thirty-nine feet up the bluff and then higher still over the forty-foot lighthouse. Her heart beat lighter. She turned toward Captain Roberts with a smile. "The last two nights I've had these bizarre nightmares about past presidents and events surrounding the American Revolution. Monday and today, I woke up feeling as though I was falling through a black hole. Or maybe that's how the nightmare ended. I'm not sure.

"But this morning, Tucker heard me moaning and came in to check on me. I was extremely dizzy, and my throat was parched. He brought me some water and made sure I was able to stand." Melissa forced herself to laugh. The conversation was getting much too serious, and she felt like a fool all over again. She didn't want Captain Roberts thinking she was into any New Age dream mumbo jumbo. "I'm fine now. Honest. Once I came up on deck and drank some water and tea, I felt better."

"Water?" Captain Roberts asked. "Melissa, maybe you've spent too much time in the sun the last few days and have not been drinking enough water."

Melissa couldn't bring herself to tell him that she had been drinking at least three large sport bottles a day, always having one nearby. "Could dehydration give you nightmares?"

Captain Roberts lifted his right hand off the wheel. "Excuse me," he said to Melissa and then cupped both hands around his mouth and called out, "Ready to come about."

Melissa watched in appreciation as the men adjusted the main sail and the inner and outer jibs. The sails began to luff, fluttering during the change in wind direction. As *Shenandoah* turned port toward the shoreline of Eastville Beach, the sails filled once again and the crew tightened the sheets. Their efforts looked nearly seamless, but she knew years of experience were necessary to understand when and how to tack, or turn, a ship.

Under Captain Roberts's expertise, they now glided across the late-morning waters, giving anyone on Beach Road a spectacular visual. The late-summer visitors were in for a special treat. Melissa could envision everyone at Eastville, whether splashing in the Sound or walking the shore looking for sea glass, rushing to their bags and blankets for a camera to shoot the famous schooner in full sail. If she were on the beach, Melissa would be doing the exact same thing.

But she was on the ship, a much better place to be. A sigh escaped.

Captain Roberts grinned. "I'm familiar with that sound. Nothing better than a strong wind and swift current."

Melissa rose and walked a couple steps toward the port rail. She observed the liberal number of colorful blankets and the families eking out every last second of summer. She pivoted back toward the captain. "Not to sound snobby, but it's rather sweet knowing people are admiring the ship you're on."

"The old girl is a grand ship. I'm a blessed man to have recovered her and restored her. She first appeared to be a lost cause, but I was persistent. To be able to sail her is a blessing from God."

Five class trips, and Melissa knew how much Captain Roberts loved *Shenandoah*. "I bet the kids will love hearing her story."

"Tonight," he said.

Seagulls were flying closer to the ship. The scavengers were most likely inspecting the vessel to see whether they were a fishing boat or a passenger transport. The Island gulls enjoyed many a snack from folks on the ferry. Some treats were freely given; others were stolen as the birds dive-bombed a sandwich put down while an unsuspecting gentleman took a sip of his soda or swooped a French fry off a plate while a child toyed with her food.

Finding nothing, the gulls flapped their white wings and made their way back to the beach. Captain Roberts waved Melissa closer.

"I don't want to beat a dead horse, and you look the image of health at the moment, but please take care to drink plenty of water today."

Melissa nodded. "I will, Captain. I've heard enough from the Colonists to last me a lifetime."

He raised an eyebrow. "Colonists?"

"The men in my dream spoke of Samuel Adams and the American Revolution. There was someone named Ben, whom I think must have been Benjamin Franklin, but what would he be doing in Boston? And in my dream?"

"Melissa, is it possible you are overthinking these dreams? I'm sure you've heard me talk about the captains of the *Shenandoah*. I've told Isaiah Reed's story a hundred times. You know that, in 1772, he turned over his captain's title to his nephew, Benjamin, who had served as Isaiah's first mate since *Shenandoah* launched in 1770. Benjamin captained her through the Revolutionary War, though some of the ship's logbooks are missing, and portions of her history are unknown."

As Captain Roberts recounted the information, a huge weight lifted off her shoulders. She had heard that story—twice. Funny how she'd forgotten.

"Now that you mention it, I remember you talking about Benjamin Reed." Melissa shifted her weight from side to side, tapping the fingers of her right hand against her thigh. Something about Ben Reed and Ben Franklin niggled at the back of her brain. Something about guns. Something about relatives. "Last night…" She grimaced. "I can't put my finger on it, but I'm missing a piece in my memory."

The captain walked two steps toward Melissa and tapped his watch. "Don't waste too much time on it. I think your dreams are merely your brain working overtime. Be grateful for the sunny day and that we're not sailing through stormy seas or gunfire."

*Gunfire?* Yes! One of the men in her dream had said there was no gunfire. And… "That's it! I've got it! Ben wasn't Benjamin Franklin. You're right. He must be Benjamin Reed. One of the men in my dream was talking about his nephew, Ben."

Captain Roberts nodded. His eyes were as soft and patient as her father's had often been when she was struggling to comprehend a math problem in junior high. "There you go. And I'm sure you've been preparing for the new school year, too. Are you teaching in your sleep?"

His joke made her feel better. Everything made sense. Well, not the dizziness. Then again, maybe she had been dehydrated. She'd drink an extra bottle of water today and hope the nightmares and nausea stayed gone. At least she knew who the people in her dreams were and why they were there.

"Captain, you are a genius. I'm going to go refill my water bottle and gather the students to make T-shirts."

"Before you begin the craft, would you mind asking Zane to join me at the helm?"

"Sure thing, Captain."

"Melissa, grab a hat and wear it," he advised.

"I will." She nearly skipped up the starboard side. Noah and Cassie, who'd been sleeping at the wheelbase the entire time she and Captain Roberts were speaking, fell into step behind her.

# 12

Melissa stood next to the water pump, her bottle refilled, and announced, "Anyone who wants to make a T-shirt meet me on top of the roof deck."

A couple of the girls squealed with delight, which set the pups to barking. When Maddie, Lea, and Shelby went off to gather their friends, the dogs were eager participants in corralling the children. Noah, his herding instincts in full gear, ran up to every student on deck and barked and licked until he had their attention. Cassie followed behind him until Lea picked her up.

"You're such a good girl, Cassie. Want to help me make a T-shirt?" Cassie licked Lea's face, though whether that meant she wanted to help was questionable.

Melissa spread the fabric paints out on the rooftop and began tearing sheets of wax paper to place between the front and back of the shirts. She'd purchased plain white tees online when she'd ordered the students their commemorative cruise shirts. She bought a dozen extra T-shirts of mixed sizes in case the chaperones wanted to get crafty, and also for the crew. The girls normally finished their projects and then wanted to make special shirts for their favorite crewmember.

The students weren't required to make one, but within ten minutes every child was spread out over the roof deck and along the sides with a brush or squeeze tube in hand and designs underway.

"Can Cassie help me?" Lea asked.

"What do you mean, 'help you'?" Melissa questioned.

"Can I dip her paws into the paint and have her walk over my shirt?"

Melissa contained her laughter. She loved the creativity of her students. She hated to squelch a cute idea, but the dog's safety came first. "I'm not sure the paints are safe for Cassie. I wouldn't want her to lick her paws and get sick. Can you draw her paw print instead?"

Pensiveness furrowed Lea's brow for a minute, then she smiled. "Could I ask Captain Roberts?"

"Sure." Melissa suspected what the outcome would be, but better to have the dog's owner decline Lea's request.

Lea lifted Cassie and cradled her as they moved toward the helm. Melissa watched, unable to hear what Captain Roberts was saying, but able to see his head shake no in response to Lea's appeal. He said something further to her, and Lea lowered Cassie to the deck and then disappeared into the captain's quarters. She surfaced with a broad grin and a stuffed toy Corgi.

Calling Cassie, Lea bounced down the starboard side. "Guess what?"

"What?" Melissa asked.

"Captain Roberts said I can use this stuffed dog someone gave him. Isn't that a great idea? Then we won't have to worry about Cassie eating paint that could make her sick." Lea was grinning, and Melissa was thrilled with the solution. Cassie seemed especially content to sleep against Lea's leg while the young girl dipped the stuffed dog's paws into various paint colors and walked the toy across her T-shirt.

Occasionally, when a student made a bawdy comment, Melissa or John had to remind one or two of the boys that the words and images they used needed to be school-appropriate. Some of the kids were gifted artistically, which further convinced Melissa that T-shirts should be a craft done on every school cruise. It was certainly her favorite craft, but she hadn't heard of any of the other schools creating clothes onboard.

An hour and a half later, thirty-some-odd shirts were spread out over the roof deck to dry in the sun. Pete called for lunch and they all ate on deck, leaning against the cap rail or sitting on an icebox, as Captain Roberts maneuvered *Shenandoah* around West Chop. A steady southeast wind filled the sails, and the captain took them for a ride, tacking back and forth across the Vineyard Sound toward Naushon Island twice before anchoring in Lambert's Cove.

When the sails were lowered, Bear ordered everyone to gather around him at the main hatch. "Today is your lucky day. You're going to learn the proper way to stow the lines when we're at anchor. Now, I need two volunteers." Once again he didn't wait for hands to go up. He pointed to Ashleen and Chris and directed them to the mess of rope in front of him on the portside.

"Flemish coils, boys and girls, are your new best friend. Once you master the skill, you can go swimming. Chris, Ashleen, and I are going to show you how it's done, and then you're gonna break off into your work groups and tidy up this deck. Ready?" Bear asked.

"Ready," the students screamed, some a little too loudly for Melissa's ears.

She slid to her left, away from a rowdy group of boys. John motioned for her to come and stand beside him by the fruit box, but she shook her head and lifted the camera hanging from its strap around her neck. He nodded.

Relieved to have the excuse, Melissa turned her attention back to Bear and waited for a movement or image to catch her eye.

"Have a seat," Bear said to Chris and Ashleen and squatted beside Ashleen. "Flemish coils start big and get smaller. I bet some of you have sat in class drawing on paper when you should have been paying attention, right?"

Melissa chuckled as more than half the students nodded.

"Ever press your pen to the page and then start making a circle, and another, and another, until you had lots of circles around your one little dot?"

More heads bobbed in agreement.

"Well, a Flemish coil is the same thing only backward. We're going to make the big circle first, and then go smaller and smaller, pressing the line tight against itself until there's none left."

Bear helped Ashleen create a large circle with the section of line closest to the sail. He showed Chris and Ashleen how to tuck the rope inside the initial loop. One after another, the work groups figured out the job at hand. Melissa shot numerous pictures of the children's faces, intent on the task, and of their hands manipulating the lines.

When every line was perfectly coiled, Bear challenged the students to a diving contest. The kids started jumping off the cap rail. Shrieks of delight left their mouths before they hit the water, though a few students surfaced with a sputter. Melissa shot dozens of pictures.

Captain Roberts joined her at the rail. "How are you feeling?"

"Fabulous. I couldn't ask for a better day."

He pointed to her water bottle. "No dizziness?"

"None. All the ill effects of the morning have completely disappeared."

Mya scampered up the ladder. "Miss Smith, I'm going to try a pike. I've been practicing all summer. Can you please take my picture?"

Melissa raised her camera to look through the viewfinder. "Of course, Mya. Dive away."

Mya climbed atop the cap rail and waited for the water below to be clear of her friends. "Come on, Mya," Lizzie cheered from the sea.

Mya was long and lean, and her dark brown skin glistened with drops of salt water. Melissa held the camera steady. Mya glanced back, gave her teacher a thumbs-up, and faced forward. She raised her arms overhead, jumped high, touched her toes, straightened, and finished the dive. She broke the water in one graceful movement. Her friends screamed and clapped. The three male chaperones all gave her nines, putting Mya in the lead position.

"Sometimes I think the term S/V should be changed to S/P," Captain Roberts said. "At the moment, I would say *Shenandoah* is more of a swimming platform than a sailing vessel."

"Would you have it any other way?" Melissa asked, knowing the answer.

"Not for a minute," he said with a chuckle. "They get such a kick out of jumping off the ship and swimming in the ocean. Few adults appreciate a swim from the ship as the children do."

Melissa pointed to John, Chip, and Larry goofing off below with the students. "I think you've got three adults on this ship who enjoy the swimming almost as much as the students."

Captain Roberts nodded. "That's why you all are chaperoning. But I know it's not easy to find parent chaperones who want to spend a week at sea aboard a working ship. Most people would rather take a free cruise to the Caribbean. I've never heard of a school needing to turn away parent volunteers."

"You know I love sailing with you, Captain. And I would love it even more if we could do a little night swimming. Not that I'm asking."

He nodded. "You've mentioned that before. I think it's time to take a group of adults for a sail under a full moon. Night swimming included."

"I'm going to hold you to that." Melissa extended her right hand. They shook on the deal, and she smiled so wide her cheeks twinged. The day had started off pretty shaky, but everything was going her way now.

She heard a motor start and swiveled to see where the noise was coming from. As she scanned the water, the yawl boat came into view. Nathan and Tucker were powering over to the sandy beach on the Island to take Noah and Cassie for their afternoon walk.

Melissa walked over to the fruit box and put down her camera. "Since they'll be no swimming tonight, I think I'll join the kids," she told the captain.

"Enjoy yourself." Captain Roberts headed toward his quarters.

Melissa slipped off her shorts and pulled her T-shirt over her head. She put them on the fruit box and repositioned her camera atop the clothes. Climbing up onto the cap rail, she scanned the water below for anyone under the surface who might not hear or see her coming and then yelled, "Look out below."

The water sports lasted for a couple of hours. Melissa's skin was beyond prune-ish when she reboarded the ship. The students were given an hour to change and relax before they would meet on deck for a navigation class. Melissa had asked John if he would mind if she skipped the class and took a nap. He'd been great, and now she was ready to stretch out with her book and read until she nodded off.

She turned on her cell phone and set the alarm for five, just in case she really zonked out. She woke at five to the noise and vibration of her phone.

*Tristan's Gap* was open on her chest, upside down. She lifted the book and chuckled. She hadn't even finished a page before she'd fallen asleep.

The bunk was stuffy, and she was sweating, though she knew it was only because the day was so warm and the air didn't circulate well in her cabin. Melissa changed her shirt and decided to finish her book before Pete called them to dinner. Hoping for some cross ventilation, Melissa walked across her floor to open the door.

It stuck. Again.

She yanked hard, and it squeaked open. She'd already asked Nathan twice to take a look at it. She wasn't going to ask again. Not today. She didn't want to be a pest. She'd wait and see if he got around to fixing it tomorrow. If not, she'd mention it on Thursday morning. At the moment, the extra air felt nice, and she wanted to finish her book before the kids returned below.

"Perfect!" She turned the last page with happy tears in her eyes. Melissa stowed her book in the locker beneath her bunk. She rummaged under her shirts to find another novel and pulled one out just as the dinner bell rang. The new book would have to wait. She put it on her pillow, slipped on her flip-flops, and walked down to the saloon. She sat at the captain's table and waited for everyone to arrive. Five minutes later, the saloon was packed.

"Are you ready for supper?" Zane asked the roomful of students, chaperones, and crew.

The students replied with multiple versions of "yes" as well as stomps on the floor and rhythmical banging on the tables. Zane walked over to the portside table and leaned hard on the inside edge. The table tilted high to one side. The kids gasped. Melissa laughed.

"Yup, it's all fun and games to bang on the tables until someone is wearing their dinner." Zane eased off of the table and brought it back to level. "I'm all for your enthusiastic responses; just remember not to tip the tables while you're eating. Especially if you're at my table." He winked and the kids laughed. "Bring it on, Pete," Zane shouted.

The galley boy and members of work group five carried in platters of chicken, rice, and vegetables.

Captain Roberts silently folded his hands in prayer, and the room grew quiet. He sang the first line of grace, and the crew and Melissa joined in. Nearly half the students had learned the song the previous night, and the others sang what words they recognized of the Johnny Appleseed grace.

*"Oh, the Lord is good to me,*
*and so I thank the Lord,*

*for giving me the things I need,*
*the sun and the rain and the apple seed.*
*Oh, the Lord is good to me.*

*And every seed that grows*
*will grow into a tree,*
*and one day soon there'll be apples there,*
*for everyone in the world to share.*
*Oh, the Lord is good to me.*

*When I wake up each morning,*
*I'm happy as can be,*
*because I know that, with God's care,*
*the apple trees will still be there.*
*Oh, the Lord's been good to me."*

As the students were finishing dinner, Melissa turned to Captain Roberts. "I'm surprised how similar Cabin 8 is to all the other cabins. I was expecting the room to be different, somehow—to look or feel older, like an antique."

Captain Roberts nodded and glanced around the saloon. "Excuse me," he said and waited for the boys and girls to shift their focus to him. "Miss Smith just asked me about her cabin. Tonight, I'm going to share with you the renovation of *Shenandoah*.

"I'm sure all of you bright young men and women are familiar with the American Revolution. How many of you know that the *Shenandoah* served as a privateering vessel to aid George Washington and the Patriots in their fight against the British?"

"I do," Amber voiced. "My dad loves that war and the Civil War. He has stuff all over the house. And he's dragged us to every museum and historic place on the East Coast, trying to make us like it, too. I like when he brings us to the Freedom Trail in Boston and we get to eat at Faneuil Hall."

The captain and Amber's friends laughed at her story. Melissa knew that Amber's father had wanted to chaperone this week but had been unable to secure the time off from work.

"Young lady, your father is a man after my own heart. I collect artifacts from the Revolutionary War and a few other significant naval pieces. This ship, though, is my favorite. When I purchased her in 1958, I had hoped to remodel her and save the original ship. The shipbuilders in Maine and those here on the Island told me she was beyond repair. I had to come up with a plan, and quickly, or she would rot and return to the sea. We hauled her into dry dock and began a complete gutting and reconstruction process."

Melissa, having heard the story before, raised her hand. "Could you save any of the original ship?"

A twinkle came into Captain Roberts' eyes. He slid out of his bench seat and stood. He stepped to his right and placed his hand on the black potbelly stove in the center of the aisle. "I salvaged everything I could. This stove here was on *Shenandoah* when I bought her. Though it's an antique, I doubt the stove was onboard during the 1700s. It is, however, a piece of history to the ship and at some point in time served *Shenandoah's* captain and crew."

The captain took two steps back to his place at the head of the table and sat down. "If you run your hand along the boards in the saloon, you might be able to feel a roughness to some of the boards while most are smooth. That's because I reused every board possible. When the ship builders were gutting the ship, I asked them to number and map every board that might be reusable."

"No way!" Jeremy, one of the quieter male students and a whiz at math, raised his hand. "How many boards were there?"

Captain Roberts chuckled. "A lot. Dozens. Miss Smith began this discussion when she asked about her cabin. Cabin 8 is exactly the same as it was when we broke *Shenandoah* down. We changed the location of the cabin to fit in with our new layout, but every board in that bunk is exactly the same as it was when the old girl was sailing during the Golden Age."

"Do you know what Cabin 8 was used for?" Melissa asked.

"No, though judging by its size, it was probably a storage room for the cook or sensitive cargo, or it might have been the slop room. We will never know the original floor plan of *Shenandoah* or when she was remodeled at any point in history before I restored her."

"Like my room," Greg announced. "My mom is always telling me I live in a pigsty. She calls my room the slop room, because she thinks I'm too sloppy."

Everyone laughed at Greg's comment. He raised one fist in triumph.

"Just be certain your cabin doesn't fail inspection," Zane offered.

Greg's arm lowered. "Don't sweat it. We've got Jeremy on the job."

Melissa noticed that Jeremy, who had been assigned bunk space in the same cabin as Greg, rolled his eyes and shook his head. She made a mental note to ask Zane later how they'd fared over the last two mornings.

"What cabin are you in?" the captain asked Greg.

"Why? Trust me, it's clean." Greg hurried to defend himself.

"I'm not concerned with your cleanliness habits. I'll leave that to Zane. I wondered what cabin you were in because some of you have original boards in your bunks, just as Miss Smith does."

"Does mine?" a girl asked.

"Which ones?" Greg questioned.

"Cabins 6, 7, and 9 each have many original boards, some on the floor and some on the walls. If you run your hands along the walls, you might be able to feel the difference between the newer boards and the originals. The eighteenth-century boards were hand-cut, while many of the new ones were machine cut. The hand-cut boards do not have the smooth surface we are accustomed to today."

"Now that's cool," Amber said. "I'm going to find one of those boards and take a picture. My dad is going to freak out."

"It is impressive." Captain Roberts sat back and crossed his arms over his chest. "Think about this: *Shenandoah* measures 108 feet long at the rail, 23 feet wide, and 150 feet long from jibboom end to mainboom end. That's a lot of wood. Factor into that the interior spaces, and we had piles and stacks of boards all over the inside of the warehouse I rented during *Shenandoah*'s reconstruction."

"I would have hated that job," Anthony stated.

Captain Roberts smiled. "You weren't the only one. Shipbuilding is hard work. Men had to lift both her masts, each 94 feet in height, from the water. Her lower masts are 20 inches in diameter as they pass through the deck, and each weighs about two and a half tons. Not a light load. Nor is her ballast. *Shenandoah* carries 37 tons of lead ballast in her bilges. Which one of you would like a job hauling the lead up and down the companionways?"

"Not me!" and "You couldn't pay me enough money" were countered by Greg's, "I could do it."

"You're hired," Captain Roberts said.

Greg beamed. "Can I raise the anchor every day?"

"A fine job." Judging from the respect in Captain Roberts' voice, Greg was earning favor. "Some of you might appreciate the fact that *Shenandoah's* anchor was found on the bottom of Boston Harbor. A salvage crew recovered quite a few anchors and parts. There are no markings or indications of what ship the anchor was once attached to, but they dated the iron and forging to the nineteenth century."

Several of the girls had folded their arms and put their heads down to rest. Melissa noticed two boys were leaning back against the wall with their eyes closed. They had all worked hard and played hard. She hoped they would sleep equally hard and wake cheerful and ready for a new day.

"And that is probably enough history for tonight. You've all had a busy day, and I bet you're pretty tired. Might be a good idea to go to sleep instead of whispering to each other all night long. Tomorrow is another work day for all aboard." Captain Roberts rose and stretched. Noah and Cassie, who had been sleeping at his feet, dashed out from under the table and padded over to the companionway. "Good night, everyone."

The students wished the captain good night and trekked back to their cabins. Within half an hour, all the students were below deck, tucked into their bunks. Melissa washed her face and brushed her teeth in the quiet of the moonlight. She basked for a few minutes under the stars and thanked God for a beautiful day.

Zane approached her while she was pulling her cell phone out of her pocket. "How are you feeling?"

"Wonderful."

"Listen, it's still fairly warm and even warmer below deck. I'd feel a heck of a lot better if you bunked in my doghouse tonight. Perhaps the cooler, fresh air will help you sleep better."

"I couldn't," Melissa said. "And I'm fine. Really."

Nick walked over and stood next to Zane. "I couldn't help overhearing. I agree with Zane. The heat seems to have done you in two nights in a row. If you're worried about kicking the first mate out of his space, feel free to have my doghouse."

Melissa dropped her gaze to the deck. She hated the worry in their voices, yet she had to admit she was a little uneasy about another night in the warm cabin.

"Take the offer," Nick insisted. "Not many people can say they slept on deck aboard the *Shenandoah*."

Melissa heard the warmth and jest in his voice. "Are you sure? I don't want to impose."

"I insist," Nick said. "The fresh air might do you good."

"Well," Melissa stood and looked between Nick and Zane, "I'd be lying if I didn't say I'd love to sleep somewhere cooler tonight. And, Nick, you're welcome to my cabin. I put clean sheets on this morning, so you're all set."

Nick shook his head. "Thanks for the offer, but I'll bunk with the guys. Give me a few minutes to go below and get you new sheets."

Melissa put up her hand. "Please, Nick, let me do it. I'm kicking you out of your house, so the least I can do is make my own bed."

"I won't argue about making a bunk. I'll grab what I need and be out of your hair." As he slid open the doghouse door, Melissa noticed that his pillow was closer to the stern...not that changing her sleeping position had helped her last night. He carried his pillow, some clothes, and a few personal items out of the doghouse. "She's all yours," he said with a smile.

"Thanks again, Nick."

"Don't worry about it. You need a good night's sleep."

Melissa went below to gather fresh sheets, her clothes, and her toiletry case. She made two trips up the companionway ladder and then set about stripping and remaking the bunk. Careful to heed the captain's advice and follow Nick's lead, Melissa faced her head toward the stern.

She turned on her cell phone and hoped Cindy was watching one of her evening crime dramas. Melissa texted:

*Hello from Lambert's Cove. Are you glued to the boob tube?*

*C: Make fun all you want, but Spike is curled up on my lap, thoroughly enjoying* The Sopranos. *How's life at sea?*

*The morning started off rocky, but the rest of the day was gorgeous.*

*C: Rocky?*

*I woke up nauseous, second day in a row.*

*C: Something you're not telling me?*

Melissa could hear Cindy cracking up as she wrote that text. Melissa sneered at her phone as she typed:

*Ha, ha. Not even a possibility.*

*C: I know. Sorry you're not feeling well.*

*I'm fine now. Captain thinks I was dehydrated. Sleeping in the cook's doghouse tonight.*

*C: A perk for being ill? Or a new friend?*

*You're a sick woman. The guy who normally sleeps there is half my age.*

*C: And?*

*You're ridiculous! But I have a favor to ask. There was a nice young man, Tucker, who helped me this morning. He was incredibly kind and caring. He's off to med school next week. I want to help him. I have the money from Bryce's insurance policy. I'd like to give*

*Tucker a thousand dollars to help him with books and expenses, but I don't want him to know it's from me. Can you ask Rick if his accounting firm can set something up for me?*

Melissa brushed her hair while she waited for Cindy's reply.
Her phone buzzed.

*C: Shouldn't be a problem. Rick will work on it tomorrow.*

*Thanks!*

*C: Don't mention it. You're the nicest person I know. Hanging around you is good for my image.*

*Love you!*

*C: Love you, too. Sleep well all alone in that doghouse.*

Melissa chuckled and shut off her phone. Nothing like a dose of love and laughter before bed. She slid between the sheets and turned off the bedside light.

# 13

A COOL BREEZE BRUSHED ACROSS MELISSA'S FACE. She rolled to her right side and pulled the blanket up over her shoulder. She stretched her legs, pointing her toes until they poked out from under the covers and over the end of the bed…into a wall.

Melissa froze. She tapped the big toe of her left foot against the solid mass and groaned. *Not again!* Opening her eyes, she found herself inches from a large, imposing white wall. She sucked in her breath. Dread seized her heart. She spread the fingers of her right hand and pushed. Nothing happened. No spinning, no black hole, no falling.

She ran her fingers across the wall. The surface didn't feel like wood, at least not the rough panels she'd encountered the previous two mornings. And this wall was white, not the natural finish the other two had been. Maybe not even natural material. Melissa poked at the surface. Not metal either.

A gust of air swirled around her uncovered arm. With none-too-small an amount of trepidation, Melissa turned in the direction of the breeze.

She laughed and exhaled at the same time.

Of course! She was in Nick's doghouse. Safe and sound on the *Shenandoah*. A peaceful night's sleep. Dreamless, as best she could remember. Certainly no dreams of falling, no dreams of Colonial presidents, no dreams of strange men. She grinned and stretched again. Wednesday was promising to be a fantastic day, and she was ready to capture the beginning rays of light waking the rest of the world.

The morning air was much cooler than yesterday. Having slept in a T-shirt and summer cotton pants, Melissa donned her lightweight fleece jacket. She listened for a moment, waiting to hear if Zane or anyone else was up and about. No noise, no talking—even the gulls were still snug in their nests. Not wanting to wake Zane in the bunk ten feet away, she quietly slid open the doghouse panel door. Zane's door was closed. Melissa tiptoed around her small quarters toward the galley.

As she stopped and observed the gray mist moving over the water, Zane came up through the galley hatch and walked toward her.

"Good morning." A wisp of steam rose from the mug of coffee he held.

"Morning, Zane. Are you always the first one up?"

He shrugged. "Comes with the job, and the quarters. Except for whoever is on morning watch, Nick and I pretty much start the day for the ship. I've gotten in the habit of rowing the dogs to shore so they can take care of business before the kids are up and we have accidents on deck to deal with."

"I wondered why I hadn't seen them the past couple of mornings. In previous years, two of the crew had rowed them ashore during morning chores. I was surprised yesterday when I saw Nathan and Tucker motoring them over after lunch while the kids were swimming. I couldn't believe they had gone all day to that point without a stinky mess or puddle of pee on deck. Your revelation makes more sense."

Zane swallowed a sip of coffee. "The first cruise I worked, I brought the dogs over during morning wash down. Personally, it was too distracting. The kids worked the dogs up and the dogs worked the kids up, and then there was the inevitable accident. The second week out, I opted to get up a little earlier and take the dogs over while the ship was still peaceful."

Melissa searched the deck for Noah and Cassie. "Did you leave them on shore?"

"Hardly. The second we get back to the ship, they scamper down to the captain's quarters and sleep for another hour or so. I think they rest up so they can bark at the students when we call for morning muster." Zane raised the mug to his lips and took another sip. "Hope I didn't disturb your sleep."

A yawn began before Melissa could clamp her mouth shut. Zane shook his head and chuckled. "Guess I'll take that as a yes?"

"No, not at all. I slept great," Melissa replied. "I just need some coffee."

"No presidents or black holes, then?"

The warmth of embarrassment tinged her cheeks. "Not one. Thank God."

Zane exaggerated a frown. "There goes my dissertation on who fired the first shot."

Between chuckles, Melissa quipped, "Sorry to disappoint you."

Placing his mug of coffee on the deck, Zane opened the lid of the fruit box and extracted an orange. "Want one?"

"No, thanks. But I'd love some grapes."

He passed her a handful of red grapes and began peeling his orange. "Joking aside, I'm glad you slept well."

"Me, too. I was beginning to think I was crazy."

Zane tossed his orange peels into the water. Two sea gulls appeared out of nowhere and dove for the discarded compost, only to fly away disappointed. "I don't think you're crazy, but you had Pete going. I'm surprised he's not up and asking you questions."

"I'm relieved to say he's going to be as disappointed as those gulls," Melissa said, pointing to the white birds rising in the air, the orange peels still floating in the water. A thick layer of fog swirled around the ship and blocked the view of the shoreline. "Might feel an ounce of dissatisfaction myself in a minute or two. I'd hoped to shoot some sunrise pictures this morning."

"Give it a while. This fog will burn off. The morning's cold air temperatures are working off the warmer ocean waters. Once the sun begins to do its job, we'll have clear skies and great sailing. You might miss the actual sunrise, but there could be some interesting images with the fog and light beams." Zane split his orange in half and popped a segment into his mouth.

Melissa stared out over the water toward the shore and then glanced up. The sun was trying to break through. "You're right. The sun is poking through the gray. I'm going to grab a cup of coffee and perch on the rail until the moment arrives. It's breezy enough that things should clear quickly."

"The captain mentioned last night that he wanted to anchor off Cuttyhunk today. If these southerly winds keep blowing, we'll have no problem getting there," Zane confided.

"Really?" Melissa was thrilled at the prospect. "In all my years on the Island, I've only been there a handful of times. Every time has been fantastic, and I always say I'm going to go back there later in the summer or early fall, and then I get busy and Cuttyhunk feels as far away as Greece. I haven't been in two or three years. I bet some of the students have never been."

With his mouth full of orange slices, Zane held up his index finger. Melissa waited for him to finish chewing. "Last kids' cruise of the summer and the first time we'll make it over there. Guess this is our lucky trip."

"Works for me. Some sun, a huge cup of coffee, and the day will be perfect."

The fog indeed started to burn off while Melissa drank her coffee. She photographed the rays of sun cutting through the gray/white mist. The pictures might not turn out, but that was the beauty of digital cameras. Melissa would go through them later before bed or during a quiet time on Thursday and weed them out. She also needed to compile a list of all the students photographed and how many pictures she had of each child. There needed to be good ones of every student to put into the scrapbooks she planned to make.

While she finished her coffee, Melissa spotted a woman running on the beach. She'd never had the slightest motivation to try the sport. Who in their right mind wanted to run when one could just as easily walk? She loved walking and hiking. Kendra had dragged her to cycling classes, which had eventually grown on her. Running, she knew, would never grow on her.

Voices coming from the bow alerted Melissa to the time. If the crew was up and wandering down to get coffee, then she had about thirty minutes to change Nick's sheets and move her belongings back down to her cabin. She stopped at the galley hatch and climbed down to put her mug into the sink.

"Thanks again for the use of your doghouse last night. I'm going to straighten up and carry my stuff below. I'll change the sheets before the kids start chores," Melissa said.

Nick waved her off. "Don't bother with the sheets. I won't tell you that I didn't even ask whose bed or how old the sheets were last night."

Melissa plastered on a smile while cringing inside. "I'm not going to ask for any further explanation."

Laughing, Nick poured two cups of raisins into his granola mix. "Let me know if you want to sleep there again tonight."

"I'm good," Melissa said. "I don't think it will be as warm today or tonight. The breeze is cool and I feel wonderful. Thanks for the offer, though."

The morning flew by. Captain Roberts had them under sail shortly after ten. Most of the students elected to make a sailor bracelet with Melissa, and all of them spent an hour in their work groups learning ship knots.

Just before lunch, the crew dropped anchor in Cuttyhunk's outer harbor and secured the ship.

"Attention," Bear yelled above the hum of voices. Excitement had been building throughout lunch and during cleanup. Everyone appeared eager to visit the second largest of the Elizabeth Islands. The students turned to face the second mate. "Alrighty, Holmes Hole, let's get into our work groups and wait for the first mate's orders."

Caleb, Roscoe, Tucker, Justin, and Avery stood in a wide circle around Bear. With a bit of grumbling, the pirate gang separated, and the girls, all ten clustered together, split and joined into their preassigned work teams.

Zane strode up from the helm and stood beside Bear. "Listen up, pirates and lasses. You're going to have two hours to explore the Island. How many of you have been to Cuttyhunk before?"

Only six hands went up.

"Okay, we're going to split you up into four groups of seven. A school chaperone and one crewmember will go with each group. You get to pick where you want to go, but we're going to do this nice and orderly. No shoving, no bickering, no complaining."

Melissa, John, Chip, and Larry stood along the starboard rail. Zane gestured toward Melissa. "Miss Smith will take her group to visit the library and the one-room schoolhouse. There's a community yard and book sale going on, in case you want to spend any of that money you brought onboard.

"Mr. Masters will be exploring the shoreline and the nature preserve. If you're curious about sea life and birds or want to try your hand at clamming, choose tour number two," Zane said.

Israel raised his hand. "If we go clamming, can we eat them?"

"Bring 'em back and I'll steam them for you," Nick answered.

"All right!" Israel exclaimed.

A few others joined in his enthusiasm, while Melissa heard one of the girls say, "I hate clams. I hope they don't find any. I'm not eating them."

A loud whistle silenced the children's conversations. Bear grinned. "Stay focused. We're losing daylight."

Everyone turned their attention back to Zane. "Mr. DeMello will take tour three over to Church's Beach for swimming, sunbathing, and walking. Tour four is heading overland in two golf carts, driven by Mr. Saunders and Caleb. Those in tour four will crawl through the graveyard, circle the island, and visit the Coast Guard station. Any questions?"

Maddie, who had been to Cuttyhunk before, raised her hand. "Can we go to the store and get ice cream?"

Zane laughed. "Oh, did I forget to mention the ice cream? Every tour will visit the store, and everyone gets a free ice cream."

Cheers and claps filled the air. Zane and Bear waited until the ice cream lovers quieted down. The first mate crossed the deck to group three. "When I walk over to your work crew, select your tour group and line up beside your tour leader. Do not run!" Zane commanded.

Work group three went first, followed by four, two, five, and one. "Hey," Greg complained. "I want to go with Anthony and Trace."

Bear clapped the leader of the pirate gang on the back. "Looks like you're going to the library. Maybe you'll find a book on pirates."

Greg scowled at Bear before stepping into line beside Travis and Victoria.

The crew lowered the yawl boat and two rowboats to shuttle everyone ashore. Melissa put a bottle of sunscreen in her camera bag and shoved her cell phone into the pocket of her jeans. She waited for John, Larry, and Chip to head over with the first groups of students, and then went with Nathan and her group in the third boat.

While Nathan was rowing them to shore, Melissa brought up her request. "I hate to be a pest, but would you mind taking a look at my cabin door? It's still sticking."

"Oh, crud, I completely forgot. I'll check on it as soon as we get back," Nathan said.

"Tomorrow is good. I'll want to change and relax when we return."

"Sure thing. Sorry I forgot about it."

Nathan rowed them to the water's edge and then pulled the boat up onto the sand. He offered Melissa his hand to help her out. The students threw their legs overboard and splashed into the shallow water.

Once the rowboat was tethered to a cement block, Melissa and Nathan led the students up the hill to the library. Almost as soon as they started walking, someone asked the inevitable child question, "How far is it, Miss Smith?"

Melissa laughed and, without turning around to see who had asked, answered, "It's less than a mile, probably closer to half a mile. Come on, we'll all make it. And the walking will make the ice cream taste even better."

About three quarters of the way up the hilly street, Melissa stopped in the road and pivoted to face a small, weathered building set back from the pavement.

"Is this their library?" Greg asked. "What do they have, like, ten books in there?"

Melissa ignored his sarcasm but answered the question. "It may be small, but they have nearly ten thousand books. When I came here awhile back, I was impressed that they had all my favorite authors and every young adult book I was planning to teach in school that year."

Maddie inched forward. "Can we go to the yard sale?" She pointed across the street to the churchyard, where locals had set up tables of goods for sale.

"Let's visit the library and the schoolhouse first, and then we'll shop. I know I'm likely to find something, and I'd rather not lug it around while we explore."

The librarian met Melissa and her students at the door. "Good afternoon, every one. I'm Mrs. Langley. Let me show you around my most favorite place on the Island." Mrs. Langley escorted them inside the narrow front passage and led them to the main room. "The library was first constructed in 1892. Back then, folks borrowed books on the honor system. In later years, we began using a card catalog, which we still use today."

Melissa's students hadn't seen a wooden card catalog desk in their computerized library on Martha's Vineyard. Travis skimmed through one of the drawers and lifted out a card. He asked the librarian where the book was located and, finding it, pulled it off of the shelf. "Hey, look," he called. "Some guy checked out this book in 1957. My dad wasn't even born then."

"Pretty cool, isn't it?" Melissa said. "Now let's play a game. Pick your five favorite books and let's see if the library has them."

The students spent fifteen minutes searching for their personal favorites. All but two were on the shelf. They thanked the librarian for her time and headed across the lawn to the one-room schoolhouse built nineteen years before the library. The school was closed for the summer, but they peered in through the windows.

"Who goes to school here?" Haley asked. "It's so small. Is there even a bathroom?"

Melissa chuckled. "I'm sure they have a bathroom, though it doesn't get nearly as much use as ours does. They have only three students enrolled for the fall, and the kids go home for lunch. If you lived on Cuttyhunk, you could attend school here from pre-school through sixth grade."

"Then you get to drop out and go fishing," Greg joked.

"I doubt their parents would consider that option," Melissa said. "If all of you finished sixth grade in this classroom, you and your parents would then have to decide whether you went to the Vineyard, Falmouth, or boarding school."

Victoria's eyes grew wide. "Boarding school? I wouldn't want to move away from home to go to school. That's so unfair!"

Melissa nodded. "I'm sure that's one of the reasons very few people live here year round. I think there's only about thirty people on Cuttyhunk during the winter months."

Shelby walked over to the stone wall bordering the schoolyard. "Can we go shopping now?"

"Absolutely. Let's go see what bargains we can find."

Nathan led the students across the deserted street, allowing Melissa to shoot pictures of the library and schoolhouse before joining them. The churchyard was empty except for the *Shenandoah* visitors.

"How can we shop when there's nobody here to sell us anything?" Shelby asked. "Maybe we should go knock on the door of that little house attached to the church and see if anyone's home."

Nathan walked across the green grass to the table where Shelby was standing. "I don't know if anyone is using it now. That's where the schoolteacher lives once the academic year starts. Most summers one of the preachers lives in there, but not always."

Melissa was curious. "What do you mean 'one' of the preachers? We've probably got more church members at my parish on the Island than they can have here if every resident attended, and we need only one pastor."

Nathan pointed to the outdoor bulletin board. "I spent a summer working on a fishing boat out of here two years ago. My first month I thought everybody was spending all day at church on Sundays. People were coming and going through the white doors all day long, or so it seemed. Then a woman at the general store explained that, though this is a United Methodist church, they also have Episcopal and Catholic masses on Sundays. The church has four different services on Sundays."

Shelby lifted her hands in defeat. "If people come here only on Sundays, how do we buy something today?"

Melissa pointed to the large coffee can with a blue plastic lid sitting in the center of a table near the stone wall. "It's the honor system. Everything for sale is a donation for the library fund. You decide how much you want to pay and put your money in the can. Someone must come by before dark and put everything away and bring the money inside."

"That's cool," Travis said as he picked up an old fishing reel.

Melissa and the students browsed for ten minutes. Nathan sat on the fence, joking with the students as they inspected different items. Greg found an old pocket-sized radio. Travis bought the fishing gear he'd seen when they first walked over. Melissa purchased a set of lovebird salt and pepper shakers for Cindy.

Half of the girls selected books. Shelby hugged a copy of *Percy Jackson and the Lightning Thief* to her chest. "I already read it twice, but I don't own it. And it's my favorite book. Do you think a dollar donation is okay?"

"Perfect," Melissa said.

When everyone had put their money into the coffee jar, Nathan led them down to the general store for ice cream and then back to the beach for the short boat ride out to *Shenandoah.*

Melissa sucked in her breath as Nathan maneuvered the rowboat around, and she saw *Shenandoah* resting on the water in the late-afternoon sun. The ship was majestic. Her wooden black hull, tall masts and sleek lines looked nothing like the modern-day fiberglass speedboats. Anchored as she was, with only the sun, sky, and the sea in view, Melissa felt as though they really were stepping back in time and rowing out to the original eighteenth-century *Shenandoah.*

She raised her camera and took pictures of the hull on the water, the masts against the blue sky, the bowsprit balanced between sea and air.

"You take a lot of pictures, Miss Smith," Victoria said.

"I know. Sometimes I think this camera should be a permanent attachment to my body."

"But what do you do with all of them?" Victoria asked.

"I'll let you in on a little secret." Melissa lowered the camera and leaned in closer to Victoria, knowing full well anyone paying attention in the boat could hear them. "First, I'm going to make scrapbooks for you kids. But I'm also dreaming of developing a line of cards to sell in the Island shops."

"That's cool." Victoria nodded, then turned to chat with Shelby.

They reboarded the ship and the students talked excitedly about their adventures on Cuttyhunk—what they'd seen, bought, and where they'd gone. Melissa caught up with the three male chaperones and heard about their tours. No one had a single complaint. The day had been a resounding success.

A couple of hours later, after Nick had served chocolate-coconut magic cookie bars for dessert, Captain Roberts shared the history of Cuttyhunk. "Who knows where Gosnold, Massachusetts, is?"

None of the students raised their hands.

"Ah, but you were just there," Captain Roberts explained. "The island you visited today is named Cuttyhunk. It is a village, but the village is part of the town of Gosnold, exactly as the village of Menemsha is in the town of Chilmark. The town, and the other four Elizabeth Islands, are named after Bartholomew Gosnold, who landed there in 1602. He stayed for only twenty-two days, but the British claimed and named the land. And I hope everyone knows who Bartholomew Gosnold was."

"He discovered Martha's Vineyard," Israel said.

"That he did." The captain delved into further history of the island, when the lighthouse was built, the great fishing and lobstering, and the building and closing of the Coast Guard station. When the children began to fade, Captain Roberts wished them all a good night's sleep and promised them another fun day of sailing on Thursday.

Melissa supervised the girls getting ready for bed and then went up on deck to do a little star gazing before she crawled into her bunk. She was texting Cindy when John came up behind her.

"Saying good night to the boyfriend?" he joked.

"I guess you could say that," Melissa replied, keeping her answer vague.

"Uh, oh. Trouble in paradise?"

"Definitely not." Melissa lowered the phone and faced John. "The 'boyfriend' is my cat, Spike. He's staying with my friend Cindy, and I'm checking on him."

"No boyfriend, then?"

The flirtation in John's voice was undeniable. Melissa glanced around the deck and wondered where everyone had gone. Where was a kid demanding your attention when you needed one? She had to end any thoughts John might have toward her. Her phone buzzed, but she ignored it.

Keeping her voice as flat and disinterested as she could, Melissa let John know exactly where she stood. "No boyfriend. No husband. I swore off men after I caught my husband cheating."

"Hey, we're not all bad," John offered in defense of mankind.

"Sorry, I don't want to sound as if I don't like men. I do. I just don't believe I'm meant to live with one. I spent thirty years comfortably on my own before I married the wrong guy. Since he's been gone, life has improved dramatically. I can't see myself going down that road again."

John stepped back. "I used to think along those lines, too. I never married…always thought it was a short walk from the wedding reception to divorce court. Lately, though, I've wondered if I'm missing out."

Melissa heard the longing in his voice, not necessarily for her, but for a special woman. "If you listen to my friend Cindy, who's been married for twenty-seven years, she'll tell you the right person will come along when you least expect it. And then you're in trouble. Life will never be the same. According to her theory, you're probably due for that woman to show up."

The cell phone buzzed again.

"Go ahead and get that. I wouldn't want to keep Spike waiting," John said, then walked toward the main hatch.

Sympathy stirred in Melissa's heart. John seemed nice enough, but she really had no interest. Cindy would tell her to take a chance, which is why she wasn't going to mention it to Cindy.

Pulling up her messages, Melissa read that Rick had been able to set up an anonymous grant for Tucker and that Spike had eaten half a side of salmon for dinner. The salmon was a joke, at least the quantity of fish. She had to smile, though. Cindy did spoil her cat rotten.

*Thanks for taking care of everything. Give Spike a big hug for me, and stop trying to steal his affections with food! Love you!*

*C: Spike has chosen to stay with me. He said to write when you can. LOL.*

The phone buzzed again a second later, as Cindy texted: *Love you, too!*

Melissa smiled and turned off the phone. She was ready for bed. The day had been fabulous, and tomorrow promised more sunshine and another fun adventure. The cool evening air guaranteed another restful night's sleep.

# 14

MELISSA SNUGGLED INTO HER BUNK, said her prayers, and closed her eyes. The cool air through the porthole brought in just enough chill that she wanted to pull the sheet up over her shoulders. In the stillness of her cabin, Melissa could hear the guys talking in the saloon. Their voices carried and echoed into her bunk. She rolled over and tried to ignore their conversation and jokes.

"You worried about her sleeping in the cabin again?"

"What are you talking about?"

Melissa rolled back over to face her door. She recognized John's voice.

"Do you wonder what dreams she'll have tonight?"

"Not at all, Pete. Melissa is fine. She was dehydrated on Monday. You saw her today. She looks great."

"Yeah, she seemed normal and all that today, but what about tomorrow?"

"I'm not sure what you're implying, Pete."

Meslissa hated that they were talking about her. Hated that Pete was insinuating she was off balance. Hated that she could hear them. On the other hand, she was surprisingly pleased to hear the edge in John's voice and that a man was sticking up for her.

"I'm not implying anything. I was there," Pete insisted. "I heard her talking. When she was remembering those dreams and telling us about the men and the acts and the presidents, she wasn't normal. She was sick and sweating and dizzy. She acted a little nuts, is all."

"Nuts—Melissa? You don't know her. She is levelheaded, intelligent, sane, and more than capable. She's one of the best teachers on the Island. She was sick. That's all there was to it."

Melissa heard the annoyance and firmness in John's words. For a second, she reconsidered going out with him. She wouldn't, and her heart had no interest in being broken again, but she did feel a twinge of happiness having a man act as her protector.

"We'll see," Pete added. "Want to place a bet on what the morning brings?"

"No!" John said, louder than he'd been speaking. A second later, someone stomped out of the saloon and faded off toward the galley. Melissa guessed it was John, especially since the men grew quiet after the person's departure.

"How 'bout them Red Sox?" one of the guys joked.
"Best team in baseball. Going all the way again!"
"If they don't choke."
"Stuff it, Roscoe."

Melissa opened her eyes and listened for several more minutes. No one mentioned her or her dreams again. Pete had been curious about her dreams yesterday morning, but he hadn't seemed mean-spirited or derogatory. She hoped he was merely goading John, trying to get a rise out of him. After all, what other purpose could there be? Her dreams weren't that interesting.

She liked Pete, and she didn't have any hard feelings toward him because of what happened tonight. She'd speak with him in the morning and let him know she felt great, that she wasn't crazy or nuts. When he saw her awake and healthy two days in a row, he'd be convinced that she'd just been under the weather the first two mornings.

A tingle spread across Melissa's arms. She shivered and rubbed them both and then tucked them back under her blankets. She wished Spike was onboard so he could cuddle up with her and keep her warm.

Minus a sweet kitty, Melissa ran through some joyful memories to help her relax and fall asleep. She couldn't help but think about John. He had been kind all week, especially tonight. She was grateful for his comments to Pete. Thinking about his statement that she was one of the best teachers, Melissa smiled and closed her eyes.

*

"I am well pleased with her."

Melissa turned away from the voices. In the recesses of her mind, she wondered how long those guys would sit in the saloon and discuss sports.

"She sails well."

"My nephew is most enamored with her."

"That he is. The lad was born to sail."

"He is a lad no longer. Twenty and five, with no wife and no declared intentions to settle. Elizabeth frets he will join with Samuel and the Sons of Liberty."

Dread sliced through Melissa's last moments of sleep. She recognized the men, recognized their accents, recognized their words.

"I perceive no occasion upon whence Benjamin would inflict violence upon another without just cause. Samuel and his mob have displayed a grave lack of character. A fault I cannot conceive within Benjamin."

"Eli has said as much to Elizabeth. The recent events have placed men and women on edge. Though it galls Elizabeth to agree with me, life at sea appears a much safer choice. Not a musket fired from Maine to Milton."

Dread gave way to fear. Melissa didn't want to open her eyes. She didn't want to see what she'd seen days before. She knew what was coming next.

"Ye must be relieved the Townshend Act has been repealed."

And there it was. The Townshend Act. Melissa knew when she opened her eyes she'd be surrounded by wood. But she also knew she had to find out how to end this crazy dream and never have it again.

"Aye, Adam, we must all be grateful. Though the cost was dear. Five men, five families. I fear the violence has only yet begun."

Counting down from three, Melissa opened her eyes. Exactly what she'd expected. If she wasn't dreaming, she'd be terrified. As it was, she was scared. She shifted her weight and got onto her knees. She was boxed in, literally. Around her on all sides were large wooden crates. She stood, and her ankle-length nightshirt brushed the tops of her feet.

She shivered as goose bumps rose on her arms. Thank God she'd worn her hooded nightie to bed. She collected her hair in her left hand and pulled the hood up onto her head, tucking her hair underneath. Her feet were freezing, but she couldn't do anything about that. She had to end the nightmare and get back to her warm bed.

Turning about, she saw no opening large enough to squeeze through and get to a door. She would have to push one of the crates and hope the effort sent her back to *Shenandoah*. She placed both hands on the crate in front of her and pushed. Nothing happened.

She braced the sole of her right foot flat on the box behind her and, driving as hard as she could, shoved the container in front of her. The crate moved about six inches, enough space for her to squeeze through.

"Did ye hear that? Something within moved about the cabin."

"There had best not be rats aboard."

Melissa's bravery vanished. She wished she was a rat and could scurry to safety, though from what she hadn't a clue.

The latch on her door clicked. She held her breath. Whatever ghost or goblin was haunting her dreams, she needed to face it and be done with it. Shaking, she waited in the space between the crates.

"I shall see to it, Captain."

The door opened and Melissa was blinded by a yellow glow.

"Go away!" she screamed. "Leave me alone!"

# 15

"Captain!"

"What have ye found, Adam?"

"A stowaway. A woman, I believe."

Melissa could hear the voices but couldn't see past the bright light shining in her face. She squeezed her eyes shut, placed her hands over her ears, and pleaded, "Heavenly Father, this is not happening, this is not happening, this is not happening."

"Be still, Adam. She is frightened."

"Madam. Madam, are ye injured?"

There was no way Melissa was going to answer the monster in her dream. She was done being brave and facing her demons. It was time for God to end this nightmare and wake her up. "Just leave me alone. Go scare someone else," she groaned.

"Adam, perhaps if ye lowered the lamp we could move the crate and see to her needs."

"Aye, Captain."

When she heard the wood scrape across the floor, Melissa froze. Whatever it was, whatever they were, they were about to get closer. Too close.

"Please, God, get me out of here, get me out of here now!" she pleaded desperately.

"Adam, let us step back. Leave the lamp so she may see about her." The soothing voice continued. "We mean thee no harm. Be at ease."

Melissa heard the footsteps move farther away. She kept her eyes closed and prayed for the dream to end. *Be at ease?* Did the creature have any idea what had been happening in her dreams lately? There was no "ease" to any of this. "God, please," Melissa whispered.

"Do ye think her harmed? What would force her to run away and hide on a ship?"

"I cannot fathom. Whatever has brought her here, she is in need of help."

"From whence did she come? We did not anchor long in either port."

"Falmouth would be my guess, though when and how I do not know."

"Mayhap the woman is a nun? She wears the robe of a monastic order."

*A nun?* The word stopped Melissa's heavenly appeal. Monsters, ghosts, or goblins would not be discussing nuns. She opened her eyes and stared at the men talking about her. Seriously? A nun? What on earth could possibly convince any man that she was a nun?

In the pre-dawn hour, the cabin lit by a kerosene lamp, Melissa knew she was still dreaming. She had to be. The two men gawking at her were dressed in Colonial clothing, right down to their long overcoats, breeches, and wool stockings. Melissa wanted to laugh. Her fantasy life had never been so rich. But she didn't laugh. A niggling of fear squeezed her neck and wouldn't let go. She shivered and pulled the hood close to her neck.

Wasn't this the moment she should fall backward or into the tunnel back to her bunk on *Shenandoah?* Why didn't they vanish? Why didn't she vanish? Why didn't they all vanish?

One of the men took a step toward her. She inched back, expecting him to lunge at her or that this would be the moment her body started falling into that black hole. Neither happened. Melissa reached out and put both hands on top of a crate on either side of her. "What now, Lord?" she asked out loud.

The younger man moved another step closer. "Madam, have ye been harmed?"

Was he joking? Melissa couldn't believe what was happening. The bad guy in her dream was asking if she was harmed. She had a brief thought that she should be frightened, and then she realized how absurd the whole nightmare was becoming. If she answered, would he vaporize and be gone? It was worth a shot. "No, I'm not hurt. But I've had enough of this dream. Could you just stay where you are until I wake up?"

The man looked back at his friend. "She believes she is sleeping."

The gray-haired man by the door nodded. The two were close in age, but the man by the door appeared a bit older. The odd thing was, he had a nice face, a kind face. They both did. Melissa couldn't picture them chasing her or terrorizing her or killing her. Except for their clothes, which belonged on the tour guides at one of many stops along the Freedom Trail in Boston, they seemed normal.

"Captain, she may have fallen or been knocked about the head. She may not be in her right mind."

Melissa cringed. First Pete, now one of the guys in her dreams was calling her nuts. "I'm not crazy," she whispered. "I don't know what's wrong with me, but I'm not crazy."

The room was getting blurry, and her stomach rolled as the blackness began to overtake her. For the first time since the dizzy spells started a few days ago, Melissa was grateful to drop into the darkness. She felt her body falling and welcomed the end of the nightmare.

A burning in her nose woke her. As she tried to draw a breath, her lungs felt as if they were on fire. She coughed, opened her eyes, and screamed. Though she heard an ear-piercing shriek in her mind, she felt only a scratchy sputter scrape through her throat and pass by her lips.

She waved her hands frantically in front of her, smacking at the hands holding the vial near her face. When the man lowered his hand, Melissa realized someone was supporting her in a sitting position. She spun her head to the right and, sure enough, the other man from her dream was there behind her. One in front, one in back. Her eyes darted back and forth between them.

"Do not fret, madam," the man in front of her said.

He was talking to her. Calming her. They were both still in the room with her. Something was terribly wrong. Why didn't the nightmare end? Was she stuck? Who were these people? Why did they feel alive and real? Had one of them caught her when she started falling? She needed to leave this dream world and get back to reality. She squeezed her eyes shut and leaned back, hoping the falling would begin again.

In a second, the burning returned. She coughed and opened her eyes. The gray-haired man was yet again waving some container under her nose. The smell was worse than bleach. She pushed his hand away. "Are you trying to kill me?"

"My apologies, my lady. I meant only to revive thee with smelling salts."

"Smelling salts?" Melissa said the words aloud as she ran them over and over in her mind. She nearly smacked at his outstretched hand a third time until she realized he was showing her a bottle. She picked up the glass container labeled *Sal Volatile.* "What is this?"

"Smelling salts, ma'am. Ammonium carbonate."

"You had them in your pocket?" she asked, incredulous and curious. Did bad guys carry first-aid kits in dreams to help revive their victims? Is that why she was having recurring dreams?

"No, madam. I returned to the galley to retrieve them."

Melissa rubbed her nose, grateful the burning sensation was fading. The movement made her aware of her surroundings. She wasn't beside the higher boxes anymore. And she was sitting. "How did I get over here?"

"I helped thee to the crate," a voice behind her stated. "Are ye able to sit without assistance?"

"Oh!" Melissa shot forward, away from the man's touch. She'd forgotten he was holding her up. No, she hadn't forgotten. She had no memory of him carrying her in the dream. "Yes, I'm fine."

*What is happening?* She fussed with her sleeves, rolling the fabric down over her partially exposed arms. She fingered the cuff of the blue cotton nightshirt and considered her situation. She was sitting on a wooden crate, her feet only inches from the floor, but with nowhere to run. There was a man in front of her and one behind her. Though they'd done nothing to indicate they meant to hurt or threaten her in any way, she didn't want to push anybody's buttons or set one of them off. She needed to figure out where she was. There had to be a logical thread weaving her outrageous nightmare together.

"Where am I?"

"Aboard the schooner *Shenandoah*, madam," the man behind her said. He rose and moved slowly to stand beside his friend.

Melissa smiled. Good to know everyone in her dream was on the *Shenandoah*. Now she had to find out who they were and why they wanted her. "Will you tell me your names?" she asked, slightly hesitant, hoping to appear meek in case one or both of them thought she was trying to get the upper hand.

The younger of the two middle-aged men bowed from the waist. "I am Captain Isaiah Reed. Allow me to introduce thee to our cook, Adam Greene."

Adam also bowed. Melissa inhaled a deep breath and exhaled slowly, counting backward from ten. She did not recall Adam Greene, but she knew full well who Isaiah Reed was. Hadn't she and Captain Roberts just been talking about him? No wonder he was standing there in her dream. So far, so good. She'd get out of this yet.

"May we have the pleasure of thy acquaintance?" Captain Reed asked.

"Oops, sorry." Melissa extended her hand toward Isaiah. "Melissa Smith, teacher-chaperone."

Captain Reed shook his head, paused, and then shook her hand. She smiled at Adam, who nodded.

Certain she was going to wake up at any minute, Melissa plowed ahead. "Do you know Captain Roberts?"

Their eyes grew wide. "Captain John Roberts?" Adam Greene asked. Melissa heard the disgust in his voice.

"Yes," Melissa replied, cautious not to say too much as Adam already seemed upset with her or her question.

"Thee cannot refer to that scoundrel of a pirate?" Captain Reed said. "The man has been dead nigh on fifty years. What concern is he to thee?"

"Pirate? What pirate? Definitely no pirates in this dream. No, I'm talking about Captain John Roberts who owns the *Shenandoah*."

Captain Reed looked down at Melissa with a perplexed shake of his head. "Mrs. Smith, it is I who own and captain the *Shenandoah*. I commissioned her and launched her. She sails this week past on her maiden voyage. She knows no other captain."

Melissa laughed softly. "Oh, I know you're the man who built the *Shenandoah* in 1770, but I'm talking about the captain who owns her now. I'm trying to get out of my dream and back to the real world." She said the words confidently, in her kind teacher voice. She had no desire to correct the images in her dream, merely to lead everyone to the accurate answer.

Adam leaned over and whispered something to Isaiah Reed. Both men frowned.

Melissa didn't want to anger anyone. Her nightmare had gone from scary to almost commonplace, although surreal. She wanted the nice men to remain nice and not morph into two three-headed, flesh-eating dragons.

"Mrs. Smith—"

Melissa cut into Isaiah's comment. "Um, would it be okay if we dropped the Mrs.? Bryce was more of a nightmare than this dream."

Adam gave Isaiah a knowing look. Captain Reed gazed down at her again. This time Melissa saw sympathy and concern in his eyes. "Miss Smith, are thee in trouble? Has thy husband whipped thee or threatened thy life?"

Melissa rolled her eyes. "Let's not rehash my marriage. He's dead, and I'm much better off without him. And I don't want to hurt your feelings, but I'd really like to go home now."

"Dead?" Captain Reed said more than asked.

"By thy hand?" Adam did ask.

"By my hand? You think I killed Bryce?" Melissa stared at him. Was he kidding? Judging by the intensity with which he watched her reaction, she guessed he was serious. She hoped Gayle Burroughs wasn't about to make an appearance in this nightmare. "I didn't kill my ex-husband, though I probably had plenty of reasons to. Bryce died drunk behind the wheel. Technically, he died a couple of weeks later from the injuries after the crash, but his death was his own fault."

For a minute no one spoke. Melissa had no desire to explain anything further about her marriage. The silence, though, was uncomfortable even in the dream state.

Captain Reed finally broke through the awkward stillness. "I am sorry for thy loss."

Melissa reached up and pushed the hood off her head. "Don't be. My life is much better now. At least it was until these dreams started. Now, I'd just like to go back. The students and crew will be getting up soon."

Captain Reed shook his head. "I regret to say we cannot return to Falmouth today. When we reach port, I shall send Jonah to inquire if any carriages or wagons are departing for northern destinations. I could not, in good conscience, allow thee to travel aboard a ship of men. There are no passenger freights departing for England at this time."

"But I don't want to go north. And though I would love to go to London one day, I don't have the money or the time off to go now. I just want to wake up on the *Shenandoah*, anchored off Cuttyhunk with all the kids and Zane and Pete and John and everyone else."

Another silence engulfed the room. Melissa waited for one of the men to agree with her. The light coming in through the porthole told her that daylight approached. Surely she'd be waking up soon. This fantasy had to be coming to an end.

"Cuttyhunk? When were ye last at Cuttyhunk?" Adam asked.

"Today—no, yesterday. Well, actually, now, right? *Shenny* should still be anchored there." Melissa heard the frustration in her voice and shut her mouth. The conversation was going nowhere quickly. She'd let the students, or in this case her dream characters, take control of the classroom, and now she was off track. Her mistake. Time to turn the ship around. "Gentlemen, you have been very kind. Would you mind if I tried to go back to sleep so I can return to my school cruise?"

Adam nodded at Isaiah.

"Sleep may prove a healing balm for thy confusion," Captain Reed said. "Would ye allow me to show thee to more comfortable accommodations?"

Melissa glanced about the room. In every dream, she had been here. "No, but thank you. I think I need to stay here. Every night I've pushed on one of these crates and fallen back into my bunk. I'll try jostling one of the boxes as soon as you guys leave."

Again, there was an exchange of looks. Melissa didn't care at this point. She wanted to go back to sleep and go home. The dream had gone from surreal to a little too real, and she was ready for the whole thing to be over.

Captain Reed offered her his hand. "I am not comfortable taking my leave with a lady on the floor amidst a room of supplies. Ye may have my cabin. I shall not be needing it further this morning."

Melissa thought of Captain Roberts' cabin. She'd been down there a few times on the annual tour. There was a large bed and plenty of pillows. She would probably dream her way back to her students a lot faster in a comfortable bed than on a cold, hard floor.

She reached up and placed her hand in Isaiah's. A jolt of electricity shot through her hand and up her arm as he helped her to stand. She wobbled as the current raced to her heart. He appeared to feel nothing. Then again, it was her dream.

He deftly tucked her hand into the crook of his elbow and took the lead. Appreciating the warmth of his body on the chilly morning, she followed him out of the storage room and into the passageway. He held the lamp in front of them and walked slowly toward the stern. He climbed up the companionway, placed the lantern on the deck, and then extended his hand down to Melissa. With Adam behind her, Melissa went up the companionway and reached for Isaiah's hand as she stepped onto the deck.

She blinked and then blinked again. Nothing changed. She rubbed her eyes with one hand and tightened her grip on Captain Reed's hand with the other. She'd never seen anything like the scene before her. But then again, she had. In textbooks and in pictures hanging in museums.

"Where are we?" she asked, her voice trembling.

"Boston. My oldest niece is to be married in four months' time, and her mother requested…"

Blackness engulfed Melissa. She didn't hear another word Captain Reed said.

# 16

"THE WOMAN IS IN TROUBLE." Captain Isaiah Reed stood at the helm, his ship at anchor, the sun rising over Boston Harbor. His lifelong friend and confidante stood to his left. In his quarters, a few feet away, a woman professing to be Miss Melissa Smith slept on his bed. When she'd swooned the third time, Adam had suggested they allow her body to rest.

"She is not well. Is there a chance she has the fever?" Isaiah spoke one of his concerns. Six years ago, the deadly disease had swept through Boston, killing many. He could not risk the lives of his crew and the families they returned to.

Adam removed his knit cap and ran his fingers through his gray hair. "I do not believe she suffers from scarlet fever."

"She is a teacher. Mayhap her students took ill," Isaiah said.

"Aye, she stated she was both teacher and chaperone."

"Thee did not believe her?"

"I know not what to believe of her comments," Adam replied. "As for the fever, there has been no word of another outbreak. If Mistress Smith's students succumbed to illness, reports would have made their way to towns and ports."

Isaiah nodded. "Aye, thee speaks truth. I should not worry over that for which I have no evidence. But, Adam, there is something amiss. I am troubled. Her presence cannot be a good portent of days to come."

"My good friend, ye know better than to question the ways of the Lord. For reasons we have yet to learn, the lady has been placed in thy care. Time shall tell whether 'tis for good or naught." Adam looked into Isaiah's eyes. "What occurred when the woman accepted thy hand?"

Isaiah turned away. He did not wish to dwell on the sensation her hand in his created. Twenty years had passed since Jane's death. Twenty years in which he had not felt such a jolt to his system. Twenty years in which he had grown accustomed to solitary life.

"It matters not," was his curt reply. He simply refused to elaborate on the experience. He did not understand it himself. Therefore, he could not be asked to explain it.

"I saw thy expression," Adam stated.

"Ye have no…" Gripping the wheel with both hands, Isaiah met Adam's eyes and sighed. He knew his friend meant well. "I am at a loss to explain the connection. When Miss Smith placed her hand in mine, 'twas as if lightning surged through her fingers." Isaiah broke away from Adam's gaze. He looked out over the harbor, observing the ships as morning dawned and the crews prepared for the day.

"Quite odd," was all Adam said. Isaiah was grateful his friend did not ask further questions.

"'Tis done." Isaiah continued to watch the harbor activity. "We sail home, and from there I shall send her onward to Falmouth."

"She believes her journey is to Cuttyhunk."

Isaiah faced his friend, a heaviness in his heart. "We know the impossibility of which she spoke. Mistress, or Miss, Smith did not board the *Shenandoah* in Cuttyhunk."

"Aye, which leads me to reflect on where thou should send her."

"The woman cannot remain aboard the *Shenandoah*," Isaiah stated hastily but firmly.

"Agreed. Now, I must see to the morning meal. If she wakes, pay heed that she does not attempt to rise too quickly." Adam was about to walk away and then paused.

Isaiah anticipated the unspoken words. In rare form, his lifelong friend refrained from speaking what was on his mind and left his thoughts unspoken to set about his task.

Isaiah was grateful. He had no desire to dwell on the past, and he was unprepared to contemplate the immediate present.

A whaling ship followed the tide and current out of the harbor. In his youth, Isaiah had crewed on a sloop that had ventured north to the Gulf of St. Lawrence in search of whales. Their seventy-ton vessel had nearly capsized during a hunt. Many had asked if he would rig the *Shenandoah* for whaling. Though there was financial gain to be had in the business, Isaiah had no desire to risk his crew or ship for monetary motivations.

He watched the topsail schooner catch the wind and disappear into the horizon while he mused over the choices he'd made. A loud moaning rose from his cabin. Shaking his head, Isaiah strode across the deck and called down, "Miss Smith, do ye need assistance?"

"Where am I?" came the frantic reply.

Facing the stern, Isaiah descended the short ladder into his quarters. He found a distraught woman sitting on his bed, his blankets covering her from the waist down. Her eyes were wide, and she was sweating and clutching her midsection. His first instinct was to run the other way. He had little to no experience calming upset women, and he had no wish to become sick if, in fact, his stowaway was ill.

Yet, instead of retreating up the ladder as was his inclination, Isaiah approached the bed. "How are you feeling?"

"Where am I?" she asked again.

He could tell she was frightened, not of him, but certainly of something or someone. "Ye are aboard the schooner *Shenandoah*."

She nodded but still looked apprehensive. "Why are you dressed like that?" The woman pointed to his clothes.

Isaiah glanced down at his attire and could not fathom the meaning of her question. His tan breeches, white shirt and cravat, green coat, and brown great coat were in fashion. Thinking she might be remarking on his wearing of the great coat below deck, he removed the jacket. "The air above is still damp and chilled," he said after hanging his outer jacket on a peg.

"But why are you wearing clothes like that?"

"Madam, I do not understand thy question. These are my clothes; hence, I wear them." Isaiah fidgeted with a button on his coat. He did not like the way her eyes were roaming over his apparel. Her dislike was evident in her frown.

"I can't figure out what is going on, why this dream isn't ending. Are you dressed for some 1776 Colonial reenactment?"

Her voice held a hint of humor—at his expense, Isaiah presumed. But he still had no idea what she was talking about. "Mrs. Smith—"

"Melissa, please. No Mrs."

"Miss Smith, I do not know what a Colonial reenactment is. Are ye referring to an activity thy students play in school?"

"No, but they could. Haven't you ever been to Bunker Hill or the Freedom Trail or the Boston Tea Party Museum? All the guys are dressed like they're in the eighteenth century."

"As we are presently in the eighteenth century, the men ye speak of would be considered appropriately attired," Isaiah stated. Her sentences made no sense whatsoever. He considered himself a well-educated man, yet he struggled to follow her train of thought.

"What?" Her words were barely a whisper. "What did you just say? What year do you think this is?"

"We are today in May in the year of our Lord 1770."

The woman put her hands over her ears and began rocking on his bed. "This cannot be happening. This cannot be happening."

"Miss Smith, what can I do for thee?"

She reached up her hands to him as though she were a beggar on the street. "Take me home!" she screamed. "Get me out of here!"

Isaiah felt helpless. Nothing the woman said was logical, yet her fear was palpable. His sister-in-law would know what to do. He would take her there before nightfall. Until then, he must do something to calm her. He scanned his cabin. He had decanters of Madeira wine, and rum on the desk to his left. He walked over and poured her a glass of Madeira.

"Sip this, Miss Smith. It will help to calm thee."

She smelled it and wrinkled her nose. "It smells like cough syrup."

Isaiah chuckled. "I assure thee this is not elderberry syrup."

She took the smallest of sips. "It's alcohol! Are you trying to get me drunk?" She held the glass out to him, wanting him to take it, but Isaiah gently touched her hand and pushed the goblet toward her.

Her eyes found his immediately and Isaiah knew that she, too, had felt the current flowing between them. He looked down and tipped the glass slightly to encourage her to drink. "Ye have suffered a shock. A drop of Madeira will help take the edge off. I shall not allow thee to become drunk."

The woman gulped down the liquid as a child swallows unwanted medicine. He poured her another glass. She drank the contents in four large sips. Her face appeared more relaxed. She looked up at him and smiled. "Maybe I am drunk. I don't remember anything. And you're telling me it's 1770. If I'm not dreaming, I'm drunker than Bryce ever was."

"Adam, our cook whom ye met earlier, believes thee has taken a knock to the head. He has no formal education in medicine, but he has gained extensive knowledge of ailments and the appropriate treatments. I shall go to the galley and ask him to come speak with thee," Isaiah said softly, hoping to comfort her.

He took the empty cup from her hand, and as he did so, she grabbed his arm. "Please, don't leave me here. I'm scared. I know something's wrong. Something's terribly, terribly wrong."

Isaiah tensed. Though his shirt and jacket lay between her hand and his arm, he felt her warmth radiating through his body. He could not fathom the woman's effect on him, and he desperately wanted to move away from her. She was tugging harder and pleading with her eyes.

"Isaiah, please, will you sit with me?" she begged him.

He flinched, taking a step back from the bed. Her use of his Christian name caught him off guard. "Madam, it would be highly improper for me to sit on the bed with thee. If it shall bring ye comfort, I shall pass the time at my desk while ye rest."

"Okay," she said. "Maybe this time I'll fall asleep and wake up in the right place."

Isaiah watched as she turned onto her side and pulled the blankets up to her chin. She appeared helpless, childlike, though he knew she was no child. She was younger than his sister-in-law, but not by many years. She was a woman in his bed, a circumstance he had not come upon in twenty years. The sight was not a welcome one.

He turned and walked to his desk, placing the glass on the silver tray. He reached for his Bible and opened to his daily reading. He began with Proverbs 3, a profound bit of wisdom. He stopped at verses five and six. "Trust in the LORD with all thine heart; and lean not unto thine own understanding. In all thy ways acknowledge him, and he shall direct thy paths."

Adam had said as much to him earlier. He glanced over his shoulder at the form in his bed and prayed silently, *Whatever thou hast planned, I beseech thee to direct my paths.*

He finished his readings and waited for Adam to bring breakfast. He needed to escape the cabin. He needed Adam to sit with this strange woman. And he needed to sail his ship home.

# 17

JOHN WALKED AROUND THE DECK, coffee mug in hand. He was surprised Melissa wasn't up yet but grateful she'd dozed well enough to sleep in. He'd walked by her cabin before coming topside. He wasn't giving Pete's rantings from last night any credence, but he had wanted a cup of joe, and it wouldn't do any harm to walk through the saloon and past her cabin to get to the galley. He was pleased when he'd seen her door was still closed.

He had slept better, too. The evening had been much cooler, a good 10 degrees cooler than the nights before. Personally, he preferred sleeping with his ceiling fan on. Life without electricity was not an experience he wanted to live every day, especially in a small cabin with only a porthole for ventilation. It's no wonder Melissa was dehydrated.

The first mate approached John. "It's ten to seven. Melissa's still below?"

"Yeah. Guess she's making up for a few rough nights."

"No problem. I'm sure she'll wake up shortly. The kids are starting to congregate at the ladder. Their ruckus is sure to disrupt anyone's sleep."

"Tell me about it," John said. "I hear everything. I don't know how you all live onboard all summer long. I'd be exhausted."

Zane chuckled. "You get used to it. Me, I can sleep anywhere through anything."

"Melissa must be equally blessed this morning. I can hear the kids from here." John glanced down at his watch: *6:58.*

"It's time." Zane left him by the galley and headed toward the generator.

Nathan was unrolling the hose. Pete rang the bell, and the twenty-eight students hurrying up the ladder and across the deck sounded like a herd of horses from the apocalypse.

As the last student rose from the hatch, John waited expectantly for Melissa's pretty blond head to emerge. He frowned when she did not appear.

He liked her. He'd finally admitted it to himself at the April staff meeting. He'd been looking forward to this cruise for months. She was sweet and kind to the students at school but had always been formal and businesslike during their interactions. Still, he'd noticed her. He'd agreed to chaperone the cruise for the sole purpose of spending time with her.

He knew the basics of her story, much like anyone else who'd read the papers after Bryce Burroughs died in the car accident a few years ago. Though he was married to his third wife at the time of his death, his divorce from Melissa and her relocation to Vineyard Haven had been mentioned in the articles. There was also the nasty gossip and innuendos Bryce's widow had spread around town to anyone who would listen.

John had admired Melissa throughout the ordeal and in the weeks that followed. Over the years, he'd caught pieces of conversations in the staff room and heard comments from other teachers. Melissa showed no signs of bitterness or anger, but she didn't date. Their staff room was news central whenever a marriage was pending, a baby was expected, illness hit, or new relationships bloomed. No one had ever mentioned Melissa seeing anyone. Ever.

She'd confirmed as much the other day, but he'd also felt her softening toward him, flirting at times. They had three more days together, and he intended to make the most of every opportunity. If she'd just come up on deck, he'd get her a cup of coffee and engage her in a conversation to find out what she liked to do on the weekends, what her interests and hobbies were—other than photography and Spike.

Water trickled down over his feet. Zane was approaching with the hose, and the students were right behind him with their brooms and brushes. John wanted to go below and see if Melissa was awake and relaxing in the saloon, but he knew he should be on deck with the students. He drank the last of his coffee and passed the mug down to Nick.

"Any sign of Melissa yet?" he asked as he handed Nick the cup.

"None," Nick replied. "She must be dead to the world if she slept through this noisy bunch."

"Yeah." John stepped up onto the roof deck as Zane pulled the hose down the starboard side. He glanced at his watch again: *7:18. Where is she?* Now he was annoyed.

He looked out over the still waters of the harbor and Buzzard Bay, trying to appreciate the view of Cuttyhunk as the sky turned a rosy pink. What was that old saying? "Pink skies at night, sailors' delight. Pink skies in the morning, sailors take warning." He believed the phrasing referred to the weather and seas, which looked calm and peaceful. But he felt disconcerted, or maybe just impatient, as the minutes ticked by with him waiting for Melissa to surface.

Lizzie came by, pushing a broom over the pine boards. "Where's Miss Smith?"

John forced a smile. "Guess she overslept."

"Uh-oh. Good thing it's not a school day," Lizzie joked, her lopsided grin giving John a moment of happiness.

"You're right. Would you do me a favor and go below and knock on Miss Smith's door? We don't want her to miss breakfast."

"Sure." Lizzie passed him her broom and took off.

John carried the broom over to the bosun box and waited.

Several minutes later, Lizzie came up through the hatch. She looked anxiously over toward the galley and then spun around until she saw John. She ran over to him. "I knocked and knocked, but Miss Smith didn't answer. I tried to open her door, but I think it's locked. Why didn't she answer? Do you think she's sick?"

John suddenly had that same thought. He'd been pacing around thinking she was catching up on her sleep, but what if she'd been dizzy again this morning and passed out?

He handed Lizzie her broom back and forced another smile. "I'll go check on her. You finish up your chores."

With a sense of urgency, John strode across the deck and dropped down the ladder. Cabin 8 wasn't more than fifteen feet from the companionway. He listened for a moment outside the door. Hearing nothing, he knocked twice and called out to Melissa.

No answer.

He tried the latch, but it didn't move. He banged on the door again, waited a few seconds, and then banged again. "Melissa," he yelled.

Nothing.

He curbed the rising panic. Sprinting up the ladder, he found Nathan supervising a handful of girls learning to polish the silver and brass. "Excuse me," he said as calmly as he could, "do you have a putty knife?"

"Of course. Follow me." Nathan led the way to the bosun box, pulled out a knife, and passed it to John. "What's up?"

"Melissa's not answering her door, and I can't get the dang thing open."

"Let me go with you. I should've fixed it Monday. I was going to do it yesterday afternoon, but she wanted to rest after we got back from Cuttyhunk and asked me to see to it today," Nathan said.

The two men stood outside Melissa's cabin. John knocked again. When she didn't answer, he pried the putty knife between the doorframe and the door, working on the latch. After a couple of hard upward whacks, the metal gave. John and Nathan pushed against the door until it flung open.

Her bunk was empty. The room was empty.

"Ah, you're sure she's not on deck?" Nathan asked.

"Positive." John looked around the cabin. Her bunk had clearly been slept in. The sheet was twisted and the blanket had been tossed to the foot of the bed. Melissa's camera bag was on the floor next to her bunk. He walked over and opened it. Her camera was inside.

Panic rose. John knew he should feel better, relieved that she wasn't passed out on the floor or worse. But he didn't feel better.

Nathan, however, didn't seem overly fazed. He pointed out the door. "You go tell Zane what's going on. I'm going to start searching the other cabins. She's got to be somewhere."

John climbed the rungs two at time and then found Zane with Caleb by the generator, rolling the hose. "Melissa's not in her room," he blurted out.

"Did you check the head?" Caleb asked.

"Ah, no," John replied, slightly chagrined. Then he realized there was no way Melissa was in the bathroom two doors down and hadn't heard him yelling and pounding on her door.

Unless she was sick and had passed out in the head.

Zane put down the hose. "First, take a deep breath. It's a big ship, but not that big. She's around. We just need to find her—without telling the children."

John nodded. Zane was right. Melissa had to be somewhere.

"I'll go below with you and we'll check the heads. Caleb, don't say a word until we come topside."

"Um, Nathan knows, too. He was with me when I opened Melissa's door. He's searching the cabins," John said.

"Okay, good. Nathan knows enough not to tell the children why he's looking for Melissa. They won't suspect a thing."

As Zane spoke, John noticed that only a handful of kids were on deck. "Let's hope we find her before one of the students does."

"Right." Zane marched toward the main hatch.

The two student heads were side by side at the foot of the companionway ladder. John knocked on one, Zane on the other. No one answered. They opened the doors simultaneously.

The heads were empty.

John turned to Zane, his heart quaking with dread. "Where could she be?"

# 18

ZANE DIDN'T ANSWER JOHN. If the man was a poker player, John wouldn't know what he was holding, but he didn't need to look in the mirror to know his own face was a frantic, worried visage. "Go above," Zane ordered. "Ask Caleb to muster the crew and meet me at the bow. We don't want our voices to carry. I'm going to stop in and talk with Nick."

John went up and gave Caleb Zane's instructions. He paced between the starboard and port sides until Zane returned and the crew assembled silently. Instinctively, every guy glanced at the water, but John knew Melissa wasn't floating anywhere visible. He'd spent a good hour staring at the water waiting for her to wake up. She wasn't there.

Zane's eyes narrowed as he neared John, but he remained cool. Melissa wasn't with Zane, and neither was Nick. Not a good sign.

"Nick hasn't seen Melissa all morning. Didn't hear anything while he was preparing breakfast either." Zane looked directly at each crew member. "Let's keep this between ourselves. I don't want to alarm the children. We'll send them down for breakfast and hope they don't ask any questions. She's on the boat somewhere, probably sick and unable to call for help. Let's work quickly and efficiently to find her. I have my cell phone. Text me if she's not in your area. Call me only if you find Melissa. Everybody clear?"

"What about those dreams she was having?" Pete asked.

"Not now, Pete!" Zane snapped. He took a deep breath and exhaled. Regaining his composure, Zane gave Tucker and Justin new orders. "You two search the crew's quarters and your head. Roscoe and Caleb, comb through the cabins and storage areas from the bow to the galley. Nathan and Avery, investigate the stern cabins through to the saloon. Listen, guys, we've got a ship full of students who do not, I repeat, do not need to know one of their teachers is missing. Pretend you're doing cabin inspection or make up anything you want. Keep it light, keep it fun. Hopefully Nick will call breakfast shortly and the kids won't be underfoot while we search. Bear, take the forepeak. If you find anything out of—"

"What's the forepeak?" John asked. He hadn't heard anything about that area of the ship.

"A storage area in the extreme bow of the ship," Zane explained. "We stash lines, lamps, extra gear, and tools there. It has its own hatch and a ladder below deck." He pointed beyond the windlass. "The hatch is just forward of the windlass. It's a great place to get lost if someone was so inclined."

"Did Melissa know about it?"

Zane shook his head. "I don't know, but Bear will find out."

Pete inched forward. John glared at him, thinking he'd better not make another crack. "What do you want me to do?" Pete asked.

A brief smile crossed Zane's face. He too must have been anticipating another flip remark and was probably as relieved as John that Pete wasn't pursuing his previous comment. "You go work the breakfast detail, just as you would any other morning."

"I want to help," John said.

Zane shook his head. "You need to stay with the children. I don't want them to suspect anything. We have to believe that Melissa is going to be okay. Maybe she was up early taking pictures and got dizzy again."

John put a shaky hand on Zane's shoulder. "Her camera is in her cabin. I already checked." Nothing Zane could say would ease John's inner turmoil.

"Don't panic, John. We've got to keep things normal for the students." Zane was matter-of-fact. John understood his reasoning, agreed with him, but wanted to scream out Melissa's name until she answered.

"I'm going down to tell the captain. The two of us will meet you in the saloon for breakfast. She's here somewhere, and we'll find her." Zane gave a quick nod and headed down to the helm.

The crew dispersed and John went below to pretend everything was normal. He took a seat. Zane didn't expect him to eat, did he? That was a joke!

Pete stuck his head out of the galley. "Mr. Masters, Jeremy is heading topside to ring the breakfast bell."

"Thanks, Pete." John folded his hands and bowed his head. He wasn't religious, not by a long shot. He hadn't been to church in over a decade, and that was for a wedding. He didn't know what to say. He heard the bell ring. "Please," was all he muttered.

The students poured out of the cabins and down the passageways from bow and stern, filling the saloon with laughter, smiles, and excitement. John wanted to tell them all to be quiet. He couldn't stand their energy and happiness. Didn't they know or sense something was terribly wrong?

Zane and Captain Roberts appeared before all the students had taken their seats. John stared at Zane, waiting for some signal. The first mate shook his head. Captain Roberts looked at John and nodded. Another man with a poker face.

Pete and work crew four carried in breakfast—heaping platters of cinnamon French toast, four pitchers of maple syrup, two big bowls of fruit, two wooden bowls of Nick's homemade granola, and two smaller bowls of Greek yogurt. When they'd placed the morning chow in the middle of each table and taken their seats, Zane and Captain Roberts began passing the food.

Looking at the hearty meal, John thought he was going to be ill. He felt Zane's eyes upon him.

"Amber, please pass Mr. Masters some French toast," Zane said.

Taking the platter from Amber, he forked two slices onto his plate. How could Zane be so calm, while John could do nothing but sit there, waiting for Zane's phone to ring? He could care less about food.

"Where's Miss Smith?" Lizzie asked.

As John flinched, Zane put down his fork. "She's busy at the moment. She'll be with us as soon as she can."

"She's probably taking more pictures," one of the girls said, but John didn't see who. Of course they would think she was doing something fun. The kids wouldn't suspect anything was wrong. Why would they? As far as they knew, sailing on the *Shenandoah* was the perfect summer vacation.

A phone buzzing jolted John's senses. Zane read his Blackberry screen. A text message, not a phone call. John wanted to ask who was checking in, who hadn't seen Melissa, but he knew better.

"Hey," Greg said, "how come you get to use a cell phone?"

"When you're the first mate, you can change the rules," Zane stated somewhat brusquely.

"Yeah, my dad says the same thing about smoking when he lights one up," Greg added.

Zane's eyes softened. "You're right, Greg. I haven't changed the rules because I'm the first mate. But we're expecting quite an important call and a few vital messages this morning that relate to the ship, and I need to have my phone on. Otherwise, it would be off."

Respect shone in Greg's eyes. He grinned. "Working overtime, huh?"

"You could say that." Zane's phone buzzed a second time, and a third. Two more text messages. Not good. That left only one option.

Slicing his toast into small pieces, John moved the bread around his plate. A million thoughts raced. Most of them he didn't want to think about, but they kept coming. He glanced down at Zane's plate. Same scenario as on his plate—lots of cut-up pieces, not too many consumed. He was worried too.

Barely a minute passed when Zane's phone went off again. John felt as though he'd been sucker-punched. That was it. Everyone had checked in. No one had found her. Zane stared at him, willing him to remain calm, but John was ready to scream.

Zane headed for Captain Roberts. "Captain, we're needed on deck."

John eyed his watch: *8:27.* The students chattered and ate. Helpless, John watched every second tick by.

One by one, the kids rose and scraped their plates clean over the slop bucket, placing their dirty dishes and utensils into the cleaning trays and heading back to their cabins. He asked Chip and Larry to oversee the boys' cabin cleanup. He said he would check on the girls. He didn't. Work crew four washed down the tables and scrubbed the dishes. John sat and waited.

At 8:43, Zane returned to the saloon. "Can you come with me to the captain's quarters?"

John rose and followed the first mate. With each step up the ladder, his sense of impending doom increased. The crew clustered around the helm, and Captain Roberts was in his quarters. Zane led the way down. The captain stood at the foot of the companionway ladder, adjusting a radio knob to Channel 16. He stepped aside to let Zane and John enter his quarters.

"Mr. Masters, we've searched the ship from bow to stern and top to bottom. Miss Smith is missing. It is time to call the Coast Guard."

As he heard the words, John's worst fear came true. He reached behind himself for the chair at the captain's desk and grabbed it for support. "Anything. Just get it done. Do whatever you have to do to find her."

Captain Roberts picked up the radio's hand microphone. "Mayday! Coast Guard, Coast Guard."

"Vessel hailing, this is Coast Guard Station Menemsha."

"Coast Guard Station Menemsha, this is the *Shenandoah*. We have a man overboard. Repeat, man overboard."

"Copy man overboard, *Shenandoah*. What is your position?"

"Copy position. *Shenandoah* is anchored at 41 degrees, 25 decimal 56 North, 070 degrees, 54 decimal 79 west."

"Copy that position, *Shenandoah*. Do you have any immediate injuries on board?"

"Negative to injuries, Coast Guard Menemsha."

"Copy negative injuries. Do you have any medical conditions?"

"Negative medical conditions."

"Copy negative medical. Sit tight, *Shenandoah*. The small boat is being dispatched. Otis will be radioed for the helo."

"Copy that, Coast Guard Menemsha."

"Over and out, *Shenandoah*."

"Over and out, Coast Guard Menemsha."

Captain Roberts set the microphone back into its resting place on the radio. He straightened, removed his ball cap, and ran his fingers through his gray hair. During the distress call, the captain seemed to have aged ten years. The smile was gone, a grim line replacing his usual friendly expression.

John felt worse than the captain looked. His stomach twisted in a knot so tight he feared he'd double over from the pain. He didn't want to ask, but he had to. "What happens now?"

Placing the cap back on his head, Captain Roberts stood taller, more formal. "The Coast Guard is sending over their forty-seven footer. It will probably be here in about forty minutes. It takes about thirty minutes to get the helo from Otis Air Force Base in the air. The small boat should arrive first. Once they arrive, they'll begin a search. The helo will fly over the water and the island. Officers from the small boat will search *Shenandoah* and the surrounding waters. Though he didn't say so, I suspect they'll also send the Coast Guard Cutter *Hammerhead*, which is stationed at Woods Hole."

John leaned back against the chair. Melissa's nightmares were nothing compared to what was happening in real life. "How long will this take?"

"There is no way to know, Mr. Masters. I've never been in this situation before. Search and rescue missions can take hours or days. Depends on when they find the missing person," Captain Roberts said.

He didn't say "body," but John knew they all had to be thinking the same thing. If she wasn't on the ship, what were the chances she was alive? "If she's…if they don't find her…"

"Mr. Masters, we have no idea where Melissa is or how she got off the ship. I'm going to question the men again, but until we know when she left and how, there is no point in guessing the outcome."

"I know," John said, "but what are the chances she's alive?" There, he'd said it. The words no one else had spoken aloud in the last hour.

"I don't know," Captain Roberts said. "If she swam to shore or floated to shore, she could be fine. The Coast Guard will most likely report our situation to the State Police on the Vineyard. There is no police station on Cuttyhunk, but the Coast Guard, Cuttyhunk residents, and the Vineyard police will do a thorough search of the island. Cuttyhunk is small and still has a fair number of people on the island for the upcoming Labor Day weekend. The locals will pitch in to help find her as soon as word gets out."

John released his hand from the chair and rubbed his palm, his mind sorting through the horrible information it was being fed. John glanced over at Zane. He had been silent throughout the emergency call and their discussions.

He stood by the trunk at the foot of the captain's bunk, cracking his knuckles one at a time over and over again. He was physically in the room, but his eyes were not focused on anything in the quarters. He stared past John and through the wall. "What are you thinking?" John asked him.

"I keep asking myself how and when Melissa left the ship. I'm trying to piece together where I was when. What time did she go to bed?"

"Around ten. I was in the saloon with Pete, Avery, Chip, Larry, and Roscoe. I left before eleven and she hadn't come out of her cabin," John said.

Zane nodded. "Tucker was on first watch from twenty-hundred to o-hundred—eight o'clock to midnight. Pete came on middle watch at midnight and was on until four this morning. Caleb was on morning watch from four to eight. I was up by five, so she had to leave sometime between eleven and five. When I rowed Noah and Cassie to shore, nobody was in the water. Nobody was awake and out as far as I could see. She had to have gone in much earlier. I need to sit down with Tucker, Pete, and Caleb. It's fairly difficult to leave the ship unnoticed, especially when she didn't use a ladder."

Captain Roberts passed Zane a legal pad and pen. "The men are waiting topside and we have children below who are expecting to sail shortly. We need to figure out how, when, and what to tell the children. No one can leave the ship until the Coast Guard arrives and gives the okay. We've got about twenty minutes before the small boat and the helo arrive. Before the chaos begins and the students witness the arrival of the police boat and the Coast Guard cutter, we need to sit them down and try to explain the situation. Let's decide on our course of action now."

"But first, gentlemen, we need to pray." Captain Roberts removed his hat and bowed his head. "Heavenly Father, we pray for Melisa, for her safety and well-being, for the men and crews who will search for her, and for the children as they learn that their teacher is missing. We ask for Your protection and grace to surround us all, most especially Melissa. Amen."

# 19

MELISSA ROLLED OVER AND SAW THE MAN CALLED ISAIAH sitting at his desk, reading a book that resembled her mother's old family Bible. For generations, her relatives' births had been entered into the front pages, as were weddings and deaths. The book had been passed down for generations. There were people listed in there from the early 1800s. It was heavy, larger than a standard sheet of paper, bigger than most of their cookbooks, and thicker than any other book in their house, including *War and Peace*.

The tome Isaiah had open on his desk resembled her mom's, right down to the gold edging on the pages, and that comforted her. A point of normality in the midst of her extraordinary circumstances. She could make no sense of what was happening at the moment. She had to be dreaming, simply had to be, yet where she was and what she was experiencing didn't feel like a dream anymore.

Isaiah had told her they were in the eighteenth century. What did that mean? A good-looking stranger from the eighteenth century was visiting her dream? Or was she stuck in her dream in the eighteenth century and couldn't wake up? Her head hurt just thinking about it.

Melissa was grateful to be lying down in a warm bed. She tugged the sheet, blanket, and quilt up under her ear. The nautical quilt was pretty—masculine, but pretty. The blue fabric had sailing images stitched on it. It looked fairly new and felt handmade, not factory-produced. Someone had spent a fortune on it. She'd have to Google it when she got home and see if she could find one and who made them. It was probably Amish.

The dizziness had passed, as had her queasiness, but her eyes were heavy, and Melissa could feel the pull of sleep. She nestled into the soft pillow. Maybe when she woke up the next time, she'd be back on *Shenandoah*, the real *Shenandoah*.

Before she closed her eyes, she saw Isaiah turn the page in his Bible. She wondered what passage he was reading. She wished she had her Bible. Why hadn't she brought it with her on the cruise this year? Every other year she'd brought it along. She would love to read through Ruth right now. Ruth's story always filled Melissa with hope. *The woman loses her husband, ends up broke, and follows her depressed mother-in-law to a foreign land. Then, because she is faithful, God blesses her with a fabulous husband and a wonderful life. They have children, and through their bloodline King David is born and, years later, the Savior of the world, Jesus Christ. Best happily-ever-after ending ever written.*

She closed her eyes and sighed. She wanted a happily-ever-after ending. Preferably immediately, which needn't be more than waking up in her own bunk. Picturing Ruth sneaking in and resting at Boaz's feet, Melissa drifted off to sleep quickly....

\*

Voices woke her. Melissa yawned and stretched. The bed was so warm, but her nose felt chilly. She should've closed the porthole all the way last night, but the cool air had felt good when she'd first gotten into bed.

She could smell the yummy breakfast Nick was cooking. Oatmeal—her favorite. The scent of cinnamon was also unmistakable. She hoped he would put some apple slices, raisins, and brown sugar on the tables, too.

The sound of footsteps outside her door brought to mind the nightmare she'd experienced again last night. Grateful to feel at peace and snug in her bunk, Melissa opened her eyes to the new day. She immediately blinked, blinked again, and then rubbed her eyes hard. Silently, she prayed, *Lord, please, please let me open my eyes and have this nightmare be over.*

Slowly, willing herself to see her craft bags lined up against the wall and her camera on the floor beside her, Melissa opened her eyes again. Isaiah, the Colonial man from her dream, was still at his desk, just as he had been when she'd fallen back to sleep. He was eating cinnamon oatmeal, judging from the aromas in the room. Not Nick's cooking at all.

Did people eat in dreams? She couldn't remember ever having a dream in which she ate or watched other people eat. Her stomach growled. She was hungry, and Isaiah's breakfast smelled delicious. Could she eat in a dream? Her stomach rumbled again, louder this time. Self-conscious, Melissa curled up under the covers, pulled the pillow out from under her head, and shoved it against her middle, hoping to muffle any sounds. Then she rubbed her belly and hoped Isaiah wouldn't hear the grumblings.

Whether it was the rustle of the sheets or the growling of her stomach, Isaiah turned around. Her nightmare man was quite handsome—rugged yet refined, black hair with mere touches of gray, and hands that emitted electrical jolts to her skin. He gave her a half-smile, or what Melissa labeled a tolerant "I'll be nice to you, but what are doing here and how quickly are you leaving" look. She'd used it with door-to-door salesmen and religious groups who knocked and hoped to convert her. Considering the unusual circumstances in her dream, Isaiah probably wished she would go away just as she wished the intruders would leave her property.

"Are ye hungry?" he asked politely.

"Starving," Melissa replied. "And oatmeal is my favorite, especially with cinnamon, apples, raisins, and brown sugar."

"I—" the captain began.

"Not that I'm asking for all that," Melissa rushed to explain, sitting up as she talked. "Anything at all will be fine."

Rising from his chair, Isaiah gazed at her. "I shall ask Jonah to bring thee a bowl of porridge with raisins and sugar. We have no apples onboard, though there are ample quantities of cider. Would ye enjoy a mug?"

"Cider sounds great. Thank you." Melissa's stomach grumbled in anticipation. Her brain was equally active but quite unhappy. There was simply too much to process. Ordering food in a dream, talking to a man who claimed to be from the eighteenth century, and sleeping in the captain's quarters that weren't really the captain's quarters was simply too bizarre, too weird, too *Somewhere in Time*-esque.

When Isaiah went up the ladder, Melissa glanced about the room. She didn't want to get caught snooping, so she sat there and tried to absorb each item. If she didn't know better, she'd say she was in a museum. Though sparsely decorated, the room contained finely crafted wooden furniture, possibly walnut. Her knowledge of older pieces was limited. Cindy would know. She loved antiques.

While all the belongings were of high quality, Melissa was troubled by one important fact: they were not anything like the items in Captain Roberts' quarters. Wherever she was, wherever her dream was taking place, she was not on her *Shenandoah*.

Within a few minutes, Isaiah returned. He bowed slightly when he reached the end of his bed. "Jonah shall bring thy morning meal shortly. Is there anything else ye require?"

That was a loaded question Melissa couldn't answer. She didn't know exactly what she wanted or needed, other than to wake up. Tugging nervously at the drawstring of her hood, Melissa became aware of the fact that she was in her pajamas, and she had no shorts, pants, shirt, or sweatshirt to put on.

"Ummm, do you have any clothes I could borrow?"

"Clothes?" He stumbled over the words. Eyes widening, Isaiah asked, "Ye wish to remove thy habit?" He spoke the words in a reverent tone.

"What?" Melissa stared at him. He was speaking oddly again. Did he think she was in the habit of getting undressed in front of men? If so, he had another thing coming! Dream or no dream, she wasn't getting naked for this man.

Isaiah pointed at her. "We have no such habits onboard."

Relief softened Melissa's indignant gaze. She smiled. "Well, that's good, because I don't go around getting naked in front of strange men, even if I am in your bedroom."

Whew. Good thing that was out there, just in case her dream characters got any improper ideas. There would be no misunderstanding now. All those movie plots with pirates and captains taking advantage of helpless women were not about to happen to her, not even in her dream.

The blush that covered Isaiah's face was nearly as amusing as the cough he instantaneously developed. He spun away from her and put both hands on the back of his wooden chair. Melissa stifled her laughter. He was pretty funny, this monster in her dream. She kind of liked him.

He straightened and erased any drop of friendliness from his face. "Madam, I never once presumed ye were anything but a woman of God."

"Great. I'm glad we cleared that up. So, can I borrow some clothes?"

He cocked his head, giving her another odd look. "Madam, am I to understand ye wish to remove your habit? 'Twas my understanding that nuns were required to wear the habit of their order."

She couldn't help it. Melissa started laughing. For the first time in her dream, the situation was hilariously funny. "I'm sorry," she said, holding up a hand and trying to suppress the fits of laughter escaping her mouth. "It's just," she snorted as she attempted to laugh, talk, and breathe at the same time, "you think I'm a nun?"

"Thy hooded robe." Isaiah pointed up and down at her pajamas.

"Wow, you're really playing up this Colonial reenactment, aren't you? Well, this is not a nun's robe," Melissa insisted, grabbing a fistful of the blue cotton fabric in her right hand. "This robe is my pajamas. I normally wear it in fall, but it was cool last night on the ship, and I hate to be cold."

Isaiah's face had drained of color. "Ye are not a nun?"

"No. I told you, I'm a teacher."

"Forgive me." Isaiah averted his eyes.

Melissa couldn't figure him out. Was he embarrassed that he'd thought she was a nun? Worse things had been assumed about her. She had lived through Bryce and his cheating and the gossip. Being called a nun was nothing. Her dream man was verging on priceless. "Hey, Isaiah, don't worry about it. I'm not offended."

Keeping his eyes on the floor, he faced her once again. "I presumed..." He glanced up and quickly back down at the floor. "Before supper, I shall escort thee to my sister's home."

Melissa was ready to change the subject and her clothes before her breakfast arrived. She flipped back the covers and scooted across the bed until her feet were on the floor. "Do you have a pair of sweat pants or something else I could put on? I can't wear my pajamas all day, and it looks like I'm going to be stuck in this dream for a while."

Waiting for his reply, Melissa noticed Isaiah's open mouth and the heat once again rising on his neck. He was staring at her legs. Not as a lech would, but in horror. Melissa tugged her nightgown lower until the hem of the jersey gown reached her feet. What was his problem? Her legs weren't that bad. Granted, she hadn't shaved them in a couple of days, but her hair was so fine and so light, she really didn't have to shave them every day as some women did. So why the look of repulsion? This was her dream. Shouldn't he be overwhelmed with her beauty or falling at her feet?

"Have ye no stockings, madam?"

Was he kidding? Before she could answer him, a knock on the roof interrupted their conversation.

"Porridge, Captain."

"Come, come, Nephew," Isaiah called up the hatch.

Melissa thought he sounded as if he were pleading. Either way, she sensed Isaiah was relieved when a young man, probably fifteen or sixteen years old, entered the cabin. He wore similar attire to Isaiah's—breeches, two coats, long wool socks, black shoes, and one of those tricorn black hats. Melissa just rolled with it. One more character in a very strange dream.

"Good morning, Captain."

"Good morning, Nephew."

The young man turned and bowed to Melissa. "Good morning, madam."

He wasn't surprised to see her, which meant either Isaiah or Adam had told him she was on board and in Isaiah's cabin, which was completely illogical. Given the way Isaiah blushed at her wish to change clothes, it was doubtful that the Colonial teenager before her would, if he were really from 1770, so blithely accept a strange woman in his uncle's bed.

Melissa grinned to herself, further proof that all that was happening around her was a peculiar dream. She'd already ruled out that she was having a nightmare, since nothing bad was happening beyond the fact that she couldn't wake up. A minor detail, but she'd have to wake up eventually.

Sooner than later, one of her students would knock on her door, seeking a brush, comb, tube of toothpaste, or permission to call home.

In the meantime, she was hungry. Melissa rose and walked to where the young man stood holding her breakfast tray. "Hi, I'm Melissa."

The boy turned quickly and peered at his uncle. Isaiah shook his head. Melissa wondered what that exchange was about but didn't dwell on it. She was hungry, and her feet were cold standing on the wood floor. She smiled, held out her hands, and waited for him to pass her the tray.

With a slight blush on his cheeks, he passed her the food. "It is a pleasure to make thy acquaintance, madam. Jonah Reed at your service. Adam sent porridge, raisins, sugar, and a mug of cider as requested. Would ye be needing anything else, madam?"

"I'm hungry enough to eat a horse, so if this doesn't fill me up, can you stop by Naturally Good and pick me up a sunrise granola bar?"

Once again, Jonah glanced over at his uncle. Isaiah again shook his head. They both wore a patient look, one she knew well as a teacher. Many times she'd had to paste on a polite smile, nod, and then calmly deal with an over-talkative or less-inhibited child.

Bowing respectfully, Jonah then straightened and looked at Melissa. "I shall do my best to accommodate thy needs." Facing his uncle, Jonah asked, "Will there be anything else, Captain?"

"Nay, Nephew. Thank you," Isaiah said.

Jonah departed up the short companionway. Melissa walked back to the bed, set the tray in the middle of it, sat down, and then shoved her feet deep under the covers. Pulling the blanket up to her waist, she slid the tray onto her lap and lifted the cloth from the bowl. Underneath was oatmeal with raisins, and on the side a small pewter bowl with brown sugar. The utensils were also pewter. Her dream was becoming more authentic as she went.

She sprinkled some sugar on top of her hot cereal and let the crystals melt. Reaching for her mug of cider, she took a long swallow of the drink she craved, hot or cold, throughout the fall months. She nearly gagged.

The juice was disgusting. She'd heard and read about food spoiling on ships, and this cider had definitely gone bad. Melissa wondered why nobody else had noticed. Was she the only one drinking it? Maybe that was why. Maybe the bottle had been sitting in the ice chest for months. Yuck!

Isaiah must have seen her mouth pucker at the sour taste. He stepped closer. "Is the cider not to thy liking?"

Melissa held out her mug. "I think it's gone bad."

Instead of taking a sip from her mug, Isaiah walked to his desk and drank from his own mug. Melissa watched him take a huge gulp, draining the contents of his morning beverage. He set the mug down and returned to stand near her. "I believe the cider is quite good."

"Really? It has that tang as if it's fermented."

"I would hope so. My orchard produces barrels of cider. We pay—"

"Oh, my gosh," Melissa interrupted. "This is hard cider."

"Aye." Isaiah gave her another patient look. She was expecting him to roll his eyes, but he didn't. Just the slow nod with his head. "Mayhap it will taste better when ye have fully recovered."

"Okay, well, I'll skip the cider and just eat my oatmeal."

The sugar had melted and spread over the top of the oatmeal in long, vein-like streams. Melissa dipped in her spoon and cautiously raised the food to her mouth. She hoped the oatmeal was normal.

The first bite was heaven. The sugar was flavored. She'd never tasted anything like it. Now her dream was getting fancy. She swallowed and looked over at Isaiah. "Where did you buy this sugar? What is the flavoring? It's divine."

He nodded, a crack of smile appearing for the briefest of seconds. "I am pleased ye are enjoying Adam's meal. The maple sugar is also from my farm."

"Where is your farm? Hawaii? I didn't know you could grow sugar cane in New England."

Once again giving her his patient look, Isaiah pointed to the bowl of golden brown sugar. "We do not grow sugar cane, Miss Smith. I have an abundance of maple trees on my property. We process the sugar from the syrup."

"You're kidding! I've heard about that, never tried it. I adore real maple syrup. Can't stand the junk made with high-fructose corn syrup and flavoring." Melissa scrunched up her nose. "But I've had maple sugar candy. Didn't love it. A little too sweet for me."

Melissa thought she saw Isaiah roll his eyes. "Certainly, madam. I shall leave thee to enjoy thy meal. I shall return shortly. Please remain in the cabin," Isaiah said before turning his back on her.

A tingle of fear inched up her spine. Was he going to hold her hostage? Keep her captive? Maybe she'd decided this wasn't a nightmare too quickly. "Are you planning to keep me prisoner down here?"

Isaiah calmly turned and met her eyes, his own brown ones brimming with compassion. "I am not holding thee prisoner. I am protecting thee. Neither thy condition nor thy attire shall be easily explained. It is best if ye remain here, safe in my quarters, until we anchor in Quincy Bay."

"Quincy Bay? Where is that? Is it near Cow Bay? Are you sailing home? I have never learned all the names of the little alcoves, lagoons, and bays the captain anchors in overnight."

"Aye, we journey home this day. Do not fret. My brother and his wife do not live far. You shall be welcome there." Isaiah climbed the ladder and left.

The fear that had scaled her spine had receded. Melissa believed Isaiah meant the words he spoke. They were going home. If she had to meet a few more people in her dream, and they were as nice as Isaiah, Adam, and Jonah had been, then she was completely comfortable with Isaiah's plans. One never really had control over their dreams anyway, so she'd ride this one out until morning. Whenever that might be.

# 20

JOHN, ZANE AND CAPTAIN ROBERTS STOOD ALONGSIDE THE STARBOARD CAP RAIL, the crew, chaperones and all twenty-eight students before them. Zane asked the students to take a seat on the deck. Though the sun was shining and the air was warm, a somber mood hung over the students, chaperones, and crew.

John noticed the girls clustered close together. Some hugged their knees to their chest with their arms looped through another's, while others sat cross-legged with their legs overlapping those of a friend. Lea cradled Cassie in her arms. Noah sat at attention beside Captain Roberts. John watched the small dog glance up at his master and then over at the children and then up at his master and over again to the children.

Captain Roberts took one step forward. Noah stood, walked up, and then sat beside his master. The captain removed his hat, folded the bill in half, and rapped the crown of the cap repeatedly onto the open palm of his left hand. John guessed he was trying to find the right words. He was relieved the captain had said he would tell the students.

John had just called Mark Maciel, their principal, and had given him the news. John had spent one minute telling Mark what he knew and another ten minutes telling Mark everything he didn't know. Mark had left the Island on Wednesday to spend the long weekend with his family, visiting his wife's relatives in western Massachusetts. Less than twenty-four hours later, he said he'd get back to the Island as soon as he could and would call John for hourly updates. That phone call had drained John's last bit of energy. Every call, every person, every action made Melissa's disappearance real. He didn't know how he was going to call all the parents.

Captain Roberts lowered the ball cap to his right side and tapped it gently against his leg. "Boys and girls, I'm sorry to have to tell you that Miss Smith is not on the ship this morning. We don't know when she left, but we are going to do everything we can to find her."

"Where is she?"

"I told you so."

"Probably went to check out the Cuttyhunk School and apply for a job."

John heard numerous comments but didn't look to see who was speaking. He was keeping his eyes on Lizzie. She hugged her knees tight to her chest and rocked back and forth, tears rolling down her cheeks. He mentally kicked himself for sending her down to knock on Melissa's door earlier. Chip DeMello stepped around a few of the boys and crouched down behind Lizzie. He rested a hand on her back, and she turned and fell into his arms, crying. Mya started crying too, which set off more children.

Captain Roberts clucked his tongue and Noah barked. The students looked up at the captain.

"I imagine this sounds a little scary to all of you. Believe me, we are doing, and are going to do, everything we can to find her—"

"Where is she?" Anthony asked.

Captain Roberts shook his head. "I don't know, son. I do know that Miss Smith loved to go for late-night swims in Lake Tashmoo. There is a chance she went swimming last night off *Shenandoah*, got tired, and then swam to shore on Cuttyhunk. For all we know, she's sleeping or exhausted and unable to contact the ship."

"Can't you call somebody?" Amber asked, her voice cracking.

"We have called the Coast Guard. They'll be here shortly to search Cuttyhunk and the surrounding Islands."

He didn't say "search the waters." John was grateful the captain had focused the rescue efforts on land. He didn't want his students leaving the ship thinking or believing Melissa had drowned.

"Captain," Nathan called from the helm, "you're being paged on the radio."

"Excuse me, children. Please listen to Zane, and help us do our best to find Miss Smith." Captain Roberts marched toward the helm.

Zane stepped up beside Noah. "Okay, everybody, let's pull together. You've all had some bad news. I want to help you in every way I can. Everyone in the crew does. What we want to do most is help you get home to your parents. We're sending a big boat over from the Island to pick you all up and bring you home. I'm sure this won't be easy, but I'm going to ask everyone to go below and pack up your gear."

He motioned for Bear and Caleb to come up next to him. "The guys are going below with you. Anything you need help with, just ask. I'll be down, too, to check on you. Take your time. If you have any wet clothes or towels, ask Caleb for a plastic bag. I'm really sorry. I hope we find Miss Smith quickly."

He paused. Every child's face was staring at him, asking unspoken questions, waiting for answers, hoping for a miracle. "Okay, let's head below. If you have any questions, we'll try to answer them while you're packing."

Most of the girls were crying, making John feel completely and utterly helpless. The boys were silent. Even the pirate gang descended the companionway quietly. One thing was certain: the students were going to need counseling. He was going to need counseling if they didn't find Melissa. First, he had to call twenty-eight sets of parents and tell them their children were coming home early and why. He'd dug the parent list out of his duffel bag when he went below to get his cell phone to call Mark.

When the deck was cleared of students, John started dialing. The Coast Guard pulled up, blue lights flashing, while he was on the phone with Amber's mother. Zane and Nathan, the only two crewmembers on deck, stood at the helm with Captain Roberts, who was standing in the companionway of his quarters, talking on the radio. John hung up the phone and Nathan waved him over.

"The Coast Guard is going to start a Victor Sierra search for Melissa. They need specifics about her to insert into their computer program. That way, they can get a baseline datum so their boat can begin its search," Nathan explained.

"Why are they sending only one boat? Hundreds of boats go in and around the Vineyard and Cuttyhunk. Why don't they ask them to help?" John asked.

"They'll probably send the big cutter from Woods Hole. For now, until they assess the situation, they sent the small boat, and the helo will be here shortly. But bear in mind, any ship in the area has heard an alert. The Coast Guard put a message out on Channel 16, stating there was a woman overboard in this area and asking everyone to be on the lookout. That's why I called the captain over to the helm earlier. Other captains of local boats were reporting in their locations, asking who had fallen overboard, what she was wearing, and other helpful questions. Everyone said they had their eyes on the water."

"That's good." John gazed out on the dark blue water and shuddered. He wouldn't want to be out there, trying to swim, trying to float. Melissa had worn a navy blue swimsuit the other day. Would she simply blend in if her arms and legs weren't moving? He couldn't stand the thought of her not being found. He turned back to Nathan. "So what is datum and what is a Victor Sierra search?"

Nathan opened a folded map. "This is a chart of the area. The Coast Guard boat will follow a specific pattern in their search and rescue mission. They have many options, the five most common being: an expanding square called Sierra Sierra; a creeping line called Charlie Sierra; a trackline called Tango Sierra Return; a parallel line search called Papa Sierra; and the Victor Sierra, a star-shaped pattern. The small boat will move in the outline of a star, forming three triangles as the vessel covers ground in search of Melissa." With his finger on the chart, Nathan drew an imaginary line of three connecting triangles. John willed Melissa to be in one of those areas.

He passed John the chart, and then he drew an "X" to indict where they were anchored. "The Victor Sierra search pattern is used most often when the search is small and the Coast Guard is fairly certain where the man overboard might be. As *Shenandoah* was anchored when Melissa went missing, datum will be able to predict the probable location."

"And datum is?" John asked.

"How technical do you want this?"

"Technical," John replied. "I'm a science teacher. Specifics will help me think better."

"Okay, technically, datum is the most probable location of the search object corrected for movement over time. They'll take the wind current, sea current, and tidal current, and then factor in the leeway, or the movement through water caused by winds, and then calculate the total surface drift."

The blue light was still flashing like a strobe light on the Coast Guard boat as it moved away from the *Shenandoah*. Captain Roberts was still on the radio. John couldn't hear him. He wondered if someone was giving him the datum. Because Melissa was still missing.

He looked at Nathan. "Just to make sure I've got this, datum is when they factor in tides, currents, winds, weather, what the person was wearing, and whether she can swim, then figure out the most likely location she could be?"

"You've got it."

John lowered his gaze to the deck. "What if you don't know whether the person is alive?"

"Mr. Masters..." Nathan placed his hand on John's shoulder. "John, we are hopeful Melissa is alive. At this time, we have no reason to presume she is dead. Which is why we're going to put as much information into the system as we can. Do you know Melissa's height and weight and what she was wearing when you last saw her?"

Holding his hand palm down and level with his nose, John made eye contact with Nathan. "I'm five-eleven, and she came up to about here on me. I'd say she was five-eight. She was taller than most of the female teachers at school. I have no clue about her weight, but she wasn't overweight, so probably, what, 140 or 150? As for what she was wearing, wouldn't you say a bathing suit?" John's last thought raised a question he hated thinking about. If she didn't go swimming, did she jump? That didn't seem like Melissa, but then again, he barely knew her.

"We believe she went swimming, so a bathing suit is logical. What was the last thing you saw her wearing?"

"I don't remember. Whatever she wore yesterday. She hadn't changed for bed when I said good night to her. She probably had on a sweater or sweatshirt last night after dinner, but I don't remember."

"No problem." Nathan smiled compassionately at John. "They will probably calculate for the swimsuit. If she was wearing a bright-colored shirt or nightgown, she might be easier to spot."

The thought of Melissa floating in the ocean overwhelmed John. He glanced out at the water, keeping his focus off Nathan. "What do you believe—really? Not what you're supposed to tell me, but what is your gut telling you? Is she alive?"

"I have every reason to believe she is alive. She is a swimmer, healthy, fit, the sun is out, the wind is light, and the water temperatures are the warmest we could hope for. Let's say she's floating in the current, too tired to swim. She's got everything on her side. Who knows? Maybe she's on Cuttyhunk or one of the other islands right now and walking to find a phone. Let's remain hopeful," Nathan urged.

Absorbing the words, John realized with mild irony that Nathan was wearing a Batman T-shirt. His affinity for cartoon characters had been obvious the first four days on board. Today, his shirt choice seemed fitting. They needed a superhero or two, and Nathan was doing his job extremely well. "You're right. Thanks for the pep talk. Guess they train you for this."

"Search and rescue is the bosun's duty, so Captain Roberts made me take a course with the Coast Guard in May, before I started working here. Maintaining morale in a crisis was covered multiple times," Nathan said.

John's cell phone rang. He looked at the screen. *Mark.* "Excuse me, Nathan. My boss."

Mark was on his way to Woods Hole and hoped to catch the noon ferry across. He wanted to be at the dock with the waiting parents when John arrived with the students. After talking with Mark, John resumed calling the parents. He'd no sooner finish one upsetting phone call when a parent would call back to check on a child or ask a question he couldn't answer.

One mother insisted that John give her son his phone so she could speak with him. When he tried to explain that he had more parents to call, she exploded. "I don't care who you have to call," Janet Pollock screamed into the mouthpiece. John had yanked the phone away from his ear. "I want to talk to Derek now. I want proof that my son is alive."

Zane had gone below, checked on the students, and had brought Derek

Pollock topside. Derek called his mother with Zane's phone.

The next thing John knew, every parent was calling back and wanted to talk with their child. Pandemonium broke out on his and Zane's cell phones. The parents had no clue that calling their children actually upset some of them more than it calmed them down. As he continued his way through the parent list, John began asking each parent if he or she wanted to speak to a son or daughter. If they said yes, he told them their child would call back in a few minutes. Zane allowed the kids to use his cell phone.

When all the parents had been called by both John and their son or daughter, John went below to check on the students and their packing. According to Nathan, the shuttle boat was about fifteen minutes away. It was almost noon. The Coast Guard had been searching for over an hour and found nothing. John didn't have any good news to tell his students.

The girls were all packed. They were huddled together in the large, four-bunk cabin at the bow end. Mya was rubbing Lizzie's back. Lea still held Cassie. The dog seemed to know the girls needed her. She didn't fuss or whine or try to get down.

"Did they find her?" Lizzie asked.

"Not yet," John answered.

"Where could she be?" Haley questioned.

"I don't know, girls. I hope she got turned around in the dark and swam to one of the smaller islands by mistake. There's no phones or houses in some locations, which would explain why we haven't heard from her." Zane had given him that answer before he came below. It was possible, and it gave the students hope.

"Is she…do you think she's—"

"Shut up, Amber!" Lizzie screamed at her friend sitting on one of the top bunks. "She's not dead! She's not dead!"

"Girls, let's try to stay positive. There are many places Miss Smith could be. Hopefully, we'll hear something soon." John forced a smile. "The boat will be here shortly to take you home."

John walked down to the boys' cabins. They were more spread out. He popped his head into each of their bunks. Most of them showed little emotion. Girls were harder to deal with but much easier to read. He gave them all the heads-up about the arriving ship. Chip and Larry were sitting with a handful of boys in Israel's cabin.

"Any word?" Chip asked.

"Still searching."

"Does anyone know when she went swimming?" Larry inquired.

John leaned back against the doorframe. "Zane estimates sometime between eleven last night and five this morning."

Travis raised his hand. John almost smiled. "What is it, Travis?"

"Will you call our parents and tell us when you find Miss Smith?"

"Of course. As soon as I hear anything, I'll start calling everyone. I promise." John liked talking about finding Melissa. He wanted that optimism to last until she was back on the ship. He straightened. "I'm going to head back up and get a status update. Won't be too long until the shuttle is here to take you all home."

Back on deck, John immediately spotted a new boat. Hard to miss as she was dropping anchor half a football field away. He recognized the boat. He'd seen it many times in the Oak Bluffs Harbor. The red and white vessel was a charter fishing boat. John figured the skipper must be a friend of Captain Roberts.

"She can take forty-five people, more than enough room for our crew," Zane said.

"How soon will we leave?" John asked.

The crew was at the stern, lowering the yawl boat into the water. "Captain just got the all-clear from the Coast Guard. They're going to conduct a post-search-and-rescue boarding after they find Melissa. There's no reason to hold the kids. Pete's going to ring the bell in a few minutes once the yawl is ready to go. We'll shuttle them over in groups of six."

Caleb and Tucker were pulling back on their line on the port side, trying to keep the yawl boat level as she hit the water. When she was down, Zane called for the guys to stow the lines.

"Are you going over with us?" John asked.

"Yes. I heard you're coming back," Zane said.

"The principal wants to come out and talk with Captain Roberts. Are we coming back on the same boat?"

"No. We'll come back on one of the company's small motor boats," Zane replied. "How are you holding up?"

John almost laughed, that snort one often hears when the ridiculous is happening and someone asks a logical question. John crossed his arms and stared at Zane. "My brain is running numbers and stats. How long has she been in the water? How cold is the water? How quickly will her body temperature drop? I can't calculate a positive outcome. I can't answer why. And I can't release a single emotion." John uncrossed his arms and pivoted. He put both hands on the cap rail and stared into the endless blue of sky and water. In the distance, the blue light of the rescue boat flashed.

"I understand, John. None of this makes any sense, but don't give up hope. People have survived in the water for days. It's unexplainable, and yet it has happened. Melissa could be—will be—one of those people."

"Zane. Mr. Masters," Captain Roberts called.

John and Zane walked over to the helm. Captain Roberts held the microphone in one hand and a cell phone in the other, and his hands were shaking. John felt the same way. His whole body wanted to shake. He couldn't wait to get home, away from everyone, so he could rage at the world without anyone seeing him lose it.

But the captain was managing the situation with great control. He lowered the microphone and faced the men. "Bear has the yawl boat ready to go. Let's bring the children up on deck and start shuttling them over. I want to address them again as a group before they disembark."

Since Pete was downstairs talking with the students, Zane rang the ship's bell. The crew and children came up the companionways with backpacks and luggage in tow. Avery, Roscoe, and Justin loaded the luggage and backpacks into the yawl and made the first trip to the shuttle boat.

Captain Roberts sat on the starboard icebox and asked the students to come sit by him. "I cannot imagine how difficult this morning has been for all of you. I am very sorry. I want to assure you that we are doing everything we can to bring Miss Smith home. You were a wonderful crew to have onboard. You will all be in my prayers and the prayers of my family."

A couple of girls stood and hugged Captain Roberts. He positioned himself by the boarding ladder as each group of six departed, saying good-bye to the students personally. Between the trips to the shuttle boat, the captain was either on his cell phone or on the radio. There was no sighting or news of Melissa.

John boarded the shuttle boat with the last group from the *Shenandoah*. Zane had gone over with the first group. He met John as he came aboard. "Quite a few of the students asked if we could look for Miss Smith as we sailed home. I didn't have the heart to tell them that if she was in the water on the way home, someone would have seen her by now. It might help them to feel useful if we give them lookout jobs. What do you think?"

"What are the chances we'll find her? Because I don't want these kids seeing her floating in the water. I'm not saying she will be, but I can't chance that. They've been shaken up enough today already," John said.

Zane nodded. "I agree, and I wouldn't have suggested it if I thought for a minute that Melissa would be anywhere in our path. It is highly improbable that she swam through the Canapitsit Channel and ended up on the Vineyard

Sound side of Cuttyhunk. The tide was flowing toward Buzzards Bay. The best of swimmers wouldn't take that challenge in daylight."

"Okay, then anyone who wants to can help look. If we don't guide them, they'll do it anyway. They're not going to ride home oblivious to the ocean," John stated.

Every one of the students took a position along the rail and surveyed the water for the entire fifty-five minute trip from Cuttyhunk to Vineyard Haven. They pulled into the second ferry slip at the Steamship dock. The gangway and loading areas were packed with people. John also spotted two news crews. They must have heard the distress calls on the Coast Guard radio and come over on the noon boat along with Mark. What a nightmare!

The Steamship guys had sectioned off an area for parents. John and Zane led the students off the boat and had them line up. Chip and Larry stationed themselves at the sides. As much as the parents wanted their children to run over, John had to make sure every child went home with the person or people on their permission slip.

Mark ducked under the ropes and came over to help John and Zane. One at a time, they called each child and their parents. Tears flowed, hugs were long, and questions were impossible to answer. The news crews were filming everything. Zane was asked for a statement. He said he had no new information. John and Mark refused to comment. Mark asked to speak with Zane away from the cameras.

When the children had left with their parents, a well-dressed woman walked up to John. "I'm Cindy Flanders, Melissa's best friend."

"The believer in love when you least expect it?" John had no clue why he'd said that. It was the only thing he could think of.

She seemed pleased, though, by his odd comment. Her tear-stained face brightened for a moment. "When did she say that?" Cindy asked.

"The other night, when she was explaining that she'd given up on relationships, but that I should not give up hope."

"Oooh, I hate when she says that. I keep telling her that one day a man is going to walk into her life, and he will be the right one, and she'll fall head over heels in…" Cindy choked up. "Where is she? What happened?"

John could physically feel Cindy's heartache and worry. Her feelings went to the depth of her soul and radiated outward. John had no answers to ease her pain, but he would try to give her as much detail as he could. As they talked, one question kept coming to John's mind. He finally had to ask her.

"I hate to ask this, but I'm trying to understand what might have happened. Is there any reason Melissa would have jumped?"

Cindy's eyes practically crossed. "You mean jump as in jump off to kill herself?"

She sounded incredulous, not angry with him. For that John was thankful, on two levels. "Um, yes, that's what I was asking."

"No way!" Cindy's response was firm. "Melissa loves life, loves her job, loves her friends. She is a happy person."

John ran his fingers through his hair. "That's my impression of her, too. She's always smiling and upbeat at school. I just don't understand why she would go swimming at night. Do you?"

"Melissa wasn't reckless—not at all. But she did love to swim at night. I can't believe she would do it on *Shenandoah*, though, going against the rules. It's not like her. I don't believe it, but I don't know what else to think." Cindy paused. "There's no way anyone pushed her, is there?"

He'd asked himself that same question but couldn't imagine it. There was no reason anyone would fight with Melissa. "No. The crew is a bunch of good guys. Plus, two guys are sleeping on deck as well as whoever was on watch. For her to be pushed there would have been a fight and shoving and probably yelling. I ruled that out earlier. Makes even less sense to me than a late-night swim."

"Yeah." Tears started rolling down Cindy's face. "Can I give you my number? Will you call me as soon as you hear anything?"

"Yes. Absolutely." John wrote down her number, promised again to call, and then walked across the parking lot to the Tall Ships' office, where Mark and Zane were talking. When he opened the door, they stopped speaking.

"Come on in. Close the door," Zane said.

"What's up?" John asked, knowing it wasn't good news.

"I just got off the phone with the captain. The Coast Guard is widening the search. There has been no sign of Melissa." Zane let the information sink in. They didn't ask any questions. "If you're ready, let's head back."

John met Mark's eyes. They didn't need to speak. No words would express their dread and sorrow.

# 21

MELISSA FELT *SHENANDOAH* GLIDING ACROSS THE WATER. In all her years of sailing on the school cruise, she had rarely gone below while *Shenny* was in motion. Not today, though. Isaiah had asked her to remain in his cabin. Isaiah—the man in her dreams. She'd never given much thought to the history of the *Shenandoah* and the men who sailed her. Melissa couldn't recall spending one minute wondering about the first captain of the *Shenandoah*. She couldn't fathom where her implausible dream had originated.

She wasn't into dream interpretations, but this one was surely one for the record books. Everything—and she did mean everything—smelled, tasted, and looked real. Felt real, too. When Isaiah had taken her hand, the current running through his fingers and up her arm had been powerful. She'd never experienced that with another man, real or imagined.

Maybe all the talk about relationships with John the night before had sparked a deeper longing in her subconscious. Was it possible to think about your subconscious while dreaming? Melissa didn't have a clue. But something had stirred this dream. Maybe she was repressing a desire to date again. Isaiah would certainly be a safe choice. When he said or did something to irritate her, she could simply dream a different boyfriend into place.

Melissa chuckled. Dream men definitely had advantages over lying, cheating husbands.

The rise and fall of the ship over a good-sized wave shifted her focus from her ex-husband to the cabin she was in. Melissa decided a little walk around the captain's quarters would be good for her. She rose from the chair, drawing Isaiah's blanket tightly around her shoulders, and walked the five steps to the opposite wall and back to the desk. She repeated the exercise six or seven times. Running on a treadmill for minutes on end didn't make sense to her. Walking back and forth, without a view or friend to talk with, was boring enough. Never mind running in place like a hamster on a wheel.

She made the bed, since she was the one who'd last slept in it. As she fluffed the pillow, she inhaled Isaiah's masculine scent, a combination of sea air, spice, and lavender. Someone must have washed his sheets in lavender.

*No. There is no someone.* This was a dream, and she was merely fantasizing one of her favorite fragrances. It was nice, though, that Isaiah was handsome and smelled good. The nightmare had definitely turned into a fantasy of sorts.

Melissa caught sight of Isaiah's boot on the ladder rung and tossed the pillow quickly onto the bed. Dream or no dream, she didn't want any man witnessing her in the vulnerable moment of smelling his pillow and going weak in the knees. She had no time to get over to the chair, so she plunked down onto the edge of the bed before he turned around.

"Ah, good. Thou are up and about. How are ye feeling, Miss Smith?"

He really was handsome. Now that she had settled into an odd comfort with her situation, to some degree, Melissa was able to appreciate the adventure. And the man. He was tall, possibly an inch or two over six feet, rugged, and outdoorsy with dark brown eyes and rich brown hair tinged with gray.

"Miss Smith?" Melissa heard her name and realized he was staring at her, once again with a puzzled look. "I asked how thee were feeling."

She flushed under his gaze. "Better, much better. I think I was hungry. The oatmeal seems to have settled my stomach."

Isaiah didn't move from the companionway. Melissa was unsure whether she should stand or remain seated. The man was impossible to read.

"I came to inform ye that we shall reach the outskirts of Quincy Bay within the hour. I shall have thee off the ship by midafternoon."

For a moment, Melissa's heart sank. Did he want to get rid of her that badly? Was he counting the minutes until he could unload her on someone else? She did her best not to sound sad or put out. "Okay, I'll just wait here." She pulled the blanket snugly against her, dropping her face behind the fabric so the man wouldn't see that his words had stung.

"Are thou chilled?" He strode across the floor to the wooden chest at the foot of the bed, reached in, and brought out another wool blanket. Shaking it out to full length, he then draped it over her shoulders. Then he took a step back and looked down into her eyes. For the briefest of moments, Melissa thought his eyes held a look of appreciation. Maybe even attraction. Then it was gone.

She glanced at his mouth and saw the grim line vacant of a smile. She didn't understand the man, or why her dream couldn't be at least a tad more romantic.

"I have two additional blankets, should ye require more warmth. Do thy best not to get chilled. Elizabeth shall have proper clothing for thee to wear. I shall inform thee when we drop anchor." Isaiah pivoted on his heel and strode to the ladder. "Until then."

"Isaiah," Melissa called, "thank you for the blankets."

He didn't face her but nodded as he exited the cabin. Not your average hero in a dream. Fortunately, not a monster either.

The extra blanket did feel good. He'd said it was May, which explained the cool air blowing through the cabin. Melissa shook her head. May in 1770. What was her brain up to? She much preferred sailing in August in 2007.

After a few minutes of quiet and no answer to her question, Melissa walked over to Isaiah's desk and sat in his chair. His Bible was open to Proverbs. She flipped back to her favorite chapter in the book of Ruth. Years ago, her broken heart had identified with the destitute widow and her plight to find a husband to take care of her.

Melissa's heart skipped a beat when she read the first verse in chapter two: "And Naomi had a kinsman of her husband's, a mighty man of wealth, of the family of Elimelech; and his name was Boaz."

Melissa had read Ruth's story so many times she'd lost count. Every time Boaz enters the scene, she feels the same sense of hope and promise. And a twinge of longing. She continued reading slowly, savoring every piece of the story. When she reached 3:18, Melissa read the words a second time aloud: "'Then said she, Sit still, my daughter, until thou know how the matter will fall: for the man will not be in rest, until he have finished the thing this day.'"

She could picture Naomi telling Ruth to be patient while Ruth paced the floor, sitting down and then getting back up, her heart hoping, her mind wishing, and her body unable to rest until she knew whether or not Boaz would prevail or whether she would be redeemed by another kinsman.

With as much anticipation as when she first discovered the story, Melissa read on. She inhaled deeply when she finally read Ruth 4:13: "So Boaz took Ruth, and she was his wife: and when he went in unto her, the Lord gave her conception, and she bare a son."

A son. A son named Obed, who fathered Jesse, who would have a son named David. King David, a man after God's own heart and destined to be the ancestor of the Messiah. From destitute widow to great-grandmother to the umpteenth degree of Jesus Christ. Perfect redemption.

Melissa ran her hands over the pages. A dream within her dream. She sighed. Dare she ask God for another chance at love? Was she ready? Would her heart survive if the relationship didn't? Could her damaged soul find a mate as Ruth's had? Maybe when she got home, she'd ask her women's small group to pray about it with her.

When her mind quieted, Melissa realized the ship was barely moving. Shifting in the chair to face the companionway, she listened to footsteps and muffled voices above but couldn't hear enough to figure out if the wind had died or the ship was coming into port. Melissa walked over to the companionway.

She put her right foot on the first rung of the ladder. A little peek through the hatch should be okay. After all, Isaiah had said he wasn't holding her hostage. She wouldn't go on deck. She'd merely look around to see what was happening. Placing her left foot on the second rung, she pulled herself up. Her eyes weren't quite level with the opening. She could see sky and aloft, but not Isaiah or any of the crew. Stepping onto the third rung, she saw Isaiah at the wheel. Her heart pounded.

He looked mighty fine standing behind the wheel, powerful and strong. The flutter in her chest was real and exciting. She stared at him, enjoying the view, taking in the dream man in front of her.

Then, a minute or so into her blatant adoration, Isaiah's gaze met hers.

She blushed. He grinned.

Then the scowl returned to his face, and he marched over to the companionway. "Miss Smith, I asked thee to remain below."

"I am below. Technically, I have not left your cabin, which is what your instructions were. I felt the ship slowing down and wanted to see where we were," Melissa rationalized.

Isaiah glared down at her, his anger way over the top for the situation. As a teacher, Melissa had learned years ago when and how to control her anger and frustration. Some kids had a knack for pushing certain buttons. The trick was to flip the internal off-switch before the child pushed the on button. Isaiah was in sore need of a few lessons on letting the small stuff slide.

"The air is cool. Thou are underdressed. Thou has no cape nor shoes on thy feet. Return below before illness overtakes thee," Isaiah ordered.

He was overreacting. Melissa knew it, but she couldn't figure out why. She'd probably be warmer sitting in the sun with her feet tucked under the blankets. She thought about explaining that to Isaiah, but the pained look in his eyes gave her cause to think twice.

"I'm fine, really. But I'll go back down. Could you just tell me how much longer until we dock?"

Isaiah's face visibly relaxed as Melissa eased back down the ladder. "We shall drop anchor shortly. If thee may practice patience, thy departure will be upon us within the hour."

His implication that she was being impatient irked her. She had been the picture of patience all day. Did he have any clue what it was like to sit around waiting to wake up and go home? She was doing her best to make the most of her time lost in this dream. How infuriating that the man she'd dreamed into being was chastising her. It was time to conjure up a new hero and get rid of this one!

"Great. Let me know when I can leave. Until then I'll just sit here grading these imaginary papers," Melissa snapped. With a huff, she spun around and walked over to the desk. She slumped into his chair, silently fuming. She glanced at his Bible, still open to the final verses of Ruth. Why were men and happy endings so much easier to experience in books?

With a sigh of exasperation, Melissa flipped a chunk of pages and landed in Jeremiah. She was no longer in the mood to read, and Jeremiah suffered too long, though he did pack some powerful messages into his prophecies. She grabbed the front cover and closed Isaiah's Bible. She wished she could close down the dream. It was time to wake up, time to watch the sunrise and shoot some pictures, time to leave 1770—and Isaiah—behind.

Melissa leaned back in the chair and closed her eyes. She concentrated on the students and what they would do today. She had purchased supplies to make sailboat Christmas ornaments. The girls would love it, and she was counting on most of the boys wanting to make at least one, as well. She was hoping they would anchor in Menemsha tonight. It was her favorite spot for sunsets. Picturing the ship, her cabin, the students, Captain Roberts, and members of the crew, Melissa willed herself to wake up.

"Miss Smith?"

She squeezed her eyes shut and visualized Nick passing her a steaming mug of hot coffee.

"Miss Smith?" A hand on her shoulder startled her. She opened her eyes to Isaiah's frown. "Are ye unwell?"

"No, I'm stuck. I was trying to go home. I thought if I focused long and hard on where I wanted to be, I might get there. No such luck." Did he hear the sadness in her voice? Was that why the frown remained on his face? He didn't look sympathetic, that was for sure.

"I have brought thee a pair of shoes and stockings. Though they be too large for thy feet, thee must wear them whilst we travel to my brother's." Isaiah placed the brown shoes and wool socks on the floor. "I shall return for thee in five minutes' time."

"How thoughtful. Thank you, Isaiah." Whatever she'd said, the man turned immediately after she said his name.

"Thou art welcome," he said in a monotone as he walked away from her.

Melissa watched Isaiah ascend the ladder. She wanted to ask how she had offended him, but she decided to let it go. She donned the socks and welcomed the warmth. Slipping her feet into the shoes, she chuckled. She could use another pair of socks to jam into the toes so they wouldn't flop around while she walked, but she would not ask Isaiah. He seemed to want as little contact with her as possible.

He returned promptly five minutes later, this time with a coat in one hand. "Thou should put this on."

Melissa folded the blankets and placed them on top of his storage chest. He waited for her to climb the ladder first.

Adam offered her his hand at the top. "Good afternoon, Miss Smith. How are ye faring?"

"I feel much better, Adam. Thank you for the delicious bowl of oatmeal."

"I am pleased ye found the fare to thy liking. May I escort thee to the skiff?"

Adam's smirk at Isaiah made her want to turn around and see Isaiah's response, but he hustled past them and departed the ship. Shuffling across the deck in the oversized shoes, Melissa threw her leg over the cap rail and climbed down into the skiff. Isaiah seated her facing away from the town. Adam stayed behind.

As she watched *Shenandoah* grow smaller, she glanced around the harbor at all the ships anchored in the water and took full note of the fact that every single boat was wooden. Not one motorboat, no fiberglass speedboats, no charter fishing vessels. Just wooden boats in various sizes and shapes.

Isaiah sat opposite her. He never looked directly at her, which was probably a good thing. The more she observed the number of wooden ships, the more unsettled she became. Shouldn't there be at least one or two normal boats? She pasted on a smile, not wanting to appear frightened or freaked out. Isaiah already thought she wasn't right in the head and was about to dump her off at his brother's house. No need to give him any further reason to confirm what he perceived as her mental instability.

Melissa inhaled deeply and exhaled slowly. She envisioned the wooden boats as part of a movie set, like John Jakes' television mini-series or the movie *The Patriot*, both of which she'd loved. If she thought about the scenery and people as the settings and characters in a Colonial movie playing in her mind, she might be able to relax and enjoy the moment. But if she spent more than a minute reflecting on how far from reality she was, panic would rise, which might result in Isaiah or Adam waving another vial of smelling salts under her nose. The movie idea was much more appealing.

A young man who bore a close resemblance to Jonah rowed their skiff. Isaiah had not introduced them and didn't appear to be heading in that direction. Melissa twisted her upper body so she could see where they were going. The scene before her was the most impressive movie set she could have imagined. Every man, woman, and child was dressed in Colonial clothing. The houses and stores were exact replicas of Plimoth Plantation or Colonial Williamsburg.

When they reached the dock, Isaiah exited the little boat and extended his hand to Melissa. She climbed up the short ladder and placed her hand in his. *Zap!* There it was again, that sensation of hot liquid rushing through her veins while her skin felt as though dozens of tiny shocks extended up her arm.

She glanced up at Isaiah and searched his face. Blank, unreadable. He seemed completely unaffected by their touch. Lucky him.

Standing on the dock, Melissa drew her hand back quickly. She brushed her palm against the coarse jacket, trying to rub off the tingling Isaiah's fingertips left behind. Without so much as a "follow me," Isaiah strode down the dock. Melissa tried to keep up, but the shoes were too big and her heel kept flopping out the back.

"Isaiah," she called. He stopped and glanced over his shoulder, a serious glower on his face. "I can't walk that fast in these shoes."

He said nothing, but at least he waited for her to catch up. He slowed his pace as they cleared the dock and started to walk up a dirt road. Melissa sucked in her breath. The roads, the houses, the people were too real, too authentic, too Colonial America.

*Do not panic. Do not panic. It's just a dream.*

Melissa averted her eyes and did her best not to notice the old homes and buildings, the people all dressed as though they were working in Colonial Williamsburg, and the lack of cars, buses, mopeds, or anything technologically advanced beyond a horse and buggy.

Jonah ran up beside them. He waved to a few people, smiling at everyone. He obviously didn't inherit his social skills from his uncle.

"Run on ahead and tell thy mother I bring a guest," Isaiah prompted him.

"Yes, Uncle," Jonah replied.

Melissa liked Jonah. His enthusiasm for life was evident in his smile and the energy he put into everything he did. As they came around a corner, Melissa stumbled in the oversized shoes. Isaiah reached out and steadied her.

Without a word, he offered Melissa his arm. She looped her hand in the crux of his elbow and gave him a thankful smile. He nodded. It was definitely time to envision another hero in her extended dream.

"How far is it to your brother's?" Melissa asked. She noticed that people were gawking at her.

"Not far. Can ye walk?"

"I can walk fine as long as you go slow. I think your neighbors might be wondering what the cat dragged in."

"Aye, tongues shall set to wagging. Pay no mind."

He patted her hand and then rested his palm over her fingers. Melissa wondered if the rush of electricity she felt whenever they touched was a physical reaction between herself and Isaiah, or if the sensation would occur if she touched another person. He seemed to feel nothing, so maybe it was a result of her dream state.

Isaiah stopped by a picket fence in front of a large white two-story home set back from the road. The house had four windows and a door on the first floor and five windows on the second floor. The windows were simple and without shutters. The only ornate presence on the exterior was the large peaked frame around the single front door. The house was larger than some, but nowhere near as large as many fancy homes she walked or drove by on the Vineyard.

Without comment, Isaiah opened the gate and waited for her to pass through. The front door opened, and a couple walked out to meet them. The man's relation to Isaiah was unmistakable, though unlike his gloomy brother, he smiled with genuine warmth.

The four met halfway up the gravel path. "Brother," the man said, hugging Isaiah and then stepping back and smiling at Melissa. "Who is thy guest?"

Isaiah glanced sideways at Melissa, then turned quickly back to his brother. "May I introduce Miss Smith?"

The man bowed. "Welcome, Miss Smith. Eli Reed. I am pleased to make thy acquaintance. My wife, Elizabeth."

The woman curtsied before Melissa. "Good afternoon, and welcome. Jonah tells us thee has experienced an arduous journey. A cup of tea and light repast is called for."

Elizabeth placed her hand on Melissa's left arm and wrapped her other arm around her. She ushered Melissa toward the house, smiling and talking. "Come inside and we shall get you settled. Our daughters are all a-flutter. Jonah set them off with the news of thy impending arrival. I fear they shall be waiting to besiege thee with questions. I have instructed them to greet thee and then retire to their sewing."

Melissa allowed Elizabeth to lead her down the path and into her home. It was easy to see from whom Jonah inherited his friendliness. Elizabeth was one of those people you liked instantly. Eli appeared kind, too. He hung back now with Isaiah. Melissa wondered what Isaiah was telling Eli about her. What could he say? Realistically, if some guy showed up in her house and claimed to be from a place and time two hundred years in the future, she'd think he was nuts. She didn't blame Isaiah, but she was tired of people saying she was crazy.

Elizabeth broke into her reverie, asking for her jacket. Melissa passed her the borrowed coat while glancing around the house. Wide, polished wooden boards stretched out beneath her feet. Two family-room-type areas flanked the entrance. The house was well decorated but not elaborate. Cindy would be in her antique glory if she could see—never mind buy—some of their furniture. A young black woman took the coats from Elizabeth and stood by the door as Eli and Isaiah entered.

"Husband, I shall see to Miss Smith's needs. Would ye like for Penny to bring cider or ale to thy study?"

"Aye, wife, a drop of ale will do us good. But do not tarry. Please see to our guest. I shall stop into the kitchen and speak with Clara," Eli said. The men turned right and disappeared into another room.

The sound of footsteps moving quickly across the floor upstairs compelled both Elizabeth and Melissa to glance up.

"My daughters have discovered a guest has arrived," Elizabeth said. Her tone was loving, and the fondness in her eyes reflected an undeniable bond between mother and children.

Two young women in their late teens reached the staircase and halted abruptly at the top. Melissa guessed they'd been told on more than one occasion that it was not ladylike to run down the stairs.

When they reached the bottom, Elizabeth opened her arms, and they came over to stand beside their mother. "Miss Smith, may I introduce thee to Miss Lucy Reed and Miss Abigail Reed."

"Are ye really a nun?" Lucy asked.

"Lucy Grace Reed, where are thy manners?" Elizabeth corrected.

"Sorry, Mother. Sorry, Miss Smith," Lucy said, her gaze on the floor.

"It's okay," Melissa replied in Lucy's defense. "I can only imagine what you're thinking. I'm in desperate need of a shower and a change of clothes. I don't blame you for wondering what I'm doing walking around town in my pjs."

"Lucy knows better than to inquire on a person's attire or profession," Elizabeth stated, her voice firm but soft-spoken.

"Please forgive me, Miss Smith," Lucy said.

"All is forgiven. Don't worry about it," Melissa offered. The more they talked about her standing there in a nightshirt, the more self-conscious she became. "Would it be possible to wash up before we have tea?"

"Of course." Elizabeth clapped her hands twice. "Come girls, let us show Miss Smith to Grammie's room. I shall have Penny bring thee a pitcher of water to freshen up as well as a clean shift and gown. Is there anything else ye might be needing?"

"No, thank you, that will be perfect."

Elizabeth led the way up the stairs to a small room at the front of the house. There was a twin bed, maybe smaller than a standard twin, an armoire, a delicate writing desk and chair, and a large sewing box. "My mother-in-law's room. She has gone to be with the Lord. Please make yourself at home. We shall have tea in the parlor when ye has changed for supper," Elizabeth said. Then she told Lucy and Abigail, "I believe thee each has a sampler to finish."

The Reed women left the room and Melissa sat on the bed. She unlaced the oversized shoes and slipped her feet out, suddenly exhausted. Everything around her felt far too real, and though she knew it was impossible to fall asleep in 2007 in her cabin on the *Shenandoah* and then wake up in Colonial America in 1770, a ball of fear was churning and building in her throat.

A knock on the door startled her. She placed her hand over her pounding heart and called, "Come in."

Penny entered, carrying a pitcher of water and an armload of clothes. "Mistress has sent me to help thee dress."

Penny poured water into a washbowl and passed Melissa a cloth. After scrubbing off the sweat, salt, and grime, Melissa dried her face and arms. She wished she could take a long, hot shower, but that wasn't in the cards. Penny held out a thin white dress, too thin for May.

"I think the other dress will be a bit warmer. Do you mind if I borrow that one for dinner?" Melissa asked the pretty young servant girl.

Penny's eyes narrowed, and she shook her head. "Thou are to wear them both, Miss. The shift shall go under thy dress."

"Oh." Maybe she looked foolish, but how was she to have known that? She accepted the shift. Penny politely faced the door until Melissa had removed her nightshirt and changed into the clean shift.

Penny then placed the dress on the floor and created a circle opening for Melissa to step into. When she was in the center of the dress, Penny lifted the gown off the floor and pulled it up for Melissa to slide her arms into the sleeves. "I would be happy to tie thy laces, Miss."

Laces? Melissa had never worn a dress with laces. These days you didn't even have to tie your sneakers. Many of her students had Velcro on their shoes and had no idea what it was to tie shoelaces. She needed to keep her dreams to the twenty-first century, where she could dress herself properly. "Thank you, Penny, that would be great."

Melissa ran her fingers through her hair after Penny finished tying off the dress. The maid leaned down to bring Melissa her shoes and then stood, holding the brown boots at arm's length. "These be not thy shoes. I shall return."

Carrying the shoes as though they were infected with the plague, Penny left the room. She returned five minutes later with a pair of women's beige slipper shoes. They resembled ballet slippers, only hardier and with a slight wedge heel. They were a tad too small, but Melissa was not going to complain for the one night she'd need to wear them.

They descended the stairs and Penny led Melissa to the front room on the right side of the house. "Thou art lovely. The blue fabric compliments thy blue eyes," Elizabeth said. She looked past Melissa. "Would thou not agree, Isaiah?"

Heat rose on Melissa's neck. She hadn't heard Isaiah and Eli come in behind her. Eli stepped around Melissa and stood beside his wife. Isaiah inched his way past her and crept into position beside his brother. "Lovely," Eli said.

"Aye," was all Isaiah managed. "Daylight is departing, as must I."

"What?" Melissa sputtered.

"Thou art in good hands, Miss Smith. Do not fret."

"But…you're going to…just leave me here?"

Elizabeth walked over to Melissa and wrapped her arm around her. "My dear brother lives in Milton. He best travel whilst there is daylight. Thou art most welcome here." Elizabeth gave her a gentle squeeze when she finished speaking.

Melissa smiled and moved toward Isaiah. "I know you think I'm crazy, and if the situation was reversed, I'd probably feel the same way. So, thanks for not throwing me overboard, and thanks for bringing me here and being kind."

Melissa pushed up onto her tiptoes and wrapped her arms around Isaiah to hug him good-bye. The blood rushed through her body and made her feel lightheaded. Isaiah stood stock-still. He did not return her hug, did not pat her back, did not respond to her in any way.

Melissa stepped away awkwardly, avoiding eye contact. "Sorry. This has been a stressful day. I don't normally hug strange men. At first I thought you were the bad guy, the monster in the dream, if you will. But you've been caring, in a removed sort of way. I don't think I'll see you again. I hope that when I wake up in the morning, I'll be back home. So I wanted to say goodbye."

Isaiah gave a curt nod of recognition to her words. "Fare ye well, Miss Smith," he said, then pivoted on his heel and strode toward the front door.

Melissa glanced sideways at Isaiah's sister-in-law and caught the smirk on Elizabeth's face. With a teasing glint in her eye, Elizabeth wagged a finger in Isaiah's direction and chuckled. "Brother, we shall discuss what I just saw when thou returns."

Isaiah stopped midstride and turned partway around. He had hints of red creeping up his neck, and he mumbled words under his breath that Melissa could not hear.

Though also bearing a grin, Eli said, "Wife, do not meddle."

"Hush now, Eli. I know what I saw." Elizabeth turned back toward Melissa. "Come, let us have tea. I am eager to hear thy tale."

Melissa kept her eyes on Isaiah's back until the door closed behind him. A sudden sense of loss and sadness washed over her. She couldn't explain the emotions. She barely knew him. He'd hardly spoken to her, and when he did, it was short and to the point. But watching him leave tugged at a place in her heart she hadn't visited for a long, long time.

As she sat across from Elizabeth, sipping tea and avoiding the facts of her life, it occurred to Melissa that when Elizabeth had put her hand on her shoulder, she had felt nothing unusual. Just a hand on her shoulder.

Only Isaiah ignited her blood to liquid fire.

# 22

JOHN, MARK, AND NATHAN BOARDED *SHENANDOAH* around three-thirty in the afternoon. Motoring across the Vineyard Sound, John noticed more boats trolling the waters. Men and women, friends and parents of students at Holmes Hole School, as well as strangers, were out searching for Melissa.

The Coast Guard had found no sign or trace of her. Captain Roberts was on the phone to his wife when they approached the helm. He waved and told Katherine he would call her back shortly.

"Mark," he said, extending his hand.

The guys shook hands. Mark pointed to the chart opened on the roof deck and weighted down by iron couplings. "Has anyone narrowed down her possible location?"

"There are logical possibilities, based on tides, currents, and wind. Melissa's ability to swim adds in a factor both for and against the calculations. The Coast Guard has computed a couple of options," Captain Roberts said.

"I'm not pointing fingers here, but how did this happen?" Mark asked.

"I haven't got an answer for you. I had a brief conversation with the crew, but no one heard or saw anything. Let's get everyone together, and you can ask whatever questions are on your mind."

The crew gathered mid-ship. Captain Roberts introduced Mark and let him have the floor.

"John has mentioned what a fabulous crew you are. Many thanks for taking care of the students during this difficult time. Did anyone talk to Melissa on Wednesday night? Does anyone have any idea what might have happened to her?"

Tucker stepped forward. "I think Melissa had cancer, or some life-threatening disease."

"What makes you say that?" Mark asked.

"The first two mornings she was onboard, she was sick. I'm talking dizzy, nauseated, disoriented. Tuesday morning I heard her moaning and thought she might be having a heart attack. I went into her cabin, and she was struggling to stand, just as my mom did in the final stages of her cancer."

Mark turned to face John. "Did you witness this? Did you ever see Melissa showing signs of illness at school? I never did."

151

John massaged his temples while he thought about the last few months of school. Melissa had not missed a day that he knew of. And she'd always dressed well and smiled and appeared happy. "I don't think she was sick during the school year. If she came down with anything over the summer, I wouldn't know. She was definitely having a tough time the first two mornings. Had we been under sail, I would have guessed she suffered from seasickness. But we were anchored. I guess she could have been sick."

"Having cancer, or anything fatal, would explain why she might have jumped," Tucker said. A few heads nodded, Mark's included. "And we all noticed there was no ladder or rope over the side of the ship."

More heads nodded. Tucker took a seat on the portside icebox.

John had to agree with Tucker's observation that no rope or ladder had been thrown over the side. He had been wondering about that since he climbed up the ladder to reboard *Shenandoah*. How had Melissa planned to get back on board? There were no stairs or exterior pegs for climbing.

"The headrig," Captain Roberts said.

"What's a headrig?" Mark asked.

Zane motioned for John and Mark to follow him up to the bow. He pointed over the side of the ship. "These chains are the headrig. They run from the bow of the boat out to different parts of the bowsprit and jib boom." He leaned over the cap rail. "Look down here."

John and Mark followed his instruction and aimed their gaze in the direction of two thick chains that descended to the water.

"These two chains are the bobstays. They run parallel to the bow, starting at the waterline. They hold down the bowsprit. A man or woman with decent upper-body strength could climb down the chains quietly and slip into the water unnoticed," Zane explained.

Mark straightened first. "So Melissa could have shimmied down these chains and gone for a swim?"

"Sure." Zane led them back to where the crew and captain were waiting.

But the disbelief on Zane's face belied his positive answer and made John want more explanation. "Why? Why would Melissa deliberately go against the captain's rules? And why would she want to climb down these chains, knowing she'd need to climb up them to get back onboard the ship? It makes no sense. No sense at all."

"It makes sense if she didn't intend to return and she didn't want anyone to know she was leaving," Tucker reasoned. "Lots of cancer patients find creative ways to end their lives."

What Tucker said sounded scientifically logical, but John wasn't buying it. Melissa had been an image of health and happiness. He'd watched her more than Mark had—watched her walk down the corridors or into the teacher's lounge, watched her interact with the students in the halls. She'd never been sick or weak or dizzy once during the school year. There had to be a different answer. Swimming he could believe. Suicide he couldn't.

"I've been thinking about this all day." Pete rose from the top of the hatch and walked to the center of their loose circle. "Melissa didn't have cancer. She was dizzy and sweating, but I don't think it had anything to do with being sick. Don't forget that two days in a row she was talking about hearing voices, seeing people, being trapped with rats, and all the history stuff with those Acts and dead presidents. When she woke up, all she talked about was being in the 1700s. She's not dead. She's gone back in time. I'd bet on it."

Mark rolled his eyes. John had all he could do to keep from laughing. He was a science teacher. Though many had done extensive research on parallel universes and crossing time lines, no one had yet to discover any means to transport through time dimensions. Fact was, if time travel were possible, companies and airlines would be making millions on it right now.

Pete narrowed his eyes, his face indignant. John did his best to remove his grin. No reason to tick Pete off again. He'd been going on about Melissa the other night, and they'd gone a round. He wasn't interested in arguing today.

Nathan walked up from the helm. Everyone focused on what he was going to say. "Coast Guard just radioed in, Captain. They're shifting the search to the southeast section by the Barnyard."

Captain Roberts nodded.

"What is the Barnyard?" Mark inquired.

Captain Roberts glanced over his shoulder at the island of Cuttyhunk. "On the other side of the island is an area with a dangerous amount of rock. Some of the rocks are large enough to have been named. For reasons I don't know, folks named them after farm animals. There can be a good deal of chop there and serious current at certain times of day."

"She won't be there," Pete stated.

Zane shook his head. "Pete, I am not going to argue the feasibility of time travel. *Shenandoah* has been sailing for nearly fifty years, and no one has ever gone missing before. It's much more logical that Melissa jumped or went for a swim."

"I would've heard her! You can't jump off the ship in the middle of the night and not make a sound," Pete insisted. "And there's no way she climbed the headrig. I would have seen her."

"Maybe you fell asleep," Zane said with not a trace of anger or accusation.

Pete strode across the deck, his finger stabbing at Zane. "Don't go there, Zane. I didn't fall asleep. This is not my fault. I was awake for my entire shift. She didn't come up on deck, and she didn't jump in."

John stood, his head pounding once again. He should have taken a couple more pills hours ago. "Captain, what do you believe happened to Melissa?"

The skipper removed his hat and lowered his head. When he looked up, his eyes were moist. "I don't know. There was no note. You and Mark have both stated that Melissa appeared to be healthy minus her morning sickness the first two days."

"She wasn't pregnant, by the way. I asked," Nick reported. A couple of the guys chuckled. Mark cracked a smile, but the captain frowned.

"Well, just throwing that out there, in case you were wondering since she was sick in the mornings," Nick defended.

The captain put his hat back on and walked over to Mark. "Melissa was a great teacher while onboard. I would not have picked her as one to sneak around or defy safety rules. However, I don't for one second believe she has disappeared to the 1700s, so I'm left with her deciding to go for a midnight swim, which we all know she loved to do at home."

Mark's gaze dropped to the floor. The captain's reply did not bode well for Melissa being found alive. John absorbed the words and images sinking into his brain. Every minute they didn't find her gave less and less chance of a rescue.

"I don't want to rush you, but you and John should think about heading back to the Island," Captain Roberts said to Mark.

"You're right. Thank you for everything." Mark faced John. "How long will it take you to get ready?"

"Five minutes." John went below, grabbed his gear, and walked through the galley up to Melissa's cabin. The ship felt eerily empty. Cabin 8 looked no different than his cabin. Maybe the wood was older, but nothing was going to convince him that Melissa had found a portal to the past in the tiny Cabin 8.

He left the door open, left all her clothes, left her camera, and headed up the companionway. He couldn't wait to get home.

*

Home didn't turn out to be as peaceful as John had hoped when he got back to the Island. People had been calling nonstop. For dinner, he scrounged up what he had sitting in the cupboards and freezer. He boiled some pasta and frozen vegetables because he hadn't wanted to face the questions and comments he was sure to hear at the grocery store or the local diner.

At midnight, John finally hung up the phone and walked into his bathroom, every muscle aching as though he'd been run over by a tank or a steamroller. His head throbbed. The pasta was rolling around in his intestines with the heaviness of lead. He found some headache medicine under his cabinet and took a couple of tablets. He brushed his teeth and got ready for bed, carrying the bottle of pain meds and a glass of water to his nightstand, just in case the pain didn't subside.

With his stomach revolting against the pills, John lay down and prayed sleep would come quickly. He didn't want to spend another waking moment wondering about Melissa. He was beyond exhausted.

*

John woke shortly after six, his head still pounding. He stared at the ceiling fan whirling round and round. He felt as though his life was being sliced by those blades and scattered to places unknown…unknown, like Melissa's location and motivation. Where could she be? Why did she jump?

The questions made his head pound even harder. He sat up, put his feet on the floor, and reached across his nightstand for the bottle of pain reliever and the glass of water. Shaking out two tablets, he popped them in his mouth, and took a drink to wash them down.

His cell phone sat on the table, silently calling his name. He knew there were no messages on it. He'd left it on with the volume as loud as it would go. There was no way anyone had called him during the night and he hadn't heard it. Without a drop of hope, he flipped open his phone. Nothing, just as he'd expected.

He needed a shower and a shave to help him wake up.

Thirty minutes later, he picked up the phone again and dialed. Zane answered on the second ring. "Any news?"

"Nothing," Zane reported. "No sign of her yet. The Coast Guard has widened the search area. Have you had the television on this morning?"

"No, why?"

"Captain's wife called. Melissa's on the news."

"Oh, great."

"It's a good thing, John. Every person at the beach and on the water who knows she's missing is one more person who will be looking for her."

An ounce of frustration erased from John's brow. "Okay, that's good then.

Have they said how much longer they'll search?"

There was an extended pause on the other end of the phone. "I don't know. The helo is back up. I think the commander in charge will call a meeting this morning," Zane said.

"Is there anything I can do? I feel useless. And helpless." John glanced at his unmade bed and started pulling up the sheet and blanket and pressing out the creases, as he had done the previous four mornings aboard *Shenandoah*.

"I hear you. All I'm doing is answering the phone. Nothing to do but wait. Captain Roberts said our main job is to pray. Some of the guys and I have prayed a few times with the captain. I don't know how much good it's doing, but it can't hurt. Captain believes it makes all the difference in the world."

"Not my thing, but I get what he's saying. At this point it's going to take a miracle for Melissa to be found alive, isn't it?"

"Let's not go there," Zane said.

John punched the pillow into place on his bed. "Yeah, right. We won't go there. So what are the plans for the day?"

"When the tide and wind are good, we're sailing *Shenandoah* home. There's nothing we can do out here."

"Makes sense." As John spoke the words, he heard the flatness in his voice. The return of *Shenandoah* was the next thing to saying Melissa was dead.

"John, our return is no indication of Melissa's whereabouts. There is simply no reason for us to be here. We can wait at home better than we can wait here. And I think it would be better for the skipper if he could be with his family. Better for all the guys in the crew. Morale is sinking as we remain anchored away from our families and friends."

"I hear you. Give me a call when you're back in the harbor." John said good-bye but still held the phone tightly, his fingers cramped around the small device. He had two more calls to make. He guessed both Mark and Cindy would be awake. He opted to call Mark first. He dreaded the call to Melissa's best friend. Thank God Mark had called her parents.

# 23

MELISSA ROLLED OVER and PULLED THE BLANKETS UP OVER HER SHOULDERS. The air was chilly, but she wasn't ready to get up yet. She felt drained, even after the night's sleep. She had dreamed last night, of that she was certain, but there hadn't been any falling into blackness or shifting floors. A relief of great proportion. She kept her eyes closed and snuggled into the pillow, opting for another ten minutes of relaxation before the students were awake and moving full-steam ahead.

The minutes passed too quickly. She heard voices talking and giggling and figured a few of the girls must be clustered near her cabin, waiting to use the head. Tired or not, it was time to get up. With a good deal of reluctance, Melissa opened her eyes.

Instantly, she wished she hadn't. Feminine toile wallpaper was mere inches from her face. She flipped over to her right side and saw a desk and chair, an armoire, a sewing basket—everything she had dreamed about last night.

"No, no, no, no, no!" Melissa pleaded, the ball of fear in the pit of her throat growing larger by the second. She closed her eyes and begged to be set free from the dream. "I'm scared and confused," she whispered heavenward. "I know these people and this place are not going to hurt me. But, Lord, I feel trapped in time. I can't explain it, but you know what I'm saying, what I'm feeling, what I'm experiencing. Something is terribly wrong. Please help me wake up. Help me get back home."

Melissa curled up into the fetal position on her right side and closed her eyes. She waited and waited, but sleep did not come. She had no idea how much time had passed, and it didn't matter. At last she gave up trying to sleep. She was stuck. As she hugged her knees to her chest, her lower lip trembled. "What is happening, God? Where are you? Why don't you help me?"

Tears started to drizzle down her face. Within seconds, she was sobbing. Tired. Scared. Alone. Her sobs turned to wailing. She couldn't catch her breath. A knock sounded on the door, but she ignored it and curled tighter into herself. Surely God would hear her. Surely he would save her.

The knock came again. Louder, more insistent. Melissa couldn't stop the tears.

The door opened, and Elizabeth stepped into the room. "Melissa, may I sit with thee?"

Melissa bawled like an eighteenth-century baby. Was Elizabeth real or part of her wretched nightmare that never ended? And if she was real, what did that mean? The fear burst forth from her lungs in one long howl.

Elizabeth rushed to the bed. She leaned over, placed her hand on Melissa's forehead, then sat on the bed. "All will be well, all will be well," Elizabeth murmured. She rubbed Melissa's arm until her sobs became a low moan. Then she hummed softly while Melissa cried herself out.

When her tears stopped flowing, and she'd blown her nose in the handkerchief Elizabeth had given her, Melissa asked what the song was.

"A hymn by William Billings. Shall I sing it for thee?"

"Please," Melissa whispered.

And Elizabeth sang:

*"When Jesus wept, a falling tear*
*in mercy flowed beyond all bound.*
*When Jesus groaned, a trembling fear*
*seized all the guilty world around."*

"That's beautiful. You have a lovely voice. I sing in the choir, but not nearly as well as you," Melissa said.

"Thank thee. My son, Jonah, possesses the true talent. Neither Benjamin nor Magnus can carry a tune. The girls be blessed with sweet voices, though none as blessed as Jonah."

"I like Jonah. He's very friendly and always seems happy. I would love to hear him sing."

"Jonah has the gift of joy. Mayhaps we can entreat him to sing for us tonight?"

Tonight. Would she still be here? Or would she simply stand and then fall into the black hole again? Or would she remain stuck in this time dimension?

"I...I don't know if I'll be here tonight. I don't know how to get home or how I got here," Melissa whimpered. Fresh tears slid down her cheeks. "I don't know what to do."

"Mr. Reed would guide us to pray. When we know not what to do or where to go, we must place our trust in the Lord. Would ye care for me to pray?"

"Please."

Elizabeth bowed her head and folded her hands. "Almighty Father, we beseech Thee to hear the prayers of Thy servant, to heal the heart and soothe the fears of Thy servant, and that Thy will shall be done. Amen."

"Thank you, Elizabeth. Praying does seem to help."

"Aye, 'tis a great comfort to entreat the One who hears all." Elizabeth stood and extended her hand to Melissa. "Shall we go downstairs and break our fast?"

The knot of fear in Melissa's body tightened. How was she going to get home if she kept getting out of bed and going about her day as though living in these new places? Maybe she should stay in bed, stay in one place, and wait to fall into the black hole and wake up on the *Shenandoah*.

"I…would it be okay if I stayed in bed? This is going to sound a little nuts, but I think I need to be in bed to go home." Melissa watched Elizabeth's eyes. They didn't roll, but her lids closed a bit, doubt reflecting back at Melissa. She understood doubt and why her new friend struggled to understand what she was saying. Since there was no logical explanation, Melissa couldn't explain her thoughts any clearer to Elizabeth, nor could she comprehend what was happening in her life.

"Mayhaps the rest will fare thee well. Shall I have Penny bring thee a tray?"

Melissa sat up in bed and tucked the blankets closer around her legs. She smiled at Elizabeth. "That would be wonderful. Thank you for not pressuring me to leave the room. I'm sure this is nearly as confusing to you as it is to me."

"I would speak false if I said I understood, but I sense thou be hurting and scared in the midst of a storm, and our home shall be thy refuge until the waters recede."

Her words were gracious and eloquent. Melissa allowed the warmth and concern to surround her and comfort her. "Thank you, Elizabeth. You have no idea how much I appreciate your kindness and compassion."

Elizabeth smiled. "I am happy to help in any way I can."

Melissa twisted the sheet in her hands. What was she going to do? She knew next to nothing about dreams. How long could one last? How did a person in a dream know how much time was passing? How could you leave a dream or end a dream from within the dream?

Melissa allowed one dreaded thought to permeate: what if she wasn't dreaming? What if she *had* awakened in 1770? What if by some fluke of nature she'd left her life and landed in someone else's?

Her heart cried out for Spike to come wandering into the bedroom, jump onto the bed, and curl up in her lap. She wished Cindy was on her way over to go for a walk on the beach and look for sea glass. She wanted the phone to ring and for Kendra to be nagging her to get out of bed and come down to the gym for a spinning class. Those were real-life moments for her. Those were the things that should have been happening. But those thoughts now seemed so far out of reach as to be implausible.

The knock on the door sounded real. Melissa called out, "Come in," and Penny entered with a silver tray. She handed the tray to Melissa.

"Master Eli's brother told Clara that ye enjoyed porridge with maple sugar." Penny finished speaking and then quietly but quickly left the room. Elizabeth probably told the servant girl not to bother her, or maybe to be careful around her and get out of the room as swiftly as she could. Melissa chuckled softly. If she got home—when she got home—she would be bursting to tell Cindy and Kendra about this adventure.

Her stomach growled at the aroma. She had barely eaten anything at dinner, or *supper,* as they called it. She had met Magnus, the second-oldest child. He had dropped off a letter from a neighbor but hadn't stayed for supper. She'd also discovered from Jonah that the man rowing the skiff to shore yesterday was Benjamin Reed, Jonah's eldest brother, and Melissa then knew the future captain of the *Shenandoah*. He had returned to the ship, but Elizabeth mentioned that everyone would be at dinner today. Dinner was to the Reed family what lunch was to her and most everyone else living in the twenty-first century.

On the plus side, Isaiah was supposed to come, too. Anticipation quickened her heartbeat. Something about that man stirred emotions she thought long dead and gone. As she ate the porridge with Isaiah's maple sugar, Melissa wondered what time he would arrive. Maybe she would leave the room for a little while to have dinner with everyone.

Last night, or last night in her dream, when she'd said good-bye to Isaiah, she hadn't expected to see him again. Now she was glad she would. She reflected on the conversation she'd had with Elizabeth as they'd climbed up the stairs to go to bed. Elizabeth had mentioned her plans for the next day, which Melissa had not paid attention to because she'd figured they wouldn't involve her, and then she'd commented about a warm bed being just what Melissa needed to feel more like herself come morning.

"You have no idea," Melissa had replied. "I've had only one good night's sleep in four nights, and that was when I slept in Nick's doghouse. But don't worry, I promise not to be one of those horrible guests who stays forever and expects to be waited on hand and foot. I'll be gone and back home by morning."

Melissa glanced at the tray in her lap. She was still in Elizabeth's home, and now she was one of those guests who had asked to be waited on hand and foot. She cringed. This was not how she normally behaved when she visited friends or family. She didn't want to scare the bejeezus out of the Reed family by vanishing in the middle of their lunch, but she figured she should take the chance, make an appearance, and stop asking to be served in her room.

She smiled. Maybe she could sit next to Isaiah and have a chance to ask him about his farm and why he built the *Shenandoah*. Who knows? Maybe the dream would be infused with a little more romance.

If she was going to see Isaiah, she needed to brush her hair, brush her teeth, and change into the pretty blue dress Elizabeth had lent her yesterday. Time to get moving.

She lifted the silver tray off her lap to stand, then paused when her feet hit the floor. *It couldn't be.* Out of curiosity, she raised the tray above eye level and surveyed the bottom. She couldn't believe it. There, stamped just as the museum pieces she'd seen on school fieldtrips, was the signature trademark of Paul Revere. She was holding an original Revere silver tray.

Her hands shook as she slowly lowered the tray, stood, and carried it over to the writing desk. Paul Revere. The Paul Revere. She wasn't dreaming. Whatever was happening to her, the chances of the last two days being a dream were dwindling faster than a gambler's money in Vegas.

Her stomach heaved. There was no bathroom inside, and she wouldn't make it to the outhouse in time. She couldn't be sick. She needed to sit down and try to relax. Wobbling over to the bed, Melissa eased herself down and then curled up once again under the covers.

"God, where are you?" she whispered.

## 24

JOHN PARKED HIS TRUCK in the grocery store parking lot and cut through the scallop-shell-lined alley between the bakery and clothing store to reach the Summer Sails Tall Ship office. Captain Roberts had called him earlier and said a Coast Guard officer, John couldn't remember the name of the guy, wanted to interview the crew and chaperones. John's appointment was at 11:15, in ten minutes.

Gratefully, he reached the office porch without running into anyone he knew. His home phone had rung off the hook until he'd finally unplugged it at 9:30 this morning. Captain Roberts, Zane, and Nathan didn't know his home number, so they would only call his cell phone. He'd called Mark and told him about the unending calls, which Mark was also receiving. They'd agreed that cell phones would be their only form of contact.

Students had called, students' parents had called, teachers, neighbors, and then there were the papers and television stations. The reporters had been the easiest to deal with. He simply told them, "No comment," and hung up. His fellow teachers were upset, concerned, and most wanted to do something to help. He was exhausted after the fourth teacher had called.

Then the first student called. "Did they find Miss Smith?" Amber had asked.

He'd hated to tell her no. She'd mumbled something and then her mother had gotten on the line. "Hello, Mr. Masters. We've been waiting 'til eight to call you. Is there any news, anything at all?"

"I'm sorry, Julie, there isn't. The Coast Guard is still searching."

He had hung up and, not a minute later, someone else was on the line. When Captain Roberts called, John had hoped against hope that Melissa had been found. Now he was waiting to go into the office and be questioned by the Coast Guard. He was okay with that. He had questions of his own.

Leaning against one of the posts, John spotted Zane motoring over to the dock. He watched the skiff ease up against the bumper pads. Zane nodded as he tied off, and then he walked toward the office at the end of the dock. "How are you doing?" he called.

"Hanging in there. How about you?" John stepped off the porch and joined Zane in the sand near the water's edge. Any other time, he might appreciate that someone had an office twenty feet from the ocean. Today it served only to remind him that Melissa was somewhere out in that ocean.

"Same. Spend nearly every second waiting for the phone to ring." Zane tilted his head once in the direction of the office. "You up next?"

"Yeah. Don't know what I can say that will help. Hoping they can answer a few of my questions so I can answer everyone else's questions."

"I can only imagine. I've had more than enough on my phone, and I barely know anyone on the Island. Friends and family have called to check in after catching segments on the news. I heard that Cuttyhunk is inundated with press people and rubberneckers in their boats. It's amazing no one has seen her." Zane finished his sentence and glanced quickly at John as he rocked back on his heels. "Alive! I wasn't implying they'd only find a body."

John shook his head. "I'm not naïve. It's been over a day since Melissa went missing. We both know her chances are dwindling with every hour that passes. What I don't understand is why someone hasn't seen something. Anything."

Zane looked down at the sand.

John's gut twisted. "What? Just say it, Zane."

The first mate met John's gaze. "The tides and the currents around Cuttyhunk are a bit like a blender. If Melissa was swimming and got pulled under, she could be carried a good distance, or directly out to the Atlantic."

"What do you mean 'a blender'? I'm from the West Coast. Tides were simple. The water moved in slow and steady, and then the water moved out slow and steady. It was gradual and predictable. Any friends who had boats said the major rule of thumb was to make sure you always had enough water between the bottom of your boat and the ground, which sounded logical to me." John pointed to some of the smaller boats tied off at the dock. "Though I do recall seeing many of the smaller rowboats sitting on the muddy bottom when the tide was out. I never heard anyone talk of unpredictable currents or tides that resembled a blender."

Zane nodded. "Those West Coast tides aren't anything like these here in New England, especially in and around Woods Hole and the Elizabeth Islands. The local tide waters not only move up and down, but also horizontally, and often at alarming speeds. At times, the sea can become a salty whitewater rapids. I've been on a boat that was sailing along at a good clip, and still going backward against the current."

John couldn't process the idea. "You're kidding me. Backward?"

"You'd better believe it. If you're in a non-motorized boat and the current is moving in one direction at five knots, and you're going against the current at four knots, you're going backward. The other day, the tidal flow was moving in three different directions. The water was flowing west in Buzzards Bay, east in Vineyard Sound, and southeast through Wood's Hole. If that isn't enough to factor in, we've got to consider that she might have been pulled into a channel."

"You mean like the ones separating the Elizabeth Islands?"

"Exactly. Those channels, or holes as they're known locally, have strong tidal currents."

John jammed the toe of his sneaker into the sand. "Okay, so the waters, or currents, are fairly treacherous out there. Is that why we didn't sail through Canapitsit Channel when we anchored in Cuttyhunk Harbor? That would have been the most direct route from Lambert's Cove."

"It would have," Zane said, "but Canapitsit Channel is impossible for *Shenandoah* to pass through. We entered Buzzard's Bay through Quick's Hole. We also could have sailed out and around the west end of Cuttyhunk, but the currents were running with us on Wednesday."

"And the currents might not have been running Melissa's way. Is that what you're saying?"

"Maybe. The currents can reach up to six knots and are driven by the different sizes and filling rates of Vineyard Sound to the southeast and Buzzard's Bay to the northwest. At high tide, water flows from Buzzards Bay to the Vineyard Sound. Near mid-tide, the water stops and reverses, filling the Bay at low tide."

"Stop." John held up a hand. "You're telling me the direction the water flows between each of the Elizabeth Islands actually changes multiple times a day?"

"Yes." Zane bent down and drew two large circles in the sand with his finger. Between the circles, he drew two parallel lines to create a channel. Zane drew a small box near the left-hand circle and then picked up a pebble and placed it near the box. "Let's say Melissa was taking her nighttime swim around the boat. It's dark, she can't see the water moving, and before she knows it, she's caught in Canapitsit."

He moved the rock forward half an inch, then back in the channel drawn in the sand. "Wednesday night, high tide was at 9:23. We know Melissa didn't go into the water until after eleven. Low tide was at 3:05 on Thursday morning. That means around midnight, the water was changing. Not a good time to be stuck in the channel. We had a full moon, which might have been part of the reason she wanted to swim, but we also had a good deal of fog. She could have thought she was fine until a fog bank and the tide change collided, and it was too late." Zane choked up.

John couldn't look at the first mate. He felt the same way. Standing, Zane rubbed his hands together, brushing off the sand. The pebble stayed in the sand channel, unable to move. The chicken-scratch drawing made John ill. He looked away, over to his right, toward the shoreline and over past the buildings where holiday weekend traffic was already backing up.

John checked his watch: *11:28.* The Coast Guard was running late. His interview hardly mattered now. He knew nothing to help them, and Zane had answered his most pressing question of how and why Melissa could have disappeared without a trace.

## 25

MELISSA LAY CURLED ON HER SIDE. She'd fallen asleep after her crying jag. Maybe she was depressed. Maybe this whole dream was a product of a screw coming loose in her brain. She could play a character in one of those television ads for antidepressants. But she'd never felt sad or lonely or experienced any of the symptoms that would have caused her to seek out help. Whatever was happening, she couldn't make any sense of it.

Judging by the light outside and the lack of sunbeams coming into her room, it had to be close to noon. She'd slept and cried half the day away. Not like her at all.

A soft rap on the door forced Melissa to sit up. "Come in."

Elizabeth opened the door and entered, smiling. Melissa wondered how she did it. There was a strange woman in her home who had yet to give a rational explanation for her presence, yet Elizabeth was always kind and gracious. Melissa couldn't envision that happening in Boston, or on the Island. Most people avoided the homeless and mentally ill as if they had the bubonic plague. Further proof, Melissa hoped, that none of this could be real.

"Did ye rest well? I checked in earlier and thou were sleeping. I pray thou art feeling better," Elizabeth said.

"I'm getting there, sort of." Melissa glanced at the Paul Revere tray on the desk. Her uneasiness returned, but it was controllable as she reminded herself that it couldn't be real. Still, she had to know. "Can I ask a slightly rude question?"

Elizabeth's eyes widened for a second; then she regained her hostess composure. "Certainly."

"Where did you buy the silver tray?"

With a wave of her hand and a chuckle that sounded more like relief than laughter, Elizabeth walked over and ran her fingers over the item in question. "At Revere's silversmith shop. My husband ordered a number of items last fall to replace older pieces we had acquired or been given in our early years of marriage. Mister Revere's craftsmanship is exemplary, is it not?"

The knot in Melissa's stomach twisted. "Yes. Very impressive. I've seen some of his silverware and teapots in the mus...on a trip from school. You're lucky to own some. Your children will be very lucky to inherit them."

Elizabeth chuckled and winked at Melissa. "I hope my dear daughters do not inherit their pieces in the near future."

"Yikes! Of course, I didn't mean today or this month. I think it's safe to say the more years the better." Melissa needed to change the subject. *Something safe. Hmmm, nothing is safe. Maybe a familiar topic.* She could think of only one. "Will Isaiah be coming for lunch? I mean, dinner?"

"He has arrived." Elizabeth walked toward the door, opened it slightly, and then closed it again. "He awaits thee in the foyer. I believe he is most impatient. At least he is not pacing in the hall."

Melissa shot to her feet. "In the hall? As in out there right now, waiting for me? But I haven't used the bathroom or washed my face or changed into something decent."

"Rest easily. He is not in the hall. He waits below." Elizabeth stepped toward the armoire and took out the blue dress. She grinned at Melissa. "I am pleased that thou cares for him."

"What? No! I don't care for him in that way. He's just a guy in my dreams." The words sounded bogus to her ears. Elizabeth probably wasn't buying it, either. But it wasn't as if she had feelings or the hots for Isaiah. He was attractive but too reserved and stuffy for her taste. Plus, she'd sworn off relationships. "I need to talk with him about getting back on the *Shenandoah*, so I can go home. That's all."

"Hmmph," was all Elizabeth uttered as she held out the dress for Melissa to step into.

"Don't get me wrong, Isaiah's nice enough…well, if you can get past the grumpy exterior. But none of that truly matters. I only want a ride home."

Elizabeth tied off the laces and patted Melissa's back. "Isaiah is a fine man. Many women have attempted to catch his eye. None has succeeded. Until now."

"Oh, he has a girlfriend?" Melissa felt a twinge of jealousy she didn't want to examine. Isaiah couldn't, and didn't, mean anything to her.

"He does not. But he has shown great interest in thee."

Melissa's heart skipped a beat or two. "Me? I know you've got that wrong. Isaiah can barely say two words to me without looking as if he wants to bolt or as if he thinks I'm daft. Chemistry is not part of the equation."

After passing Melissa a beautiful ivory comb, Elizabeth rummaged through a basket of ribbons. "We shall see," she said as she found a blue one that matched the dress. Her smile was a good indication she was pleased with her discovery. "My brother is very fond of blue."

Melissa clamped her lips to resist her happy reaction. She continued to comb her hair, hoping to appear not to care one iota whether Isaiah liked blue or not. She would not allow herself to smile or get sucked into thinking of him as anything more than a friend to help her get home. Plus, she didn't want Elizabeth to believe she was falling for her brother-in-law.

When Melissa finished working the knots out of her hair, Elizabeth tied it into a low bun wrapped with the blue ribbon. In spite of not showering in a couple of days, Melissa felt pretty…not that it mattered to anyone other than her. She eased her size-seven feet into Elizabeth's size-six shoes and took a deep breath. As she exhaled, she wondered what Isaiah would be wearing. Did men wear formal clothes to lunch? Her floor-length dress was more formal than any dress or skirt she'd worn to church on Sundays.

"Ready," she said, hoping to sound light. The morning had been a shaky one. She wanted to have a better afternoon.

When she reached the bottom of the stairs, her heart fluttered as Isaiah came into view in a dark green coat or suit coat. She'd have to ask Elizabeth what they called men's indoor, everyday jackets in 1770. Whatever it was, the green flattered him. Suddenly conscious of wearing the same dress as the day before, she brushed a hand over the gown, focusing intently on a pretend spot of dirt.

"Thou looks even more lovely than yesterday, Miss Smith. I believe the rest has done thee good," Eli complimented.

"Thank you," Melissa said to Eli but shifted her focus to Isaiah.

When he said nothing, she looked away and headed toward the kitchen. She heard Elizabeth's harrumph as she marched by Isaiah.

Lunch, or dinner as she kept forgetting to call it, was a drawn-out meal of multiple courses. Melissa hadn't doubted the Reeds' comfort in life, but the meats, cheeses, breads, vegetables, and sweets were another indication of their status. Isaiah barely spoke to her, though both she and Elizabeth tried to engage him in conversation. Why he bothered coming over was beyond Melissa. She had tried three times to start a conversation with him, hoping to ease into discussion on the *Shenandoah*, and he had ignored her every time. Not quite ignored, but he gave her one-word answers and then turned away.

Though everyone else around the table chatted and laughed amicably, Isaiah uttered few words, and those he did speak were not directed at Melissa. He left immediately after they ate. Elizabeth insisted he return tomorrow for dinner, but Isaiah mumbled something about not knowing if he'd need to travel to Boston. As the door closed behind him, Melissa resolved not to think of him again.

# 26

JOHN LEANED ON THE WINDOWSILL and stared out at the ball field and the school playground below. At midmorning, there should be children outside for recess, playing and talking. They should have started school today. The other Island schools had commenced, but Mark had postponed Holmes Hole's start of the new school year until Monday. And that was fine with John. He'd barely made a dent in setting up his classroom, never mind having to teach anyone.

It had been a week today since he'd spoken to Melissa. Last Wednesday, they were taking the kids for adventures on Cuttyhunk. He'd been happy. She'd been happy. At least she'd seemed happy. They had talked on deck after the students had gone to bed. John had gone so far as to hint that he was interested in her…that after nearly half a century, his heart longed for marriage. She'd told him she would never marry again. Then she was gone.

The police had acquired her medical records. There was no report of any kind that indicated physical or mental illness. No cancer as Tucker had suspected. The young man, all of them in fact, had been surprised when Cindy's husband, Rick, gave Tucker a check for a thousand dollars to use toward his college expenses. Cindy explained that Melissa had called her Tuesday night and asked Rick to set it up. On Wednesday, she'd confirmed with Melissa that it was a done deal. Though Melissa hadn't signed off on the paperwork, Rick had honored Melissa's request.

That one act gave some people cause to think Melissa was planning to kill herself, but Cindy had quickly and adamantly squashed those rumors. Melissa hadn't made a will, hadn't done any end-of-life planning, and hadn't left a note.

With vehemence Cindy insisted, "There is no way she took her own life. I know Melissa. She loved life, loved teaching, and loved her family and friends. She also loved Spike, and she wouldn't have up and left him for anything. She hated leaving him for a week, never mind a lifetime. I don't see it, and you'll never convince me."

John pounded his fist on the white windowsill. *What happened?* he shouted inside his head. The question had blared in his mind dozens of times during each day over the last week. He had no answer.

Neither did anyone else.

"Knock, knock."

Startled out of his deep thoughts, John turned to find Mark standing in the hall outside his classroom.

"Want to head out and get some fresh air?" Mark asked.

John heard it—the finality and resignation in Mark's voice. Whatever he wanted to talk about while walking wasn't going to be good news.

"No. Just tell me."

Mark walked over to the window and stood beside John. Both men looked out at the playground, avoiding eye contact.

"Captain Roberts just called…"

John's chin collapsed to his chest. "Did they find her body?"

"I'm sorry, John. They didn't. The Coast Guard is calling off the search and rescue at noon today. They will officially declare Melissa's search a *no joy*."

"What does that mean, exactly?" John clenched his left hand into a tight fist. He knew Mark would ignore the anger and sarcasm in his voice.

"*No joy* is the phrase the Coast Guard uses when they don't find a missing person. It means they didn't have the joy of rescuing Melissa."

John slumped against the window. Tears built inside, but they did not fall. None of his anger, hurt, sadness, or frustration showed. On the surface, he was numb, and too many emotions were trapped inside. He knew why. He'd been expecting this news for days, bracing himself. "What happens now?"

Mark turned to face him. "The Coast Guard will make an official statement to the press and public. Melissa's family has already been called. Her parents, as I think you know, are staying with Cindy Flanders. The Tall Ships operations have been shut down for further investigation."

"What?" John exclaimed. "Why? Captain Roberts isn't responsible."

"You've heard Pete Nichols' story. The police are going to do an investigation. They have to. And Captain Roberts said he understands. I don't think he's up to sailing at the moment anyway. He sounded pretty beat up when he called."

"I can't believe Pete Nichols is still talking about Melissa disappearing to Colonial Boston. What is his problem?" John wasn't asking a question.

"Pete's going to have his own set of problems soon. Captain Roberts said Pete is going to be questioned as a suspect for foul play. His Jules Verne tale is causing people to look closely at him and the fact that he was on watch that night. He might regret spinning that crazy story when all is said and done. I'd hate to think he had anything to do with Melissa's disappearance."

"I don't think he did. His explanation is ridiculous and makes him look like a fool, but I don't believe he killed her or pushed her overboard." John walked toward his desk. He picked up a yellow pencil and tapped it on the large desk calendar. "What will happen at school?"

"I'm going to call a staff meeting in an hour. Everyone is at school, and I want all the teachers and staff to hear the news from me first. You don't have to be there."

"Thanks. I think I'll skip it."

Mark nodded. "Good. Go home and rest, or get on your bike. I'll call the parents of the students who were on the ship with you. We'll post a notice on the school website to explain what we can to everyone else. We'll close the school tomorrow and reopen on Friday for teachers and staff to finish preparing their classrooms. I'm going to arrange for grief counselors to be at the school once the students return next week. If you want to talk with someone, which I suggest you do, the school will pay for it."

"Not now. Maybe later." John glanced at the pencil in his right hand. He hadn't realized it, but he was circling August 30, the date Melissa disappeared, on the calendar over and over. *Died. Not disappeared.* He dropped the pencil and stepped back from his desk. "I've gotta get out of here."

# 27

MELISSA ROSE WITH THE SUN, donned the coat Elizabeth had found for her, and headed downstairs. She stopped in the kitchen to put some water on to boil over the fire and then slipped through the back door to the outhouse. Day three at the Reeds' home, and she wished for indoor plumbing every hour of the day. A long, hot shower would be one of the greatest, most wonderful luxuries she could experience. Instead, she sponge-bathed in the morning and again at night, trying to stay clean and healthy until she could return home. Which hopefully would happen soon.

She had a plan, and a favor to ask Isaiah. He had been stopping by Elizabeth's house every day. Elizabeth never failed to mention that she hadn't seen that much of him in years. Melissa couldn't help but feel pleased, but she was also cautious not to show any feelings. Her plan was to go home. Tonight.

She hurried back upstairs with a pitcher of warm water she'd carried from the kitchen and then began her morning routine. She was back downstairs and ready to help by seven. Elizabeth was teaching her how to cook, how to sew, and how to do needlepoint. Her hosts had determined that she must have fallen and hit her head, which explained to them why Melissa couldn't remember where she was from or how to function as a woman in the eighteenth century.

Melissa had settled into an uncomfortable routine. She enjoyed Elizabeth's company, and Abigail and Lucy were wonderful—full of life, laughter, and dreams of love. She enjoyed learning the ways of a Colonial woman and had decided to dedicate a semester to reading about the time period in the coming school year. But she didn't enjoy waking up every morning, hoping she'd be home, and then spending the rest of the day wondering how long until she would be.

The hardest part of her day was the pretending. She pretended to plan a new wardrobe as the four women sat in the parlor and sewed, pretended to have an interest in the summer and fall harvests while planting and hoeing a garden she would not see sprout, never mind bear fruit. She even pretended to be happy about the numerous invitations to tea, card games, and future engagements that many of Elizabeth's friends had extended. Too much pretending.

Today, when Isaiah arrived, she was going to ask to speak with him before they sat down to dinner. He normally arrived around noon. She had plenty of time to rehearse her words and how she wanted to ask him.

By ten, Melissa was so distracted watching the clock for Isaiah's arrival that she'd had to tear out her stitches three times.

"The joy of new love," Elizabeth stated.

"Who is in love, Mother?" Lucy asked.

"I cannot say for certain. Mayhaps we should ask Miss Smith."

"With Uncle Isaiah?" Abigail squealed in delight.

Melissa felt the warm flush spreading up her neck and over her cheeks faster than a Colorado wildfire burns up brush. "No, no, no. I have no interest in your uncle."

"Three nos. Me thinks the lady doth protest too much," Elizabeth teased.

"Would it not be a wonderful match if thou married Uncle Isaiah? Thou and mother would be sisters as well as friends," Lucy said in the voice of young girl fantasizing about happily-ever-afters.

Melissa put her sewing in her lap. "Girls, your uncle is a nice man. I appreciate him bringing me here to rest while I, ah, healed. But other than gratitude, I don't feel anything much for him."

"Of course not," Elizabeth said swiftly. "Back to our sewing, all." But her tone was amused.

Melissa jabbed her needle into the worsted wool and felt the tip stab into her index finger. "Ow," she exclaimed.

"Mind thy focus, Miss Smith. Would not do to poke one's finger and find blood on the fabric because one's attention was elsewhere," Elizabeth replied as sweetly as could be.

Melissa gave her a friendly glare. "My eyes are tired, nothing more. I think I need glasses."

Elizabeth let the reply go, and the four of them went back to work, Melissa unable to stitch anything worth keeping. When the front door opened an hour later, Melissa jumped to her feet and started to sprint to the foyer.

"Miss Smith," Elizabeth called, stopping Melissa as she was about to exit the parlor, "'tis best to let the gentleman come to thee, especially when one is not interested in the man in question."

The words caught Melissa by the hand and dragged her back to her chair. Elizabeth, Lucy, and Abigail exchanged knowing looks, but fortunately said nothing. Of course, they didn't know what Melissa was feeling. They assumed she was eager to see Isaiah because she was interested in him. They had no idea she was planning to ask him to bring her back to the *Shenandoah* so she could live on the boat until she went home. She wasn't the least bit interested in him as a man…at least that's what she kept telling herself every time he crept into her thoughts.

Within minutes, Eli and Isaiah entered the women's parlor. "My dear Mrs. Reed, we are famished. When will thou be available to dine?"

Melissa loved Elizabeth's laughter and the casual flirtations between her and Eli. "Dear husband, we shall dine shortly. I shall speak with Clara now. Thou and thy brother might enjoy a beverage whilst ye wait, if thou is not about to faint."

Lucy and Abigail giggled. Elizabeth kissed her husband on the cheek as she walked to the kitchen. Though it seemed such a little thing, a pain of longing struck as Melissa witnessed the moment. It had been years since she'd been married, longer still since she'd shared tender moments with a man.

Eli and Isaiah followed Elizabeth out of the room. Melissa wanted to go with them, to ask to speak with Isaiah, maybe have a private moment, but his cold shoulder moments ago told her to wait until lunch. Maybe a good meal would lighten his mood. She couldn't count the times her mother had said that the way to a man's heart was through his stomach.

Abigail gathered their sewing items and stored them in the large sewing box in the corner of the room. "When Father is hungry, Clara serves quickly. We should adjourn to the dining room before Mother calls for us."

Lucy led the way. Abigail fell into step beside Melissa. "Thou may have my seat next to Uncle Isaiah if it pleases thee," she whispered.

Melissa coughed, the girl's matchmaking intentions making her more nervous than she already was about talking with Isaiah. "Won't your brothers be joining us?" Melissa asked, trying to change the subject.

"No, they shall take dinner at their work locations today. Therefore, thou may have my seat at the table and sit next to Uncle Isaiah."

Melissa placed a hand on Abigail's arm. "I think I'll sit next to Lucy, okay?"

Abigail nodded. "Thy choice shall be equally pleasing, as thou may gaze upon thy heart's desire." Her eyes twinkled.

Blood pumped exceedingly quickly through Melissa's veins. Warmth spread through her again. She might not make it through lunch at this rate. She wanted to speak with Isaiah, but she couldn't have anyone believing she was falling for him, or worse, trying to match them up.

When they entered the dining room, Isaiah and Eli were standing behind their respective chairs. Clara and Elizabeth came through the swinging door, carrying platters of food. Elizabeth placed hers in front of Eli's spot at the head of the table, and then she went to the chair at his right.

"Ladies," Eli said and held out Elizabeth's chair. Isaiah attended to Abigail's chair. Lucy looked at Melissa, grinned, and then went behind her chair to hold it out. Everyone laughed and the meal began on a happy note after Eli said the blessing.

Eli asked about their morning and discussed plans for the garden they would plant shortly. There was a lengthy discussion on who wanted which vegetables and why. Apparently Lucy hated every vegetable known to man.

"Father, please tell Mother we need only plant corn and potatoes," Lucy whined.

Elizabeth shook her head. "We shall plant beans, cabbage, kale, greens, and turnips, as well as onions, parsnips, and peas next week."

Lucy rolled her eyes.

Ignoring her younger daughter, Elizabeth asked, "Miss Smith, does thou enjoy tending a kitchen garden?"

"I tried to grow squash and tomatoes once in planters, but they didn't do well. I do better with flowers and herbs. They need less care," Melissa answered.

"On the morrow I must address the savory, thyme, chives, and sage. The pennyroyal and valerian are growing well, as are the garlic and comfrey. I fear the rosemary may need to be replanted. Mayhap ye can help me when I tend to the herb garden?"

Melissa smiled. "I would enjoy that."

"Mother, may I try my hand at carrots and melons this summer?" Abigail asked.

"I love melons! I shall purchase thy seeds on the morrow," Eli said, clearly delighted with his daughter's request.

"Do you have a garden?" Melissa asked Isaiah.

"Yes," was his curt reply.

"What do you grow?"

"Vegetables."

Melissa felt everyone's eyes on her. Isaiah was being rude and his family knew it. She looked down at her plate and stabbed a potato. She wanted to stab Isaiah with her antique Paul Revere fork, not to draw blood, per se, but to let him know how utterly contemptible he was. Instead she chewed and swallowed the starch past the lump in her throat.

When dessert arrived, Melissa knew she needed to speak her piece or wait another day. She didn't want to wait, especially after Isaiah's rude behavior today. She looked across the table, willing him to look at her.

"Isaiah, um, Mr. Reed, can you please take me back to the *Shenandoah?* I am feeling much better and think I should return home. If we can't go today, maybe tomorrow?" Melissa held her breath as she watched the grim line return to his face.

"Thou wishes to sail on my ship?" he barely choked out.

"No, not necessarily. Just live on it until I go home."

The room had become uncomfortably silent. Everyone else had stopped eating and put down their utensils.

"Live on my ship?" Isaiah's eyes bulged and it appeared as though he might be having a heart attack. "Such a concept is impossible. There is a schedule, never mind propriety. No, Miss Smith, I will not allow thee to live on my ship. Ye shall need to find another way home if thou insists on departing." Isaiah pushed back his chair and rose abruptly. "I must leave. Brother, Sister, please forgive me."

Elizabeth jumped up to see him to the door.

"Sister, will thou speak with her?" Isaiah insisted. "She speaks nonsense. I fear she is still unwell."

Though Melissa couldn't see them, she and everyone else at the table heard Isaiah's loud, angry comment.

"I shall do as ye request as I can see thou cares for her."

*Bless Elizabeth.*

"Do not read more into my words. I care to understand how she came to be on my ship and why she wishes to return to my ship. And if she is unwell. Nothing more."

Melissa flinched at the brusqueness of Isaiah's words. He'd expressed his feelings clear as a bell. She'd have to find another way to get back onboard *Shenandoah.*

# 28

MELISSA WOKE THE NEXT MORNING WITH A NEW RESOLVE, and she was determined to keep it. Even if that meant wearing a bonnet. Yesterday she'd come close to telling Elizabeth that she wanted to work on her tan. Thank God her brain had kicked in before she opened her mouth. Melissa wanted everyone to think she was normal, and no right-minded eighteenth-century woman would willingly expose her skin to the sun. So here she was, in her guest room, about to put on a bonnet on a gloriously sunny day when she'd rather have the sun on her face and her hair loose in the breeze.

Yesterday, Isaiah had hurt her so much and made her so angry she'd barely spoken to anyone after he left. Elizabeth hadn't mentioned his parting comment, nor had she given Melissa the third degree about her mental health as Isaiah had asked her to. They had spent the rest of the day turning over the garden and preparing the soil for the season ahead. Now they would trim back the herbs, cut away the dead leaves and branches, and plant new seeds.

Though early May, the morning was warm and her room was getting stuffy. Melissa raised the window about three inches to let in the fresh spring air. She spied a familiar-looking bush and lifted the window higher for a better view. Bending at the waist, she braced her hips against the sill and leaned over as far as she could toward the six- or seven-foot shrubbery growing near the side of the house.

*Lilacs!* Every year, her mother said they were the first sign of summer's pending arrival. Crocus heralded the ending of winter. Daffodils and tulips were spring's showstoppers. The purple lilacs had bloomed in their yard in western Massachusetts in late May, always before Memorial Day, and their heady scent had wafted in through the screens. For weeks she would wake, take a deep breath, and sigh in contentment.

*These bushes are a week or more from blooming. As much as I love their scent, I hope I'm not here when they're in full bloom.* Determined to have a good day, Melissa reined in her thoughts of family and friends back home and stepped back into the room. She lowered the window and walked to the desk. Placing her hands on the back of the chair, she bowed her head.

"Lord, grant me the serenity to accept the things I cannot change. The courage to change the things I can. And the wisdom to know the difference. I have no idea what is happening to me, but today I give it all to you. You know my heart, what I want, but also what I need. Please help me to trust when I start to panic. Amen."

Melissa straightened and smiled. *God is in control.* All she needed to do was stay focused on him...but also behave in such a way that everyone would believe she was on her way to total health and could be trusted to venture into town alone. Once in town, Melissa would somehow find a way onto the *Shenandoah.* Perhaps she would see Jonah and be able to convince him that she needed to be rowed out. If she had to, she could always swim.

Until then, she needed to help Elizabeth with the garden. Melissa searched through the drawers in the armoire and found the bonnet Elizabeth had offered. One more article of clothing to wear! How did women do anything with all the layers of clothes, the dresses down to their ankles, the hairpieces, and the hats and bonnets? Oh, and the long apron she would tie on before they headed outside. She missed her jeans and T-shirts.

And her family. And her friends. And Spike. *No, no, no! Don't do that. Focus on God. He will see you through this.*

Melissa nodded once. Firmly. She couldn't dwell on those she loved at home. She put the green and yellow print bonnet on her head and tied the strings. "Lord, I trust you. Help my heart to get through this day." With her hat on and a prayer sent heavenward, Melissa joined Elizabeth in the yard.

"A beautiful day we have been blessed with," Elizabeth said, her face tilted toward the sun, while her bonnet ensured she would not tan or burn.

Melissa held back the chuckle that built inside. At least she was finding humor in the circumstances. "Where shall we start?"

They stood just inside a large, square fenced-in area. The garden was laid out much like the pictures Melissa had seen of formal English gardens, but on a smaller scale. In each corner stood a three-foot boxwood shrub. The garden itself was set up with raised beds in geometric patterns. Melissa could envision how pretty it would look in the summer, especially from an upstairs window where you could see the full layout of the beds.

Elizabeth walked to her right. "Let us begin with the medicinals. The pennyroyal appears to have survived the mild winter. I covered the herbs with leaves and sackcloth in November past. All but the rosemary appear to be greening well."

Melissa pinched off several brown leaves from a sprig of pennyroyal. Even wilted, the scent of mint was strong, and not in a good way. "I haven't grown this before. What do you use it for?"

"Mosquitoes. The oil in the leaves repels the insects. One should not be without pennyroyal." Elizabeth turned over the soil at the base of the plant, aerating the dark loam. "What herbs do ye grow?"

How to describe her window boxes? She hadn't walked around the neighborhood yet to notice if anyone had anything that resembled a twenty-first-century window box. Many older homes on the Island had them, especially in Edgartown, but she hadn't a clue when they were added to the houses.

"I guess I grow the basic ones—basil, oregano, thyme, sage, parsley, and some catnip for Spike. He'll play in the stuff and make himself silly." Melissa chuckled. She could picture Spike on his back, rolling back and forth in the catnip patch.

"Do ye have a cat?"

"I think he has me, but yes. Spike wandered into my life seven years ago, and now I can't imagine being without him."

Elizabeth smiled. "Thy memory is returning. This is good."

Melissa didn't say anything. What could she say? Her memory was fine. Her location and state of existence were the problems. Avoiding any further talk about her life on the Island, Melissa worked side by side with Elizabeth, chatting amicably as they pruned.

From their location in the side yard, Melissa could see the white fence Isaiah would walk past as he approached the house. A few times, or maybe more than a few, she'd checked to see if anyone was nearby. Where were the guys? She and Elizabeth were almost done with the herbs, and it had to be close to lunch—no, dinner, she reminded herself.

She broke off another handful of dead stems from the thyme plant and glanced toward the gate once more as she tossed the debris into the basket.

"My husband shall be home soon. Are ye hungry? I cannot fail to notice the number of times thy eyes have sought the gate," Elizabeth said.

Something about the way Elizabeth said "my husband" alarmed Melissa. She stood, bracing herself for Elizabeth's response. "Will Ben and Jonah and Isaiah be with him?"

Elizabeth must have heard the anxiety in her voice. She set down her tools and rose to face Melissa. "They have gone sailing. Jonah did not say where they were going, but did say they would return in two days' time."

Melissa couldn't help it. She started to shake. *Shenandoah* was gone. Without *Shenny*, Melissa was lost. Stuck. She didn't know how and she didn't know why, but Melissa did know she'd never get back home without *Shenny*. Tears rolled down her face unchecked. She placed her hands on the top rail of the fence for support.

Elizabeth rubbed a hand on her back. "Shhh, all will be well. Two days is hardly any time at all."

"Nooooo," Melissa whispered through her tears, shaking her head back and forth until the movement made her nauseated. Everyone back home would be so worried about her. She was worried about them and her future. She lowered her head to her hands, beseeching God without speaking a word aloud. From the recesses of her mind, she heard the lyrics of a Bebo Norman song: *"God, my God, I cry out. Your beloved needs you now."*

She hummed the beginning of the song and peace immediately settled into her heart. Melissa could wait two more days. God was in control. The lyrics of the song buoyed her spirit. She straightened and gazed up at the cloudless blue sky. "I will lift my eyes to the Maker of the mountains I can't climb." Melissa sang the first line of the chorus. She would be okay. God knew the plans He had for her, and she trusted they were for her good.

And she didn't have to worry about anyone at home. No one had ever known she was gone the first two nights, so no one would be worried about her now. Everything would be fine in two more days.

Yes, she would lift her eyes to God and trust Him to bring her home. "I'm okay," she said, giving Elizabeth a quick hug. Whether such displays of gratitude were normal in 1770, Melissa didn't know or care, and Elizabeth treated her as though every word and action was acceptable. Elizabeth never condemned her or criticized her, despite what must appear to be very odd behavior. A remarkable woman, for sure.

Elizabeth patted her back and then moved toward the garden gate. "A lovely song ye sang, though I do not recognize it. Do ye know who wrote it?"

Fortunately, Melissa could answer that question truthfully. "I haven't a clue. But I've heard Bebo Norman sing it, and it's one of my favorites. He has an incredible voice, masculine yet with great range."

Elizabeth accepted her answer without questioning who Bebo Norman was. They each gathered their tools.

Elizabeth opened the gate for Melissa as she lugged the basket of debris out of the garden. "Ah, here comes Eli. Leave the basket by the gate, and he shall empty our morning's work after dinner. I am suddenly famished."

"Me, too."

Surprisingly, she was. The peace she'd been determined to keep had stayed with her through a minor setback. A hearty meal sounded fabulous. And maybe she could pump Eli for information on Isaiah. Melissa quickened her step and beat Elizabeth to the back door.

# 29

ISAIAH STOOD AT THE HELM and watched the island grew larger as they sailed closer. He had questions, and he wanted answers. His blood boiled yet again today as he considered her request to reside on his ship just as it had yesterday when she'd first posed the question at Eli's home. "The temerity of that woman! I hath provided her with safe refuge. A ship is no place for her."

"Captain?" His nephew Benjamin, his worthy first mate standing with him at the helm, stared at him. If he was waiting for an explanation for his uncle's outburst, he would not be satisfied with an answer.

"Prepare the men to lower the sails. We shall drop anchor once we reach the inner harbor," Isaiah ordered.

Benjamin nodded and headed toward the bow, but not before Isaiah caught the amused expression on his nephew's face. Benjamin's arched eyebrow and slight smirk told Isaiah his nephew was most likely fully aware of whom and what he was thinking about. The thought irked him. He had no time for notions of being with a woman. He had finally built the ship of his dreams. The seas were his to sail.

He turned the wheel starboard tack and angled *Shenandoah* toward his purpose. Miss Smith was not the woman for him. He intended to find her family or prove that Cuttyhunk was not her home. Either way, he would have his answer today.

"With whom are thou angry?"

Isaiah snapped his head to the right and glared at his friend. Adam knew him too well and rarely held back his thoughts or opinions. "No one."

"To lie is a sin." Though spoken in jest, Isaiah recognized the truth in Adam's words. He would not lie to his friend, but neither did he wish to discuss his thoughts on Miss Smith.

His friend was goading him. He knew better than to take the bait. The ship's cook could serve words with more skill than he served food. Isaiah would not win a debate with Adam, nor would he be able to conceal his thoughts. They had known one another too well and too long to pull the wool over each other's eyes. If Adam inquired about Melissa, then he already knew too much.

*Miss Smith,* Isaiah corrected himself, *not Melissa!*

"Aye, if I were to lie to the Lord, 'twould be a sin. Our Father knows my mind. Others have no business meddling." Isaiah did not make eye contact with Adam. He suspected a smug grin would be on his leathery visage. The snicker he heard confirmed his suspicion.

"Miss Smith is a fine woman."

"Thou hast no concept of whether she be fine or fickle, sane or insane, maid or married," Isaiah growled. There, he'd lost his temper over her once again. She provoked his sensibilities, whether in his presence or not.

"Ah, I see."

"I doubt it!" Isaiah had lost control of the conversation, as he'd known he would. Ignoring Adam, he called out, "Benjamin, the halyards."

"We have sailed to Cuttyhunk to determine if Miss Smith is married?" Adam probed.

Isaiah gripped the wheel so tightly his knuckles turned white. He counted to ten, then twenty, then fifty. *Blast that woman. Why the devil did she choose his ship?*

"Foresail," he shouted to Benjamin. He eased up on his hold, and the circulation returned to his fingers. Now what could he say to Adam to curtail his incessant questions?

"Miss Smith is residing in my brother's home. I brought her there; therefore her presence is my responsibility. I must ascertain how she came to be on my ship, the condition of her mind, the accuracy of her claims, and what is to be done with her."

Isaiah felt pleased with his response. He showed no emotion, no attachment, because there was none, and no remark that needed further explanation. And, glory be to heaven and Lord God Almighty, his friend was silent.

"One could also determine if Miss Smith's husband is deceased, and she is free to be courted by another," Adam stated bluntly.

For all of two minutes! Why for all that was holy could Adam not have refrained from speaking for another two minutes? Isaiah kept his mouth closed for fear he would loose his tongue on Adam.

Watching the sails lower, he decided on a new tact that would preserve his countenance. "Miss Smith's marital status matters not to me. If thou wishes to court Miss Smith, then thou should inquire as to her husband's whereabouts."

Adam laughed. Not chuckled, but a full-blown guffaw. "'Tis not I who shall be courting Miss Smith."

"Captain," Benjamin called from midship, "shall we drop anchor?"

"Drop anchor," Isaiah returned. He ignored Adam, who leaned against the cap rail with his hands relaxed by his side and a grin on his face—the kind of grin one would want to wear, not be on the receiving end of.

When the ship was secure, Isaiah called for the crew to lower the dinghy. He went below to his quarters to retrieve his gloves, hat, and some coins. When he returned topside, Adam was no longer at the helm.

Isaiah strode down the starboard side and peered into the galley. "Are thou joining me or not?"

Adam climbed up the short companionway. "Ye needed to ask?"

Isaiah would not gift Adam with the pleasure of spoken words to confirm he wanted him along for the endeavor. His friend had gloated enough for one day. Jonah and able seaman Hugh waited below in the small boat. Isaiah followed Adam down the gangway ladder. Jonah sang a rousing sea chantey while he and Hugh rowed to shore.

Once they hit sand, Jonah jumped out and pulled the rowboat onto the beach. Isaiah and Adam stepped over the side and surveyed the land before them. The island was small. There could not be many people about. Whomever they encountered might be able to answer Isaiah's questions or guide him to the person who could.

"Remain with the dinghy," Isaiah ordered Jonah and Hugh. "I suspect we shall not be gone long."

A group of men worked on a fishing boat down the beach a ways. A young African maid, perhaps twenty, strolled across the upper beach, carrying a large wicker basket.

"Pardon me," Isaiah called to her. The woman stopped and turned toward them. "I am looking for the family of Miss Melissa Smith. Do ye know where they might be? Do they reside on thy island?"

"I do not know, sir. The Slocum family owns the land. I do not know a Smith family."

"I would be indebted to thy kindness if thee could direct us to the home of the Slocums," Isaiah said, handing the servant girl a halfpenny.

"Please, follow me. Ye may speak with my mistress. She shall know best the answers to thy questions."

Isaiah and Adam followed behind the young lady. Adam offered to carry her basket, which contained three good-sized bass, but she declined and sung gaily as they walked across the fields to a large house sitting on a hill.

The lady of the house was in the front yard, picking wildflowers with two children running about. When she saw them approaching, she stood and waited.

"Thee has brought guests, Hannah."

"Yes, Mrs. Slocum. They are searching for a Smith family."

Hannah continued into the house. Mrs. Slocum curtsied, and Isaiah and Adam bowed. "Good day, Mrs. Slocum. I am Captain Isaiah Reed, and may I introduce thee to my good friend Adam Greene?"

"Welcome, kind sirs. How may I assist you?" The children continued running about, playing a game of tag and giggling as they circled trees to dodge each other.

"My brother has a guest in his home in the North Precinct of Braintree. She is unwell, and we are seeking her family. She has mentioned Cuttyhunk in reference to a location she recently visited. Have ye met a Miss Melissa Smith?"

"I have no recollection of a Miss Smith, nor of a Melissa visiting here this spring."

"What of thy servants? Maids? Relations? Might they have guests staying with them?"

"I am sorry, but I fear thy trip has been for naught. Any company that might come to the island would greet my husband and myself."

A wail interrupted their conversation. The three adults turned toward the children. The little girl was on the grass, crying, apparently having tripped and tumbled to the ground. Seeing she had her mother's attention, she sobbed louder.

"Excuse me, Captain Reed." Mrs. Slocum walked over and picked up her daughter. She brushed off the child's knees and kissed an outstretched palm. Taking hold of the young boy's hand, she walked both children over to Isaiah and Adam. Isaiah smiled at the girl, who buried her face in her mother's neck.

"I believe they are in need of some quiet time. Ye gentlemen are welcome to join us for supper."

Isaiah shook his head. "Thank thee for your kind offer, Mrs. Slocum. We have a crew awaiting our return. We shall anchor overnight and take our leave in the morning. If thou or thy husband recall any information that might be helpful in our search for Miss Smith's family, please send word to my ship."

"Certainly, Captain Reed. I am sorry for thy trouble. I pray Miss Smith recovers from her ailment and that ye are able to locate her relations."

Isaiah and Adam bowed and headed back to the ship. When he left Milton this morning, he had not expected to find Melissa's family or friends on Cuttyhunk. Now, faced with the reality, Isaiah was less certain what to do next and what to believe about her.

Melissa had said she was on Cuttyhunk as recent as this week past. She had insisted she was on a ship named *Shenandoah*, anchored in Cuttyhunk Harbor. Though he knew she spoke inaccurately, the conviction of her words did not appear false, nor did her eyes reflect deceit. Her eyes were...

He pictured her face before him, smiling at him, thanking him. Her blue eyes were quite lovely and enchanting, drawing him to a place he dare not go.

But he did not want to think about the attraction he felt toward her. He could not think about it. She was not who she said she was, and therefore not a woman to be attracted to—no matter that he hadn't felt the emotions in twenty years. *Guide me, Lord. I know not where to seek the answers.*

Not fully true. He did know where to seek wisdom and direction, and he knew from whom all truth came. Isaiah trusted the Lord. He distrusted his emotions, or maybe he did not trust himself. He had failed Jane. He dare not fail another.

He picked up the pace, striding toward *Shenandoah* as quickly as he could without running.

Adam kept pace with him. "A word before we reach the ship."

Isaiah exhaled heavily. The day Adam said "a" word would be the day Isaiah sprouted wings. Nonetheless, he stopped.

"Thou knew we would not find Miss Smith's family on Cuttyhunk. The journey proved only to confirm what thou knew. We may not discover her past. She may never regain her memory. But, my friend, she is here. Miss Smith has entered thy life for a reason. The emotions thou may have toward her are true, regardless of her circumstances."

Isaiah strode six steps away from Adam, then spun around and marched back. "I shall not discuss this. Nor shall I befriend Miss Smith."

Adam closed his eyes briefly, then rested a hand on Isaiah's shoulder. "Thou may deny thy feelings day and night until thee be blue in the face, but those feelings will not change. Thou has avoided love for twenty years; now it may have found thee. Do not be so foolhardy as to cast it aside."

"I cannot," Isaiah snapped.

"Thou can."

"I shall not."

"Then thou art a fool." Adam stalked toward the ship.

Isaiah followed at a distance. Adam knew what he was suggesting, what he was asking of Isaiah. But the risk was too great. Jane had been frail, as Miss Smith seemed to be. An image of Melissa in the blue dress, her eyes sparkling, emerged. She didn't seem frail. *But she is unwell,* he reminded himself. He had not been able to save Jane. He could not risk Miss Smith's life. Or his.

\*

Isaiah guided *Shenandoah* into the harbor and ordered the crew to drop anchor. Adam had left him to his thoughts since yesterday afternoon, but peace had not yet settled upon Isaiah. He knew not what to think, though he had determined his next course of action.

He would drop anchor and go speak with Eli. Then tomorrow he and the crew would sail for Falmouth. He'd pick up another shipment of white pine, and while he was in town negotiating with the merchants, he would question the good people of Maine about Miss Smith. Surely someone would know of her.

As the crew secured the lines under Benjamin's direction, Isaiah went down to the galley to speak with Adam. "We sail tomorrow for Falmouth."

Adam stowed the sack of porridge oats in the cask next to Isaiah. After fitting the lid onto the barrel, the cook stood and faced his friend. "The quest continues."

"Aye. I must discover who she is and where she came from." Isaiah needed to pace, to move and release the tension, but the galley was too small. He should have built Adam a larger space.

"Isaiah, I do not need to tell thee, when ye cannot see the course through the storm, to trust the Lord to guide thee. Seek His will before ye do thy own." Adam did not smile. In fact, he looked worried. He rarely frowned, but he was now. "Will ye speak with thy brother on the matter today?"

"Aye. Miss Smith resides in his home. He, too, deserves the truth."

Adam shook his head. "I do not believe Eli is concerned. 'Tis only thee who carries this heavy load. Though I understand thy reasons."

Isaiah opened his mouth to deny the words Adam had not fully spoken, but thought better of it. Adam was correct, and they both knew he was. Instead, he ascended the companionway and called back, "I shall see thee on the morrow."

"God's speed," Adam said before Isaiah stepped onto the deck.

After informing Benjamin of the plans, Isaiah gathered his bag and departed *Shenandoah*. He wished he could go directly home, skipping the visit to his brother's and the questions he'd be asked and the answers he would give. He walked down the dock, up to the main road, and turned right toward Eli's. Miss Smith would be there. Her blue eyes may even welcome him home. And he would need to look the other way and pretend he did not care.

# 30

MELISSA SAW ISAIAH WALKING UP THE ROAD from her window on the second floor, and it made her ridiculously giddy. She ran down the stairs and burst through the front door. He was home, or at least he was at Elizabeth's.

She stopped about ten feet down the path and watched him approach. Would he be happy to see her? Maybe he missed her and would go wild and crack a smile her way before she went home.

*Home.* Home was good, or should be. She should want to go home. Her life was at home. And she could only imagine the concern her disappearance would be causing everyone she knew if this dream wasn't a dream. So why was her heart pounding for Isaiah and not for *Shenandoah?* The ship was back in the harbor, and Melissa could probably get aboard today. Once onboard, who knew how long it would be until she dropped into the black hole and fell into the twenty-first century?

*If I leave here, if I wake from this dream, I may never see Isaiah again.* Melissa didn't need to search her heart too long or too hard to admit she could care less that *Shenandoah* was back, but she was thrilled Isaiah was home. She hadn't seen him in two days. Watching him unlatch the gate made her heart beat several thuds quicker.

He saw her then, and she waved, probably a little too enthusiastically for the time she was in, but she wasn't an eighteenth-century woman. Back home, women had been known to ask men out. Waving was a given. Elizabeth and the girls would probably faint if they learned that a twenty-first century woman could and would ask a man on a date.

Isaiah raised a hand briefly, showing next to no emotion, and then closed the gate. He was an eighteenth-century man to the "T." And judging by the snail's pace at which he was moving, Isaiah was either exhausted from his journey or had little interest in seeing her. Part of her wanted to run toward him; the other part wanted to back away. If he smiled, she would be less uncertain.

Perhaps because he was taking forever to reach her, her stomach flipped and fluttered. When he finally stood in front of her and smiled, she gave in to her heart and threw her arms around him. She had nothing to lose. It wasn't as if she would be around next week to face the neighbors at church or tea.

She heard his startled intake of breath whistle past her ear as their bodies molded together. The sound ricocheted exhilarating tingles down her spine. A few seconds later, his hands found her hips. The contact sparked a shot of electricity, and happiness raced through her bloodstream.

"You're home. Thank God! I thought you'd never get back," Melissa whispered, holding him now in a not-so-brotherly way.

Isaiah returned her hug, tentatively at first. Then he pulled her tighter into his embrace, pressing her against the length of him. The sensations between them were heady, less electric this time, more like warmth flowing through her and raising her body temperature to a comfortable sauna.

She sighed. He felt good, strong, and safe. She could feel his heart pounding against her body. She liked the phenomenon.

"I was worried you wouldn't be back in time," Melissa said.

He leaned back slightly and gazed down at her. Melissa met his eyes. The intensity bore into her soul, jarring her heart to a split-second stop before beating again at an elevated staccato.

It was a strange mix of fear and protection.

"In time for what?" he asked.

"Brother...," Eli called from behind Melissa.

Isaiah stepped away from her as though they'd been hit with one of those thick black thunderbolts in a Saturday morning cartoon. She lost her balance and wobbled for a second. Isaiah hurried past her without offering her a hand. Melissa blinked and then blinked again. One second she was in his arms, staring up into his dark brown eyes, and in the next second he was gone.

*What just happened?*

She turned to find Elizabeth walking toward her with wide eyes and a broad smile. Her friend looped an arm through hers, and the two women strolled back to the house. Melissa kept glancing at Isaiah's back and then over to Elizabeth.

"I have no idea what just happened," Melissa said.

Elizabeth patted her arm and grinned. "We shall talk about yer greeting inside over tea. I want to hear everything, but we must let the men retire to my husband's library before we speak. I shall go and speak with Penny and Clara. I am eager to hear how ye became so bold."

Melissa chuckled at Elizabeth's hushed, conspiratorial tone. Did they really need to sneak off and whisper? She'd hugged Isaiah; that was all. Nothing more. She looked out the window at the blue sky and beautiful spring day. What was his problem? The man had gone from drawing her closer to tossing her away as if she were a flea-infested rug. Where did that come from?

Penny entered the parlor, carrying a tray with cups and saucers, a pretty teapot with pink and yellow roses on it, and biscuits. Elizabeth followed behind with cloth napkins. She wore a smile that bordered on wicked. Elizabeth and Cindy would get along great. Both seemed intent on finding Melissa a suitable boyfriend. No, not a boyfriend—a husband.

Melissa would have offered to help set the table, but Penny and Elizabeth seemed to have an unspoken system. When Penny left the room, Elizabeth fussed with the silverware, putting each piece in its proper place. "Sit and tell me everything. How did ye know Isaiah was arriving?"

Melissa took the chair opposite Elizabeth, who poured them both a cup of tea. Picking up her dainty teaspoon, probably made by Paul Revere, Melissa couldn't help her grin. "I saw him from the bedroom window."

"Which caused thee to run downstairs and outside?"

When she said it like that, Melissa had nowhere to hide. But she couldn't feel anything for Isaiah. She had to go home. Isaiah wouldn't want her staying anyway. He'd shown her that yet again a few minutes ago. "Well, I was happy to see him…because the *Shenandoah* was back."

Elizabeth laughed. "Of course. Thy reaction is about a ship. Nothing to do with the man."

"I, well, it's not possible, you see." Melissa stumbled over the words. Her reasons for not getting attached to Isaiah could not be explained. She could spill the beans and tell Elizabeth why feeling anything for Isaiah was pure stupidity on her part, but she didn't want to ruin a new friendship by mentioning her little problem of being from two hundred years in the future and not knowing when she would fall into the black hole again.

Elizabeth started talking, but Melissa couldn't focus on her words. She swirled the spoon in her tea. When would she go home? She'd been here five days, almost a week. At times she thought it was real, but she knew everything had to be a dream. A woman didn't fall asleep in her bed in 2007 and then wake up in 1770 with a handsome man who made her feel emotions she hadn't experienced in years, if ever. That didn't happen in real life.

Then again, maybe lonely divorcées did dream about finding the perfect guy. But that was where her dream became less dream-like. Isaiah wasn't perfect, far from it. He sure wasn't sweeping her off her feet. If today was any example of his feelings, he couldn't stand to be around her.

So what did that mean? Her dream wasn't a dream? Not possible. Or, that she couldn't even find a good man in her dreams? That she could believe. But when Isaiah touched her, everything felt real. He stirred sensations in her that she wanted to feel daily.

*Which is why I can't allow myself to go there. No man I know back home will be able to compete with my dream man.*

"Is the tea not to thy liking?"

Melissa stopped stirring and put the spoon on the table. "I'm sorry. Lost in thought."

"About Isaiah, perchance?" Elizabeth's tone was light. It held that teasing lilt women so often use when chatting with girlfriends who are falling for a new guy, as if trying to wiggle an admission out of a love-struck friend.

There was no point denying her emotions. Melissa simply had to be careful how she said things. "I am thinking about Isaiah. I thought about him all day yesterday when he was gone. I was angry and hurt after he left the day before, but when I saw him walking down the street, I…"

Hmmm, what had she felt? *Happy. Excited. Giddy. Warm all over. Butterflies in my stomach. Heart palpitations. And that urgent desire to run downstairs and be with him immediately.*

"Oh, my gosh!"

"What?" Elizabeth leaned in.

"I think…but I can't…but I might be…falling in love with Isaiah." Melissa spoke the words in shock. The realization fell into the category of bad decisions that would come back to haunt her. And haunt her Isaiah would. She had to go home. Now. Today, before things got worse.

"Wonderful!" Elizabeth clapped her hands.

"No, it's not wonderful." Melissa rose from the table and hurried to the nearest window. Why hadn't she fallen for John? He was real, and he lived near her, in the same century and a couple miles down the street. What was wrong with her? Why was she having this dream? She needed to wake up. "I have to go home."

"Of course ye do. Ye must let thy family know ye be well and have met an honorable man."

Elizabeth sounded so confident, but she had no clue where home was. And tell someone? Melissa wasn't planning on telling a soul about this dream. This would be her secret. Not even Cindy or Kendra could pry it out of her. She would bury it in the recesses of her mind and never think about it again.

"You don't understand, Elizabeth, and I can't explain it to you. But when I go home, I won't be able to come back." The last seven words stuck in Melissa's throat and choked her up.

Elizabeth moved to stand next to Melissa. "Art thou married?"

"No."

"Be thou in servitude?"

Melissa could have made a joke about all teachers being slaves working for peanuts, but Elizabeth wouldn't understand the humor. "No. I'm single and free."

"Then I do not understand."

"I want to tell you, honest I do, but I would sound crazy, and you won't believe me," Melissa said. She needed to tell someone, needed someone to know what she was going through, needed Elizabeth to understand why she would disappear. She stepped closer to her friend and whispered to her, "I am not from here. I live in the twenty-first—"

Eli and Isaiah sauntered into the room, catching Melissa and Elizabeth whispering with their heads together. Melissa jumped away from Elizabeth much the way Isaiah had bolted from her earlier.

Elizabeth swiveled toward the men. "Hello, Husband, Brother. Is thee departing so soon, Brother? Can ye not join us for supper?"

"Nay, I must take my leave and be home before nightfall." Isaiah stepped toward the window and faced Melissa. "Miss Smith, thou stated earlier that I had arrived at my brother's home in time. In time for what?"

"Before I had to leave."

"I see."

Isaiah's curt reply stabbed into her heart. He had no idea what she was feeling. It wasn't like this situation was her doing or her choice.

"I don't want to leave. I like...I like being here." Melissa glanced over at Elizabeth, who nodded for Melissa to continue. "I would like to stay. There are, ah, things I don't want to leave, but I don't have a say in the matter, which I can't explain to you right now."

"A safe journey to thee then, Miss Smith." He looked through her—not at her, not into her eyes, not into her heart, but through her.

Melissa's happiness drained from her as though she was bleeding out. *So be it. I was going to wake up one day, and all of this would have been nothing but a memory. This way will be easier. It would be ridiculous to miss someone who didn't care that I was gone.*

Forcing herself to be strong, Melissa studied the man she thought she was falling in love with and hid those feelings deep in her heart. "Thank you for the safe travels. If you could take me to the *Shenandoah,* I shall try to be gone today."

Elizabeth sighed loudly. Melissa glanced at her and had to turn away quickly before tears threatened to roll down her cheeks.

Isaiah started to walk away. "If thou art determined to leave, thou shall need to find another way. I have ordered *Shenandoah* to Falmouth."

The words hit Melissa full force, as though a truck had plowed into her. "What?" she yelled at his back. "Take me with you. Please. Falmouth is minutes from my home."

He didn't so much as slow his pace. If anything, he moved faster, walking away from Melissa and her heart.

Elizabeth rushed toward her. Melissa couldn't process the overwhelming dread that threatened to consume her. Isaiah didn't care about her, and she was stuck in her dream turned nightmare.

*I don't belong here. I'll never get home.*

Elizabeth wrapped her arm around Melissa as the door slammed behind Isaiah. Melissa fell onto Elizabeth's shoulder and sobbed. She didn't know what hurt more—not knowing how to go home or that the man she was falling in love with had just walked out of her life.

*God, why is this happening? What do You want from me? What did I do wrong? How can I make it right? How can I get home?* Melissa prayed through her tears.

"Come, let us go for a walk. The girls will be home shortly from Mrs. Barwick's, and we shall not have a moment of privacy." Elizabeth patted her back, her compassion soothing Melissa's wounded heart.

A walk would be good. She needed time to think and plan. When she straightened, she noticed Eli was no longer in the room. He'd probably made his escape as soon as she shed her first tear. Or maybe when she was yelling after Isaiah.

"Getting outside would be nice. Is there a park nearby or a hiking trail?" Melissa didn't ask if they could stroll down to the beach. She had no desire to look out over the water and be reminded that Isaiah had sent *Shenandoah* to Falmouth without her.

# 31

MELISSA AND ELIZABETH WALKED OUT THE FRONT GATE, past the hitching post, and turned left—away from the *Shenandoah*. Melissa was too upset to fully appreciate the houses and lawns. She loved spring back home, especially the greening of the grass and the leafing out of the trees. Life was blooming here too, but it wasn't her life.

As they strolled, neighbors called hello or waved to Elizabeth. Melissa kept her head down. She needed to leave. She didn't belong in this time or place, and her heart would only be shattered all over again if she stayed here much longer. The whole concept of living in a dream no longer felt practical, but the alternative was more farfetched than living in fantasyland for a week.

Time travel. Crossing centuries in her sleep. That was impractical and improbable. But how else could she explain her arrival in 1770? *Lord, I can't grasp the idea of traveling back in time any more than I can believe being stuck in a dream for the rest of my life. Show me what to do. Please.*

"Elizabeth, I need to find my way home. If Isaiah will not help me, I don't know what I'll do."

"I believe he suffers from injured pride."

"What? How so?" Melissa held back the sarcastic retort that was forming.

Elizabeth slowed their pace to a shuffle and glanced at Melissa. "'Tis my belief that Isaiah felt he was thy protector, as he found thee on his ship. Thy announcement that ye intend to depart suggested he was not providing thee with adequate security. Alas, I am guessing and cannot say for certain. I do know I have not seen him storm from my home on any other occasion. Then there are his feelings for thee, which he has yet to express."

Melissa nearly burst out laughing but managed to merely roll her eyes and wave off Elizabeth's notion. "That's crazy! He wants nothing to do with me. And, at this point, I only wish to go home. If Isaiah really wanted to protect me, he would have taken me on the *Shenandoah* when she sailed for Falmouth. He could have dropped me off on Cuttyhunk or, better yet, the Vineyard. I'm from Tisbury. If Isaiah had taken me with him to Falmouth, it might have been that much easier for me to get back to where I belong."

"I believe thou misunderstood Isaiah. *Shenandoah* shall be sailing north to Falmouth, Maine."

"Why is he going to Maine? What was so urgent he couldn't help me?"

Elizabeth stopped and looked at Melissa. "I believe Isaiah is certain that his decision shall help thee. He sails to Falmouth to find thy family or acquaintances who could be of assistance."

Melissa shook her head. "Why on earth would he go to Falmouth, Maine, to find my family? I never said I was from there. Did I?"

"I have not heard thee speak of Falmouth. I do know that Isaiah launched *Shenandoah* last week. They visited two ports, Falmouth and Boston. Isaiah and Adam were convinced ye did not board the ship in Boston Harbor. Therefore, Isaiah has presumed ye boarded the *Shenandoah* while he was anchored in Falmouth."

"Oh." Melissa glanced at the Colonial homes on either side of the road, some large and stately, others modest and unpainted, none belonging to a time and place she knew. *What now?*

Melissa started walking and Elizabeth joined her. The sea was somewhere off to their right, not more than a mile away. If she stood by the shore, would the water carry her back?

"Thou speaks of going home. Do ye remember where home is?" Elizabeth asked, her words gentle.

Though she had just mentioned the Vineyard, Melissa knew this was the moment she could tell Elizabeth who she was and where she needed to go. She swallowed the pit of anxiety lodged in her throat and contemplated how to begin her story. At last she said, "What do you think about time travel?"

A single horse and rider trotted toward them at a good clip. Melissa and Elizabeth dashed to the edge of the nearest fence. Whoever was at the reins was in a rush, oblivious to anyone else. If he'd been driving a car, he might have hit them.

Elizabeth shook a finger at the backside of the man spurring his horse on. "If by time travel thou refers to a person moving from one place to another without riding his horse through the streets with complete disregard for others, I believe the roads would be a safer place for all."

Melissa chuckled. If Elizabeth only knew what modes of transportation were coming, she'd be grateful for the less-deadly horses. "That, or people traveling back or forward in time, say between centuries."

Elizabeth seemed to consider Melissa's question as she leaned back against the fence's top wooden rail. "One night last week after supper, Eli read from Revelation. The apostle John was in prison on Patmos when he wrote the book. He was visited by an angel and shown the future. I asked Eli if John dreamed the vision or if he ascended and saw the future for himself. Eli said that the Good Book instructs us that God told John to come up hither and that He would show him things of the hereafter. I do not question the Lord's ability to bring a man where He desires him to be."

Elizabeth patted the rail and motioned for Melissa to sit beside her. "We know from the Book of Matthew that Jesus visited with Moses and Elijah, and they were deceased. Eli teaches us that we shall not question the ways of our Lord, but rather strive to follow in his path. I trust the Word of our Lord. In the same breath, I say to thee that I have not pondered whether an errant horseman, a neighbor, or a child of mine might travel to another time. Why do ye ask?"

There it was, the open door. Now all Melissa had to do was walk through it. Would Elizabeth think she was crazy? Or a witch? Or would her friend go on believing she'd taken a bump to the head and had lost her memory? If the situation were reversed, Melissa knew she wouldn't believe Elizabeth. Time travel seemed a great adventure in movies and books, but no scientist or inventor, nor any person Melissa knew, had disappeared from the day and time they were living in. Yet here she was, sitting on a fence, staring at Colonial homes that weren't part of a movie set or located in Plimoth Plantation.

Melissa looked directly into Elizabeth's eyes. "I have traveled in time."

Without so much as a gasp or wide-eyed expression, Elizabeth asked, "Where did ye go?"

Melissa suspected from Elizabeth's question, and the riveted tone that she asked it in, that her friend was placating her much like a parent listens to a child's tales of whimsy. Elizabeth surely thought Melissa was still suffering from the ill effects of the knock to the head they all deduced she'd suffered.

To sound credible, Melissa started with her first day on the *Shenandoah*. "I am a teacher back home on Martha's Vineyard. Every summer, the students from the five Island schools sail aboard a square topsail schooner for a week. It's an amazing experience for everyone, made more so because the ship is over two hundred years old." Placing both hands on the fence, Melissa added, "I live in the twenty-first century, not the eighteenth century—2007 to be exact. The ship we sail on each year is Isaiah's *Shenandoah*."

Elizabeth's hand flew to cover her open mouth. Melissa expected worse, so minor shock was a good thing. After a minute or so of disquieting silence, Elizabeth lowered her hand. "How is that possible?"

"I don't know. This year was my fifth summer chaperoning the trip, and I'd never had any weird dreams or experiences before. The first two nights, I thought I was having strange nightmares about sailors on a ship. The third night, nothing strange happened. On Wednesday night, I fell asleep in my cabin in 2007 and woke up on Isaiah's ship in 1770. That's all I know."

Elizabeth stared at her. Melissa knew she sounded crazy. Only she wasn't. Just her life was. "I'm sorry to burden you with this. I needed to tell someone. For days, I've wondered if I was dreaming, but I can't deny this bizarre reality any longer. I'm sorry that I brought my problems into your home. When Isaiah first said he was taking me to his brother's house, I thought for sure I would be gone in the morning."

"Aye." Elizabeth nodded. "I recall thou expressed as much to Isaiah when ye bid him farewell that first night."

"Do you…" Melissa clasped Elizabeth's arm. "Do you believe me?"

Elizabeth covered Melissa's hand with hers. "I believe that thou believes. May we begin with that?" Her request was more than Melissa had hoped for. Elizabeth wasn't calling for a witch-hunt. She wasn't kicking her out of her home. And she wasn't running in the opposite direction. Anything else was a plus Melissa would latch onto and hope for the best.

"Of course! Thank you. I imagine this sounds pretty far-fetched, and it is. So I'm grateful you're still willing to sit here with me and listen. Is there anything you want to know, something I might be able to answer?"

"Will ye share with me memories of thy life, as we walk for a bit?"

Both headed up the street, away from Elizabeth's home.

"I grew up in western Massachusetts in a small town where local parades and church socials were important occasions," Melissa said. "I couldn't wait to get away from there and go to college. I could have gone to school closer to home. Lord knows there are plenty of great colleges in and around Massachusetts, but I took off to Indiana to study at Purdue University."

Elizabeth reached out a trembling hand. Melissa slowed her pace, praying she hadn't said something to offend her friend. "Thou hast gone to university?" Elizabeth asked, her voice filled with wonder.

"Yes, most women back home go to school. Very few women graduate from high school and skip college. Continuing education is encouraged and insisted on by many parents. Mine included."

"Unfathomable," Elizabeth murmured. "Please continue. Did thou obtain a teaching position after university?"

They strode ahead once again, their pace determined by the topic Melissa discussed and whether they huddled close and whispered about a life not many would believe. Melissa shared the bulk of her life history with Elizabeth in about forty minutes. The houses and people they passed became a blur as she related her story and Elizabeth asked questions.

"Thou petitioned for a divorce?" Elizabeth spoke with such shock that Melissa didn't dare mention how easily one could end a marriage in the twenty-first century. She wasn't proud of her divorce, and the months leading up to it were painful and filled with remorse and regret.

"The decision was the most difficult one I'd ever made. I waited a long time to get married. I dated, but not often. My parents had a beautiful marriage. It wasn't perfect, but they were perfect for each other. In my early twenties, I never found anything close to what they had, so I waited. Then Bryce came along. He was handsome, funny, tall, and full of adventure. Too much adventure, as it turned out. His idea of exploring became exploring other women's bedrooms."

Elizabeth's sharp intake of breath halted them both in their tracks. "Oh, my dear friend. I cannot imagine the pain."

There were no tears this time, though Melissa remembered the days when every memory of that first affair shattered her to pieces. "I stayed with him through the first and second affair. When I caught him the third time, with a woman named Gayle, I kicked him out and filed for divorce."

"How ever did ye survive?"

Melissa smiled at Elizabeth, hoping to quell a bit of the jolt she'd given her. "I was blessed with a great job and wonderful friends, and my parents helped me to relocate down Island to a small home closer to the school where I now teach. As fate would have it, Bryce died several years later from injuries he sustained in a driving accident. Rumors had it that he was out cheating on Gayle, who had become his third wife."

"A vile scoundrel."

Melissa had used a variety of words to describe Bryce. Elizabeth's selection worked well, too. "He was. Unfortunately, he hurt many people. Kendra, one of my closest friends, dated him years before I knew him. After my divorce, she broke down one afternoon and confessed to me that her son, Mike, was Bryce's child. She had a brief relationship with Bryce, but not brief enough. She survived the gossip, then carried the guilt and shame for years. But she has never told her son who his father is. She confided in me that she has written Mike a letter that she will give to him after he turns twenty-one."

"A tragedy. Mr. Shakespeare did not pen such a heartbreaking tale." They resumed their walk. "Thou hast not married another?"

"The right man never came along."

"Until thou met Isaiah."

The mix of joy and dread once again churned in Melissa's heart. "I can't be with Isaiah, even if he wanted me, which he doesn't. Don't you see? At any time, I could disappear and never return."

"If what thou hast said is fact, mayhap thou are destined to remain."

"I can't stay here! I have no job, no home, no way to support myself. My family and friends will be worried. And Spike will think I deserted him."

"Where is Spike? Thou did not bring him aboard the ship, did thou?"

Melissa chuckled. "No. I left him with my friend Cindy. She loves Spike almost as much as I do. He's in good hands." In the distance, she could see Elizabeth's home. They had walked for over an hour, Melissa pouring out her story and Elizabeth receiving it with compassion and understanding.

"What thou hast shared is material for books, yet I believe. I cannot pretend to comprehend thy circumstances, though I offer thee my home and my friendship for as long as ye may wish them."

Tears pooled in Melissa's eyes. She let them roll gently down her cheeks as she sought to find the words to thank Elizabeth for her kindness. Overwhelmed, Melissa hugged Elizabeth tightly and whispered, "Thank you."

When her tears subsided, Melissa stepped back and looked around from the spot where they stood on the side of the road. The homes, yards, people, horses, and carriages were foreign to her. *What if Elizabeth is right? What if I am destined to be here? What if a new life begins today?*

Melissa held her fear at bay, forcing herself to focus on one positive aspect of her situation. Elizabeth immediately came to mind. A roof over her head, food to eat, and clothes to wear were her next thoughts. *Eli, Lucy, and Abigail—more positives. Isaiah.* Melissa pressed the internal pause on her brain pathways. *Isaiah?* If she stayed, could she give her heart to another? Would he give her his?

Elizabeth must have sensed her internal struggle. She gently rested a hand on her shoulder. "Before we enter the house, shall we cast our cares upon the Lord?"

"Yes, please."

The women bowed their heads and Elizabeth began, "We beseech Thee, Lord, that Thy abundant mercies shall flow freely upon Melissa. May Thy eternal peace provide her comfort. May she find wisdom within Thy Word. And may Thy will be done. Amen."

"Amen." Melissa lifted her eyes to the heavens and offered a silent prayer of gratitude for her new friend. As she had the other day, Melissa heard the lyrics to one of her favorite songs play in her head: *"I will lift my eyes to the Calmer of the oceans raging wild."*

# 32

Four days passed quickly. Each night, Melissa went to bed wondering where she would wake up, but by morning she was still safely tucked into the narrow bed in the cozy room in Elizabeth's home. She was becoming more comfortable in her new role as houseguest and student of Colonial ways and life.

She'd never been a fancy chef, but she'd managed to prepare herself and friends decent meals at home. Learning how to make apple pies the true old-fashioned way was a task Melissa had no previous skill for but now wanted to perfect. "Isaiah is known for his predilection of sweets and pastries," Elizabeth had disclosed the day before, "his favorite being apple pie."

At breakfast, Eli had mentioned that he expected Isaiah and the crew to return today. Melissa's heart raced whenever she pictured him walking through the gate. She cut the lard into the flour, sugar, and salt, imagining the perfect apple pie she could give Isaiah. *If Elizabeth is right, and he does have feelings for me, maybe a slice of yummy pie will break the ice.*

"Mind the dough, Melissa. Thou hast sliced the same section of lard nine or ten times," Elizabeth kidded.

"Oops. I was thinking." The heat of embarrassment rose on her neck.

"Aye, and I can gather on whom thy thoughts were directed."

Clara, the Reed's cook, chortled while she added more dried apples to the bowls of boiled water on the table. Elizabeth had been quick to point out that the apples had come from Isaiah's farm. The warmth on Melissa's neck spread across her cheeks. Everybody knew Elizabeth was intent on pairing off Melissa and Isaiah. Everyone but Isaiah.

"Is there any word on their arrival?" Melissa no longer wasted time denying her interest in Isaiah.

"Nay. Mayhap Jonah and Isaiah will join us for supper. Benjamin shall take his meal on board *Shenandoah* with Adam, I am certain." Elizabeth sprinkled flour on the wooden table and began to roll out her pastry dough.

"Has Benjamin always liked to sail?"

"'Tis in his blood. Jonah, too, I fear. Isaiah has raised them on his ships. Magnus shares Eli's passion for the Word. He shall make a fine preacher one day. His apprenticeship in Boston suits him."

Melissa added a few drops of water to her piecrust as Elizabeth had done and worked it into the dough with her fingers. Clara now had two large bowls filled with dried apples rehydrating. A small container of cinnamon sat beside the apples. Melissa's mouth watered. She could almost taste the pies.

Hours later, with four pies cooled or cooling, Melissa and Elizabeth were talking in the parlor when Jonah walked in.

"Good afternoon, Mother, Miss Smith. Do I smell apple pie? Hast thou made my favorite?" Jonah grinned and kissed his mother's cheek.

Elizabeth hugged her younger son and took his jacket. "After ye cleanse thy hands, I am certain Clara will allow thee into her kitchen to sample what cools in the window."

"Jonah," Melissa said in a decibel above a whisper, "is Isaiah on his way?"

"Nay. My dear uncle was in a most foul mood and has gone directly to his home. Ye would not wish his company this night."

Melissa shuffled back to her chair and slumped down. Jonah hurried toward the kitchen and the desserts they'd baked—the apple pies she'd made for Isaiah. Her soul hurt. Why were men such impossible, annoying creatures? Especially Isaiah!

Elizabeth sat across from Melissa, reached over the table and squeezed her hand. "Thy heart must be aching. Ye gave thyself to preparing his favorite sweet, and he shall not be here to enjoy thy efforts. Shall we save a pie and bring him one on the morrow?"

"I don't know. What if he didn't come because he doesn't want to see me? Going to his house would only make things worse. And I don't need the rejection. Could we set one aside for dinner or supper tomorrow in case he joins us?"

"For certain. Now let me fetch the girls, and we shall sit down with Jonah and Eli and listen to Jonah's tales of his days at sea. After supper, Eli shall provide us with another reading and food for our souls. Do ye have a favorite story in the Good Book?"

Melissa forced a smile. She knew Elizabeth was trying to cheer her up, and she didn't want to bring everyone down at supper. "Ruth."

"'Tis a fitting choice for thee." Elizabeth walked out of the front parlor and went upstairs to summon Lucy and Abigail to the table. Melissa paced the room, kicking herself for anticipating Isaiah's return and then trying to remain hopeful about his arrival the next day.

*

Three days later, a week since she'd last seen him, Isaiah marched through the front gate, bypassed the front door, and walked around to the back of the house. He'd been avoiding her, but Melissa was past being hurt and had attained a finely tuned state of being ticked off. She tossed her sampler into the chair she recently vacated when she caught sight of Isaiah on the road.

"Miss Smith?" Elizabeth asked, though she, too, had witnessed Isaiah's avoidance of her.

"I'm going upstairs for a bit."

"A fine idea. I believe it is time for me to have a word with Isaiah."

"Oh, no. Please don't, Elizabeth. He already hates me."

"His problem is not hatred, dear friend. And his behavior has gone on long enough. My fuse is not often a quick wick, which he knoweth well. However, today I shall hold his feet to the fire of said flame."

Melissa thought she was angry, but if Elizabeth were a cartoon character, she'd have steam coming out of her ears. The thought gave Melissa a chuckle, and she nodded at Elizabeth. "Maybe I'll sit here and see how it goes."

Her friend exited the room as a woman on a mission—anything in her path would be stormed over. For a split second, Melissa felt sorry for Isaiah. *Ha! He deserves whatever she throws at him.*

Elizabeth's wedge heels clicked and clacked, echoing the pointed frustration both women felt. Melissa knew she shouldn't leave the parlor—listening in on their conversation wouldn't be polite—but she'd had it with Isaiah and was dying to hear what Elizabeth was going to say to him. She slipped off her shoes and tiptoed down the hall to the dining room, which resided conveniently next to Eli's library.

Melissa missed whatever Elizabeth had said when she entered the room. She heard Eli ask what time they would partake of dinner.

"We shall dine in two hours' time. Before then, I require a word with thy brother."

Melissa smiled, recalling the numerous times her father would arrive home from work and her mother would say, "Your daughter was a hooligan today." If her mother said "your daughter," Melissa knew she was in trouble. She found it rather amusing to have Elizabeth turn that table on Isaiah. She stepped closer to the dividing wall and listened.

"What vexes thee, Sister?" Isaiah asked.

"Thou art what vexes me, Brother. Thy behavior toward Miss Smith is unpardonable. I have never taken thee for a fool until now."

"Wife—" Eli tried to intrude.

"I shall speak my peace, Husband," Elizabeth stated firmly. "Miss Smith is a guest in our home and has become a friend. Thy brother has been rude and stubborn."

"Rude and stubborn? I have done no such—"

Melissa wanted to scream through the walls that he'd been a jerk, but she waited for Elizabeth's retort.

"Thou has, without a doubt, been most unkind. Thy foolish pride builds a wall where none should be. Thou cloaks thy feelings and hides them amongst thy wounded pride. Thou hast judged her without hearing her story. Thou hast has been wrong, though I shall not disclose a confidence. In spite of thy indifference, Miss Smith baked thee apple pies, yet thou was too prideful to enjoy them. The pies have been consumed, and thou doth not deserve Miss Smith!"

Melissa heard Elizabeth's heels thud over the rug in the library and strike the wooden floorboards. She wished she could see the shocked expressions on Isaiah's and Eli's faces. Holding her own shoes, she hurried across the floor to meet Elizabeth in the hall.

Her friend was grinning as though she'd just won the Mass Lotto and was about to burst with excitement. Melissa covered her mouth with her right hand to stifle the bubbles of laughter building within. Elizabeth grasped onto her arm and they dashed to the parlor, closing the door behind them. Once safely inside, they erupted into laughter.

"I hath set him straight," Elizabeth exclaimed between chuckles.

"To say the least. You were brilliant. God help any man who crosses Lucy or Abigail."

Elizabeth pointed toward the front window and laughed harder. Isaiah was scurrying down the path toward the gate. For the first time since she'd known him, Melissa was not sorry to see him leave. Elizabeth had given him an earful and more than enough to think about. One way or another, Melissa's relationship with Isaiah was going to change. Even if he only addressed her politely as a houseguest from this point on, it would be better than wondering what he was thinking.

"Mark my words, on the morrow he shall be a new man." Elizabeth turned away from the window and stepped toward her favorite wing chair. She sat with the confidence of one who knew without a doubt that she was right.

# 33

*WAS IT ONLY YESTERDAY? Feels like forever!*

The morning had passed slowly. Melissa was grateful Elizabeth hadn't mentioned Isaiah or asked how she was feeling. Truth was, she'd been sitting on pins and needles since breakfast, waiting and wondering if and when he would arrive and if today he would act any differently toward her.

Lucy and Abigail had left over an hour ago, Elizabeth sending them to a neighbor's house for a young ladies' game of cards. "I remember well those days of games and gossip. My friends and I spent more time engrossed in discussions on the handsome men we swooned over than we did on a game of cards," Elizabeth had confided as she passed Melissa a cotton dress.

Day by day, the conveniences of the twenty-first century became fond memories, or eager longings as the case was today. Melissa despised sewing. She'd hated it in home economics when she was in junior high and high school, and then she'd at least had a sewing machine. Elizabeth had the patience of a saint, teaching her the painstakingly slow method of hemming a dress with merely a needle and thread.

"The colors of the print will highlight your eyes. Blues flatter your coloring and blond hair," Elizabeth said.

"Let's just hope my stitches hold, and I don't trip over a loose hem and fall flat on my face." Melissa pulled the needle through, tugged lightly as Elizabeth did, and then threaded the needle into the next section of fabric. She understood now why women wore thimbles. Her fingers were sore from the number of times she'd pushed the needle through the fabric with more force than necessary.

"Mrs. Reed, mum, Mr. Isaiah has tied his horse to the hitching post," Penny announced while she dusted the parlor windows.

Melissa's pulsed quickened at the mention of his name. *I'm not ready.* Melissa looped the thread through and drew the needle up with a steady hand. *Yes, I am.* She heard the front door open and stabbed her finger as she pushed against the needle. *Um, maybe not. Lord, steady my heart. I don't want to look like a schoolgirl crushing on the quarterback.*

"Thank thee, Penny," she heard Isaiah say.

Elizabeth motioned for her to look down and focus on her stitches.

"Let him believe ye hath not noticed his arrival. Shall serve him well." Elizabeth grinned and threaded her needle perfectly through her side of the hem.

Melissa heard Isaiah's boots on the wooden floor and dropped her eyes to the tedious task she would be relieved to have any excuse not to be doing.

"Good morning Sister, Miss Smith."

"Brother," Elizabeth said with pretend surprise, "thou startled me. I did not hear thee arrive."

Melissa focused hard on the blue, yellow, and indigo floral print and had to bite her lip to keep from chuckling. Elizabeth would have made a marvelous actress.

"A fine piece of handiwork, Miss Smith."

*Maybe he does like me. That's the first compliment he's given me that hasn't been forced from him.* "Thank you, Isai...um...Mr. Reed."

Elizabeth secured her needle in a section of fabric. "Brother, would thou have the time to escort Miss Smith down the lane to Mrs. Thatcher's to acquire a yard of velvet ribbon she has for me? I fear the noonday hour is nearing, and I must tend to our dinner. Thou art welcome to join us upon thy return."

Melissa silently cursed the warmth spreading across her cheeks. She wanted to kick Elizabeth under the table.

"I would be delighted, Sister."

*Or maybe I'll hug her later.*

"Thank thee, Brother. I shall fetch a parasol for Miss Smith."

Isaiah stood silently in the center of the room. Melissa didn't know whether to stand or stay seated and wait for Elizabeth. She was relieved to give up sewing, so she secured the needle and folded the dress onto the table before rising. Thank God Elizabeth returned before the two minutes of silence became even more awkward.

Elizabeth passed her the umbrella and ushered them toward the door. "Enjoy the walk," she said, smiling to Melissa as she passed by her.

Once on the path, Isaiah offered Melissa his arm. The instant her fingers touched him, the electric currents once again shot through her veins. She glanced sideways at him to see if his face gave away any similar reaction. Nothing. He stared straight ahead.

Determined to make the most of their time alone, Melissa asked, "How far is it to the Thatchers'?"

"'Tis only five houses."

"Oh." Melissa had assumed Elizabeth was sending them out for at least a half hour. After a few minutes, in which neither spoke again, she understood why ten minutes would be more than enough time together. She was happy to be with Isaiah, but she had no idea what to say—or not to say.

"We have arrived." Isaiah released her arm, opened the gate, and led Melissa up to the front door of what she guessed was a modest home. The wood was not painted, but the house was a decent size. He knocked, and an older woman answered.

"I saw thee approaching, Isaiah. Welcome, Miss Smith. Abigail has mentioned thy recent arrival." She passed a cloth bag to Melissa. "Please convey my good tidings to Elizabeth. Mayhap we can have tea next week?"

"I would like that. Thank you."

Melissa turned and accepted Isaiah's arm, relishing the tingles spreading through her body. Even though he wasn't talking with her, she was glad to be next to him as they spent another ten minutes in silence on the way back. When they entered the Reeds' yard, Isaiah stopped abruptly about fifteen feet from the front door. Melissa looked up at him, waiting for whatever he was going to say, hoping he was actually going to say something.

"Miss Smith, may I accompany you on another walk tomorrow? Perhaps of greater length, if thou art so inclined?"

*Yes! Yes! Yes!*

"I'll double check with Elizabeth to make sure we don't have any plans, but I'd like to go if I can." Melissa knew Elizabeth would kick her out the door and into Isaiah's arms if she even thought about saying no to him, but her friend had also advised Melissa to play hard to get.

Isaiah nodded. "I shall return on the morrow then, and hope to find thee free."

"You're not…aren't you going to have dinner with us?" *So much for playing hard to get.*

Isaiah smiled, and for the first time, Melissa saw the light of happiness reach his eyes. "I must return to *Shenandoah* and see to her preparations. Tomorrow, Miss Smith," he said with a bow, and then he walked with a lightness in his step toward the gate.

He untied his horse from the post and led him out from under the shade tree. Once astride the big bay, Isaiah met her eyes and waved. Her heart skipped a beat, and she rushed inside to tell Elizabeth that she had a date tomorrow.

\*

When Isaiah arrived the next day, Elizabeth made sure they were in the kitchen working on another project so they appeared busy and somewhat indifferent to his arrival. "Elizabeth, I can't cut another biscuit. My heart is pounding so hard I think I'm going to break a rib."

"I am happy for thee, though it would not do to reveal thy sentiments too soon. Isaiah must be made to pursue thee. His heart will yield a greater emotion for the effort." Elizabeth passed Melissa the rolling pin. "Look busy in case he does not wait as Penny will instruct."

Penny came to get Melissa, leaving Isaiah in the foyer. Elizabeth helped her untie the apron and fasten a bonnet on her head. "Thou art lovely. Today ye might try to engage him in conversation."

"About what? He doesn't speak more than five words at a stretch." Melissa needed to quell her apprehension before she left the kitchen. "What does he like?"

"The sea and his orchards."

Melissa wiped her flour-covered hands on a damp kitchen towel. "I think I can handle fruit trees and sailing."

The day was warm and sunny, and Melissa smiled as they headed toward a large grassy field speckled with wildflowers. "You mentioned you had apple trees. Are they starting to leaf out?"

"Aye. The flowers are blooming. Thousands of pink and white flowers to behold."

"That sounds beautiful."

"Would ye like to see them?"

Melissa squeezed his arm. "I'd love to."

Isaiah gave her another joy-filled smile that had his eyes twinkling. "I shall return for thee tomorrow with my carriage."

"I can't wait." Truer words she had not spoken. She was eager to see his farm and his home. She wondered why he'd never married. If he was available back home, he'd have every single woman on the Island chasing after him.

*Good thing I'm here instead because I'm a goner and wouldn't want all that competition vying for his affections.*

As they reached the center of the field, Isaiah leaned down to pick some flowers. He passed the bouquet to Melissa and then extended his hand. "May I call thee Missy?"

The question caught her by surprise. Her heart pounded. Though she'd been in the eighteenth century for only a couple of weeks, she knew his question was asking more than her name. Only family members or those courting addressed one another by their first name.

She looked up into his eyes and smiled. "I'd like that. May I call you Isaiah?"

He nodded, another gorgeous smile creasing his handsome face. "I would be pleased if thou addressed me so."

Melissa slipped her hand into his and prayed her heart's fondest wish. *Please, Lord, let me stay. Let this be real.*

They walked holding hands until they reached the edge of the field, when Isaiah offered her his arm once again. It would take her a while to get accustomed to his old-fashioned ways, but she liked it. She felt honored and respected, as she'd always believed her mother felt with her dad.

*

As the days passed, Melissa fretted over when and how to tell Isaiah who she was and where she was from. Elizabeth encouraged her to wait, until one day her friend said, "I believe thou should speak with Isaiah before dinner."

"Really? Things are going so well. Maybe there's no need to after all." But Melissa knew that would be wrong. She had to be fully honest to have a healthy relationship. She had to risk losing him in order to keep him.

"Ye both have pasts to disclose."

"Isaiah? A past? But you never said…."

Elizabeth shook her head. "'Twas not my place. 'Tis Isaiah's story to tell. Begin by asking him of his recent trip to Falmouth. The ice shall be broken."

By the time Isaiah arrived for dinner, Melissa was filled with dread. *Dear Lord, I'm so nervous. What if Isaiah doesn't accept me for who I am? What if he wants me to leave? What if he walks out the door and never speaks to me again? Please give me your peace. I trust that I am here in this time for a reason, and I pray that reason includes Isaiah. Amen.*

Elizabeth glanced at Melissa when she heard the front door close. "Mayhap a short stroll would enable thee to talk freely?"

Melissa thought she might be sick as Isaiah's footsteps grew louder. Fresh air might be her only saving grace. "I'll ask him. Then I'll lead him like a lamb to slaughter."

"Hush now. All will be well. He loves thee, and ye love him. 'Tis time for the past to be laid to rest." Elizabeth was so sure of herself. Melissa wished she had an ounce of her friend's confidence.

Isaiah entered the kitchen looking incredibly handsome in beige breeches, a white shirt, and dark blue jacket. Melissa barely contained her sigh at the sight of him. *I can't lose him. Please don't let me lose him.*

"Hi," she blurted out, grabbing his arm, "can we go for a walk?"

He chuckled. She didn't know if he was laughing at her abrupt request or the way she talked. They'd all joked with her about her odd expressions. She sometimes wondered, as she did now, if it was her words or the way she said them that made Isaiah laugh.

"Good day to thee, too, Missy."

Melissa stopped pulling on his arm and forced a grin. "Sorry. Good day, Isaiah. Would you care to take me for a walk before dinner?"

His eyes crinkled as he smiled at her eager request. She wanted to melt into his arms and forget about the reason she needed to go for a walk.

"I would be pleased to escort thee." He offered her his arm. Melissa raised a brow at Elizabeth, who nodded and shooed her out of the kitchen.

They went out the front door and Melissa led him right to walk around the house. No matter how hard she tried, she couldn't force the words on her tongue to flow out of her mouth.

"Art thou troubled, Missy? Is there something on thy mind?"

She kept her eyes straight ahead, afraid he might spot the fear growing inside her. "May I ask you a question?"

"Anything." He patted her hand as they strolled toward the kitchen garden.

"How come you never got married?"

Isaiah froze in his tracks, his arm muscles clenching under her fingers. She'd hit a nerve. This is what Elizabeth hadn't told her.

The man she loved gazed up at the sky. She waited, understanding how difficult the words might be to express.

"I was married, over twenty years ago. I brought Jane home with me from South Carolina, but she did not adjust to the northern clime. She was frail and caught the fever. There was nothing I could do for her. I tried. The doctor stayed with her for a week. There was naught to be done."

The pain in his voice tore at Melissa's heart. She reached up and rested her palm against his cheek. "I'm so sorry. I can't imagine losing someone I love."

"Ye said thy husband died. Did thou not love him?"

Melissa shuddered. Memories of Bryce were never pleasant. "When Bryce died, I had stopped loving him years before. He was with another woman, one of many."

Isaiah gasped. "A scoundrel of the worst sort. I am sorry, Missy. Ye deserve to be honored and cherished."

"My dad always says that, too. He would like you."

Isaiah's eyes widened. He tipped Melissa's chin and looked into her eyes. "Missy, thou remembers thy family?"

"I do. But first, why did you go to Falmouth?"

Isaiah locked his gaze on hers. "Thou spoke of thy father a moment ago. I sailed in search of thy family. I was certain you boarded the *Shenandoah* while we were anchored in Falmouth Harbor. Alas, I found neither family nor friend. Hast thou remembered where thou is from?"

Melissa nodded, doing her best not to cry the tears forming in her eyes. "I've always known. And I tried to tell you. Well, technically I did tell you, but you and Adam thought I'd hit my head and was not in my right mind."

He took both her hands in his. "Missy, I also sailed to Cuttyhunk. Not a soul on the island knew thee."

*No kidding.* "They wouldn't. I *was* on the *Shenandoah* off Cuttyhunk, but not in the eighteenth century. I live, or lived, in the twenty-first century. One night I went to bed on a school trip aboard our *Shenandoah*, and then I woke up on your ship."

"Missy! Cease. What ye speak is impossible. Please, do not utter these words to another. Thy life could be in danger." He squeezed her hands and looked down at her with such care and tenderness. "'Tis only the head injury. Give it time, and thou shalt remember."

Melissa hated to argue with him. He was being kind, trying to protect her. But she couldn't stop now. He had to know who she was. "It's not a head injury. I am telling you the truth. Ask me. Ask me anything about the future. Ask me about the Boston Massacre. Ask me about the trial. Captain Preston gets off. John Adams defends him. Only two of the eight men who will stand trial in the fall will be found guilty of manslaughter. Ask me about the coming war. Ask me who wins. I know! I'm telling you the truth."

Isaiah stepped back and held her at arm's length, his hands shaking.

She surged ahead, unable to stop until he believed her—or until he left. "I don't know the streets in Quincy well, but I know who lives here, who is going to build here, and who will have fame and political success. Dorothy Quincy has a home nearby. Her house is still standing over two hundred years later. Do you know why? Because she married John Hancock, and he is going to become the president of the Second Continental Congress, the first signer of the *Declaration of Independence,* and the first governor of the Commonwealth."

Melissa paced in a circle around Isaiah. "Josiah Quincy will build a famous house around here, too. And one day there will be twelve acres set aside in town called Adams National Historic Park that will include the birthplaces of John Adams and his son, John Quincy Adams, because they both serve as presidents of this country after we win the war against the British."

Melissa stopped moving and drew in a deep breath. Isaiah's eyes were so wide she couldn't bear to look at him.

"I implore thee to cease. This is witchcraft. Ye cannot know of what ye speak."

She wanted to scream—not at him, but at fate. "I know it sounds crazy, but I do know these things. I'm telling you the truth. You can believe me or not believe me, but I cannot change who I am or where I came from." Melissa stood her ground. If he sensed or saw her trembling, he didn't comment or move to comfort her.

"I shall not consider what thee has said. Thou hast suffered an injury to thy head. Come, let us go inside so thou may rest."

He reached for her arm, but Melissa jerked away from him. "It's not a head injury. You can try to understand or not, but I am from the twenty-first century!"

Isaiah took one large, hasty step back from her. "Enough. I hear no more!"

"Then go," Melissa said, waving him off, "because I can't change who I am."

Isaiah spun around and strode across the lawn faster than a rabbit chased by a dog.

Melissa dropped to the ground and sobbed. *Why, Lord, why?*

# 34

"Have a relaxing vacation, John," Marjorie Jenkins called from her classroom.

"You, too, Marj. Hope you don't end up cooking for half the Island." John heard her laughing as he walked down the school hallway lined with numerous Thanksgiving decorations. He was grateful Mark had given him an extra two days off so he didn't have to work Monday and Tuesday of next week. He couldn't wait to board the plane tomorrow morning and head to California for an entire week with his family.

The first three months of school had been hard. Granted, each day got easier, but he hadn't gotten past Melissa's accident. She was officially a missing person. The Coast Guard had never recovered her body. Unofficially, they had said she died from an accidental drowning. Her parents were waiting a little longer to request an official death certificate.

Captain Roberts had been cleared of any fault or wrongdoing related to Melissa's disappearance. Though he had closed down for September and October, the Tall Ships would open again in the spring, and *Shenandoah* would sail the Island students again next summer.

John wouldn't sail next summer or anytime soon, but he was relieved Captain Roberts would be able to continue doing what he loved. He wondered how the school would handle the trip next year, but that was too far away to worry about. This year's fifth-grade class had not begun their fundraising or parent meetings yet. He guessed they were all waiting until after Christmas, letting the shock wear off. *When will it wear off? When will I wake up and not wonder what happened to her and why?*

The school board had hired a temporary language arts teacher. She was older and had come out of retirement to help the Holmes Hole community through the transition period while Mark did a formal search to replace Melissa. John had wanted to shout, "It's too soon," but life went on even when one moment in time stood forever at a standstill.

Mark walked out his office door as John was heading to the large double doors and his week of freedom. John stopped but gazed out the window at the field across the road.

"When are you leaving the Island?" Mark asked.

"In a couple of hours. Spending the night at a friend's in Boston, then catching the first flight out in the morning."

"Glad to hear it. You need this break."

John grunted and turned halfway toward Mark, his feet still pointing toward the doors. "That bad, am I?"

"You know what I mean. It's been a tough quarter. Wish I could go on an extended vacation myself. Better yet, I wish I could turn back time."

John scrutinized Mark's appearance. The principal had aged over the last three months. His usual jet-black hair was streaked with gray. His boyish face had developed worry lines around the eyes. John hadn't noticed the changes; he'd been so wrapped up in his own unresolved grief.

"Maybe you should take a vacation with your family."

Mark rolled his eyes. "My wife said the same thing. She gave up counting my new gray hairs."

"Yeah, well, gray hair is the least of our worries." John pointed to his own head of salt-and-pepper hair. "We're breathing."

"You still talking to the counselor?"

"Once a week."

"Helping?"

"Some. Time is probably the real cure."

"Agreed." Mark clapped John on the shoulder. "Have a great visit with your family. Come back with a tan and a crate of oranges."

"Will do. Enjoy your Thanksgiving." John pushed open the blue door and stepped out into the chilly fall air. The cold shocked him at first, and then he felt that tingle of being alive. The wind tousled his hair and lifted his red scarf. He knotted the scarf and jogged down the cement steps.

*Alive is good. Difficult at times, but good.*

# 35

Two days had passed since Melissa had seen or heard from Isaiah. Elizabeth told her he came by late yesterday to speak with her and Eli. He couldn't have known she'd be off with Lucy delivering supper to an elderly neighbor who was sick, but it hurt that he hadn't waited to talk with her.

"Please tell me what Isaiah wanted. Did he ask about me? Were you talking about me?" Melissa had begged Elizabeth for details.

"I shall not break his confidence. Trust that all is well. Isaiah shall speak with thee on the morrow." Elizabeth had smiled reassuringly, but Melissa's heart hadn't wanted to wait another minute, never mind another twelve or so hours.

Eighteen hours later and not a sign of Isaiah. Today! What time today? It was already eleven in the morning—today—and he wasn't there yet.

Melissa circled past the front door of the Reed home for the third time. She'd been pacing inside until Elizabeth sent her out to get some fresh air. *More likely to get me out of her hair.*

Melissa glanced at the street every time she heard a horse trotting down the road. She needed something to do, but the idea of sewing or baking made her cringe. She stopped by the garden fence, dropped her parasol to the ground, and rested her arms on the top rail. The seeds they had planted were now three- or four-inch seedlings shooting up from the soil. Summer was just around the corner. But where would she be? Would she be with Isaiah? Or had he closed that door?

She wanted to weep, but she couldn't give up that easily. She had to believe Elizabeth had talked some sense into him. Isaiah's sister-in-law had accepted Melissa and her bizarre, nearly unbelievable story. Elizabeth had believed, regardless of the improbability. *And she will help Isaiah to understand, right, Lord?*

Waiting was hard enough. Waiting for a man to decide whether or not he still wanted to court you because one day you might vanish into thin air or be burned at the stake as a witch was torture.

Melissa rested her head on her arms. Sometimes, when she thought about her old life and her new life, she questioned her sanity as well as God's perfect plan. She missed her family and friends, and they must be worried sick about

213

her. Her poor students probably thought she drowned or was kidnapped. And here she was fretting over a man, who may or may not love her. She was grateful Elizabeth reminded her as often as necessary that they must always trust in the Lord and not their own understanding. Good advice, especially today.

"Missy."

Melissa jerked upright, her hands still on the top rail. "Isaiah! I didn't hear you arrive."

"You were lost in thought."

He was smiling at her and holding a bouquet of wildflowers. That had to be a good sign. Men who were about to break up with you probably didn't smile and bring you flowers. At least not that she knew of.

"My thoughts were getting the best of me."

Isaiah held out the bouquet and closed the gap between them. "I owe thee an apology. I am sorry if I gave thee cause to doubt my intentions. I reacted without honor. Even before I spoke with my brother and sister yesterday, I knew thy word, as incredulous as it may be, was true. Can ye forgive me?"

Tears rolled down Melissa's cheeks. A man had hurt her and was asking for forgiveness. Not because he was caught cheating or lying, but because he felt badly about the way he'd treated her. Her heart filled to overflowing.

"Yes, I forgive you. It's not your fault, Isaiah. My story is unbelievable, even to my own ears."

His gaze dropped to the grass, his regret palpable. It was wonderful and comforting, giving her hope for a life with a man she'd never thought to meet. "I should have stayed beside thee and listened, Missy. I allowed my fear and anger to get the best of me."

She reached for his hand and breathed a peaceful sigh as his fingers enclosed hers. "All that matters is that you're here now."

Their gazes held, and Melissa was positive he wanted to kiss her as much as she wanted to kiss him. The anticipation was more than enough, more than she had ever known.

He smiled tenderly. "What I would like to do is not possible at this moment in my brother's yard."

For a second, Melissa wished they were in the twenty-first century, where Isaiah could kiss her in anybody's front yard, side yard, or back yard. Just as quickly, she decided life was far better here. Kisses should be more precious than they were back home. And Isaiah made her feel precious, something she had not known in any relationship before.

"It's a lovely thought, though," she said, staring into his eyes.

"Aye, that it is."

For a minute they stood gazing at one another. He cared enough to apologize. He cared about her. She believed he cared in a way that meant he loved her. Melissa opened her heart and mind to every sensation. This moment was a gift, and she wanted to remember the drumming of her pulse, the warmth of her skin, and the breathlessness of wanting and needing.

His horse nickered and broke the spell. "Would ye accompany me through town? I have a surprise for thee."

"A surprise?"

"Aye, but ye shall not pry it out of me."

Melissa twirled the parasol in her left hand, hoping she looked nonchalant. "I can wait. I don't peek at Christmas presents. Surprises are much better when one is surprised."

Melissa said the words, but she wasn't entirely convinced this was a time she wanted to be patient. What would he consider a surprise for her? "Let me run into the house and tell Elizabeth where I'm going."

Isaiah pointed to the kitchen window. "There is no need. I believe my dear sister knows I am here and that ye are with me."

Melissa chuckled and waved joyfully at Elizabeth. Taking Isaiah's offered arm, they walked toward his carriage. He helped her into the buggy, jumped up, and clucked to Gabriel to walk on.

"How far are we going?"

"I thought ye said ye could wait," Isaiah teased.

"I didn't ask about the surprise. I merely asked how long the drive would be."

Isaiah's grin let Melissa know she wasn't fooling him one bit. He winked at her for extra measure. "'Tis but a brief ride. Ye shall have thy gift in ten minutes' time."

Melissa bit down on her lips to keep from smiling and to contain the eagerness she felt. She couldn't believe Isaiah had a surprise her for. A gift. Something he had chosen specifically for her. Ten minutes, he'd said. Ten minutes was nine minutes too many.

They rode east and then turned left onto a street Melissa didn't recognize. Isaiah pulled up the buggy in front of a sweet little farmhouse, much like Cindy's place on the Island. Animals and children ran around the fenced yard. Smoke billowed through a chimney in the small building to the right of the barn out back. Melissa could hear a man banging on metal, the sound similar to the one a blacksmith produces when he's pounding out a horse's new shoes.

*Maybe Isaiah had him make me a lucky horseshoe.*

Isaiah escorted her toward the family's home. Children waved and dogs barked. A flock of chickens flapped their wings and scattered as a ball rolled through their pecking area. Isaiah knocked on the front door. A pretty brunette balancing a baby on one hip answered the door. "Good day, Mr. Reed."

"Good day, Mrs. Knox. Is my package ready?"

The busy mom smiled. "Aye, it is. I shall return in but a minute."

Mrs. Knox came back with a basket in her free hand. Isaiah relieved her of the burden and quickly shifted it to his left side, away from Melissa. She couldn't see what was inside, as Mrs. Knox had placed a cloth over the top.

Isaiah tipped his head. "Thank thee, Mrs. Knox. May the Lord bless and keep thee and thy family."

Walking back to the carriage, Melissa kept glancing over to catch a glimpse of the basket. Isaiah was grinning with every step he took, clearly pleased with whatever was hidden under the towel. She was guessing he'd asked Mrs. Knox to pack them a special picnic, but if that was the case, why hadn't he asked his own cook or even Elizabeth to do that for him? But she didn't care. A picnic with Isaiah would be the best way to spend a beautiful, sunny day.

Once he'd helped her into the carriage, Isaiah sat beside her and placed the basket on Melissa's lap.

The cloth covering moved. Melissa pushed it a few inches away but kept her eyes on the kitchen towel. It continued moving, as though something, hopefully not a mouse, was squirming underneath.

Isaiah laughed. "'Twill not bite."

Melissa pinched a corner of the towel between her thumb and forefinger and carefully lifted the covering. A white, furry fluff ball meowed at her.

"A kitten!" Melissa reached in, scooped him up with both hands, and buried her face in his soft fur. "Oh, Isaiah, he's perfect!"

"Though the name perplexes me, I thought mayhap ye could name him Spike."

A mixture of joy and sorrow pooled in Melissa's eyes. Spike. Her wonderful stray cat who'd made his home in her heart over seven years ago. She missed him every day, but she knew he was happy.

"I'm not worried about Spike. He has a great home with my friend Cindy." Melissa rubbed her nose against the kitten's nose. She could hear him purring. It was one of her favorite sounds. "This little guy deserves his own special name. He's as white as freshly fallen snow and as fluffy as a cloud. I think I'll name him Nimbus."

"Nimbus?"

"Yes, after the clouds that produce snow." Melissa held her new kitten at arm's length and spoke to the adorable baby. "What do you think? Do you like the name Nimbus?"

The white fur ball meowed, and Melissa and Isaiah laughed. She drew Nimbus close and snuggled him to her chest. "I hope Elizabeth doesn't mind if Nimbus lives with us until I find a teaching position or a governess job."

"I have spoken with her, and she is agreeable for the next month."

A needle of fear poked its way into Melissa's happiness. "A month? Do you think I'll find a job in such a short time?"

Isaiah reached for her free hand. "Two days past, I deserted thee in a time of need. I promise thee, if ye will have me, that I shall henceforth never leave thy side. Thou hast captured my heart when I believed I no longer had a heart to give. I respect that ye wish to seek thy fortune, but thou alone, without a shilling, are a fortune to me. I love thee, Missy. I would be honored, and forever in thy debt, if ye would do me the great privilege of becoming my wife a month from Sunday."

He loved her. This incredible man from the eighteenth century loved her. She could feel the smile spreading across her face. She could taste her tears of joy on her lips. She could feel her heart pounding inside her chest. Through all the emotion, her mind was shouting, *Yes!* while her voice remained speechless. In shock. In joy. In love. The feelings were too overwhelming to comprehend.

"Missy?" Isaiah squeezed her hand. "Do ye understand my ques—"

"Yes. Oh, Isaiah, a million times yes."

Isaiah drew her toward him and lowered his lips to within inches of hers. "It is permissible on such an occasion."

His lips met hers with a gentle brush. The contact created a searing heat that flowed through Melissa faster than lightning strikes the ground. She leaned into him, needing more. He smelled of sea and earth, an intoxicating mixture that was more masculine than she had ever experienced.

Isaiah deepened the kiss, pulling her closer. He tasted of apples and spices. Through the fire raging within her, there was also the comfort of home, a home with him, a home where she baked apple pies and tarts. Thoughts of life with Isaiah overwhelmed her emotions as his lips astounded her physical senses.

Melissa surrendered to the heat and desire. She wanted more and pressed herself against Isaiah's strong chest. His hands tightened their hold. Melissa's heart pounded to the point of bursting. She needed air, but she needed Isaiah more.

Nimbus let out a loud meow. Melissa rocked back, on fire, her hands shaking. No wonder the little guy was scared. She lowered him to her lap and tried to catch her breath.

"A most worthy chaperone ye have, Missy." Isaiah scratched Nimbus's head. "I believe we had best return ye both to my sister's home and safekeeping. Though I fear our young friend is in for a bit of shock when the news of our betrothal is announced and the women begin shrieking."

"Our betrothal. I can't believe I'm hearing those words. I can't wait to tell Elizabeth." Melissa leaned over and kissed Isaiah on the cheek. If she spent the next week explaining the details of her life with Bryce and her previous dating experiences, she would not have enough time or words to explain to Isaiah how grateful she was to him and to God for the gift of his love. "Thank you."

He gazed into her eyes. "It is I who must thank thee. Ye saved me from a life of loneliness."

Tears misted Melissa's vision once again. Maybe he could understand. He'd remained single after his wife's death, just as she'd remained single after Bryce. Maybe he needed to be saved from loneliness as much as she did. Maybe they were perfect for each other. "Me, too, Isaiah. You saved me, too."

He kissed her softly on the lips. "We are truly blessed, Missy. I intend to spend the rest of my life showing thee how much ye mean to me. Now, however, I must drive us home before Mrs. Knox reports to her husband and neighbors that I sullied thy reputation."

Melissa laughed, her heart full. She cuddled Nimbus and relished the feel of the sun on her skin, the kitten in her arm, and the man beside her. Never in her wildest dreams could she have imagined Isaiah and his love.

Elizabeth had been right all along. God knew what He was doing. She and Isaiah belonged together.

Forever.

# Epilogue

*October 1781*

Melissa dropped the last of the beans into the basket, thankful for the second crop. She would shell these tonight while Isaiah read their evening Scriptures. She surveyed what remained in her garden. The October weather left little growing—just the spinach, beets, garlic, onions, squashes, and Brussels sprouts. The herbs were in great shape, ready to be cut and dried later in the week.

The orchard was being harvested daily, the many trees laden with ripe fruit. She'd spend the next several weeks picking, preserving, and storing the apples, pears, quince, and pomegranates. The cider press would be in full swing once the apples were picked. Isaiah had promised her he'd make some plain cider as well as his hard cider, and she'd promised to bake.

Isaiah loved her apple pies. Thank God Elizabeth had taught her how to cook in a Colonial kitchen eleven years ago. Even though they had Gertie, Melissa enjoyed baking treats for Isaiah. The man had a sweet tooth sweeter than any child she'd ever taught. Chuckling, Melissa exited the garden and headed back toward the house.

"Come on, Nimbus. Let's bring these beans inside." Melissa's large white cat rolled over in the grass and then ran to catch up with her.

Off in the distance, about a quarter of a mile away, she caught sight of someone walking toward her. She recognized Rebecca, her young friend and fellow time-traveler who had arrived five years after her. No one was more shocked than Melissa. She'd never imagined someone else would travel back in time from the *Shenandoah*. After she and Isaiah were married, she'd pleaded with him to give up sailing on the *Shenandoah*. He agreed and gave the wheel over to Benjamin, his nephew and first mate.

For years nothing happened. Melissa remembered the day Eli knocked on their door and asked them to come with him to the *Shenandoah*. "There is a woman aboard, from Martha's Vineyard, and I believe ye may know her, Sister." Eli's words had both frightened and excited Melissa. She didn't want to go back to the twenty-first century, but she would love to see a friend from home.

Their carriage ride to the ship was tense. Eli had explained the young woman's predicament while they covered ground as quickly as they could. "Miss O'Neill faces charges of treason. The patriots could hang her if she is found guilty. I do not believe she is a spy. Within minutes of making her acquaintance, I decided she arrived in the same fashion as thee, Sister. If thou can vouch for her, a life will be spared. A life I believe has become dear to Benjamin."

Eli's news of Benjamin's feelings for Rebecca had made their mission all the more urgent. Isaiah had not wanted Melissa to board the ship for fear she would disappear. He had stated he would go alone and speak on her behalf.

But Melissa knew she must be there in person. A woman's life rested on her testimony that they were friends, and she had come for a visit. Melissa hadn't known or taught Rebecca, but she knew of her family. The second they laid eyes on each other, a friendship formed. Melissa was thrilled to have someone from home, someone who understood the changes in their way of life, and someone who understood why, as much as she loved her friends and family back home, she never wanted to go back.

Rebecca explained to Melissa that Cabin 8 was the time portal. "The only way to get back and forth is to be in the cabin at night. I figured that out the night we slept on deck, and I woke up on Ben's shoulder. It's not just that the cabin is the portal or transport, but you actually have to be inside the cabin at night. I'm guessing you have to be sleeping, too, though I haven't tested that theory."

The night after Melissa met Rebecca, her new friend slept in Cabin 8 one more time. That time, she went back to tell Captain Roberts, his daughter, Tess, and son, Andy, about the cabin and that she had fallen in love with Benjamin Reed and wanted to go back and stay forever. They helped plan a rouse that Rebecca left on the spur of the moment to be a missionary in Africa.

The next morning, Becca woke aboard *Shenandoah* and walked into Benjamin's arms for life.

The Reed men were convinced no further guests would be appearing from the future.

A year later, Benjamin was flabbergasted when Rebecca's best friend, Tess, woke on his ship. She had traveled intentionally and was soon followed by the *Shenandoah's* first mate, Hawk, who intended to bring her back to the twenty-first century immediately. Rebecca was staying with Eli and Elizabeth because she was pregnant with her first child, and Benjamin had not wanted her to stay home alone. So she didn't know Tess was onboard until after her friend had returned to the twenty-first century. That was five years ago.

It was now 1781, and no one else had appeared since Tess's brief stay. Rebecca had written to Tess a few times, asking Benjamin to hide the letters in Cabin 8, where Tess might find them one day in the future. For years the letters remained untouched, and no return letters had ever been found. Melissa and Rebecca were certain Cabin 8 had been remodeled and the time portal dismantled, as Tess had said was going to happen.

"Melissa," Rebecca shouted, running the last couple of yards, "it's here! It's here!" She was waving a white piece of paper, though Melissa had no idea what "it" was. Judging from the smile on Rebecca's face, though, the paper held good news. "You'll never guess!" Rebecca's excitement bubbled over.

"Tell me."

"A letter about Tess. From Andy."

"You're kidding me. After all these years ..."

Finally. She knew Rebecca's heart had ached for months after news of Tess's visit and departure. A couple of weeks before their baby girl was born, Benjamin presented Rebecca with a gift that he said Tess had ordered him to find. Melissa had cried along with Rebecca when she opened the parcel to discover a stuffed rabbit dressed in a blue jacket. An eighteenth-century version of Peter Rabbit, Rebecca's favorite childhood toy.

"I still can't believe it. I had to rush over here to share it with you. Do you want to read it?" Rebecca held out the precious letter to Melissa.

"Why don't you read it to me?"

"I can probably repeat it word for word without opening it. I think I've read it a dozen times since Ben brought it home earlier."

Melissa lowered the basket to the grass while Rebecca removed the pages from the envelope.

*Hey, Girlie,*

*Cute kids. Guess the African missionary life is working out for you. Glad to hear it! We were stunned to find your letters today. Very clever. Always knew you were smarter than the average. Tess is going to be thrilled. Dad is going to give her the letters this Saturday on her wedding day. Yup, you read that right. Tess is getting married—to Hawk. Never thought I'd see the day. And guess where they're going to live? Your house!*

Teary-eyed, Rebecca glanced up at Melissa. "Gets me every time. Isn't that wonderful? My best friend living in my little house with the man she's loved for years."

"It's perfect," Melissa said. She'd heard the stories of Tess and Hawk. Their love story was as unique and special as hers and Isaiah's, and Rebecca's and Benjamin's. Fortunately, neither Tess nor Hawk lived in a different century. "Does Andy say anything else?"

Rebecca nodded and dried her tears.

*Dad has been paying the taxes and upkeep on your house, and no one's questioned him since "your" emails left clear instructions. (Thanks to my genius. You're welcome!) He offered the house to Hawk, who said yes, knowing Tess would love it. At the moment, Tess doesn't know. Another surprise she'll get this weekend.*

*As for me, I am officially off the market. Did you pass out? It's true. I'm dating Allyson deBettencourt. Can't believe that incredible woman wants to be with the likes of me! I'm going to pop the question at Christmas, if I can wait that long.*

Melissa and Rebecca laughed.

"Andy did have quite the reputation, but he was a good guy. Tess and I never heard a woman complain about the way he treated her, only that he wouldn't commit. He'll make a great husband," Rebecca said.

"He's had the best example. Captain Roberts and Katherine are one of the all-time great couples." Melissa nodded at the paper, urging Rebecca to continue.

*The other startling news is that Dad is retiring. Last night, Hawk turned in his resignation so he could marry Tess. Dad refused to take it and instead told Hawk and Tess that he was ready to drop anchor at home with Mom and wanted Hawk to step into his place. Hawk accepted, so Tess will get her long-time wish after all. She'll be sailing on* Shenandoah *with her husband.*

*I printed off a picture of Hawk and Tess from dinner last night. Sorry it's on paper instead of photo print. I had to send it from my phone to the office computer and then motor back to the office, print it, and motor back out to* Shenandoah *so we could leave it in Cabin 8 tonight before we begin construction tomorrow. I don't think Tess has ever been so happy. Me, either, for that matter!*

*That's all the news from the Vineyard. Did I mention how happy I am for you? Enjoy your life, Becca. Say hello to Melissa for us....Love, Andy*

Rebecca passed the photo to Melissa. Tess was standing in front of Hawk, wrapped in his embrace and smiling so brightly her joy jumped off the page.

Melissa saw the tears in Rebecca's eyes, tears of happiness, but also tears of sorrow. This one letter would be the only one. No reply would be delivered to or from the twenty-first century.

"I'm still amazed Tess made it through. I thought for certain there would be no further travel after Ben enlarged the small cabin into the medical area during the war," Melissa said.

"I think Ben thought the same thing. I so wish I'd gotten to see her. Now it is done. Andy's note said they were changing the boards the next day."

The longing in Rebecca's voice touched Melissa's heart. She clasped her friend's hand. "I'm sorry."

Tears pooled in Rebecca's eyes. "I wouldn't trade my life for anything. It's selfish to want all this and a visit from Tess, too."

"I know what you mean. I wish I could visit my parents, talk to Cindy and Kendra."

"Oh, Missy, how selfish of me. Your friends and parents don't even know you're alive and well. I was thoughtless."

She was right. They had all decided years ago that she shouldn't attempt to hide a letter aboard *Shenandoah* as Becca had. If anyone found out Melissa had time-traveled, Captain Roberts would have more publicity and hassles than he could handle. Melissa had accepted the heartache of missing her family and friends along with the blessings of marrying Isaiah and finding a new family and friends.

She hugged Rebecca. "It's not always easy to love people we'll never see again."

Rebecca sniffled. She stepped back and studied the picture. "It's not easy, but I'm glad Andy wrote. I'm thrilled for Tess. She's been in love with Hawk since the first day she met him. I'll treasure this picture for the rest of my life."

Melissa smiled. "Who would've thought that an old boat would bring love to three women?"

"No kidding," Rebecca replied, and the two friends laughed. "We could rename *Shenandoah* the *Love Boat*. It's better than any movie or book."

"Beyond my wildest dreams," Melissa mused. "Only God could have planned this for us."

Rebecca smiled. "All of it. Your journey, mine, and Tess's too. He brought us all to the places we needed to be. It's incredible, isn't it? His love for us is so great He pours out blessings we couldn't imagine."

"It's perfect. He is perfect." Melissa leaned down and picked up her basket of beans. She scanned her home, where she lived with a man who cherished and adored her. She loved him more than she'd ever thought possible. Whatever life would bring, Melissa knew God was with her, and He had blessed her with more than she deserved. Her heart swelled in gratitude. She wrapped an arm around Rebecca and started walking toward the back door. "Let's have a cup of tea and reread Andy's letter."

They walked in quiet awe, each understanding the truth that God can and does move mountains.

Melissa paused on the back step and looked up at the sky. *Thank You!*

\* \* \*

"Trust in the Lord with all your heart,
and do not lean on your own understanding.
In all your ways acknowledge Him,
and He will make your paths straight."

PROVERBS 3:5-6

# Author's Notes

The *Shenandoah* is a real and magical ship, though her magic lies in her ability to transport you back in time through your imagination, not in actuality. Captain Robert S. Douglas dreamed of, designed and commissioned the 108-foot square topsail schooner in the early sixties. She was launched on February 15, 1964, from the Harvey Gamage Shipyard in South Bristol, Maine. I took the liberty of dating the fictional ship's origins to a 1770's cargo vessel commissioned by the fictional Isaiah Reed. In reality, the *Shenandoah* was created to resemble the fast U.S. revenue cutter, *Joe Lane*, from the nineteenth century, "America's Golden Age of Sail."

Moored in the Vineyard Haven Harbor and sailing from Martha's Vineyard, the *Shenandoah* is truly one-of-a-kind. She is the only non-auxiliary square topsail schooner in the world and she boasts the longest-standing captain and schooner tandem in the nation. The kids' cruises mentioned in the book are the *Shenandoah*'s primary function.

Captain Douglas offers a reduced-rate charter to the students from the five Vineyard elementary schools. Island fifth graders raise money all year long and then enjoy a special week on the water between the summer of their fifth- and sixth-grade years. The kids learn how to raise and lower sails, the art of coiling tight lines, what it means to flake, the importance of wind direction, the indications if there is enough wind to sail, the strength and teamwork needed to raise and lower the anchor and the effort involved in keeping a beautiful boat ship shape. With no electricity or modern conveniences to distract them, the students work hard and play hard, spending hours in the water swimming, diving and jumping, and even catching the occasional baby sand shark. As my youngest daughter can tell you, sailing on the *Shenandoah* is an unforgettable experience.

To learn more about the *Shenandoah*, please visit her websites: **www.theblackdogtallships.com** or **www.shenandoahfoundation.org**.

All the characters in *Shenandoah Dreams* are fictional, although some of the names used are those of family and friends. I attempted to be as accurate as possible with the historical references and the time frame of the setting. Any errors are mine. The story, however, is a work of a fiction and I took great liberty creating characters from Colonial America, as well as transporting *Shenandoah* into the Revolutionary War time period. Many of the events portrayed in the book happened during America's fight for independence. Anything relating to the *Shenandoah* in the eighteenth century is merely a product of my imagination.

WINDS OF CHANGE

1

# SHENANDOAH NIGHTS

## LISA BELCASTRO

Could this all be a bad dream? How was she to know?
Rebecca had far more questions than answers.

*Tisbury, Massachusetts, Martha's Vineyard*

The last thing sixth-grade teacher Rebecca O'Neill wants to do during the final week of her summer break is chaperone twenty-five kids on a six-night, seven-day trip aboard the schooner *Shenandoah*. But after a desperate phone call from the school principal, she doesn't have a choice. Worse, the ship is rumored to be "haunted." Five years ago, during the Holmes Hole student cruise, teacher Melissa Smith complained about hearing voices and seeing visions, then disappeared without a trace—from the very same cabin where Rebecca will be staying.

Everything seems normal on Sunday as Rebecca boards the impressive *Shenandoah*. But as she sits in Cabin 8, she hears hushed voices that don't sound like they're from this century. Mike, a crewmember, insists he believes the crazy Island story that Melissa time-traveled to Colonial Boston. His eerie interest in constantly tracking Rebecca's whereabouts rattles her nerves.

Her first night onboard, Rebecca drifts off to sleep…and wakes the following morning with memories of a secretive conversation about a battle with Britain. Monday night Rebecca crawls into her bunk after an adventurous day of sailing, swimming, and overseeing students. She's startled awake when a man grabs her and yells, "Stowaway!" Dragged in front of Captain Benjamin Reed, she looks up into the most gorgeous brown eyes she's ever seen….

**www.lisabelcastro.com ▪ www.oaktara.com**

# WINDS OF CHANGE
## 2

# SHENANDOAH CROSSINGS

### LISA BELCASTRO

*Spunky Tess Roberts is more than ready for a grand adventure—and a lasting love—of her own. And the* Shenandoah *might be her last chance.*

*Tisbury, Massachusetts, Martha's Vineyard*

Tess Roberts may live on Martha's Vineyard, vacation spot for movie stars and presidents, but the Island feels anything but idyllic. Tess has had it with lousy dates, lying, cheating men, and the rules that forbid her from working on her family's centuries-old schooner, *Shenandoah*.

Lucky for Tess, she knows a secret—the *Shenandoah* has magical powers. Her best friend, Rebecca O'Neill, once stayed in Cabin 8 and discovered a time portal that transported her to 1775. A month after Rebecca's "disappearance," Tess's father, brother, and *Shenandoah's* annoying first mate, Hawk, plan to shut down the time travel for good by dismantling the cabin. But what if Rebecca might someday need to come home? What if Tess isn't ready to say good-bye forever?

Sneaking onto the ship late at night, Tess slips into Cabin 8 and drifts off to sleep. She wakes anchored off the New England coast amidst the American Revolution in 1776. The British frigate HMS *Greyhound* has seized *Shenandoah* and taken the crew, cargo, and all onboard hostage. To make matters worse, Hawk is relentlessly tracking her, determined to bring her back to the twenty-first century against her will. Sparks begin to fly, from more than cannonballs and gunpowder….

www.lisabelcastro.com ▪ www.oaktara.com

# Acknowledgments

*Shenandoah Dreams* and the *Winds of Change* trilogy would not have been written if Captain Robert Douglas had not designed the schooner *Shenandoah* and then graciously extended a discounted charter rate to all the elementary schools on Martha's Vineyard. My chaperone experience on the *Shenandoah* was unforgettable. Thank you again to Captain Douglas and his son, Morgan, for allowing me to use your beautiful ship in my story. I can't thank Morgan enough for answering my seemingly unending stream of questions. Morgan, your patience and quick replies are greatly appreciated!

I am extremely grateful to Fireman Luis Santana and Petty Officer 2nd Class Eric Tavares of the United States Coast Guard Station Menemsha. Fireman Santana and Petty Officer Tavares answered my many questions on the proper procedures for Search and Rescue, and also gave me extra details that I worked into the story. Any mistakes on procedure, codes, or nautical points are mine. Fireman Santana and Petty Officer Tavares, thank you for help with my research, and for your service to our country!

A warm thank you to my publisher, Ramona Tucker, for your enthusiasm for *Shenandoah Dreams* and for encouraging and believing in the Winds of Change trilogy. I am also grateful to Christina Miller for her superb editing skills, as well as her support, prayers, and friendship.

A huge THANK YOU to my Wednesday night writers' group led by mystery writer Cynthia Riggs. Erin Block, Stephen Caliri, Catherine Finch, Amy Reece, Linda Wilson, Nancy Wood, and Cynthia encouraged, critiqued, tweaked, and applauded throughout the writing of *Shenandoah Dreams*. Wednesday night remains my favorite night of the week!

An extra big hug to Stephen Caliri, Catherine Finch, and Nancy Wood for the days you spent proofing the chapters I couldn't read in group. Your edits, suggestions, and kindness are greatly appreciated.

If I didn't run, I probably wouldn't be able to function the other hours in the day. Hugs to my friend and running partner Allyson Metell Cook. You are a fantastic mom, a terrific friend, and an awesome marathoner. The talks we have while running lift me and encourage me. You inspire me in so many ways. And I'll be forever grateful that you are the world's best masseuse. Congrats on being voted *Best of the Vineyard* once again.

My family is my greatest blessing and deepest joy. My mom and stepdad, Betty Belcastro and Jack Kobelenz, are generous, kind, loving, supportive, and, to top it off, amazing grandparents. We spend a lot of time together, and it still isn't enough. I keep hoping you'll move next door. Thank you for always encouraging me!

My brother filled my growing years with friendship (and the occasional, or not so occasional, sibling conflict) and he continues to be a godly man I can trust, confide in, and laugh with, especially when I need to laugh at myself. I'm grateful for the days I spend with him and his beautiful family.

The children in my life are my true treasures, though they are more young women than children now. Kayla, my baby girl, is finishing her junior year in high school. I don't know how that happened. I remember being pregnant as if it was yesterday. My Little Pumpkin has matured into a smart, generous, talented, and lovely young woman. As we look at colleges and she thinks about spreading her wings and leaving home, I hope she knows that I am always here for her, always loving her, always praying for her. Kayla is the best thing I ever made! I love you, Pumpkin!

Starr Starr, my 16-year-old Disney princess. When I look at pictures of her and Kayla, I see adorable little girls who have grown into talented, kind and beautiful young women. As Starr considers where she wants to go to college and what she wants to major in, I know that whatever she chooses to do, she will give it her best and succeed beyond her expectations. Remember always, Daddy is looking down from heaven, watching over you and loving you. He's walking slower than everybody else up there, but this time it's not because he's dawdling along and driving us crazy, but rather so he can enjoy every moment of your life. I love you, Starr Starr!

Hugs and love to Ashleen—so far from home, yet never far from my heart. I can't believe she has been married for over a year and last week became a mom! Zoey is perfect, and so lucky to have you to love her. I pray God's abundant blessings on your marriage, your daughter, and your future. I love you, Ashleen!

Above all, I am grateful for God's unending, unchanging, unbelievable love. His love story for us is the greatest love story ever told. He is our safe harbor, our beacon in good times and bad. It is with a humble heart that I try to serve Him and create characters and situations that will reflect God's love and promises. I hope this story will touch your heart, and God's light will shine on you.

# About the Author

Lisa Belcastro lives with her family on Martha's Vineyard. She was inspired to write *Shenandoah Nights,* the first book in the Winds of Change trilogy, while chaperoning two Tisbury School summer sails with her daughter, Kayla, aboard the schooner *Shenandoah*. The weeklong adventure, sans electricity, Game Boys, iPods, and modern conveniences, kindled her imagination to dream of an altogether different voyage.

In addition to writing *Shenandoah Nights* and *Shenandoah Crossings,* Lisa currently pens the cuisine column for *Vineyard Style* magazine. She has worked as a staff and freelance reporter and photographer for *The Chronicle of the Horse* and as assistant editor at *The Blue Ridge Leader.* She has written articles for *USA Today, Dressage (London), USA WEEKEND Magazine, The Blue Ridge Leader,* and *Sidelines.*

*Shenandoah Nights* won Romance Book of the Year, Christian Small Publishers Association (2014), and Reader's Choice Award in Speculative Fiction, New England Chapter RWA (2014). *Shenandoah Nights* and *Shenandoah Crossings* are currently finalists in the SELAH Award, Speculative Fiction Book of the Year; The Carolyn Readers Choice Award, Inspirational

Romance category, as well as the Golden Quill Award, Inspirational Romance. *Shenandoah Nights* is also a finalist in the Grace Awards, Speculative Fiction category.

When she's not at her desk writing, Lisa is living in paradise, volunteering at her daughter's school, serving in her church community, planting and weeding her numerous gardens, or walking the beach looking for sea glass. Lisa recently completed her goal to run a marathon in all fifty states. Now she's training to run a 50-mile race with fellow TEAM 413 members who are also turning 50 in 2014.

www.lisabelcastro.com ▪ www.oaktara.com